⇋FIRE ARROW⇌

⇋FIRE ARROW⇌

A Novel by
Franklin Allen Leib

Presidio

Fire Arrow is a work of fiction. Any resemblance between characters in this novel and persons living or dead, other than historical figures, is coincidental and unintentional.

The United States military, naval and air force units are real, and might very likely be the ones called upon to perform the mission described, should it ever be needed.

Published by Presidio Press
31 Pamaron Way, Novato, CA 94949

Library of Congress Cataloging-in-Publication Data

Leib, Franklin Allen, 1944–
    Fire arrow : a novel / by Franklin Allen Leib.
    p.   cm.
    ISBN 0–89141–333–2 : $17.95
    I. Title.
PS3562.E447F5   1988
813'.54—dc 19   86–12484
                                             CIP

ISBN 9–89141–333–2

Printed in the United States of America

This story is dedicated to the memory of
Robert Dean Stethem
17 November 1961 – 15 June 1985
Navy Diver
Brother in Arms
Victim of terrorism.

Acknowledgments

The author wishes to thank the many people who gave this work critical readings, and who provided support during the difficult process of getting it published. Deserving of special thanks are Jim and Marian Adams, John Ehrlichman, Carole Hall, Adele Horwitz, Bob Kane, Lee Matthias, and Carl and Patricia Morton. Special acknowledgment to Major Stewart Brown, Armor, United States Army, for his invaluable assistance as to Armor weapons and tactics.

Special thanks to Major Mike Nason, Public Affairs Officer of the 82nd Airborne Division, and to Colonel Franklin Hartline and the officers and men of the 3rd Battalion, (Airborne) 73rd Armor, who welcomed me to Fort Bragg and gave generously of their time and expertise to show me how it is really done.

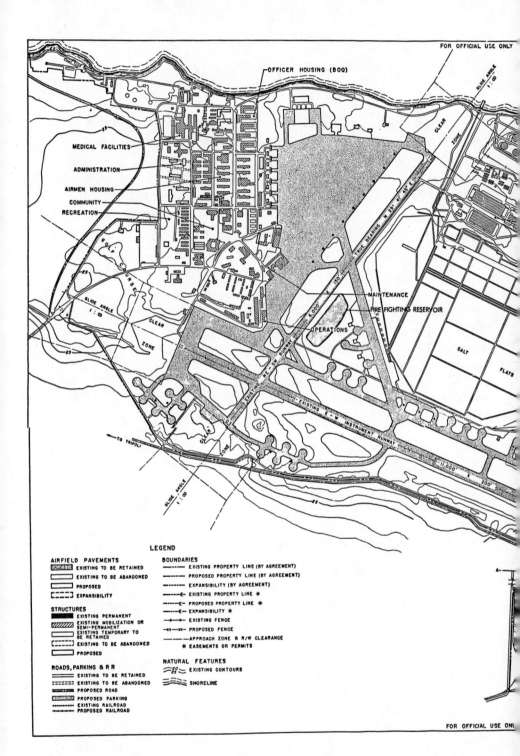

OFFICER HOUSING (BOQ)

MEDICAL FACILITIES

ADMINISTRATION

AIRMEN HOUSING

COMMUNITY

RECREATION

MAINTENANCE

FIRE FIGHTING RESERVOIR

OPERATIONS

SALT

FLATS

TO TRIPOLI

GLIDE ANGLE 1 : ∞

CLEAR ZONE

CLEAR ZONE

GLIDE ANGLE 1 : ∞

GLIDE ANGLE 1 : ∞

CLEAR ZONE

TRUE BEARING N 83° 47' 45" E

EXISTING N—S RUNWAY

EXISTING C—W INSTRUMENT RUNWAY

LEGEND

AIRFIELD PAVEMENTS
- EXISTING TO BE RETAINED
- EXISTING TO BE ABANDONED
- PROPOSED
- EXPANSIBILITY

STRUCTURES
- EXISTING PERMANENT
- EXISTING MOBILIZATION OR SEMI-PERMANENT
- EXISTING TEMPORARY TO BE RETAINED
- EXISTING TO BE ABANDONED
- PROPOSED

ROADS, PARKING & R R
- EXISTING TO BE RETAINED
- EXISTING TO BE ABANDONED
- PROPOSED ROAD
- PROPOSED PARKING
- EXISTING RAILROAD
- PROPOSED RAILROAD

BOUNDARIES
- EXISTING PROPERTY LINE (BY AGREEMENT)
- PROPOSED PROPERTY LINE (BY AGREEMENT)
- EXPANSIBILITY (BY AGREEMENT)
- —E— EXISTING PROPERTY LINE *
- —E— PROPOSED PROPERTY LINE *
- —E— EXPANSIBILITY *
- —x—x— EXISTING FENCE
- —xx—xx— PROPOSED FENCE
- APPROACH ZONE & R/W CLEARANCE
- * EASEMENTS OR PERMITS

NATURAL FEATURES
- EXISTING CONTOURS
- SHORELINE

KEY MAP

CRASH BOAT SITE
STATIC SITE
TRIPOLI
RECEIVER SITE (SITE 4)
WHEELUS AIR BASE
TRANSMITTER SITE (RADIO RANGE S.E. TAGIURA)
MEDITERRANEAN SEA
BEACON LIGHT SITE
IGLOO AREA
TRANSMITTER SITE (SITE 6)
B. EL ASCIAR

N

0 1 2 3 4
SCALE IN MILES

P.O.L. AREA

RECREATION

AIRMEN HOUSING

FAMILY HOUSING

SUPPLY

APPROX. MAG. DECL. 2° 30' W

400   0   400   800   1200

SCALE IN FEET

CONTOUR INTERVAL - 5 FEET

REV.	DATE	DESCRIPTION	INITIAL

PLAN REVISIONS

AIRFIELD ELEVATION..........36 FEET

DEPARTMENT of the AIR FORCE
DIRECTORATE OF INSTALLATIONS, DCS/O

WHEELUS

AIR BASE

LIBYA

SCALE: GRAPHIC	DATE 1 OCTOBER 1957

WILLIAMS, COKE & BLANCHARD
WASHINGTON, D. C.
NEWPORT NEWS, VIRGINIA

AIRWAYS ENGINEERING CORP.
1212 18TH STREET, N.W.
WASHINGTON 6, D. C.

CLEAR ZONE

GLIDE ANGLE 1 : ∞

APPROX. 1800' TO MELLANA WAREHOUSE

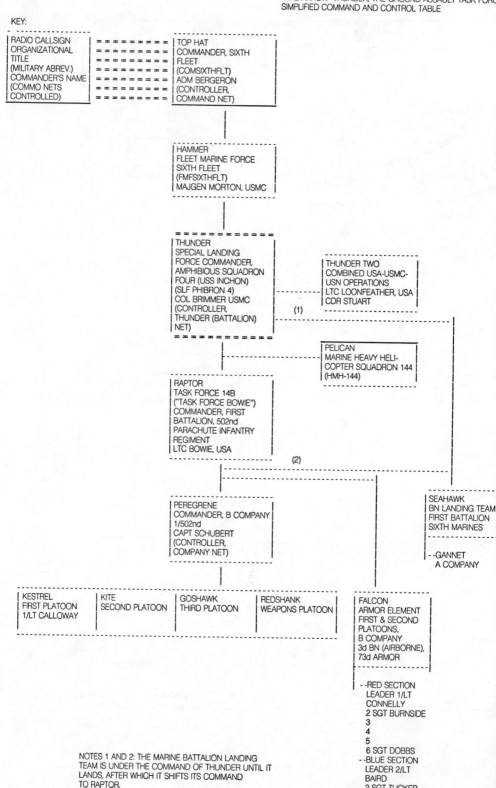

KEY:

RADIO CALLSIGN
ORGANIZATIONAL
TITLE
(MILITARY ABREV.)
COMMANDER'S NAME
(COMMO NETS
CONTROLLED)

TOP HAT
COMMANDER, SIXTH
FLEET
(COMSIXTHFLT)
ADM BERGERON
(CONTROLLER,
COMMAND NET)

HAMMER
FLEET MARINE FORCE
SIXTH FLEET
(FMFSIXTHFLT)
MAJGEN MORTON, USMC

THUNDER
SPECIAL LANDING
FORCE COMMANDER,
AMPHIBIOUS SQUADRON
FOUR (USS INCHON)
(SLF PHIBRON 4)
COL BRIMMER USMC
(CONTROLLER,
THUNDER (BATTALION)
NET)

THUNDER TWO
COMBINED USA-USMC-
USN OPERATIONS
LTC LOONFEATHER, USA
CDR STUART

(1)

PELICAN
MARINE HEAVY HELI-
COPTER SQUADRON 144
(HMH-144)

RAPTOR
TASK FORCE 14B
("TASK FORCE BOWIE")
COMMANDER, FIRST
BATTALION, 502nd
PARACHUTE INFANTRY
REGIMENT
LTC BOWIE, USA

(2)

PEREGRENE
COMMANDER, B COMPANY
1/502nd
CAPT SCHUBERT
(CONTROLLER,
COMPANY NET)

SEAHAWK
BN LANDING TEAM
FIRST BATTALION
SIXTH MARINES

--GANNET
A COMPANY

KESTREL
FIRST PLATOON
1/LT CALLOWAY

KITE
SECOND PLATOON

GOSHAWK
THIRD PLATOON

REDSHANK
WEAPONS PLATOON

FALCON
ARMOR ELEMENT
FIRST & SECOND
PLATOONS,
B COMPANY
3d BN (AIRBORNE),
73d ARMOR

--RED SECTION
LEADER 1/LT
CONNELLY
2 SGT BURNSIDE
3
4
5
6 SGT DOBBS
--BLUE SECTION
LEADER 2/LT
BAIRD
2 SGT TUCKER

NOTES 1 AND 2: THE MARINE BATTALION LANDING
TEAM IS UNDER THE COMMAND OF THUNDER UNTIL IT
LANDS, AFTER WHICH IT SHIFTS ITS COMMAND
TO RAPTOR.

⇌DAY ONE⇌

⇆1⇌

Over the western Mediterranean, 15 February, 0010 GMT

The chartered World Airways DC-8 passenger aircraft climbed out of the pattern at Torrejon Air Force Base in Spain on the final leg of its flight 41a from Norfolk, Virginia, to the NATO base at Catania, in Sicily. The night was fine and clear, and the flight crew talked softly and drank coffee as the plane settled into her cruising altitude of 33,000 feet, flying on autopilot along the path dictated by the on-board computer. In the passenger cabin, sixty-one people dozed or slept in the narrow seats. They were sailors bound for the carrier *America*, and a few dependents out to visit their men on the carrier and supporting ships. The *America* and her battle group had been deployed in the Med for nearly seven months.

The cockpit radio on the DC-8 beeped. The copilot, Peter Jackson, picked up the red handset. "Worldair 41Alfa, roger."

"Worldair, this is Touchdown. We have a problem."

Jackson pulled his clipboard onto his lap. Touchdown was the day code for the controllers at Catania. "Go ahead, Touchdown."

"Worldair, we have a threat, unconfirmed, that there's a bomb aboard your aircraft. It's supposed to be in the forward cargo bay, right below you. The callers identified themselves as the Abu Salaam faction, over."

Holy shit, thought Jackson. He tapped the dozing aircraft commander, Robert Maldonado, who woke up quickly. Jackson handed Maldonado the handset.

"This is the AC, Touchdown. What is it?" Jackson was out of his harness and unbolting the narrow access hatch to the cargo bay. "OK, OK. What did they tell you?"

"This is Touchdown. They say the bomb was loaded at Torrejon. It will go off when you descend below five thousand feet, unless they shut it down by radio signal from the ground."

Jesus, Mary, and Joseph, thought Maldonado. Jackson stood by the open access hatch and pointed downward. Maldonado nodded assent, and the copilot disappeared into the

3

cargo bay. "OK, Touchdown, my copilot is going down to take a look. What are you doing?"

"You will have escort from us in three minutes. You have to tell us what you find, over."

"Roger." Maldonado checked the instrument panel; everything normal. He twisted around in the seat and stared at the open hatch, willing Jackson to return. He unzipped the collar of his flight suit and felt the slickness of sweat in the cool cockpit.

Jackson emerged through the hatch just as the four F-14 Tomcat fighters formed up, two on either side of the DC-8, flashing their landing lights in the black sky. Jackson regained his seat on the right side of the aircraft. Jackson looked scared, his black face shiny in the red lights of the instrument panel. "Bob, there is a case down there, right up front. Looks like a Samsonite briefcase. There are copper wires around the locks, leading into the case. I put my ear against it, and it's humming, man."

"You sure? Not the hum of the engines?"

"No, Bob, it's high-pitched. Shit, man, I think it could be a bomb."

Maldonado swallowed, but the bitter taste stayed in his throat. "Touchdown, Worldair. Copilot thinks he has a bomb in the forward bay." Maldonado reached forward and touched the photo of his wife and infant son, which he had taped to the panel.

"Roger, Worldair, stand by."

"Standing by," said Maldonado bleakly. Jackson shrugged back into his harness.

"Worldair, Touchdown, over."

"Worldair."

"Can you defuse or jettison the bomb?"

"Hell, no, Touchdown!" Maldonado felt the fear in his tight throat and forced himself to be calm. "We have no idea how it works, and no way to get it out." Jackson had tuned his headset to the navy frequency and smiled slightly at the aircraft commander. "What do these terrorists want from us, anyway?"

"Stand by."

Maldonado looked across at Jackson, who shrugged and began to fiddle with the instruments in front of him. The aircraft flew on, computer-guided, unmindful of the problem.

"Worldair, Touchdown, over." Maldonado gripped the handset. "The Abu Salaam say in their message that they can shut the thing down by high-frequency radio signal, but you have to be near them."

"So where the hell are they?" Maldonado broke in.

"They are at an airfield they call Uqba ben Nafi. It is the old Wheelus Air Force Base, near Tripoli, Libya."

Oh, God, thought Maldonado, again touching the picture of his wife and child. "What are we going to do?"

"Command says we have to go with it. We have been in touch with the Libyan government, through the Italians. They want you to land. The terrorists will shut the bomb down after you are overhead."

Maldonado looked out the window at the F-14s. They must be kidding. "You want us to set down in *Libya?*"

"We have to go with it. The Libyan government says it has no knowledge or involvement in the plot, but it will allow you to land and will protect your passengers. The airfield will be lighted, and ringed with Libyan tanks."

Maldonado felt his guts loosen and fought it back. "We have to do this? You can't get us out?"

"Negative. We can't protect you over Libyan territory. Your fighters will break away at the coast. Steer one-seven-zero. That should bring you over the Libyan coast in about eighteen minutes. Tripoli will be on your right. Once you cross the coast, you'll be overhead Wheelus. Circle once, counterclockwise, with your landing lights on, remaining above five thousand feet, then land on runway 29—that's the long one."

"What happens to us then?"

"I have no idea, Worldair. We just have to keep you alive."

Maldonado nodded to Jackson, who broke out of autopilot and made the course change. The Libyan coast was lit at intervals, beckoning. The fighters broke off as the DC-8 descended. They circled the huge, brightly lighted air base, both pilots watching the altimeter, dipping no lower than six thousand feet. They lined the aircraft up with the long runway and began their final approach. The pilots held their breath as the plane dropped through five thousand, feeling for the explosion, but it did not come. Minutes later they touched down, flashing past the huge black tanks that stood beside the runway.

⇌2⇌
London, 0230 GMT

William Stuart lay in the warm darkness of his flat on Cadogan Square in the Knightsbridge section of London. Alison reached across his chest and hugged him, and he turned and kissed her fine, slightly perfumed hair. Alison made small mewing sounds into his chest, as she always did after they made love. Little Aliba is becoming a bit of a fixture, thought William absently. He stretched a bit and dozed. Pretty, sweet, boring Alison.

He was awakened suddenly by the harsh ring of the bedside telephone. Alison pushed herself away from his chest with a grunt of annoyance, and rolled away as he picked up the receiver. "Hello?"

"William, it's John. Sorry to wake you so early."

William recognized the voice instantly. John was Capt. John Harris, United States Navy, the Defense Intelligence Officer at the U.S. Embassy. John was a good friend, but not someone you wanted to hear from in the middle of the night. Stuart swung his legs out of bed and stood, then picked the phone up and carried it into the living room, trailing the long cord. He sat in his easy chair and placed the phone on the low table in front of him, found his cigarettes, and lit one. "John, it's 2:30 A.M., I just dragged in from Annabelle's, and I'm slightly drunk and very sleepy. I suppose it's too much to hope for that you're waxing melancholy in some club and need a friend to talk to."

"Sorry, old man. I need a friend, all right, but at the office." The office meant the quiet room at the embassy, though no one ever said that on the phone. "There is a fire."

Oh, shit, thought Stuart, stubbing out the cigarette and rubbing his temples. That awful, melodramatic phrase every officer long away from active service hoped he would never hear. "There is a fire" meant something dreadful had happened, and somehow the government was going to drag him into whatever operation was necessary to clean up the mess. "Can't you tell me any more than that, John?" Stuart knew the answer and wondered why he had asked, except perhaps to delay the inevitable.

"At the office, William. We're starting to brief in fifteen minutes."

"OK. I'll throw some clothes on and call a cab."

"You won't need a cab. Sergeant Hudson is waiting downstairs."

"Now?" This was beginning to sound important, and Stuart felt a kernel of excitement growing within his feeling of dread.

"Now," said Harris, and hung up.

Stuart sat in the left front seat of the small car as Sergeant Hudson, impeccable even at three in the morning in marine dress blues, drove the short distance to the embassy in Grosvenor Square. Alison hadn't stirred as Stuart slipped through the bedroom into the bath and took a brief, very cold shower. No soap, just icy water over his face, neck, chest, and crotch. He toweled himself vigorously, shivering, then dressed rapidly in an old crew-neck sweater and jeans and struggled into socks and loafers. He grabbed his old leather flight jacket from the end of the closet and shrugged into it. He kissed the back of Alison's perfumed head, but she slept on. Stuart's business was oil; he ran the engineering services department of the London office of Western Petroleum, and middle-of-the-night calls were frequent, with Stuart being roused to deal with a rig that had gone down or a key part that had to be found to repair one.

Hudson pulled into the alley behind the main embassy building and stopped. Stuart got out, pulling together his light leather jacket against the early morning chill, and followed the tall marine into the building. Stuart presented his red inactive-reserve identity card to an armed corporal, who checked it against a list and handed Stuart a clip-on badge, red again, with the words "Code 1 Access" on it. Hudson led him to the quiet room and left him at the door. Stuart entered and saw John Harris, two other men in uniform, and two apparent civilians seated around a table littered with coffee cups and full ashtrays. Stuart closed the door behind him.

The quiet room was in the central core of the embassy building. It had no windows. Outside the room, on all sides and over the ceiling and under the floor, there were baffles, both physical and electronic, designed to make sure that words spoken within stayed within. Even if somehow a transmitter could be smuggled in, its signal would be contained, lost in the lead and the concrete, or turned to muted static by the electronic traps.

Stuart was offered coffee and introduced to the others. He had met Harris's assistant, Navy Lieutenant Bill Forrest, at embassy parties. The others were a marine captain, Joe Panos, head of embassy security, a Doctor Masad, from American University in Washington but currently doing unspecified research in London, and Fred Maniero, the deputy cultural attaché. Stuart smiled and sat. He pegged Maniero for CIA and thought anybody would. Harris stood and turned to a large map of the Mediterranean pinned to the cork wall. There was a blue line made of string on the map from Torrejon in Spain to a point just west of Sicily, which then bent sharply south and ended slightly to the east of Tripoli. At the end of the string was a tiny toy airplane.

"Hijacking," said William to himself but loud enough to be heard.

"Right, William, a bad one," said Captain Harris. "It's one of ours."

"TWA again?" said William. Poor TWA had the routes in southern Europe, Spain, Italy, and Greece that seemed to attract the most attention of terrorists.

"Worse, William, much worse. The aircraft is a World Airways DC-8, under charter to the Navy."

William sat bolt upright in his chair and stared at the toy airplane stuck to the map. Fred Maniero got up and ran down the facts that were known, and then Bill Forrest described the available U.S. forces in the immediate area. The major force was the carrier *America* with her battle group, which had sailed from Sicily at 0200. Dr. Masad identified himself as a specialist in Middle Eastern affairs, then talked at some length about the Abu Salaam faction, its aims, and its demands, and about the Libyan Revolution and its charismatic and some said crazy leader, Col. Hassan al-Baruni. When the doctor sat down, everybody looked at Stuart.

Stuart took a sip of cold coffee. "So, it's a bad one, but why am I here, John?"

"Because, my friend, in 1971 and 1972, in your third tour in Vietnam, you went into Laos once, to a place called Lak Sao, and into North Vietnam once, to a place called Vu Liet, and both times you cracked enemy prison camps and brought out American aviators, alive."

Stuart felt his eyes narrow as the image rose in his brain of wet, sharp-edged leaves cutting his cheeks, and the strong, rotting odor of the jungle floor as his search team had crawled into those camps, and the stronger smells of human feces and of death they had found. More than ten years ago, he thought, but fresh and foul as yesterday. "I'm surprised you know that, John. The records of those operations are sealed, top secret."

"I received a précis of your closed record when you first came to London, William." Harris reached back and tapped the map just under the toy airplane. "We need to crack that camp and bring those men and women out alive, William, and we need you to help us do it."

"Jesus, man, that was fifteen years ago, and in the jungle!"

"You got people out then. Few others ever found anyone alive."

William frowned, remembering why the records remained sealed, and the indifference received in place of honors. The men who had fought in Nam at the end of the American involvement had it the worst, and no one had wanted to know. "Well, maybe I can help a little with method."

Harris stood, as did the others, except Forrest. "That's all we have now, except Maniero's pictures. Start thinking about the problem, William, while I organize some breakfast."

William nodded. Maniero handed him a thick folder and departed. Inside the folder were aerial and satellite photos of the Uqba ben Nafi Air Base, once Wheelus Air Force Base. Stuart spread them out and began to look for he knew not what.

⇐3⇒

Uqba ben Nafi, Libya, 0445 GMT (0545 Local)

Seaman Barbara Cummins, USN, looked out the window of the World Airways DC-8 through a long tear in the plastic window curtain. After the aircraft had landed more than four hours ago, she had seen what appeared to be a confrontation between a small group of men in jeans and red and white checked head scarves over their faces and a larger group of men in dark fatigue uniforms. The soldiers had parked next to the plane in a large, faintly boat-shaped vehicle, which had eight huge rubber tires, and a machine gun on the top. After a lot of shouting and arm-waving, a stairway had been pushed against the side of the plane and the pilot had opened the door. Two men entered—one of the ones with the scarf over his face and a man in uniform. Both carried assault rifles. Barbara recognized the soldier's weapon as an AK-47. The terrorist—Barbara assumed the man with his face covered must be a terrorist—carried a similar weapon but without the wooden stock. An AKS, she thought.

The soldier spoke into the intercom handset next to the

forward hatch of the aircraft. His first command was for all passengers seated next to windows to lower their window shades. Barbara thought his voice soft, almost musical, as he seemed to sing in English very slowly. He said he was Lieutenant Rahman of the Libyan Army. He identified the other man as Walid and said he led the freedom fighters who had commandeered their aircraft. He apologized and said that they would have to wait to disembark until a senior official from the government arrived from Tripoli. Food and water would come soon; everyone was please to remain seated. The terrorist, Walid, remained silent and scowling as the lieutenant spoke. Barbara supposed he spoke no English.

Barbara Cummins had been in the Navy only six months, and her assignment to Fleet Support Activity, Naples, was her first real job. She was a cryptography and communications specialist who had joined the Navy fresh out of high school in Zanesville, Ohio. She was a pretty, dark-haired woman, with creamy pale skin and large brown eyes, tall at five-seven and slender. She had been popular in high school, and her friends had been surprised when she had joined the Navy. She didn't tell them, or her parents, that she had been thinking about it for years. There was no money for college, and Barbara desperately wanted to leave Zanesville and her family's small and unprofitable dairy farm. She was thrilled to be ordered to Naples right out of Crypto School.

Barbara thought about the other passengers. She had spoken to many of them during the long flight and the many layovers. About half were sailors of various ratings, most of them in the Navy no longer than she, going out to the fleet for the first time, and three marines, all headed for the detachment on *New Jersey*. There was another woman sailor, a personnel yeoman, going to Naples. In the front of the plane were two mothers, one of whom had a small boy and the other two little girls. Both women were married to officers stationed in Naples. The rest were dependent wives, out for a visit to their men with the fleet.

Barbara had felt more detached than scared when the pilot announced that they were being forced down in Libya. It just seemed like another of the many delays in the long flight from Norfolk. The men with guns around the plane were more comic than threatening; even the soldiers couldn't seem to stand up straight, and several on top of the vehicle grinned and waved to Barbara before the lieutenant had told them to close the shades. Barbara was glad the Libyan officer was on the plane; he seemed a figure of legitimacy, of authority. Even the terrorist with his stockless rifle seemed no more than a boy, trying hard to look fierce.

Major Abdel Salaam Jalloud sat in darkness in the back seat of Colonel Baruni's personal Mercedes limousine as it raced along the good road from Tripoli to Uqba ben Nafi. Major Jalloud had been with Baruni in the Free Officers' Movement, which had planned and carried out the overthrow of King Idris and his corrupt government in 1969. He had served on the Revolutionary Command Council, which governed the nation after the coup, and had served as prime minister until Baruni proclaimed the Jamahiriya in 1977 and called upon the masses to rule themselves. Some said Jalloud was Baruni's designated heir and successor, though nothing official was said in a nation declared to be without formal governance.

Jalloud thought of himself as an administrator who could carry out Baruni's visions of nationalism and Arab socialism. He also thought of himself as a troubleshooter, and it was he who had suggested to Baruni that it would be prudent for Jalloud to go to the air base to find out what the Abu Salaam faction was up to. Jalloud felt he was protecting Baruni, especially if things went wrong.

Major Jalloud was convinced that the situation was very dangerous. Colonel Baruni had seemed untroubled; he had known Abu Salaam when he had trained his cells in the Libyan desert. Jalloud believed the stories that linked the faction with the violent hijacking of the Italian cruise ship

Achille Lauro; Baruni had not. Baruni agreed that having an American military chartered aircraft brought to Libya represented a dangerous provocation to the American fleet, but he also believed that the main demand of the faction would be the freedom of Abu Salaam himself, currently in an Italian prison, and that the Italians would quickly agree. Jalloud's orders were to convince the kidnappers of the Libyans' good offices, to keep them calm, and to build a dialogue. Jalloud hoped he could do all that as the limousine turned onto the brightly lighted apron and stopped beside the Russian-built BTR-60 armored personnel carrier, which was parked alongside the DC-8.

Barbara Cummins watched the black Mercedes stop next to the high-wheeled vehicle. A tall, thin man dressed in an open-necked khaki uniform with collar tabs got out of the rear of the car. This must be the government official, she thought, yawning and shifting in the cramped seat. It will be a relief to get off this airplane, she thought, even if we are in Libya.

One of the head-scarfed terrorists raced up the ladder and entered the aircraft. There was an animated conversation in a sibilant, euphonic language Barbara assumed to be Arabic. Walid smiled briefly, his teeth gleaming white against his smooth brown face, then he ran down the stairway to meet the government official, leaving a slight, scared-looking comrade standing awkwardly in the front of the cabin with the Libyan lieutenant. Barbara smiled to herself. When he smiled, the boy terrorist was really quite handsome.

Major Jalloud introduced himself to the boy who led the freedom fighters. Jalloud made it a point to smile, to put his arm around the boy's thin shoulders, and to listen. Walid explained, very confidently, that he had received a message from Abu Salaam himself, from prison, to carry out the hijacking, and that he and some friends in Spain had done so. "What is wanted of the Libyan people?" asked Jalloud.

"Sanctuary, Comrade Major," said Walid, stoutly. "Protection, until our leader is returned to us."

"And then?" asked Jalloud.

"And then our leader will lead us, Comrade Major."

"What do you mean to do with these Americans? Surely you realize you can do them no harm."

"We will do as our leader directs, Comrade Major."

"Surely you know the Sharia, the Holy Law of Islam, forbids the harming of hostages?" The major tightened his grip on the younger man's shoulder and leaned close.

Walid bowed his head. "We love Islam, Comrade Major. We respect the Libyan People's Jamahiriya. We honor the Sharia." And we love Palestine more than any of those, thought Walid, full of sorrow.

The major held Walid by his thin shoulders and looked into his black eyes, squinted in the bright lights above the apron. "Then you will act with responsibility, with caution?"

Walid didn't understand. "Comrade Major?"

"Colonel Baruni wishes to give you his support, despite the fact that you came here and brought this American aircraft here without consulting him."

Walid nodded. "We did as we were commanded, Comrade Major."

"I understand. I want to know, Comrade Fighter Walid, that no harm will come to these people, here in Libya, as long as they remain."

Walid nodded, thinking of Amin, with the radio-controlled detonator for the bomb on board the aircraft, watching from the roof of the nearby Operations Building. Amin was waiting for a sign that something was wrong, a signal to blow the aircraft. "We will act with due care, Comrade Major, and due respect for the Libyan people."

Major Jalloud smiled. This young man scares me, but what can I do, given my orders? "Very well, Comrade Fighter Walid. My troops will not impede your transfer of the prisoners to the Operations Building."

The unloading of the aircraft had taken another hour and a half. The terrorists would allow only ten passengers off at a time. Barbara Cummins was near the rear of the plane and was among the last to leave. As she reached the bottom of the stairway, a terrorist, his nose and mouth covered with his scarf, stepped behind her and roughly tied her hands. She was then prodded toward the brightly lighted building. She noticed the limousine was gone and that the eight-wheeled vehicle, along with another like it, had been pulled back away from the aircraft. So the Libyan Army has given us to the terrorists, she thought, and for the first time she was afraid.

Inside the building, Barbara saw the passengers seated in folding gray metal chairs, which looked like U.S. government issue. All their hands were tied behind them, at the wrists and at the elbows. They looked tired; some looked defiant, more looked beaten. Barbara was shocked. She was led to a chair in the front row and pushed into it. A scarfed terrorist, one Barbara had not seen before, scuttled along the row, tying each person's ankles to his chair.

When at last all the passengers were positioned and tied, Walid placed himself in the front of the room, his back to the windows. He spoke in slow, singsongy Arabic. The short, slight terrorist who had replaced Walid in the front of the plane translated, stammering frequently.

"We wait here for the return of our leader. All of you will be kept tied, until he determines otherwise. During the day, ten of you at a time will be untied and allowed to eat, wash, and exercise in this room. None of you may speak to another. Violators of these simple rules will be further bound and gagged." The slight terrorist's voice fell off to a whisper as he translated the last few phrases. Walid continued to stare at them with his exaggerated scowl.

Barbara looked around her at the other scared faces. She fought against panic. Surely the United States will get us out of this? She tried to force the question mark away from her thought, but it would not go.

⇋4⇋
Tripoli, Libya, 15 February, 0800 GMT (0900 Local)

PRESS RELEASE—ALL FOREIGN

In the name of Allah the Merciful, the Compassionate! Fighters of Islam have brought to our desert base at Uqba ben Nafi an aircraft of the American Imperialists. It rests here with us, and under the care of Allah. The band of freedom fighters who have captured the Imperialist aircraft are unknown to us, but we cannot refuse them sanctuary, as they are servants of Allah.

The revolution of the Libyan Arab People will protect both the freedom fighters and the aircraft. The passengers and crew, all military spies of Imperialist America, are in the custody of the freedom fighters, under the hand and protection of Allah. The freedom fighters have asked us to transmit their legitimate demands in exchange for the safe release of the Imperialist spies. These demands are simple and just:

1. That the leader of the freedom fighters, Abu Salaam, currently unjustly imprisoned in Rome, be returned, safe and unharmed, to his followers now at Uqba ben Nafi;

2. That brothers of the freedom fighters currently unjustly imprisoned in Kuwait, falsely accused, be released and delivered to a religious Muslim country, such as Libya or Iran;

3. That if these demands are not met, as per agreements negotiated through the good offices of the Libyan Arab Jamahiriya and whatever agency the Imperialists may select within forty-eight hours from the time of this communique, the freedom fighters will begin the execution of the Imperialist spies captured aboard the aircraft. The people are vigilant in the cause of Arab brotherhood;

4. Finally, no overflight of Imperialist or puppet aircraft, or any aggressive movements of Imperialist ships into sacred and sovereign waters of the Libyan Arab Jamahiriya, will be tolerated, and if such occur, the safety of the Imperialist spies cannot be guaranteed.

Colonel Hassan al-Baruni, Guide of the Jamahiriya

⇋5⇌
London, 0800 GMT

Stuart rubbed his tired eyes and sipped his umpteenth cup of chalky embassy coffee. He got up from the photograph-covered table and began to pace around the quiet room. His mind raced, running the images of the rescue missions in Southeast Asia at high speed, interspersed with pictures of the Libyan air base. It's the coffee, he thought to himself, but he knew it wasn't. It's like I'm right back in it, feeling the adrenaline-driven excitement of stark terror of the night and the enemy, and the certain knowledge that American prisoners could never be left in enemy hands. He had been reprimanded for the ruthlessness of his assaults, though never by his colleagues and certainly never by the men he rescued. He remembered the helpless feeling as he had crouched in the rain outside the first camp, in North Vietnam, listening to the gut-wrenching cries of a prisoner and the loud laughter of the guards as he and his team waited for the camp to fall asleep so the tiny team could slip in. Stuart had never feared anything as much as the thought of changing places with one of those tortured American pilots, and while he waited in the wet jungle, often listening to the cries of pain, he had thought of little else.

Stuart turned back to the table, sat down, and began again to look through the photographs. Oh, yes, he would help the Navy with method and anything else he could. He thought of the men and women at the Libyan base, tied and probably blindfolded and being harangued and abused by the Palestinians, themselves so brutalized as to be beyond caring for any human dignity. Stuart closed his eyes and fought back a sob of rage and terror, then shook his head and went back again to the photographs.

Bill Forrest and Fred Maniero returned at 0830, the former bringing air force reconnaissance photos from an SR-71 overflight and thick English pastry, and the latter satellite images and a carton of Dunhill cigarettes.

"Any preliminary thoughts, Camp Cracker?" asked Maniero, his voice pushy. Stuart squeezed his eyes and confirmed his earlier decision not to like the Agency spook. "The base is huge," he began, looking across the array of photographs in different resolutions on the table. "The Operations Building is here, alongside the northeast-southwest runway, labeled runway oh-three-slash-two-one. There is what appears to be an office block immediately behind Operations. You can see the DC-8 parked on the apron directly in front of the Ops Building. The prisoners have to be in one of those buildings. There are literally acres of ground around the buildings, all paved and lighted in the night photos."

Maniero and Forrest followed Stuart's pointer as it played over the features of the sprawling air base. "You can count the tanks," said Forrest.

"Yes," said Stuart, "at least two full companies, mostly dug into the sand, outside the base perimeter."

"And aircraft," offered Maniero. "Recon, tell us what type."

"The six parked in the open tarmac near runway 03/21 are identified as MiG 23s. These, in the revetments in the triangle made by the two runways and the main taxiway, are a section of four MiG 25s, most likely flown by Russians, North Koreans, or Cubans. The majority of the aircraft are in open revetments north and south of the main runway, runway one-one-dash two-niner. There are more than thirty revetments, some covered with camouflage netting. Photo interp says these are MiG 23s," Stuart swept the pointer past a long line of concrete revetments, "and the others old Mirage Five fighter-bombers."

"You'd think that asshole Baruni would get them back to other bases," said Maniero.

"Except that if he did, we could bomb them in the first minutes of a rescue raid. Besides, at least with them there, he'll have quick air cover if we come in out of the Med," said Forrest, rubbing his unshaven chin.

"That's the way I see it," said Stuart. "Those planes near the intersection will have to be dealt with by whoever is first in, so they can't take off, and maybe more important, so they can't block the runways trying."

"So how do we get in?" asked Forrest.

"We have to secure the prisoners and neutralize the terrorist guards with a quick strike, then hold the buildings and protect their lives until a larger assault can break in and get everybody out."

"You got any kind of an idea how that might be done?" asked Maniero.

"Maybe the beginning of one. We need plans of the base and all the buildings, and plumbing, fire fighting, fuel, electric, everything. And we need to know the dimensions and contents of that reservoir." Stuart pointed to the bermed pond in the center of one of the high-resolution SR-71 photos. The reservoir was near the intersection of the two runways, across the shorter one from the Ops and Admin Buildings. The surface of the fluid reflected moonlight.

"How, pray, would you like us to get plans of a Libyan air base?" snorted Maniero.

"Shit," said Stuart quietly, "it used to be Wheelus, man, U.S. Air Force. Place must have been built by Bechtel, or Fluor, or Lovell. The Agency ought to be able to get plans from one of them." Stuart set the pointer down sharply and went to look for the head.

⇋6⇌
Washington, 1100 GMT (0600 EST)

Admiral Archer Daniels, the Chief of Naval Operations, sat quietly while his N-2 Intelligence staff continued to add information about the hijacking at Uqba ben Nafi. He was a spare man, with a hawkish face and hollow cheeks. His skin had an unhealthy pallor, and his eyes were a watery pale blue. He chain-smoked unfiltered Camels.

The rest of the Joint Chiefs sat at the long table beside the admiral in the Pentagon situation room. With the exception of the two men and two women of the World Airways aircrew, all the hostages were Navy or Marine Corps, and the Navy had the forces closest to the Libyan coast. The Chiefs of Staff of the Army and Air Force and the commandant of the Marine Corps sat in respectful silence as the naval officers briefed and updated. Each chief took notes. The last item up on the enlarged, lighted computer displays was the translation of the communique from the government of the Libyan Jamahiriya, stating the demands of the terrorists.

"Shit," said General Vaughn, the Chief of Staff of the Air Force. He sat erect, cool and military in a uniform that resisted the efforts of seven hours in a chair to make it look wrinkled. "The bastards have this pretty well figured out. Wheelus is right on the coast. Even if we jam, incoming attack aircraft will be seen and heard from the ground in time for them to kill our people."

General Klim, Chief of Staff of the Army, got up and straightened his rumpled uniform. "They will be much tougher to deal with if they get that murderous bastard, Abu Salaam, back from the Eye-talians. Where in the hell is State?"

The door at one end of the oval room opened and the Secretaries of State and Defense entered with their scurrying groups of aides. Admiral Daniels looked up through tired, red-rimmed eyes. Haven't seen those two REMFs walk into a room together in months, he thought. Probably doesn't betoken any agreement.

The Secretary of Defense, small and dapper with black swept-back hair and shiny dark eyes above his prominent nose, moved rapidly into the midst of his military chiefs, who stood. The Secretary of State, a great, rumpled bear of a man with a high, shiny forehead surmounting intelligent blue eyes and a sad, heavy face, sat at the end of the table, reading the briefing papers, which explained the photos and the computer displays and which detailed the Baruni statement with commentaries.

To the Secretary of State, Henry Holt, the rapid-fire exchange of talk between the Secretary of Defense, David Wasserstein, and his staff seemed almost boisterous. The Joint Chiefs had sat down again and were conferring in low tones, ignoring the civilians and ignored by them. The Secretary of State sighed. "Dave, we ought to bring this to order. We have to brief the President again in one hour."

The Secretary of Defense turned and smiled winningly. "Of course, Henry. Why don't you bring us down to date on the political alternatives, and then we'll speak to the military options?"

Ought to be the other way around, thought General Klim, putting a new cigarette in his already sour mouth. The Secretary of Defense was liked because he would fight hard for military appropriations up on the Hill, but mistrusted because he always resisted military options. The Secretary of State, on the other hand, had openly and publicly disagreed with David about the need to use military force where appropriate to deter and suppress terrorism.

The Secretary of State walked to the front of the room and sat on one haunch on a front-row desk. "We don't have much to offer. Politically, this couldn't be worse timed. We're trying to get the Italians to hold Abu Salaam, or give him to us; his people did murder an American on that Italian cruise liner they hijacked. He is very unstable and highly dangerous, and the Italians know it, but my guess is that they'll give him up; Nino Calvi is a friend of the U.S., but he's under a lot of pressure from the leftists in his coalition. They've wanted Abu Salaam out of Italy from the first moment he was captured, and fear repercussions in the Arab world, not to mention terrorism in Italy, if they keep him in jail or try him."

"They could give him to us. We had Justice file on him," suggested the Secretary of Defense.

"We shoulda just kept the sum-bitch," growled Admiral Daniels. "When we forced him down in Sicily, the goddam Eye-talians took an hour to find *Carabinieri* to escort the bastards off the plane."

"Yes. Well, gentlemen," continued the Secretary of State, "we will continue to *encourage* the Italians to hold firm, with dubious chance for success. We have asked the Soviets to urge Baruni to contain and if possible disarm the terrorists, again with little hope of more than clucks of sympathy from behind hands held up to conceal giggles of glee. We have no channel to Baruni other than the Italians, who, for political reasons already outlined, will be of little use, and none whatsoever to the hijackers. We will advise the President to make a strong denunciation of the crime, and then see what we can develop. That's political, Dave. I hope the military has more answers than we do."

David stood and pulled down at his gray vest, smoothing it over his stomach with both hands. "Thanks, Henry. Admiral Daniels has taken the point on this problem; Navy has all the assets looking at Baruni. Admiral?"

Admiral Daniels stood and coughed as he stubbed out his cigarette. "The situation has me worried, gentlemen, for two reasons. One, even though we know we can evade the rinky-dink radar their Russian friends have given the Libyans, and can attack through it, we can't do it without their knowing we're coming. Two, we know Baruni has at least two companies of tanks and two squadrons of aircraft on the base, and the last SR-71 photos indicate that another company of T-72s is approaching from Tarhunah, the training base seventy kilometers to the southeast."

"That's the base where we believe Soviet Spetznaz commandos have been training terrorists," interjected the Deputy Director of Central Intelligence, seated with the Defense Secretary's staff.

"Quite," continued Admiral Daniels, irritated at being told something everyone in the room already knew. "Third, the base at Uqba ben Nafi is immense. Its perimeter is more than twenty miles around. Unless we have precise knowledge of where the hostages are, and where the terrorist *and* the Libyan strong points are, it will take an impossibly large force to secure the base, find our people, neutralize the terrorists, and bring our people out."

"And that's if the terrorists don't simply kill the hostages at the first shadow on a radar screen, or the first sound of an aircraft engine over the coast." David Wasserstein's voice had an edge on it.

"Yes, sir," said Daniels.

"So what's the good news, Arch?" said the Secretary of State pleasantly. There were a few soft chuckles.

Admiral Daniels smiled. "We have set up a planning group, in London, and another with Admiral Bergeron, the commander of the Sixth Fleet aboard *America*. We would like to suggest the other chiefs put in experts they think might help us solve this problem."

"A joint-services operation?" Wasserstein's voice held more than a hint of sarcasm.

"I believe my colleagues and I agree," Daniels looked at his fellow chiefs and received nods—enthusiastic from the commandant of the Marine Corps, skeptical and reluctant from the Army and Air Force, "that there isn't time for the joint approach to go beyond planning. Navy will run this, with the help we need from Air Force and Army."

"We sure as hell can't afford another screwup like that Iranian debacle several years ago," Wasserstein reminded everyone, none of whom wished to be reminded.

"Yes, sir," said Admiral Daniels, fighting his contempt for the little sharp-tongued civilian. "We intend to avoid those mistakes by uniforming command and control on the navy–marine corps methods. Our army and air force brethren have agreed." Again, the Commandant of the Marine Corps nodded enthusiastically, and the Chiefs of Staff of the Army and Air Force smiled faintly. "When you joined us, we were just on the point of appointing appropriate planning coordinators for the London group, which is forming now."

General Klim rose and spoke quickly. "Lieutenant Colonel Rufus Loonfeather, commander of the 3d of the 73d Armor, just finished observing a REFORGER exercise in Germany." Klim was amused as the bluff admiral took charge. "He should be in London by now."

"Colonel Ian Wight, for Air Force," said General Vaughn.

"He has the F-111 wing at Upper Heyford in England. Also, already there."

"So we will have options in one or two hours, Mr. Secretary," said Admiral Daniels, glad that his fragile coalition was holding together.

The Secretary of Defense heaved his small body out of the deep chair. "We had better go and see the President, Henry." The civilians filed out of the war room. The military men grinned at each other, glad they hadn't been asked to go along to explain the extreme difficulties of the problem.

⇌7⇌
London, 1400 GMT

Captain John Harris strode into the quiet room and stopped. Stuart and Forrest sat talking quietly, poring over plans of the Uqba ben Nafi Air Base that had been faxed via satellite from Langley. Maniero talked softly on the phone.

Harris looked at Stuart for a long time. He's a good-looking man, and solid, he thought. Stuart was tall at six-feet-one, and his body looked athletic and trim, although conditioned from a squash court rather than hard training. He had thick, unruly blond hair, a shade too long, deep blue eyes, regular features. Good record in Vietnam, good civilian career; messy divorce, probably drinks too much. Harris wondered how much they could trust Stuart's ten-year-old skills.

Typical Vietnam vet, thought Harris with bitterness. They're all bruised, flawed men. We all are. "Stuart, got anything?"

Stuart and Forrest looked up. They both look tired, thought Harris, but they're alert.

"Maybe, Captain," said Stuart with a faint smile. "The bermed pond in the middle of the airfield is a reservoir; stores water for fire fighting. Photo recon and SIGINT [signal intelligence] have taken precise measurements and conclude that the reservoir is 110 meters long, 70 meters wide, and at least 5 meters deep to the top of the berm, and they reckon that it's full of water to a depth of no less than 4 meters."

Harris looked at the photos, the plans, and the marked-up computer calculations from the tech people. "How does this help us?"

"We have to get people into the center of the base," said Stuart, "to hold the hostages while the major break-in occurs. If that reservoir checks out, and the next pass of the KH-11 surveillance satellite gives another picture good enough to confirm the water depth of at least 3 meters, we could drop a SEAL* parachute team into the reservoir. The reservoir is 200 meters from the Operations Building, where the prisoners are almost sure to be held, and even closer to the line of ready fighter aircraft in revetments near the crossing of the two runways."

Stuart pointed at the shimmering surface in the photograph, then at the plans. "Moreover, the reservoir is *across* the northeast-southwest runway—runway 03/21—from the Ops Building, and therefore in darkness to an observer in the lighted area all around the Ops Building and the tarmac in front."

Harris rubbed his rough-stubbled chin. He felt as tired as his small task team looked. "The Libyan message said that any overflight would be taken as cause for executing the hostages. How are you going to get jumpers in?"

"Well, Captain, we think a HALO drop. We're still flying SR-71 recon flights, and they aren't picking those up."

"True," said Harris. "But they go by at 70,000 feet."

"The HALO could be made from a B-52 from 40,000. That was standard altitude in Nam, because the radars the Soviets provided for the SAM-3s could only acquire up to 35,000 feet."

"Haven't the Russians given the Libyans better gear?"

Stuart smiled. "Not says our Agency friend."

Harris looked across at Maniero, who nodded but looked very worried. "So Stuart, that's a plan?"

* SEa, Air, Land. Navy commandos.

"An element, John, just an element."

Harris smiled. "OK, William, keep working on it. The good news is that you are recalled to active duty in our beloved Navy, with the temporary rank of commander. Indefinite assignment."

Stuart felt a rush of emotions, contrary to one another. Probably cost me my job, and most certainly Aliba. But I want to be in on this, he thought. I didn't love the Navy, but I felt purpose and pride. I could use a dose of purpose and pride. "Aye, aye, *sir!*" Stuart snapped a salute in jest, but Harris returned it. "Just get my tailor to throw another thick stripe over the two of my old lieutenant's rank on my dress blues."

Harris stood. "Shit, *Commander,* where you're going, you will *not* need dress blues!"

Stuart stood and watched Captain Harris depart the quiet room. Where am *I* going? he thought.

⇋8⇋
Washington, D.C., 1400 GMT (0900 EST)

The President got up slowly from behind the ornate oak desk in the Oval Office. He was a big man, broad in the shoulders, slim through the waist and hips. His hair was thick and dark and his eyes were clear despite his seventy-two years, and his jaw was set in a determined cast.

His back was acting up from a near fall he had taken riding at Camp David on the weekend, and he felt stiff and old. There was nothing about the job of President of the United States that he didn't like, except having to get up far earlier than his normal rising time of eight o'clock, and to think clearly through a complex briefing. The briefing about the hijacking had made him very angry.

The President liked his Secretaries of State and Defense. He trusted them, and he knew that they knew he preferred simple options assessments to detailed briefings of the sort they had just delivered, supported by numerous aides, who had just departed. The President rubbed his eyes and sat again behind the historic desk, touching it fondly with his fingertips. He put his hands behind him to massage his back through his suit jacket. "Well, men, what in the hell are we going to do about this outrage?"

Henry Holt answered. "The timing is especially bad, with the Russians just about willing to come to a summit." The burly Secretary of State was sweating in the close air of the office, and would have loved to remove his jacket. In all his years in office, the President had never taken off his jacket in this room, and the Secretary knew he never would.

"Well, I'm sure you'll both agree that getting our people back is far more important than any summit," said the President pointedly, knowing that the two cabinet officers probably didn't agree. "And I hope you have a better set of plans for us to consider than what your predecessors gave President Carter during the Tehran hostage problem."

"As we indicated, Mr. President," began the Secretary of Defense, "we have planning groups in London and Washington, as well as Admiral Bergeron's team with Sixth Fleet." The Secretary paused; then continued. "The operation is under the overall guidance of the Navy. Tripoli, unlike Tehran, is close to the sea, and reachable by navy and marine corps forces of all types, without resort to the heroic measures that were necessary, and ultimately unsuccessful, in the Iranian situation. Militarily, the operation is doable, though extremely risky."

"Because the terrorists may kill the hostages while the raid is in progress," commented the President, reviewing his notes.

"Yes, sir. That, and the risk to our political interests in the Middle East and with the Soviets," said the Secretary of Defense.

The President looked at the Secretary of State, who looked pained. The President reflected with sadness that the relationship between the two men had never been good, even though they had once worked for the same major construction company in California. "Henry?"

"We have to get those people out, Mr. President, and

unharmed, if possible. They are not only Americans, but American military personnel and families. As much as we want that summit, we cannot deal in a friendly way with the Soviets when a planeload of our people is being held by one of their clients."

"And?" said the President, toying with a long, sharp letter opener.

"And I think the Russians understand that, sir. Ambassador Dobrynin was outwardly truculent, but he almost smiled beneath it."

The President turned back to his Secretary of Defense. "Dave, if we need one, have we got a military option?"

The Secretary of Defense looked at his watch. "In an hour or two, Mr. President, the planning groups in London and at Sixth Fleet and here in Washington will have something preliminary."

"Make sure we can do it, Dave," said the President, rising once again, rubbing his back. "And make sure our friends in the region are prepared to help us, Henry."

The Secretary of State felt the force of the President's words. Who are really our friends in a situation like this, he wondered, and more important, whom can we really trust?

⇋9⇋
London, 1500 GMT

Stuart left the embassy by the side entry after a dreary lunch of the dry bread and cheese disasters the English took for sandwiches. John Harris had told him to go home and sleep and to come back to the embassy at 7 P.M., when the London group for the whole operation would be convened and task groups formed.

Stuart unlocked his flat and opened a window to let in a bit of the cool, damp air. Alison always insisted on keeping the windows tightly shut, and the flat was dry and stuffy from the ancient, noisy steam radiators. He took off his clothes and lay naked on top of the rumpled bed. He had a sharp pain behind his eyes from studying the detailed photographs and a duller, throbbing ache at the back of his head, which, together with his slight fever and deep feeling of fatigue, told him to expect a visit from his old Vietnamese malaria.

Stuart had left the Navy in 1973, when it became apparent that the war in Vietnam was going to be abandoned by the United States and never won. His mind traveled back to the images and feelings of the time, raced along by the familiar buzz of the malaria.

Stuart had come from a family with a long military tradition, and had grown up in the serene and genteel countryside of Virginia. He had been commissioned after graduating from college and been assigned to an amphibious assault ship, the old *Valley Forge*, operating off Vietnam. When he returned with the ship, he married and prepared to settle down and forget the boredom and the terror of his war. After six months in the States, he had received orders back to Nam as officer-in-charge of an ANGLICO* team, spotting air and naval gunfire for the Army and marines, working in the jungle and along the rivers and, during the Tet Offensive of 1968, even in the cities that were temporarily occupied by the Viet Cong and the NVA. It seemed so long ago.

Against all reason, he had extended his commitment after serving nine months in Washington with Naval Intelligence and returned to the jungle once more. He knew as he lay in his bed in London, the fever rolling through his body in waves and the pain seeping from his bones into his flesh, that he could never have explained why he went back, not then, and not now. But he had gone, and he had crept through the choked jungle streams and across dewy, moon-silvered paddies in North Vietnam and Laos, following rumors of imprisoned American flyers. Twice, out of the many times, he had found skeletal men, alive but unseeing, and he had quietly led his team through the camps, killing the guards, every one, and then leading the poor, weeping, frightened men out of hell and back to their homes.

Stuart got up and went to the bathroom and swallowed

* Air and Naval Gunfire Liaison Company.

three aspirins with a whole tumbler of water. I hope the malaria just takes a bite and leaves, he thought. I want to go back to the embassy in a few hours. He took his temperature, watching in the mirror as sweat coursed down his face and chest. He looked at the thermometer, 39 degrees Celsius. About 102 Fahrenheit, he figured, and already sweating freely. The attack is almost over.

He returned to bed and pulled the sheet and blanket over him as he shivered with alternating waves of hot and cold. His mind slid away from him, and he thought about returning home from Vietnam each time he had done so, and how each time it had been worse. Stuart's wife had left him in 1968, cursing him for leaving her alone while he returned to the war the nation had rejected. By 1973, absolutely *everybody* hated the war, although the vociferous demonstrations of the late sixties had ended abruptly once the threat of the draft was removed. Stuart had felt alienated even from people who had been close friends. It seemed that people, *American* people, hated him and rejected him because he felt too attached to the war and the men who had died there to denounce it and them and wear flowers in his hair.

The first job offer he had received after he resigned his commission had been from Western Petroleum, with the promise of posting overseas, and he had taken it, glad for the sands of Kuwait and then the offshore rigs of Indonesia. In the last ten years he had spent eight months in the United States, and although he had seen people soften, he still felt denied and alone and angry every time he went "home."

Stuart tossed underneath the blanket. He pushed the sheet away as it became soaked and tangled and cold against his skin. Now, I'm going to help plan a desperate raid into a heavily fortified base in Libya, an operation that looks close to impossible on paper and would be worse if actually tried. And I feel good about it. I've missed feeling American, and patriotic, and proud.

The fever folded through his brain in viscous waves, and the pain increased. He shivered and wrapped the woolen blanket more tightly around him. The dream began, haunting and lovely, painful and familiar. Flames circled him and engulfed him, and he was in the jungle near the DMZ once again, and he was dying again, but he wasn't afraid. The dream had different endings, and now as the flames died he could see the silhouette of a slender, long-legged woman, her image distorted in the shimmering heat. He couldn't see her hair, but he knew it was thick and blond, and he couldn't see her face, but he knew it was the beautiful face of the woman who had been his wife.

Stuart rolled to the dry side of the bed and fell into a dreamless sleep.

⇋10⇌

Uqba ben Nafi, 15 February, 1800 GMT (1900 Local)

Lance Corporal Craig Stevens waited while the small terrorist untied his ankles and motioned him to stand and turn around. Stevens fought the urge to drop the little shit with a kick and then stomp his lights out. He felt the bonds on his wrists release, and he rubbed his tingling hands as the small man motioned for him to walk to the head in the rear passageway.

Stevens squared his shoulders and marched toward the head, watching the slouching terrorists around the room, making himself different. Stevens had grown up in the ghetto on the South Side of Chicago, a brawling, unruly street kid with a reputation for violence. At five feet ten inches and 160 pounds, Craig wasn't big, but he was cat-quick, and his smooth, handsome black face was unmarked, although he had a six-inch-long ropy knife scar on his right shoulder blade.

If it hadn't been for the fight that left him with that scar, Craig reckoned he would still be on the streets, committing petty crimes or maybe dealing drugs. Craig had been arrested numerous times, the first at the age of eleven, but the overworked cops never had anything solid enough on him to make sure of a conviction, so they usually just slapped him around and let him go. Craig had long since ceased to be impressed by these minor beatings, and he had laughed at the cops' threats.

Two years ago on the day after Christmas, a night when the wind blowing in off the lake was wet with heavy gobs of snow, Craig followed a staggering man down a quiet street and relieved him of his wallet. As he turned to leave, he was set upon by four boys, members of a Mexican gang, who beat him and kicked him and stabbed him in the shoulder. Craig was sure they would have killed him, except for once the cops showed up when you needed one. Craig ended up in the hospital with broken ribs, bruised innards, a big bandage on his shoulder, and, for the first time in his life, a sense of fear and despair for the way he lived. Craig Stevens was seventeen.

Craig had never known his father, and he hadn't seen his mother in years. When he needed a place to lie up, he usually went to his sister's apartment in a housing project called Cabrini Green. When he was tossed out of the hospital he was still almost too hurt to walk, so he went to Clara's. She was out when he arrived, so he went back down into the street to find something to eat and a place to sit and rest. He felt dizzy after the short walk from the bus stop to Clara's building. He crossed the street and walked toward a coffee shop on the corner, which suddenly seemed very far away. He was almost there when the world began to spin away from him, and he fainted in the doorway of a storefront.

Craig awoke lying on a bench inside the store, covered with a thin gray blanket. When he stirred and tried to sit up, he felt his shoulders supported by a fearsome-looking black man in a khaki uniform, Gunnery Sergeant Jack H. Tucker, United States Marine Corps. Craig Stevens had collapsed into an armed forces recruiting office.

The sergeant had given him soup and let him stay and rest. After an hour, Craig felt strong enough to walk back to his sister's, but he was fascinated by the sergeant in his neatly tailored uniform as he went about the business of talking to the kids who wandered in from the project and wanted to talk about the Navy and the marines. The office was empty except for Craig and the sergeant as Craig got up to leave. He approached the sergeant's desk.

"Hey, thanks, man, for letting me rest up."

"No problem, Craig. Feel better?"

"Sure. I'll go back to my sister's. She'll be home by now."

"She in Cabrini Green?"

"Yeah."

"Well, good. Maybe you come back and talk to me, when you get your strength back?"

Craig smiled. "You ain't thinking of talking me into joining the marines?"

Sergeant Tucker frowned. "You're in no shape to join my Marine Corps, Craig. The training alone would kill you."

Craig snapped into his badass street scowl. "Hey, *sergeant*, I'm tough! Just had a little trouble in the street."

Tucker smiled and looked skeptical. "Maybe. You play any sports?"

"No time for that shit."

Tucker smiled. "Like I thought. Well, if you ever think you *could* get me to let you into my Marine Corps, you'd have to get into shape."

"I'm always in shape, man. Two weeks, I'll work off this hospital; I'll be fine."

"I run in the mornings, Craig. I start from here around 6 A.M. I got a shower in back."

Craig grinned despite himself. "Thanks, man. I know how to run already."

"Suit yourself. You don't look strong enough, anyway."

"Ha!" said Craig, thoroughly amused. He went out into the icy wind and walked carefully back to Clara's.

Two weeks later he started running with Gunnery Sergeant Tucker. Two months after that, when he could keep pace for the whole six miles, Tucker let him join his Marine Corps.

The terrorists had removed the outer door from the small two-hole bathroom and had removed the swing doors to the individual stalls as well. The fat one called Amin watched as Stevens sat to take a shit. Stevens fixed Amin with his fiercest street stare and pinned his eyes the entire time he sat. Amin stared back insolently and pointed his AKS at Stevens's crotch.

Stevens flushed the toilet. The tiny room stank from so many people using it. He turned to the sink and quickly washed his hands and face. There was nothing to use as a towel. He didn't want to soil his uniform, so he shook off his hands and wiped them on his sock. He patted his face with his issue o.d. handkerchief. He looked in the mirror at Amin, who still smirked. I'll bet old Amin really gets off watching the women use the head.

Stevens didn't want to stay in the head with so many waiting, but he straightened his field scarf* and gave his sharply creased gabardine shirt a quick tuck, pulling it tight around his waist from behind. Gotta look good, he thought; Marine Corps good.

Amin gestured with his carbine for Stevens to move on to a table where two women in navy uniforms were serving tea and dates and some kind of flat unleavened bread to the ten prisoners currently allowed to move about. Both girls were pretty, and both looked scared. The terrorist leader leaned against the wall behind the women and watched the hostages, his AKS loose in his hands. He seemed bored. Stevens looked some solid hatred into Walid's eyes, and he thought he saw the terrorist flinch and look away.

There are four, thought Stevens, looking around carefully, swinging his arms, doing allowed "exercise." Walid, the leader. The wimp, Ahmed, who spoke English; Amin, the

* Necktie.

toilet-watcher; and the other kid Stevens hadn't heard a name for. Four only. We're going to have to organize something, find some way to talk to each other. Half of these people are families or women, but there are two other marines and some of these sailors look pretty fit. Six or seven guys out of the sixty-five, and a little leadership. . . .

Walid stepped from behind the table and shouted something at Lance Corporal Stevens, then swung his carbine at Stevens's head. Stevens's arm came up instinctively and warded off the blow. He gasped at the sudden pain in his forearm.

Little Ahmed rushed up as Walid continued to shout in Arabic. He pointed the AKS at Stevens's gut, and Stevens felt his stomach muscles tense. Ahmed asked a question of the leader, then turned to the marine. "Walid demands to know why you are looking at us. He says you must return to your chair to be tied up and blindfolded."

"I didn't do nothing," said Stevens quietly.

"Come, go back to your chair." Ahmed's voice was almost pleading.

Stevens began to twist his body and swing his arms, staring at Walid, whose face was flushed with anger. "Just a little more exercise, Ahmed."

Walid shouted again, and once again swung his carbine at Stevens. Craig moved quickly to his left and grabbed the barrel of the gun and pulled. Walid lost his balance and fell toward Stevens, still holding onto the pistol grip of the weapon. Craig almost had it when Amin stepped behind him and clubbed him down.

Stevens was stunned, but conscious. He put his hand on the back of his neck and felt the warm, sticky blood. The terrorists continued to shout, and Stevens heard the hostages scurrying back to the metal chairs and saw Ahmed rush to tie them. Amin emerged from a storeroom tearing up sheeting, and he and Ahmed quickly blindfolded the bound hostages.

Stevens forced himself to his knees, fighting the pain.

Walid placed the muzzle of his carbine against the marine's neck and shouted. Amin and Ahmed picked Craig up by his shoulders, pressed him into a chair, and swiftly tied and blindfolded him. Walid fired three bursts from his AKS into the ceiling above the hostages, causing broken plaster to rain down on their heads. Craig heard hostages gasp. Some were sobbing, as many men as women. Walid began to speak, more softly, and Ahmed translated.

"Walid says there are sixty-five of you. He does not need so many. From now on, any who do not obey orders instantly will be shot."

Walid walked behind Stevens's chair. Craig couldn't see him, but he could hear his harsh breathing. I'm going to die, he thought.

Walid kicked the back of Stevens's metal chair, sending it and the bound man sprawling. Stevens's head and neck were on fire. His mind tightened in hatred. He thought of Parris Island and his sadistic drill instructor. I'm not going to make a sound, he thought. I can take this, Walid.

Walid fired another burst into the ceiling. All around him, Stevens heard the hostages moaning.

⇋11⇌
London, 15 February, 1900 GMT

Stuart showered quickly, shaking off the residue of the fever. He felt weak from the malaria attack, but his mind was clear after nearly three hours of sleep. Alison had returned to the flat while he was dressing, and when told of his sudden recall to active duty, and nothing else, she quickly gathered her things and left without a word. Stuart couldn't decide how he felt about that. The Wheelus situation had driven his problems with Alison out of his mind.

Stuart dressed carefully in a quiet gray wool suit, light blue cotton shirt, and dark blue tie bearing the device of the Royal Ocean Racing Club. He would have liked to wear a uniform, but his blues were in storage in New York, and anyway, the rank devices would have been wrong even if the trousers had fit. Stuart took a cab to the embassy and presented his ID and his newly issued orders. The marine guard had him sign the duty roster and sign again for his new ID. Stuart hung the embassy Access 1 ID around his neck and proceeded as directed to the third-floor conference room.

Men in various uniforms and in civilian clothes were milling around, getting coffee and shaking hands with each other. Stuart nodded to Captain Harris, who was talking with a rear admiral in the front of the room. Stuart waved to Forrest and nodded to Maniero and to Professor Masad. A huge, heavy hand dropped on his shoulder and spun him around. Stuart looked up into a face that seemed to have come from a Frederic Remington bronze sculpture.

"Hello, White-Eyes!" boomed the bronze giant cheerfully.

Stuart grinned and shook the hand that dropped from his shoulder. "Why, Rufus Loonfeather! I haven't seen you since Nam in, I guess, early sixty-eight. I'm glad to see you!"

Loonfeather grinned. He was a full-blooded Indian of the Dakota Nation, with a nose hooked like the beak of a hawk, dark mahogany skin, and deep-set black eyes. He smiled, his teeth gleaming white as they shone against his dark, thin lips. Loonfeather's uniform, that of lieutenant colonel in the Army, was covered with decorations and badges. "That's right, William. The famous battle for Horsehead Mountain. But I'm not glad to see you! You were bad medicine for me that day; I lost many coups because your navy assets chewed up my targets."

Stuart laughed. He remembered Loonfeather had liked to put on the accent and manner of a Hollywood Indian, especially when telling war stories. "And I never apologized."

"That's all right; *we* always expect *you* to speak with forked tongue. Besides, when I first met you, in that hokey survival school when we were both newly commissioned butter-bars,

you and that insane marine friend of yours got me a beating
and a trip to the box. *Very* bad medicine! No, sir, Commander,
I'm not glad to see you." His grin belied the statement.

Stuart's own smile faded momentarily. He remembered
that marine well; Billy Hunter had engineered their escape
from the prison camp of SERE training and had later been
killed while under Stuart's command on the first night of
the Tet Offensive of 1968. Before the end of Tet and the
counterattacks that followed, Stuart's small unit of air and
naval gunfire spotters had been virtually wiped out.

The rear admiral rapped on the lectern in the front of
the room, and the men quickly found seats and were quiet.

"Good morning, gentlemen," began the admiral. "I'm
Rear Admiral Wilson, N-2 for Admiral Lee at CINCUSNAV-
EUR." CINCUSNAVEUR was Commander in Chief, U.S.
Naval Forces, Europe, as only the military could compress
it. "You all know why you're here, in general, so let me go
briefly through the Table of Organization, and then we can
split up and try to do some useful work." The admiral went
through a series of flip charts, obviously hastily prepared,
showing how CINCUSNAVEUR himself, Admiral Lee, was
in charge of organizing the task force, reporting to the Joint
Chiefs, and Admiral Wilson was head of Plans. Everybody
in this meeting belonged to Plans. Other charts set forth
the forces that might be brought into the actual operation,
if one were needed. The combat operation was under the
overall command of Admiral Bergeron, commander of the
Sixth Fleet. The forces included one carrier battle group
around the *America,* one more around *Nimitz,* now crossing
the Atlantic from Norfolk at high speed, and two marine
battalion landing teams, embarked on two naval amphibious
squadrons that had been steaming off Lebanon, complete
with their helicopter squadrons. These forces were expected
to do the extraction itself, but several specialized units from
the Army and Air Force were also listed, including Airborne
units, Rangers, helicopter gunship squadrons from the Army,

and fighter-bomber and heavy transport squadrons from the Air Force.

Clearly enough force to obliterate Wheelus and the entire Libyan military, if it came to that, mused Stuart as the briefing droned on, but we still need a scheme to protect the hostages from the terrorists until they are actually lifted out.

Admiral Wilson finished with the overview and returned to the detailed chart for Plans. Stuart saw his own name and Loonfeather's in a box marked "On the Ground Tactics," along with the name of a Colonel Brimmer, USMC.

When the admiral came to that box in his briefing, he said that "On the Ground Tactics" was meant to devise ways and means of securing the hostages at the onset of the operation, and of neutralizing threats to them from either the terrorists of the Abu Salaam faction, who were presumed still to be holding the hostages, or from the Libyan forces on the air base. Simple enough, thought Stuart, grinning at Loonfeather, who shook his head.

The briefing broke for supper, which was sandwiches and coffee served by embassy staff in the conference room. During the meal, Doctor Masad briefed on political developments.

Doctor Masad was a short, energetic-looking man, slightly stout, and fifty years old. He had weak, red-rimmed eyes behind half-glasses, smooth, sallow skin, wooly graying hair, and a short-trimmed beard. He looked like the professor the briefing list said that he was. He spoke slowly, in Oxford-accented but slightly singsong English.

"Gentlemen, this part of the briefing is also top secret," Masad began. "Naturally, the U.S. government would prefer a political, and bloodless, solution to this problem."

Doctor Masad drank some coffee, picked up the admiral's pointer, and referred to his own flip chart, headed "The Abu Salaam Faction." The professor tapped the chart and looked sad. "These men are fanatics of a particular order, gentlemen. They are Shi'ites of an especially orthodox bent.

To die in the defiance of God's enemies, they believe, will grant them immediate entry into paradise. And to die for Abu Salaam amounts to virtually the same thing." The professor took another sip of coffee. "Abu Salaam, whose nom de guerre, gentlemen, means Father of Peace in Arabic [there was a murmur of anger in the room] was born, we think, in Bethlehem, on the West Bank, in nineteen-forty-five. We don't know his true name. It's unlikely that he was originally Shia, coming from that area.

"His early political career began with Al-Fatah, the group headed by Yassir Arafat. But in the sixties, he moved to the side of Dr. George Habbash, a Lebanese physician and the leader of the Popular Front for the Liberation of Palestine, where he pledged himself and his growing group of followers to terrorist activities inside Israel. Later, we think about nineteen-eighty, he abandoned Habbash, considering him too moderate, and moved his group to Libya and into the sphere of Colonel Baruni."

Loonfeather got up quietly and brought back a full pot of coffee. The room had become very still, the men totally absorbed.

"Baruni, and more recently, Khomeini, have spread the doctrine that the true enemy of Islam, the Great Satan, is not Israel alone, but the superpower the Shi'ites view as Israel's partner and protector, the United States." Doctor Masad paused and drank some water from a glass on the podium.

"So his operation has two goals, gentlemen. To embarrass the United States and to publicize the power of the terrorists of Abu Salaam. And, gentlemen," the professor took off his half-glasses and paused, rubbing his red eyes, "the more violent the end of this drama, the better they will like it."

Admiral Wilson rose. "Professor, what about Baruni? Where does he fit in all of this?"

The professor had picked up his notes. Clearly he had thought he was finished, and was glad to be going. He put the notes down. "Admiral, Baruni has been ruler of Libya,"

Masad paused and rubbed his tired eyes, "*my* country, since the coup in 1969. Nevertheless, little is known of him. He was born in Surt, of Arabized Berber parents, in approximately 1942. He was educated by Arab tutors." The professor seemed to be rushing, and his voice was taut. "He was a member of the Free Officers' Movement, which studied together in the now-closed Benghazi Military Academy, and later plotted to overthrow, and indeed overthrew, the government of King Idris. He is very religious. He believes he guides a sacred pan-Arab crusade against the Great Satan, the United States. That he supports Arab, and indeed, non-Arab terror is beyond dispute. Whether he has any control over Abu Salaam, we can only speculate." The professor looked pained.

"Speculate," directed Admiral Wilson.

"I would say not, Admiral," said the professor, as he seemed to shrink into his rumpled suit. "Abu Salaam is unmindful of the influence of any man, even Baruni. It is even said that he believes he is the Mahdi, the Messenger of God."

"Thank you, Professor," said the admiral very quietly. Doctor Masad nodded and shuffled out of the conference room, his head bowed.

⇋12⇌
Moscow, 2000 GMT (2300 Moscow Local)

Ilya Antonovich Doryatkin, the Foreign Minister of the Union of Soviet Socialist Republics, lifted the bottle of Polish herb vodka and filled the glasses in front of the three men seated around the end of the huge conference table. The General Secretary of the Communist party of the Soviet Union and the chairman of the Committee on State Security (KGB) each raised his glass and drank, and then the stocky, red-faced Foreign Minister resumed speaking.

"Comrades, this incident in Libya comes at a bad time. We have been trying to move the Americans to a more reasonable posture on arms control, and on trade and technology."

"Nevertheless, it has happened," commented Mikhail Ivanovich Nevsky, the head of the KGB and always the hardest line against improving state relations with the U.S., "and we might as well make the best of it."

Doryatkin glanced at the General Secretary, looking for support. He saw a tired old man, fighting against emphysema for each succeeding breath. Doryatkin continued. "Agreed, Comrade, but what good can be made of this? We have told Baruni to end this crisis, to force the terrorists to send the Americans to some neutral country or to neutralize the terrorists himself. He refuses!" The Foreign Minister waved his arms above his head and paced the room. He stopped in front of a map of North Africa and jabbed at the area around Tripoli with a thick, nicotine-stained finger. "What the fuck do we support these petty dictators for if they won't do as we wish?" The last was a swipe, however feeble, at the head of the KGB, who had long been a supporter of Baruni in that he willfully, even gleefully, transhipped Soviet materiel to movements of "national liberation" from El Salvador to the Philippines. Nevsky smiled coldly, and the General Secretary continued to breathe noisily, while dabbing his watery eyes with a handkerchief.

The Foreign Minister ran his finger around the outline of Libya on the map. "We now have Baruni giving the Americans a perfect reason to invade Libya, and to eliminate its airstrips and its ground-to-air defenses—the only things in the entire country worth having should we ever want to attack the Middle East or deep into Africa."

"If the Americans attack," said Nevsky carefully, "what assets do we have at risk, Comrade?"

Doryatkin wished the Defense Minister, old Marshal Tikunin, were present at the meeting, but he was attending a Warsaw Pact exercise in Hungary. The old man was an ally, at least most of the time, against the ambitious head of the KGB. Doryatkin answered carefully, "We have three Spetznaz teams in Libya, training various groups of freedom fighters [Doryatkin regretted his earlier slip in calling them terrorists] and we have sixty pilots attached to their Air Force, supporting North Koreans and Cubans who would fly actual combat missions. Also, we have advisers in their armored and mechanized units, from commanders down through the company level."

"These men will be in harm's way if the Americans attack," said Nevsky without expression, hiding his pale, thin face behind his hands as he lit a cigarette.

Doryatkin lit a cigarette for himself. "Yes, Comrade?"

"Then we must support the Libyans," said Nevsky with a slight smile.

Doryatkin opened his mouth to speak. The General Secretary intervened. "Yes," he wheezed, "we must."

Doryatkin smiled politely, picked up his papers, and spoke. "I will send a strongly worded message to the Americans, Comrade General Secretary, but I cannot believe they will be deterred."

"We will announce our support for a peaceful solution," said Nevsky, relishing his victory, "and we will condemn hijacking, as always. But we must be ready to defend the sovereignty of our brothers in Socialist Arab Libya."

"Mumpf," said the General Secretary, coughing wetly into his handkerchief and nodding. Doryatkin gathered the last of his papers and left the room.

⇋13⇌
Washington, 2300 GMT (1800 Local)

"What do the Russians say?" asked the President. He had felt the entire day weighing on him since early morning.

The Secretary of State spread his large hands open before him. "Dobrynin says that they will not stand by—his words—stand by for a violation of the sovereignty of Libya."

"And what of the goddamned terrorists?" spat the President.

The Secretary of State was startled. The President rarely

used profanity of any kind. The Secretary sighed. "The Soviets condemn the hijacking in a TASS statement, sir, as well as to us privately, but they will not condemn the Libyans for giving sanctuary."

"Ach," said the President, rising and walking to the windows to look out at the rose garden illuminated by dim floodlights. "What's their game? They know we cannot stand for this."

"Sir, we have to keep this in proportion to other events," put in the Secretary of Defense.

"God*dammit*, Dave!" exploded the President. "Right now, there *are* no other events! We have an American plane forced down in Libya, and sixty-five American people, most of them servicemen in uniform, held hostage! There is *no proportionality!*

"Sir," began David, drawing a breath. "We have many things on the table before the Russians at this time, not the least arms control."

The President turned from the window and pointed his finger at the Secretary of Defense like a gun. "I want military options, Dave, to get those people out of the hands of those terrorists and back into ours. And I want them tomorrow, at breakfast, here, in this room."

"Yes, sir, but we should consider—"

The President cut him off. "Something that will work, Dave. Tomorrow, eight in the morning."

The Secretary of Defense nodded, then rose and stood at what he thought was attention. "Yes, sir, Mr. President."

The President nodded curtly to the two cabinet secretaries, his face set in a grim mask, and left the office.

⇋DAY TWO⇋

⇋1⇋
London, 16 February, 0015 GMT

Loonfeather and Stuart were assigned a small office on the first floor of the huge Chancery Building. Stuart collected all the maps and plans of Uqba ben Nafi he had obtained from the Air Force and the CIA, as well as the satellite and SR-71 photographs from the safe in Captain Harris's office, and found his way to the new space. Loonfeather was already there, pushing filing cabinets around and clearing one wall so they could pin up the charts. A compact marine colonel stepped into the room, identified himself as Bob Brimmer, and shook hands with Stuart and Loonfeather. Stuart took a roll of masking tape and arrayed the topographical charts of Wheelus along the bottom of the wall, with the most recent photographs above them.

"Jesus, these pictures are clear," said Loonfeather, making notes on a clipboard. "Two platoons of T-72s dug in at each road entrance, east and west. Six tanks each group, with towed antitank guns maybe three hundred meters behind them, just inside the perimeter fence. I count eighteen more tanks, spread out along the southern perimeter of the base, all dug into shallow fighting positions, some facing inland and a few facing the base. Ten more—a full company— in positions on the beach, here, near the end of runway 03/21, and in these shallow depressions east of the POL area."

"Wouldn't you think they'd keep some up on the tarmac," asked Colonel Brimmer, "to block the runways?"

Loonfeather nodded. "I sure would, Colonel, and I'd expect them to keep moving around. Those fixed positions are all right if your enemy doesn't know where you are, and can't spot artillery onto you."

"We'll have massive firepower from the guns on the destroyers and the battleship," said Stuart, following Loonfeather's right hand as it flew from one photo to another, as his left traced the positions on the plan of the air base.

"Massive," said Loonfeather, "and very accurate. And we'll have fighter-bombers and helicopter gunships. As a

47

defensive setup for the base, these tanks are very poorly deployed."

"How does that change our planning?" asked Stuart, seating himself on the table in front of the photos and maps.

"The problem of those tanks is not so much that they can keep us from taking the base," said Loonfeather slowly, "but that they can reach the Operations Building quickly once we show our hand. We'll get no praise for killing tanks if one or two get into that building and shoot up our people."

"The second problem is that any tank we don't see or don't kill will have a turkey shoot with our helicopters," said Colonel Brimmer.

"So we have to plan to eliminate all the tanks before we can go in?" asked Stuart.

"We probably can't wait that long," said Brimmer, squinting at the photos. "Anyway, we should have some surprise going in. But we sure as hell have to deal with them before we extract."

"Hm," said Loonfeather. "Let's see what they have for air defenses." With his felt-tipped pen, Loonfeather made circles around three whitish objects that looked to Stuart like the business ends of pitchforks. "These are SA-3 missiles, NATO-designation GOA, here below the intersection of the runways. The trucks neatly parked behind each are the FLAT FACE–LOW BLOW radars, the target acquisition and guidance system. Those missile launchers are hard to move, but you'd think they would at least disperse the radar trucks."

Brimmer and Stuart made notes. "What about guns?" asked Brimmer. "Guns worry me more than missiles."

"Out here, at both ends of runway 03/21 and at the eastern end of runway 11/29, Bob," Loonfeather pointed with his pen. "These are Russian S-60s, 57mm automatic cannons. It's a 1950s weapon, but dangerous against low-flying aircraft. Like the SAMs, they're not mobile."

"Another target for the ships' gunfire computers," noted Stuart, writing quickly.

"Exactly," said Loonfeather.

"So what do you think, Colonel?" asked Brimmer. "Seems a pretty naive setup. Is this standard Soviet doctrine?"

"Far from it, Colonel," said Loonfeather. "The Russians are a lot better than this. They would concentrate their tanks in maneuver units, and they'd hide what they couldn't keep moving. This almost looks as though the Russ have washed their hands."

"We'll have to keep up with the recon photos," said Brimmer, writing.

"What are these vehicles near the aircraft, Rufus?" asked Stuart.

"Armored personnel carriers. Those, and the ones parked on the apron near the Maintenance Building, are Russian BTR-60s. The two little ones with the tanks on the beach are Brazilian EE-9 Cascavel armored scout cars, and the small tracked vehicles mixed in with the tanks on the southern perimeter are Russ BMP-76s."

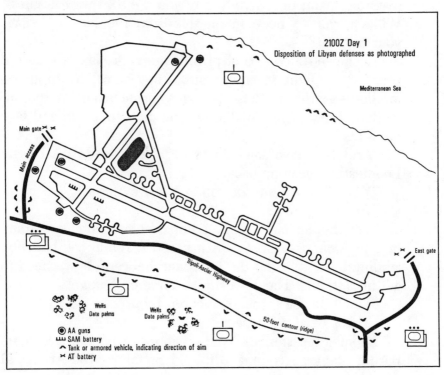

21OOZ Day 1
Disposition of Libyan defenses as photographed

Mediterranean Sea

Main gate

Main access

East gate

Tripoli-Asclar Highway

Wells
Date palms

Wells
Date palms

50-foot contour (ridge)

● AA guns
⊔⊔ SAM battery
⌃ Tank or armored vehicle, indicating direction of aim
⋊ AT battery

"Sounds like you have done a fair bit of photointerpretation work, Rufus!" laughed Stuart. The photos were clear, but not that clear, he thought to himself.

"Yeah. 'Bout all we do in Europe is look at pictures of the Soviets and their allies," said Loonfeather, too absorbed to notice the laugh. He was running his long fingers over the curves of the topographical maps as Brimmer crouched beside him. Loonfeather suddenly stood and turned his back on the charts and pictures. He stepped to the steel table on which Stuart was seated, gesturing for Colonel Brimmer to take the straight-backed wooden chair at the head of the table.

Colonel Brimmer shook his head, "No, thanks, Colonel. You run the brief while my thoughts catch up." Stuart slid off the table and sat across from Brimmer. Loonfeather sat, steepled his long fingers in front of him, and grinned happily. "Gentlemen, no one has actually told me why I'm on this planning team, or why either of you are, but we can guess. William, you've been in on this from the outset. What's your interest?"

"I cracked a couple of prison camps in Nam a hundred years ago. Quiet in, quiet out. They want my input on method—getting to those hostages and neutralizing the immediate threat long enough for you guys to get in and take them out."

"And you have some ideas as to how to do that?" said Loonfeather, leaning back.

"Yes. I'll lay it out for you in a few minutes."

"Good. Colonel?"

"I'm the Special Landing Force commander embarked in USS *Inchon*, with the Sixth Fleet. A reinforced battalion landing team, plus all the boats and helicopters we need to get in, and out. There's a similar force on *Saipan*."

"You'll do the actual extraction, then."

"That's what we expect."

Loonfeather smiled. "And my job, gentlemen, is Colonel Baruni's tanks. I command the 3d Battalion, 73d Armor, at

Fort Bragg, North Carolina. We have the only air-droppable armor capability in the U.S. Army."

"You parachute with tanks?" asked Stuart, taken aback.

"Not exactly parachute, and not exactly tanks. M-551 Sheridans; fast, big 152mm gun, but no real armor. Hit and run weapons."

"Can you break through those T-72s with such a light force?" asked Brimmer.

Loonfeather's smile expanded. "Not if we play fair, gentlemen."

Stuart frowned. "Rufus, the kind of unit I think we could get into the middle of the base should be able to handle the hijackers, and we would figure to spread enough light demolitions to prevent the interceptors from getting up, but there's no way they'll be able to stand off any sort of assault while you're parachuting into the desert and forcing the perimeter of the base."

Loonfeather positively beamed. "Quite so. We will therefore just have to land our men and equipment in the middle of the base, then let the Libyans worry about breaking through us."

The three men leaned forward and began talking in earnest. Stuart told how he was planning to get the SEALs in via the water reservoir, and how naval gunfire would be prespotted to take out the tanks and antiaircraft guns and missiles as soon as the SEALs had control of the hostages. The Navy would establish immediate air superiority over the base with carrier-based fighters, while navy and marine attack aircraft and helicopters aided the Airborne in destroying or driving off the Libyan armor and infantry. Loonfeather described how the first paratroopers would be on the airfield less than three minutes later, and the Sheridans off-loaded and cranked up before the Libyan tanks could crawl out of their fighting positions, once they discovered they were mostly pointed in the wrong directions. As soon as the Airborne had secured a defensive perimeter in the area around the Operations Building, the marine assault force would land in sufficient strength to assure the area was secure against counterattack, and the SEALs would have the hostages ready to go out on the first returning assault birds. Then the big marine helicopters would return, load the soldiers and marines, and be gone.

When Captain Harris entered the room at 0220, he found the three men of the planning team laughing and slapping each other on the back. He poured out coffee from a thermos. Whooping with the enthusiasm of schoolboys, the three field-grade officers outlined the plan. Captain Harris was impressed, if politely skeptical. "Very ambitious, from a command and control standpoint."

"Oh yes, Captain, it will be a bitch," said Loonfeather, "but we have something special going on here, perhaps unique in the history of joint operations. The men doing the planning are the ones who will actually coordinate the fighting units."

"And you think the Airborne can get in there, smack in the middle of that air base?" asked Captain Harris.

"Hell, yes, Captain," said Loonfeather, standing next to the largest map of Uqba ben Nafi. "My troopers will hit the center of that base like a fire arrow landing on the roof of a sleeping pony soldier's pup tent!" Loonfeather turned and drove his fist into the center of the map with enough force to shake the wall. He turned back to the room, his eyes bright and his grin lopsided.

Stuart looked at the big Indian and started to laugh. Colonel Brimmer and Captain Harris looked startled and a little worried. Stuart threw his arm around Loonfeather's shoulder. "Gentlemen, you have to get to know this officer. He isn't mad, he's acting." Stuart stage-whispered in Loonfeather's ear. "Rufus, try to remember *you* are the cavalry."

Loonfeather straightened up and replaced his mad grimace with his broad grin. "Right. In this life, I'm a bluebelly."

"I must say I like it," said John Harris.

"The op? The op will be dynamite," said Loonfeather.

"I like the name, anyway."

"What name?" asked Bob Brimmer.

"Operation Fire Arrow," said Harris as he left the room.

The planning groups reconvened in the embassy's third-floor conference room at 0400, and individual teams made quick reports of progress. Secure satellite voice and data links were established with the Sixth Fleet group on the *America* and with the Joint Chiefs in the Pentagon. Much of the information, especially recommendations for moving forces and materiel around, was able to be exchanged by computers talking directly to each other. Information was processed and displayed as options on monitors in the three locations simultaneously, though the embassy had far less computing and display capability than either of the military facilities. London's role was planning and political, so London led off.

The terrorists' original deadline for the beginning of execution of hostages was less than twenty-eight hours away, said Admiral Wilson as he began his brief. The Italian government continued to press Baruni to ask for more time, and the Libyan leader had expressed willingness to help, but said he hadn't the power to force the Abu Salaam. Baruni had suggested a gesture of good faith, perhaps just acceding to one demand, for the release of Abu Salaam himself. The Italian cabinet had reportedly been meeting all night in closed session, refusing to admit either the U.S. Ambassador or his Libyan counterpart. Admiral Wilson was interrupted by a voice on the voice scrambler from Washington, its tone flat and tinny from the electronic coding and decoding.

"Admiral, Jeffrey Laird, National Security Adviser to the President. We think it likely that Abu Salaam will be released, despite two calls from the President to Premier Calvi. At best, they may buy us a little time."

Admiral Bergeron broke in from *America*. "The question then becomes whether we try to interdict his passage from Rome to Uqba ben Nafi."

"It is not under consideration, Admiral," replied Laird. "Given what we know of the Abu Salaam, any attack on their leader will result in an immediate slaughter of our hostages."

The room in London grew noisy with murmurs of frustration. Stuart dozed in his chair. He thought this topic would drag on for many hours before they got to his team's plan, which, upon reflection, he thought would be rejected anyway as being impossibly complex.

He was wrong. The political brief was brought to a swift conclusion by General Elmendorf, the chairman of the JCS, who had reached Washington only that evening following a hasty return from meetings in Japan. The chairman wanted to know his military options, and his first question was how the hostages could be kept alive long enough to get them out. Stuart faced the microphones that fed the local loudspeakers and the scrambler net, and spoke very briefly about how a bomber at high altitude could precision-drop a SEAL team into the reservoir from above Libyan radar coverage. The team could then move to neutralize some ready aircraft and vehicles and secure the hostages from the terrorists. Brimmer and Loonfeather briefed together, describing the complex command and control problems, along with proposed solutions in what Stuart thought was impressive detail. The room was completely silent as Loonfeather described how his Airborne Armor and infantry would hold the center against four companies of T-72 tanks, and keep them out in the open until they could be killed by naval gunfire and aircraft. The air was electric with tension, and Stuart imagined that the crackle of static in the Washington and *America* speakers had increased. There were remarkably few questions, most of them technical. General Elmendorf once again closed debate. "OK, people, say we go with this. It's crazy, and it could get bloody, but I think we would stand at least a fair chance of getting those dependents back alive. Colonel Loonfeather, the extraction of your troops worries me the most."

"It's the diciest part, General, but we have planned for this, and practiced it, for years," said Loonfeather, returning to the podium.

"I know. The official designation is an Airborne Armored Raid, is it not?"

"Yes, General," Loonfeather smiled, "and it has almost worked, in practice, twice!"

Laughter cut into the tension, but it ended quickly. Loonfeather continued. "Fact is, General, we'll lose some of the vehicles on the drop, maybe as many as a third, but we'll be behind the Libyans, and their lack of readiness and our air power should do the rest while our marine corps friends dip in and grab the hostages."

"You going to try this at night?" General Elmendorf was an ex-paratrooper, and he had always hated night airborne operations.

"Hell, no, General. Dawn. We can parachute infantry at night, and in fact would prefer to, but the Air Force needs daylight to land the armor. But, hell, the most terrifying thing to those Libyans is just gonna be seeing us come down."

"OK, gentlemen. We have to pull all this together and get it to the White House by 0800, just eight hours' time. Needs? Navy?"

Stuart stepped forward. "We need an eight-man SEAL team, preferably familiar with over-water HALO drops, and a place to build a mock-up of the central areas of Wheelus for detailed training. Ideally that training base should be in Europe or North Africa, so we can deploy quickly if needed. The SEALs will be going in at night. And then we'll need a B-52 with an outstanding aircrew, sir."

Loonfeather and Brimmer had much longer lists.

⇌2⇌

The Negev Desert, Israel, 1115 GMT (1315 Local)

The U.S. Air Force C-140, a military version of the Lockheed Dash-8 Jetstar executive jet, taxied to a stop in front of the spartan terminal at the secret Israeli training base deep in the Negev. The place had no official name, but was called Tzafon may Eilat—North of Eilat. Stuart had been told that one of its uses had been to rehearse the successful

Israeli raid on Entebbe Airport in Uganda in 1976. Maybe the place has luck, he thought, as he picked up his small carryall and filed off the plane into the glaring heat.

Stuart had been very glad of the three hours of sleep he had picked up on the flight from London, and he felt energetic, ready to get started, despite the enervating heat. The other passengers on the flight with him were engineers and construction specialists who would build the replicas of the central structures of Uqba ben Nafi along the northeast-southwest runway of the Israeli base, exactly to the plans of the original Wheelus except modified to correspond to details picked up in the reconnaissance photographs. The Israelis had supplied four tanks and six armored personnel carriers, with crews, for training the Americans. Stuart noted that all were Russian, the same models as in the Libyan inventory. That surprised him, though he knew it shouldn't; the Israelis had captured much Russian equipment during their frequent battles with their Soviet-supplied neighbors. Good news, though, he thought, as he walked around an eight-wheeled BTR-60 armored personnel carrier. The SEALs will be able to familiarize themselves with important details of the vehicles, especially things like location of guns and lights, vision blocks, and blind spots.

An Israeli Defense Force captain, an exceptionally pretty woman who looked about thirty, walked up to Stuart, saluted, and smiled. She was petite and olive-skinned, with huge, liquid brown eyes. Her hair was glossy black and rather too long to look military, and her body was full of curves that could not be hidden by starched fatigues. The Sam Browne belt, which supported her pistol holster, fitted tightly around her waist and nicely separated her breasts. Stuart returned the salute a bit self-consciously, and grinned. He was in U.S. Army sand, pink, and gray desert fatigues, and for the first time since he had been involved in the operation, wore the silver oak leaves of a navy commander on the collar points.

"Welcome, Commander Stuart," smiled the tiny officer. "I am Captain Leah Rabin, the IDF liaison officer."

Liaison, thought Stuart. Don't I wish. She would probably break my spine with a judo chop if I even suggested it. Nevertheless, he smiled again and tried to look charming. "Thank you, Captain. I hope we will not be in your way very long."

"Israel is a very informal country, Commander. Call me Leah."

"OK, Leah, I'm William." They shook hands. Her grip was firm, but undeniably feminine. Jesus, she's lovely, thought William. I had better get my tiny mind back on the business at hand.

They walked together down into a concrete blockhouse a short way from the runway. Its roof was level with the desert. Inside it was very cool and dry, though there was no evidence of air-conditioning. Leah stopped before a mock-up of the base, which was presented on a table approximately twenty feet long and eighteen feet wide. Brad Collins, a senior engineer from the American construction company that had built Wheelus, and who had visited the base several times in the late sixties, was conferring with the head of the Israeli construction crew. They were referring to the plans Collins had spread out on a smaller table.

"How does it look, Brad?" asked Stuart. They had talked briefly while they waited for the plane to leave London.

Collins smiled, his deeply tanned face breaking up into hundreds of fine lines, the marks of a lifetime of working in strong sunlight. "No sweat, Commander. The runways here intersect at about the same angle as at Wheelus, though the orientation is a little different. My new friend Yitzak, here, tells me we have all the materials we need, and plenty of men and equipment. We'll have it laid out by late afternoon, and then we'll build it at night. You'll have a workable mock-up of the central part of Wheelus, accurate to the half meter, by sunrise tomorrow."

"Good, good," said Stuart, smiling at Collins and Yitzak, and especially at Leah. I just can't help feeling good about this, he thought. The SEALs arrive later this afternoon; I hope they're a good group.

⇆3⇄

Washington, 1300 GMT (0800 EST)

The Secretaries of Defense and State stood as the President entered the Oval Office. The President looked crisp and rested in a pressed blue suit and white shirt and small-figured red tie. The Secretary of State felt a sudden awareness of his unkempt appearance and great fatigue; the senior staff briefing had begun at 3 A.M. and concluded just twenty minutes ago. He looked sideways at the Secretary of Defense and noted the bastard had somehow found time to shave, and smelled faintly of after-shave lotion.

The President motioned his cabinet officers to a small table that had been set up for breakfast before the fireplace. A navy steward swiftly served juice, eggs, sausages, rolls, and coffee from silver serving pieces onto blue- and gold-edged china, which bore the seal of the President of the United States. Only after the steward had departed did any of the three men say a word beyond "good morning."

"Well, Dave, Henry, where do we stand?"

The Secretary of State leaned forward. "The political news is mostly bad, Mr. President."

"Shoot," said the President, sipping his orange juice.

Henry Holt glanced hungrily at the full breakfast before him, then continued. "The Italians have informed us, a scant fifteen minutes ago, that they have agreed to release Abu Salaam—".

"Damn!" said the President, shaking his head. "And?"

"Well, they think they bought us some time, sir; seventy-two more hours, to meet the rest of the hijackers' demands before any executions take place."

The President ate a forkful of scrambled eggs. Holt's

stomach growled audibly. "What else did the Italians give away?"

"They promised to deliver Abu Salaam to Tripoli, in an Italian Air Force aircraft, and they promised to refrain from any actions against the terrorists, or against Libya, unless the hostages are harmed."

"White-livered socialists!" spat the President. "Dave?"

The Secretary of State fell gratefully to eating his eggs and savoring the always-excellent White House coffee. It was Wasserstein's turn, and as usual, he had staged a small triumph. "Mr. President, we, that is London, and Sixth Fleet, and the Joint Chiefs, think we have, ah, the beginnings of a workable plan to extract our people, if political means fail."

"Lay it out, Dave," said the President.

Fuck you, Dave, thought the Secretary of State.

⇋4⇌

Uqba ben Nafi Air Base, 1400 GMT (1500 Local)

Colonel Hassan al-Baruni sat in the rear of the air-conditioned Mercedes limousine, which was parked immediately in front of the Operations Building. A BTR-60 flanked the car on either side, each with the markings of Baruni's elite bodyguard unit, which was made up entirely of young, attractive women. The BTRs had escorted the colonel's limousine down from Tripoli and would go with him when he departed. The two BTRs of the regular Army had pulled back to positions in front of the Maintenance Building, across the apron to the north.

Baruni watched as the small jet with Italian Air Force rondels on its wings descended over the Mediterranean and landed to the southwest on runway 21. The American DC-8 had been towed away to a parking spot on the north end of the apron, so the Italian jet could taxi as close to the Operations Building as possible. Abu Salaam had insisted on that.

He is afraid we might shoot him, thought Colonel Baruni. Perhaps we should.

As the aircraft taxied to a stop in front of him, Baruni
climbed out of the car and adjusted his dark glasses against
the glare. Television cameras whirred, and the colonel waved
to the reporters and smiled his handsome smile.

The colonel was above medium height, with strong features, especially his nose and the line of his jaw. His skin
was tanned and faintly pitted over his high cheekbones. His
eyes were dark and deep set, but now hidden behind the
very dark aviator-style sunglasses. He looked trim in a tailored, open-necked khaki uniform, the two stars and eagle
of a colonel, or *aqid*, on each shoulder board. His wave to
the cameras was a clenched fist. His honor guard crashed
to attention and presented their AK-47 assault rifles. Other
soldiers ringed the Italian aircraft, weapons held at the ready.
The door of the aircraft opened and Abu Salaam, born Ali
Hassan Nazim, walked the short distance and embraced the
colonel. The troops around the aircraft were waved away,
and the Italian jet began to taxi immediately. Baruni smiled.
It had been part of the deal that the Italians would get minimum television coverage of their plane.

Baruni held Abu Salaam by the shoulders, smiling at
him. In fact he was not at all glad to see his former pupil.
Abu Salaam was at least six inches shorter than Baruni, skinny
and hollow-eyed. His nose was a great, protruding beak,
and he wore a scruffy, tangled beard. His mouth was wet,
his black slacks and white shirt were dirty and wrinkled,
and he smelled. "Come and sit with me a minute in the
car, Ali," said Baruni softly.

Abu Salaam sank into the soft leather of the Mercedes
with a sigh. The windows of the car were black and reflective
on the outside, and the honor guards deployed themselves
to keep the reporters at a distance. Baruni sat beside the
terrorist and frowned. "You should have consulted me about
this operation, Ali."

Abu Salaam smiled, revealing crooked, stained teeth.
"Would you have agreed?"

"No."

"But now you will help us, my brother?"

Baruni turned in the seat and leaned toward the smaller man. "You leave me little choice. The Libyan Arab Jamahiriya stands with freedom fighters and against imperialism and Zionism, Ali, but this operation is too exposed to retaliation! It must be concluded quickly."

Abu Salaam's smile decayed into a sneer. "You grow fat, my Colonel, in your soft limousine with all your oil money and so few people to care for. You forget the masses who confront the Zionists from squalid camps in the Lebanon, and from concentration camps in the occupied territories."

Baruni pulled off his black glasses and glared at Abu Salaam. "You will not talk to me in this manner! We support the struggle in all possible ways, but this is foolhardy! The American Sixth Fleet is on the horizon, and growing bigger every day. They have been aching for an excuse to strike us, and now you have given it to them!"

Abu Salaam giggled. "Then your fine armed forces must protect us, until our demands are met."

Baruni sat back in the cushions. How to *reason* with this *fanatic!* he thought. "Ali, in the West, they say I am mad. Mad to believe in God, mad to believe in the union of all the Arab peoples as one nation. I have given money and support to those who confront the Zionists and the West directly, and arms, and training. I have supported attacks by freedom fighters in Israel and in Europe, even against civilians, so that the peoples of those lands should suffer while Arab brothers and sisters suffer. I do this gladly, Ali, the Libyan people do it gladly. But to bring this plane *here*, into *Libya,* Ali! This risks the destruction of all we have built here, for the good of all Arabs! This *is* madness!"

"But Colonel, already we have achieved much!" Ali's voice was soothing, unctuous. "I am free, and soon reunited with my fighters! The Kuwaitis will have to release my other fighters from their stinking prison. We have divided NATO, and the Americans' puppets in the Arabian Gulf are shaking in their boots! Iran will win the Gulf War, with your help, while we are showing the Americans to be weak and helpless, because they will *not*, my Colonel, *not* risk even the few lives of those pawns," he pointed emphatically toward the Operations Building behind him, "to strike at us! We will win, Hassan, because we have the will, and the courage to be martyrs!"

Baruni shook his head sadly. Ali was right, or at least ideologically correct, and yet the colonel had an awful feeling that this insult would just be too much for the Americans to bear. "Just promise me that we will end this quickly, Ali, and that the lives of the innocent will be protected."

"There are no innocents in this struggle, my Colonel, not Arab children in Gaza, not American children."

"Nevertheless, these people are under your protection, and mine, and God's, Ali. And you and I have specifically pledged to harm no one for four days while the Americans discuss your other demand with the Kuwaitis."

Abu Salaam smiled. "Let us go join my fighters now, Hassan."

The television cameras followed the two men from the limousine to the doors of the Operations Building. Inside in the central hall were the sixty-five passengers and crew members of World Airways flight 41a, seated in four orderly rows of metal folding chairs, all unbound for the first time since they had been brought into the building. Behind them, their faces covered with red-checked *kaffiyia*, were the four fighters who had infiltrated the base and awaited the American aircraft.

I should take them right now, thought Baruni. I have my guards. Blow these fanatics away, right here in front of Libyan and Western pool television cameras, then put these dangerous Americans back on their jet and send them away. But all Arabs must sacrifice for the struggle against Zionism and imperialism, and Abu Salaam has struck many hard blows at the enemy with his small band.

Abu Salaam stood aside, conferring with his young followers. He accepted a kaffiyia and wrapped it around his head and over his face. He had avoided facing the television cameras on the tarmac, and he avoided them now.

Baruni strode among the hostages, smiling and greeting them in his heavily accented English, telling them that every effort was being made to get them home, and that they shouldn't worry, they were in God's hands. Abu Salaam watched Baruni work the crowd like a Western politician, glad that his own expression of contempt was concealed by the kaffiyia. Baruni was once a great leader, thought Abu Salaam, but he has grown soft and rich, far from the pain of the actual struggle. Soon he will see that pain up close, very close. I hope he has the guts for it.

Abu Salaam looked at the faces of the Americans with curiosity. Some showed interest in the bizarre show; many showed fear. Two women were weeping soundlessly. Walid has already begun the teaching, he thought. There was one man alone who returned Abu Salaam's gaze with power, even defiance. A young black marine. Abu Salaam remembered the efforts of radical Arabs to forge ties with American blacks in the 1960s, especially the so-called Black Muslims. Well, no more, Marine. The uniform you wear makes you my enemy. But I can see you are brave, so you will be honored. You will be the first to die. The thought made Abu Salaam feel serene, and he smiled.

The young commander of the freedom fighters read a communique to the television cameras in high-pitched Arabic. He reiterated the demands made earlier through the Libyan leader, and added that once the fighters from Kuwait were delivered to Iran or Libya, the Abu Salaam faction would require forty-eight hours to travel unmolested to a place where they would be given sanctuary, and that then the hostages would be released.

The television crews were escorted from the building, and the doors were closed. Libyan troops once again surrounded the building. The journalists were loaded onto buses and then taken to Tripoli to file their stories. The buses

were held just long enough for Baruni's motorcade to leave
the base ahead of them.

⇌5⇌

Tzafon may Eilat, Israel, 1400 GMT (1600 Local)

Commander Philip Hooper dropped his heavy gear bag
on the tarmac of the secret Israeli base and looked around.
Behind him his seven SEALs hefted boxes of heavy equipment
onto a flatbed truck, and behind them, the U.S. Air Force
transport that had brought them from Norfolk wound up its
engines and accelerated toward takeoff. Hooper was a big
man, over six-feet-three and 220 pounds, with a florid face
under thinning blond hair and small, pale blue eyes. He
was stiff from eleven hours in the cramped seat of the aircraft,
and he felt every one of his forty-three years.

He turned to the smiling officer in army utilities and
the attractive female Israeli officer beside him. Both saluted.
Hooper returned the salute, but his scowl, pressed into his
face on the long flight from Norfolk, did not soften. "Stuart."

"Hoop!"

"Who's the bird?" Hooper noted that the Israeli officer's
smile disappeared as she completed her salute.

"Captain Rabin, IDF," said Stuart, his own smile brittle.

Hooper turned to his seven-man team, then looked
around. The engineers and construction crews were busily
erecting structures where the two runways of the Israeli air
base intersected. "OK, *ma'am,* sorry. Now look, Stuart, we
were friends, lotta years ago, in the Real One. But why in
the fuck—excuse me, ma'am," Hooper bowed with elaborate
courtesy to the Israeli captain.

"Commander Hooper," Stuart felt Leah's voice cut like
a razor. Hooper became suddenly silent. "I can handle military profanity, and *anything else* you can think of, as well
as you. Welcome to Israel, and fuck your mother."

Like it, thought Stuart, grinning. She didn't even raise
her voice.

Hooper reddened, then he smiled. "OK, Captain, I'm sorry. Stuart, why in the fuck are we here to train under a civilian like your long-gone reservist self?"

Stuart grinned. "*Method,* man. Navy brought me back to teach you sledgehammers method. Name of the game here is to bring somebody back alive."

Hooper smiled despite himself. "Not, to be sure, our usual mission. We had best get started."

"Follow me, *gentlemen,*" said Leah Rabin as she turned and strode rapidly toward the concrete bunker. Hooper took a long look at Leah's swinging hips and winked broadly at Stuart.

Inside, the SEALs stacked their gear in a room assigned to them, then gathered around the big table where the base layout was displayed. The layout had been altered since earlier in the day, and now reflected the changes that were in progress to duplicate as nearly as possible the position of key buildings and other facilities of the central part of Uqba ben Nafi Air Base. Red and blue tapes were pinned through the sand on the table, marked with distances from the reservoir to the Operations Building, and to the nearest revetments that contained fighter aircraft in all the photographs. Distances to the big, open tarmac north of the Ops Building were also measured. Stuart let the SEALs look at the mock-up for several minutes, then led them into an adjacent room where he had pinned up the latest recon photos, plus the detailed plans of Wheelus and the rough Table of Organization for the operation. The T/O was prominently marked, "Top Secret—Fire Arrow." The men sat in metal chairs, and Stuart picked up a pointer. "Hoop, why don't you tell us what you know, then I'll try to fill in what I can."

Hooper got up and took the pointer. "OK. Yesterday I get a call. Assemble an eight-man team with HALO experience, the best I have. Naturally I decided to lead it personally." Hooper was grinning now, and much more the man Stuart remembered from twelve years previously in Vietnam. Hooper had run the SEAL detachment in Da Nang in '67 and '68, and had been many times decorated, including a Navy Cross for leading a counterattack against a vastly superior enemy force during the Tet Offensive. He now commanded all SEAL and UDT (underwater demolition team) units in the Atlantic Fleet. "The team here is Feeney, electronics; Jones; Ricardo, commo; Cross; Miller; Osborne, night ops." Osborne raised his hand and grinned. He was very black. "And Goldstein, the medic and our Arab-speaker. We were told we had to do a night HALO into a defended shallow-water target, take and hold some people, and wait for pickup. We were not told where, but being resourceful and able to read newspapers, albeit slowly and with moving lips, we suspect the target is in Libya." Hooper tossed the pointer back to Stuart and sat down. His men applauded.

Leah Rabin stood to one side of the picture board. "Commander, what is a HALO?"

"High Altitude, Low Open, ma'am—"

"Please call me Leah."

"Fine, I'm Hoop. A HALO drop is simply the most terrifying way of getting into someplace undetected ever devised by man. First they load you into the belly of a bomber, stacked on top of each other like logs. Then the bomber gets as high as it can, to get over most radars. The aircrew then tracks onto your drop zone, using the same visual, radar, and computer equipment they have on board to drop a bomb, then they dump you out, wearing more equipment than you can imagine."

"Can you describe the equipment, please?" asked Leah.

"Mighty curious, aren't we?" Hooper looked the question at Stuart.

"Leah will be sharing your training here, Hoop."

Hooper looked back and forth between Stuart and the trim Israeli captain.

"It's part of the deal, Hoop," said Stuart.

Hooper looked back at Leah, whose face was devoid of expression. "Parachute, Captain?"

"Fully qualified, Commander. Also demolitions, night infiltrations, and underwater operations."

Hooper smiled. "OK, we'll show you the gear when we finish here. It's all in the other room, and fortunately, we have extras of everything."

"Please continue about the HALO drop," said Leah, sitting down next to Hooper. She looked at him intently and smiled a little, and Stuart felt a twinge of something like jealousy.

"OK," replied Hooper, all his irritation gone. "The technique was perfected by SEALs to mine Haiphong Harbor. They dropped us out by the sea buoy from B-52s, usually from forty thousand feet, almost always at night. We would free-fall all the way to twenty-five hundred, maybe two thousand feet. Two-stage chutes. We have on wet suits and full scuba gear, and over all that a pressure-envelope suit, and on our chests oxygen to breathe on the way down. Beginning to sound like fun?" Hooper grinned at Leah and Stuart felt irritated and upstaged by his swashbuckling friend.

"Tell me about landing," said Leah. Her expression shifted between fascination and horror.

"Absolutely the best part! We're very heavy with all the gear, but it's a two-stage chute, and the second is big, so the landing is soft. The problem, as you will have already anticipated, is that you have to get rid of the chute—which is weighted to sink fast, by the way—and out of the pressure suit and air-breathing tank, and then reach back and start your scuba air and blow up your buoyancy compensator, all the while sinking toward the bottom of the ocean."

"What about your mask?"

"Low volume. Put it on after you get air going."

"So you take off your helmet—"

"Usually do that in the air, as soon as the chute opens. Also dump the chest pack, which is mounted on the front of the parachute harness. The harness itself has a quick-twist release, and that goes as soon as your fins hit the water. The tough part is the pressure suit, but as soon as you get it unzipped in front and the hood off, you can reach back and get air flowing. Then, you can buddy up to get the rest of it off."

Leah frowned. "How could you count on landing close enough together to find each other underwater to buddy up?"

"Well, remember, we were free-falling in formation. Besides, we had these low-intensity chemical lights attached to our tanks. Very visible under water."

"Then what did you do?"

"Oh, the rest was easy. Swam in six miles, placed a few limpet mines on the ships at the docks, swam back, and got picked up before dawn by high-speed patrol boats."

"But if *anything* malfunctioned," Leah shook her head.

"Yeah, or even got stuck," said Hooper amiably, "but we never lost anyone in an actual operation. We'll show you the gear later. Anyway, that's a HALO, and that is absolutely all I know about why we're here."

Stuart tapped one of the blown-up SR-71 photos with the pointer. "That's a reservoir, used to hold water for fire fighting. We'll drop you in there, at night. We figure that you'll be nearly impossible to see from the Operations Building, here," Stuart moved the pointer, "two hundred meters away from the edge of the reservoir."

"Control tower on top of the Ops Building?"

"Yes."

"So we have to cross two hundred meters of lighted tarmac."

"Lines and shadows, Hoop. What you guys do best."

"Hm," said Hooper. "That pond looks bigger here in the photo than it did on the sand table outside."

"It is. We're duplicating only the southwest corner of the reservoir, still plenty big enough to jump into. The Israelis are naturally reluctant to use any more water out here than they have to."

"Are you actually going to do a HALO drop into that mock-up, here?" asked Leah.

"No," said Stuart. "It's the only part of the mission we can't practice, which is why we needed men with prior operational HALO experience."

"How deep?" asked Hooper, looking at the photo.

"At least three meters. Enough for concealment; you can stay underwater for awhile in case anyone sees or hears the splash and comes to investigate."

"We can get rid of a lot of gear, then," said Hooper, beginning to write on a clipboard. "Won't need wet suits or fins or weight belts; we can use weapons and munitions for weight. One eighteen-cubic-foot tank per man. No buoyancy compensators." He looked at Stuart, a hint of a grin forming. "So then we slip, unseen and Ninja-like, across the tarmac, and enter and secure. What's the strength of the opposition?"

"We think there may be four to six terrorists, either with the hostages or in the tower."

"You sure they're in the Ops Building?"

"Well, they were. Baruni went out and visited them earlier today, and took the TV crews along. By the way, the leader, Abu Salaam himself, is with the terrorists. Said to be a very crazy dude."

"The *Achille Lauro*," said Leah.

"Yeah," Stuart nodded. "Intelligence expects executions. If you can shoot an old man in a wheelchair, shooting sailors and marines should be much more satisfying. That's why this operation has to be ready to go ASAP."

"So we get in and kill the terrorists, and somebody, presumably a lot of somebodies in green suits screaming 'semper fi,' comes and springs us, pronto." Hooper paused and studied the photographs. "Not easy, but possible. Very possible, in fact, but maybe better done with a smaller team."

"Actually, we'd give you more men if we could, but eight is the maximum the Air Force has ever tried to drop from one aircraft at one time. Unfortunately, you'll have a few other tasks besides securing the hostages."

"Like blowing up tanks and planes and stuff."

"Like that."

"You're right, eight won't be enough. What you're saying is that the Libyans will crash in after we grease the terrorists."

"We have to assume so."

"So after we stir up the tanks and troops and planes, which would appear to be *all over* the air base, by blowing up a *few* of them, who keeps the rest of them off our asses so the jarheads can come and get us?"

Stuart told them about Loonfeather's Airborne Armored Raid.

⇋6⇌

Fort Bragg, Fayetteville, North Carolina,
1500 GMT (1000 Local)

Lieutenant Colonel Loonfeather sat at the long table in the operations office on the second floor of the 82d Airborne Division Headquarters on 91 Gruber Road at the end of the old All American way. He closed and rubbed his tired eyes, then opened them again. He had not slept in over thirty hours, other than the few hours of fitful dozing in the cramped seat of the air force transport that had brought him back from London. His eyes felt itchy and he had a throbbing pain in his neck, but it didn't matter. What did matter was that in the less than four hours since landing at Pope Air Force Base, adjacent to Fort Bragg, he had managed to get his op-order out and have it approved, with maximum priority by the long chain of command all the way through the Joint Chiefs, and disseminated. All the units, all of the men and equipment he would need to execute the Airborne Armored Raid on Uqba ben Nafi, were pledged to him, either at Pope or Bragg or on their way, moving toward him.

The operation as conceived was not large. The Airborne Armored Raid had been around, as a concept, for years, and one of its intended missions was to seize and hold an airfield intact. The concept had always had its detractors, most of whom thought the force was too light to get the job done. Most airfields were very large in area, and an enemy would be able to reinforce or render the airfield useless by means of standoff weapons. Still, the Fourth of the Sixty-eighth, the only unit in the Army with the air-droppable M-551 Sheridans, kept practicing.

Shit, it was a long shot, mused Loonfeather. The Sheridans were no match for anybody's main battle tank, but hell, Libyans? It was certainly clear from the dispositions of the Libyan armor that they expected any attack to come from outside the perimeter. The most recent satellite and aerial recon photos showed some tanks and more guns being moved toward the north end of runway 03/21, probably expecting an assault from the sea. Anyway, Loonfeather knew his operation had to be limited to the area in the immediate vicinity of the Operations Building, where the hostages were being held, and had given his reasons to the senior planning group in London, and they had been accepted.

Loonfeather would land his force, consisting of A Company, First Battalion, 502d Parachute Infantry Brigade, and eight Sheridans from his own 3/73 with their eight four-man crews, on the long runway, 11/29. The men would form the defensive perimeter, surrounding the area of the Operations Building and securing the northern three-quarters of runway 03/21 for the marine rifle company to come in and for everyone to go out. As soon as the paratroopers and the Sheridans were assembled and disbursed into fighting positions, the Navy would crater both runways south and east of their intersection, to prevent tanks from crossing from their positions to the south in any kind of order.

Rufus Loonfeather propped his feet on the desk and closed his eyes. He sensed that his whole military career, even his own life, had been preparing him for this single, unique operation. He drifted back to his childhood, to being raised by his grandfather, John Walking Wolf, after his mother and father had both died while Rufus was very young. His grandfather had raised him in the old ways, as much as he still knew them, and the two of them had hiked and camped and trapped and hunted the wild country around Manistique Lake and along the Tahquamenoc and the Fox Rivers, in the birch and evergreen woodlands of the Upper Peninsula of Michigan.

Walking Wolf claimed ancestry from the Dakota Nation of the West Rivers, which had roamed the territory of Montana and Idaho and the Dakotas, and north into Alberta and Saskatchewan, long before the white men had come and named those places. Walking Wolf had been brought to upper Michigan by his own grandfather, a man already old, in the great dispersion of the Plains Indians, which began in 1876, after the battle the white soldiers had forced on Red Cloud and Sitting Bull at the Little Bighorn.

Rufus smiled as he remembered long evenings with Walking Wolf, sitting close to the crackling fire wrapped in their robes of wolverine and badger fur against the bitter cold of early spring or deep autumn. Walking Wolf taught Rufus how to remember the Old Ones and how to call their spirits. Walking Wolf told Rufus of the Ghost Dances, as he had heard of them from his own grandfather, and he taught the boy that the Old Ones would never disappear as long as living people needed them and remembered them. When Rufus went to school, and later to the University of Michigan, he had told the others, the whites, about the Old Ones. Some had laughed, but not many. Some had asked him whether he *believed* in the stories and the magic. Rufus had never understood the question. One did not believe or not believe; one kept the Old Ones, or one lost them forever. Rufus would not lose them.

Rufus became a second lieutenant in the Army Reserve in the summer of 1965, receiving his commission through the ROTC program at the university. He had never thought to make a career in the military, but he had enjoyed the training and the spartan life, and he had done well, first commanding a cavalry platoon in Vietnam and later an Armor company. He found that in the Army his race was an advantage; it made him a curiosity. In Vietnam, Loonfeather had a reputation for knowing where the enemy was and where he wasn't, and when he told other soldiers that the sensitivity came from the Old Ones, they didn't understand, but respected it, because it worked. Rufus's sureness had allowed him to dash across places where the enemy wasn't and concentrate his tanks and his men where the enemy would be.

He discovered another fact of life in the military: an officer or man who did his job well could pursue other interests without regard to any military peer pressure to conform. Rufus Loonfeather left Vietnam in 1974 a very young major with important battlefield decorations. It was recorded in his service record that he had learned, and could speak fluently, Spanish, French, and German. It was not recorded that he wrote poetry and played the piano exceptionally well. Rufus Loonfeather had applied for transfer into the regular Army and was one of not many Vietnam-era reserve majors to be accepted and promoted thereafter. Rufus Loonfeather was an achiever, and he knew that it had all come down to Fire Arrow and the deadly challenge of Uqba ben Nafi Air Base. For as long as he had commanded the 3d of the 73d, he had pored over maps of air bases in Poland and Czechoslovakia and European Russia, training himself and boring himself to distraction, and now he had a shot at a real live air base, defended by enemy tanks.

Loonfeather opened his eyes, yawned, and picked up the top secret op-order. His eight Sheridans would be carried by eight C-130s. Two larger C-141s would drop the paratroopers. Marine Sea Cobra helicopters and navy carrier–based bombers were receiving additional antitank munitions, and a squadron of air force A-10 Warthog antitank aircraft was already at Rheinmain, awaiting permission from the Italian government to move to the Italian air base at Brindisi, close enough to attack inside Libya. The German government had quietly given approval for use of its facilities for assembly, but not for the launching of the actual attack, unless the hostages were seen to be in imminent danger of harm. Same with the Italians. So where the hell else do we launch from? wondered Loonfeather. Still, he figured that unless the politi-

cians pulled a rabbit out of a hat, the Abu Salaam crazies
would begin killing the hostages, and that should be enough
"imminent danger" for the most squeamish NATO government.

Loonfeather had briefed his officers on the operation at
morning officers' call. The briefing had taken less than an
hour. They had been over it so many times, they just had
to learn the locations of the objectives and the specific assign-
ments of the individual units. There had been few questions
and many smiles.

Rehearsals on the mock-up of the area of operation (AO)
of the mission, which had been set up on the western end
of Pope, would begin at 1300.

Damn, thought Loonfeather, shaking his head to clear
the fatigue, we can do this!

He emptied his mind and called out to the Old Ones.

⇆7⇄

**USS *Inchon*, fourteen nautical miles northeast of Tripoli,
1500 GMT (1600 Local)**

Colonel Bob Brimmer left Flag Plot, the compartment
just below the bridge on *Inchon*. He had gone over the
operation minutely with the commodore of the four-ship amphibious squadron. It had been decided by Sixth Fleet to
land one rifle company from *Inchon*, holding her other rifle
companies and the entire battalion landing team aboard *Saipan* in reserve. The marines would hold an expanded perimeter around the Operations Building as the Army moved out
and fought the Libyan tanks. The marines would carry a
large assortment of antitank weapons, but would have to
depend on the Army to keep most, if not all, of the Libyan
tanks well away from the helicopter operations.

The carrier air groups, now two, with *Nimitz* joining *America* earlier in the day, promised to clear Libyan aircraft from
the skies above Wheelus in the first few minutes of battle
and to shoot up any that tried to move toward the runways.

Navy bombers from the big carriers and marine helicopters operating from *Saipan* and *Inchon* would be able to range inland, identifying and attacking Libyan vehicles and troop concentrations.

The whole thing is just so fragile, thought Brimmer; everything has to work, and on time. Twenty years in the Marine Corps had taught him to expect problems, even in simple operations, and this one was as complex as he could imagine. The SEALs had to get into the Ops Building, kill the terrorists, and hold. They also had to blow up enough aircraft and vehicles to create confusion and panic. The Airborne had to get down, get their vehicles down, and shoot the tanks before the tanks could shoot up Brimmer's helicopters. If it worked, the hostages and the SEALs would fly out within three minutes of the first marine helicopters landing, and then the marines would coordinate their own extraction with the Airborne, by helos back to *Saipan* and *Inchon*. If nothing went contrary to the careful planning.

Brimmer wondered just how much would go wrong and whether there was anything else he ought to have thought of. He knew what he didn't anticipate would cost American lives.

⇋8⇋
Washington, 2300 GMT (1800 EST)

The Secretary of State stood up from behind his large Louis XV desk and moved to greet the Soviet Ambassador. Anatoli Dobrynin had given his coat and hat to an aide before entering the Secretary's cavernous office, and he smiled thinly as he shook hands with the American. The Ambassador was a big man, with a perpetually jovial expression from behind steel-rimmed glasses, but he could look dour or severe when the diplomatic necessities arose.

The Secretary ushered Dobrynin to a comfortable, intimate place in front of the low-burning fireplace. There were deep, comfortable chairs, and on a low marble table between them glasses, ice, vodka, scotch, and a pitcher of water. The Secretary prepared scotch and water for them both, measuring carefully the Ambassador's drink the way he knew Dobrynin liked it. The Ambassador's sunny expression became composed as he polished his glasses on a pocket handkerchief, put them on, and accepted the whiskey glass.

"Thank you for coming to talk privately, Anatoli," said the Secretary of State.

The Ambassador smiled and held up his glass, to be touched by that in the hand of the Secretary. Dobrynin appreciated the tact, since it had been he who had requested the private meeting. "Thank you for making time to see me, Mr. Secretary, in these difficult times."

Holt leaned back in his deep chair and sipped his drink. He knew the Russian would begin when he felt ready.

Dobrynin sighed, put his drink down, and once again began to polish his glasses. "Henry, this afternoon, you made some pretty strong demands upon us, in the matter of this affair in Libya."

"Our people are in deadly peril, Anatoli."

"Perhaps, although you have not, apparently, convinced your allies in NATO of that." The Ambassador spoke very softly.

Holt leaned forward, his brows arched. "If the intent of this gambit is to divide NATO, Anatoli—"

Dobrynin raised his hands, palms toward the Secretary. Holt stopped speaking in midsentence. "Henry. Henry! There *is* no intent, from our side. No gambit. We don't control this; even Baruni does not. That you *must* believe!" The Ambassador lowered his hands to his knees. His expression said sorrow.

The Secretary looked at the veteran ambassador, wanting to believe him, yet inevitably suspicious. Holt had come to Washington two years before, expecting to be able to use his natural instincts of honesty and candor; it hadn't taken him long to learn he was routinely lied to by friends as well as adversaries, and worse, he had learned to lie himself.

Only in the national interest, he reminded himself, suppressing a grimace.

"There must be something you can do to help us get those hostages out of there, Anatoli."

Dobrynin shrugged. "We have refrained from any but the most moderate expressions of support for Baruni, and said nothing about Abu Salaam. We are not countering your buildup in the Mediterranean, despite the fact that it violates previous understandings—"

"Dammit, Anatoli. Baruni is your client! He belongs to you. Without your support, even his own people, even his own *military*, wouldn't put up with him!" The Secretary fought back the heat in his voice.

Dobrynin leaned forward in his chair, picked up his drink, and sipped it. "Henry, things are not that simple. The Politburo is divided as to how we should handle this situation. Powerful forces want to help you with Baruni, to the extent that is possible; other powerful forces want to prolong your embarrassment."

The last word stung like a whip. Holt sipped his own drink, buying time. "Where does the General Secretary stand on all of this? Surely he wants better relations?"

"Henry, the General Secretary is dying."

Holt inhaled a sip of his drink and almost choked. The General Secretary's poor health had been known since before he had taken office, but there had been no intelligence to indicate that the man was close to death. The Secretary fought for composure, struggling within himself to understand how this would impact on the hostage situation and the larger relationship between the two nations. "Anatoli, I am saddened to hear that, truly."

"Henry, I am telling you this, because it is *imperative* that you move with care, and that you interpret reactions of my government with caution."

Holt looked at his hands. "You are telling me you cannot predict the reaction of your government to actions we may feel compelled to take."

"That is correct." The Ambassador's despair seemed genuine.

"And we won't know whether your government will help us with Baruni, whatever they may say."

"I am sorry, Henry."

"Even what they may say through you?"

"I am sorry, Henry."

The Secretary of State sighed. He knew that the Ambassador was identified with the moderate, pro-détente faction, thought to be led by the Foreign Minister and the younger members of the Politburo. He also knew the Ambassador would serve well whomever he believed to be his masters in the Kremlin. "Can you tell me who in the government takes the hard line against us in this affair?"

"No, Henry, I have said all I can." The Ambassador rose. "Thank you for seeing me, in private, and at such short notice."

The Secretary rose and offered his hand. The Ambassador took it. "Thank you for coming, Anatoli. I'll walk you to the elevator."

⇋DAY THREE⇌

Tzafon may Eilat, Israel, 17 February, 0400 GMT (0600 Local)

The SEAL team stood in front of the operations bunker, marveling at the overnight transformation of the Israeli base. The desert sky was black, changing to gray-blue in the pre-dawn. Haze on the eastern horizon was turning pink.

The men were dressed in their parachute gear, minus the chutes themselves. They were glad for the lined immersion suits, as the desert air was cold. Leah Rabin was equipped the same as the SEALs, including the CAR-15 carbine and the mixture of M-67 fragmentation and MK-3A2 stun grenades. Stuart stood next to Hooper, pointing out the newly constructed buildings, light towers, revetments, and the truncated fire-fighting pond across the runway. Stuart was wearing desert utilities and a warm, quilted Israeli Air Force jacket.

"Your guys actually built this overnight," said Hooper.

"Yeah, and it looks good, down to the last detail." Stuart was comparing locations to the blueprints he had laid out on the hood of a parked IDF pickup truck. "When the lights are on, the angles of the shadows here should relate to the pond and to the buildings exactly as they will in Wheelus."

Hooper tapped the operations plan summary on his clipboard, which described how his team would carry out its mission after landing in the reservoir. "We never did anything like this, man," said Hooper, shaking his head.

"Want to give it to the Delta Force?" grinned Stuart.

"Fuck, no. This will make history." Hooper ran his fingers over the chart, then looked at the Ops Building. It was built of plywood, its windows roughed out but without glass. A framed control tower poked up on top of the building, but there was no roof. Hooper pointed to the empty windows. "We go in there, right?"

"Right," replied Stuart. "We work this morning on getting from the pond across the apron to the building and in. We'll also train at shooting terrorists inside and not shooting hostages. Captain Rabin has had useful experience in this area, which she'll share with us. We'll take the control tower, and we'll work out how to take out the ready APCs. This evening we'll jump into the pond and do it from beginning to end, over and over."

"And then?" Hooper was grinning his maximum crazy grin.

"Tonight we'll do it with glass in the windows and Israeli crews in the BTRs. We'll practice until we go or are told to stand down."

"Bet, Stuart," said Hooper, moving his grin up close.

"What, Commander?" Stuart smiled in return.

"Bet you a dinner at Simpson's on the Strand when this is over that we in actual fact run this drill for real on the sands of Libya!"

Stuart laughed, but he felt cold inside. "You're on."

Hooper gave a bark of joyful laughter and punched Stuart on the shoulder hard enough to sway him sideways. He turned to his seven big men and the tiny Israeli woman. "All right, children, let's get into the pool."

The SEALs drilled all morning, with Stuart watching and taking notes. They taped black plastic over their dive masks to simulate total darkness and practiced getting each other out of the pressure suits under the turbid water. Leah had a difficult time at first, as even the smallest pressure envelope was much too big for her. The suits, affectionately known as "body bags," were not meant to fit tightly, so hers was huge, but the SEALs worked patiently with her. By midmorning, Hooper was satisfied that his team would be free of the encumbrances of the drop itself, and ready to emerge from the pond, less than three minutes after hitting the water.

The SEALs could not drill properly for the crossing of the runway and the apron until they had darkness, and the lights on, to create the pattern of bright light and deep shadows. They spent an hour lizard-walking across the vast open area, moving from one point of presumed shadow to another, to get a rough idea of the timing. Osborne and Miller had been detailed to emerge from the east side of the pond, away from the Operations Building, and set charges around the fighters in the revetments north of runway 11/29 and on the transverse taxiway. They practiced their approach, which would be in almost total darkness, measuring distances, angles, and heights of the revetments. Feeney and Jones had responsibility for disabling the two BTRs they expected to find in front of the Operations Building. They crawled up to and around the high-wheeled vehicles while amused Israeli crewmen either sunbathed or looked on.

The actual assault on the Operations Building would be undertaken by Hooper, Goldstein, Ricardo, and Cross. Ricardo and Cross carried the unit's two radios. The central tower of the building extended onto the apron like a large bay window, with high, narrow windows on either side of the main doors and on each angled side of the bay. The control tower rose above the flat roof of the building.

Immediately inside the main doors was the only large room in the building, which had been used as a ready room for military flight operations and as a passenger waiting room for personnel flights. It was in this room that Baruni had been shown on television talking to the hostages some eighteen hours earlier.

The doors in the mock-up were solid plywood and couldn't be opened. Original specifications for the building indicated steel doors strong enough to be easily barricaded, so the entry into the building would be made through the windows, one man each through the bay side windows and one through the window to the left of the doors. The fourth man, Cross, would climb an iron staircase in the back of the building and reach the control tower at the same moment Hooper, Ricardo, and Goldstein tossed stun grenades over or through the windows and then crashed through after them, helmets strapped tight and high-impact plastic visors closed over their faces, their CAR-15s held in front of them to deflect the breaking glass.

"Are we sure the windows have just plain window glass, Stuart?" Hooper was scribbling on the margin of the op plan.

"That's what the original specs called for. No laminate, no wire core."

"I'm not going to be pleased if we slither all the way to these windows and find nice, strong wire screens."

"Photo interp claims they could pick out screens, Hoop, but how will you get in if you find screens or reinforced glass?"

"We'd better take some extra C-4 and detonators. I guess we'd have to blow both the front and back doors, but that's sure to take more time, and let the terrorists have a few bursts at the hostages, and at us." Hooper flipped a page on his clipboard, to his equipment list, and made a note. "We're going to be jumping in really heavy."

Hooper stepped through the window to the left of the door and paced the distance to the door at the back of the big hall. He made several more notes on the op plan, then stepped back into the sun, shaking his head.

"You look worried, Hoop," said Stuart as he removed his jacket and tossed it into the pickup truck. The day had grown warm very quickly once the sun popped up over the haze.

"This is going to be a bit close, my civilian friend," said Hooper as they walked around the mock-up with the three other men of the penetration team. "We really need four more guys; two to cover the back with Cross and two to cover our tails as we go in."

"I know, but we don't have them," said Stuart. "Hopefully, Feeney and Jones can set their charges in the BTRs, and at least one can help Cross."

" 'Hopefully' was not one of Clausewitz's favorite words when he wrote about the importance of military planning," observed Hooper, measuring the height of the windowsill. It was about thirty inches above the tarmac.

"True, Hoop, there's a lot of shit you have to do. Miller can come across behind you after the fighters on the other side of the reservoir are rigged."

"Leaving Osborne to set it off by himself, and then run

in with all hell breaking loose! Jesus! If there's one patrol, one alert *Libyan* to give the alarm before that first stun grenade deafens the world and then wakes it up, we are, to coin a phrase, fucked."

"I'll be happy to forward your ideas for improvement to the admiral. Really, I take no pride of authorship in this." Stuart was increasingly unhappy with his plan as they walked it through in the bright light of the desert sun.

Hooper turned, scowled, then grinned and slapped Stuart roughly on the shoulder. "Shit, man, SEALs have done *far* crazier things than this! Your plan is probably *fine!* But to make sure your fertile brain doesn't miss any chance at improving it, I do have one suggestion."

"Sure, Hoop."

"When we begin again, after lunch, I want you to suit up and move with us, each element in turn, step by step."

Stuart smiled. Hoop just wants to see me sweat. "I might slow you shark commandos down."

"We'll ensure that you don't, old buddy."

The three elements separated to work out their individual problems. Osborne and Miller worked their way along the line of revetments, crawling up each and placing the shaped charges low on the inside rims. The charges, shaped like Claymore mines, would spew hot metal fragments in a wide arc under the aircraft, and were designed to do maximum damage to tires, external fuel tanks, and weapons slung beneath the fighters' wings. There were six revetments to be checked, and any containing an aircraft would be mined. After all the mines were in place and wired together, Miller would move around the southern end of the reservoir to watch the backs of the penetration team. Osborne would blow the mines electrically when he heard the stun grenades go off in the Ops Building. Osborne would then make his way to the Ops Building as quickly as possible, following a smaller transverse taxiway that led from the main runway to the Ops Building.

For there to be any chance at all of either Miller or Osborne crossing the north-south runway and the apron after the base was awake, Feeney and Jones had to take out the two BTRs that had been identified as positioned on the apron north of the Ops Building in every recon photo taken since the hijacking. Those vehicles had heavy and light machine guns and would be able to drive right through the front door of the Ops Building if they chose to do so. Feeney and Jones had two options, depending upon how alert the BTR crews appeared to be, how far they were from any shadow deep enough for concealment, and timing. If they could approach the vehicles, they would attach magnetic limpet mines to the lightly armored undersides, which could be set off by remote radio detonators. If the vehicles were positioned to make a direct assault impossible, or, worse yet, if they were moving, Feeney and Jones would each be carrying a Dragon wire–guided missile—a shoulder-fired rocket with a shaped charge powerful enough to penetrate most armor plate. Hooper hoped that Feeney and Jones would reach the Ops Building with their two Dragons still available to stand off any armored cars or tanks that attacked the Ops Building before the paratroopers and heliborne marines landed and made fighting enemy armor their own problem.

Hooper looked at his equipment list on his clipboard. It was impossibly heavy, yet it was not nearly enough for safety. What if a detonator didn't fire? What if the seals on one of those Dragons leaked underwater? Those armored cars *have* to be knocked out. I have to think about that element a bit more, he thought, and then he turned his thoughts to penetration of the Ops Building and the securing of the hostages. The entry of the building was the last element to be walked through before the team broke for an early lunch and began putting the whole plan back together. Stuart directed three Israeli soldiers in setting up chairs and tables inside the main hall, and putting cardboard cutouts of men, women, and children in various positions. Six terrorist cutouts were placed among the hostages, the only difference being that the terror-

ists held guns or grenades. Cutouts with guns or grenades
were to be shot; others were not. Very simple in theory,
thought Hooper bleakly, as Leah gave the penetration team
some pointers about posture and movement that might draw
their attention to the terrorists, but bloody difficult in practice.
Between each run-through, Stuart repositioned the cutouts.

They drilled and drilled. They approached the windows
in sprints and crawls, using the lines and the shadows where
they guessed they would be. They lobbed the stun grenades,
which made deafening loud bangs and were intended to cause
both the hostages and the gunmen to freeze for a second or
two, then leapt through the windows, carbines at the ready,
selectors on single fire. Cross raced up the ladder in back
and threw a dummy frag grenade into the control tower.
Hooper, Goldstein, and Ricardo all fired before their feet
hit the ground inside, each taking a third of the room. The
first time in, they killed five of the six terrorists, but missed
one with a pistol and a grenade, and shot up eight hostages.
By 1100, they were doing a little better, and they broke
for lunch.

⇆2⇄

Moscow, 0900 GMT (1200 Local)

"We have to tell the Americans something, Comrade General Secretary," said Doryatkin gently. He and Nevsky had
just been admitted to the General Secretary's overheated
office, with its special vaporizer hissing and making the air
feel even hotter and very damp. The windows ran with water
vapor, and Doryatkin felt his shirt clinging to his chest and
armpits as his sweat dripped within it.

Nevsky looked cool and disinterested. Somehow these
KGB executioners never sweated, thought the Foreign Minister. The Defense Minister still had not returned from his
inspection tour of Warsaw Pact exercises in Hungary, though
he had been summoned. Doryatkin missed the bluff old marshal; he would know enough to avoid adventuresome mischief

in this situation. The marshal knew the Americans well enough to believe that they would have to act if the hostages were not released, so the Defense Minister would agree with Doryatkin that Russian units should be pulled back and out of harm's way. The Spetznaz teams were too good to waste pulling the Libyans' chestnuts out of the fire, especially since they could do little if the Americans came in with a major assault. Soviet reconnaissance overflights had confirmed that the American Sixth Fleet was now at twice its normal strength, with the entry into the Mediterranean yesterday of a second carrier battle group.

The General Secretary dabbed his watery eyes with a handkerchief. He sat slumped in a large leather chair, laboring to breathe. He looked at Nevsky, who nodded and opened a leather portfolio on the table in front of him.

"We have prepared a series of responses, Comrades, to various aggressive and provocative actions we may expect the Imperialists to threaten, or even undertake." He passed single sheets to the General Secretary and to Doryatkin.

Doryatkin winced as he scanned the sheet. The KGB nearly always opposed the Foreign Ministry; they were natural enemies in that the Foreign Ministry sought to gain favorable positions for the *Rodina* by negotiating with her adversaries, whereas the KGB preferred to undermine and weaken adversaries directly by means of deceit, disinformation, and espionage. And the KGB had a natural enemy in the Soviet armed forces as well, since the KGB not only had its own military units, but also the right and the duty to infiltrate and spy on the armed forces by means of its Third Directorate. The KGB therefore often proposed policies that frustrated the careful initiatives of the Foreign Ministry, and as often sought to embarrass the military and weaken its influence. Nevsky's paper, beautifully written in careful socialist logic, sought to further both these objectives at once.

"Comrade Chairman," Doryatkin looked hard at the head of the KGB, "if we do any of the things you suggest, the Americans will view our actions as provocative! At the same time, since we all agree the Americans *will* attack if political means fail, our actions will not be effective in deterring them, and we will lose what little influence we retain in the Arab world by looking powerless to defend our friends. We lose both ways."

Doryatkin carefully turned the KGB option paper around and pushed it halfway across the table toward Nevsky, who reddened, though his expression remained one of bland amusement. The General Secretary looked a bit shocked at the Foreign Minister's sharp words. Good, thought Doryatkin. Maybe I have got his attention.

The General Secretary heaved his frail body up in his chair and reached for the glass of tea in front of him and took a sip. Nevsky and Doryatkin watched as his trembling hands spilled tea on his shirt as he drank. The old man coughed deeply and spat into a folded handkerchief as he slowly ran his finger down the five numbered points of the KGB paper. "Mikhail Ivanovich's recommendations seem sound, Ilya Antonovich. Surely they will discomfort the Imperialists." His voice was a querulous wheeze.

Nevsky smiled. Doryatkin spoke quickly. "Just my point, Comrade! Discomfort them, but not deter them! Cause them to trust us even less than they presently do! Cause them to withhold trade, especially in the technological items we desperately need. And *when* they attack, and we do nothing except lose a few brave Soviet soldiers who we do not even admit are in Libya, the black-asses from Morocco to Afghanistan will laugh in their filthy beards!" Doryatkin did not hold the "black-asses," as all Muslims were disparaged by Russians, in contempt, but he knew that the General Secretary did, after his long experience in the Soviet Republics east of the Urals. Another blow, however weak, at Nevsky's ties to Arab revolutionary movements, especially the Libyan Jamahiriya.

The old man blinked and dabbed his eyes. Once again, he seemed startled. Even Nevsky's expression lost a bit of its composure. The General Secretary pushed the KGB paper

gently to one side. "What, then, do you suggest, Ilya Antonovich?"

Doryatkin straightened in his chair. "Since we cannot
oppose effectively an American attack upon our miserable
Libyan ally, we must make every effort to see that the attack
does not occur. We must intervene with Baruni, and anywhere else we have useful influence, to get those American
hostages out of Libya. Our public posture will of course be
quite different," Doryatkin paused and favored Nevsky with
an agreeable smile, "but we must assure the Americans privately that we will do everything we can to get their citizens
out unharmed."

"Assuring the Americans is, of course, one thing—" began
Nevsky.

"No, Comrade, excuse me, but we must do more than
give assurances; we must act effectively to get those Americans
out."

"Suppose you succeed, Comrade?" asked Nevsky, quietly
and without inflection.

"Then we will have shown ourselves helpful to the Americans and responsible to a world fed up with terrorism."

"And to the Arabs?"

"The Arabs give lip service to Baruni's revolution, because
they fear him. If we deny him a portion of the stage, the
others will thank us, although of course, not publicly. Moreover, if we fail to act and the Americans give Baruni, with
his Soviet arsenal and his Soviet advisers, a severe mauling,
the other black-asses will thank the Americans, and not us."

The General Secretary nodded with a shadow of his old
vigor, and smiled. "Your ideas deserve consideration, Ilya
Antonovich! Don't you agree, Mikhail Ivanovich?" Nevsky
nodded dutifully, his slight smile fixed. "Good. Let us meet
and talk further this evening. And now, you are closest to
the sideboard, Ilya Antonovich. Why don't you bring us some
vodka?"

Doryatkin rose and smiled broadly as he turned toward
the sideboard to pick up the tray with the three different

bottles of vodka and glasses. He hadn't won yet, but he had scotched the KGB paper. Later he would present his own, and with any luck at all, the Defense Minister would be at the meeting and would support him.

⇋3⇌

Uqba ben Nafi, 0900 GMT (1000 Local)

Abu Salaam had set himself up in a small office in the south wing of the Operations Building. At his request, all Libyans who normally worked in the building had been removed to other locations. He wrote slowly on the lined tablet before him, putting together a statement for the press. He wrote in Arabic, a difficult language even for an educated man. Abu Salaam's early life in refugee camps had included little formal education.

He looked up from his work as the commander of the tiny infiltration cell entered with two glasses of tea. The young Palestinian was known only as Walid. Abu Salaam smiled and took the tea. All of Walid's immediate family had been killed by an Israeli bomb in their hovel in a nameless camp in southern Lebanon, and Walid had never used his family name after that. Walid lived only for the struggle, driven by his hatred.

"How are our *guests*, Walid?"

"Calm, but a little apprehensive, Naqib," replied Walid. He and the other fighters always addressed their leader as *naqib*, Arabic for captain.

"I will wish to begin interviewing them this morning, Walid."

"As you wish, Naqib, but why?"

"I want to know a little about each one. We must choose carefully which are to be executed first."

Walid smiled crookedly. "There will be executions, then, Naqib?"

Abu Salaam shrugged and smiled a little at the young fighter. "Do the Americans meet our just demands? Are our brothers to be returned to us from Kuwait? Yes, Walid, most assuredly, there will be executions."

Walid rose from the scarred metal table. "I will send Ahmed to you. He will organize the interviews, and he will translate." Ahmed had had two years at the American University in Beirut and was proficient in English.

"Good. I will finish this," Abu Salaam tapped the tablet in front of him, "then we will begin with the aircraft's commander, in about an hour."

"Ahmed will be ready, Naqib."

Abu Salaam nodded and went back to the difficult writing.

⇋4⇌

Moscow, 1400 GMT (1700 Local)

The afternoon meeting in the General Secretary's office began precisely at 4 P.M. The General Secretary had napped for two hours after lunch, as his doctors required, and looked fresh as he presided. Marshal Tikunin, the Defense Minister, had arrived at Domedovo Airfield in central Moscow at three and had been driven directly to the meeting. As Doryatkin had expected, the marshal had opposed any effort to tweak the Americans' noses ineffectively, and he had supported Doryatkin's arguments in favor of pushing Baruni to take the situation in hand and defuse it. Doryatkin had been surprised, however, to hear the old soldier's vehement arguments that the Russian advisers help the Libyans if the Americans did attack, albeit anonymously. And so a compromise was reached. Baruni would be told in no uncertain terms to control his protégé, Abu Salaam. Soviet advisers would prepare the Libyans for battle as best they could and manage the battle if it occurred. Nevsky thought better of provoking a confrontation, believing he had won half a loaf.

After the meeting adjourned, Doryatkin and Tikunin hurried back to their offices in the Kremlin and Nevsky to his in Dzerzhinsky Square. In all three offices, communiques were drafted and encoded. The Foreign Ministry sent its cable first, to the Ambassador to Libya, Fyotr Aleksandrovich Timkin, which began:

TOP SECRET EYES ONLY
AMBASSADOR ONLY
PRIORITY IMMEDIATE
SEE COL. BARUNI AND PUT IT TO HIM IN THE STRONG-
EST TERMS THAT THE SOVIET UNION VIEWS THE PRES-
ENT SITUATION AT UQBA BEN NAFI WITH ALARM AND
DEMANDS. . . .

The Defense Minister's message was for the senior military adviser in Tripoli, General Koslov:

DEFENSE MIN MOST SECRET
IMMEDIATE PERS GENERAL KOSLOV
IMPERATIVE YOU TAKE CONTROL DEFENSE OPERA-
TIONS UQBA BEN NAFI. IMPERATIVE YOU ESTABLISH IN-
DEPENDENT SOVIET REPEAT SOVIET MANEUVER CAPA-
BILITY WITHIN BASE STRONG ENOUGH TO SEIZE
CONTROL OF HOSTAGES IF INSTRUCTED. PROCEED
WITH EXTREME POLITICAL CAUTION. . . .

The KGB's message was the longest and was addressed to the senior KGB officer in the embassy, Colonel Ychengko:

KGB MOST SECRET
IMMEDIATE YCHENGKO ONLY DECODE
REQUIRE YOU IDENTIFY BEST INSTRUMENTS FOR
UTMOST KGB LOYALTY WITHIN THIRD DIRECTORATE
ATTACHED FORCES UQBA BEN NAFI AND ESTABLISH SE-
CURE COMMUNICATIONS FOR USE KGB ONLY. OPERA-
TION INDEPENDENT SOVARMY MASTERS POSSIBLE. UT-
MOST CARE. . . .

Each of these messages was sent in a completely different code.

⇋5⇌

Wadi Rum, the Libyan Desert, 1600 GMT (1700 Local)

Colonel Hassan al-Baruni stood alone in front of his dark brown Berber tent, watching the Soviet Ambassador's Zil limousine heading north on the dirt track toward the Tripoli highway, trailing a long plume of fine dust. Baruni wrung his hands and shook his head, then began to walk along the edge of the dry wadi. His elite guards watched him from the middle distance. He noticed that two armed female guards began to follow as he walked, while the rest remained around the three parked vehicles: two BTR-60 troop carriers and a Soviet-built ZSU-23-4, an ugly tracked vehicle with four 23mm automatic antiaircraft cannons mounted on a boxy turret on top.

It is good that they watch, thought Baruni, good that they are loyal.

Ambassador Timkin had been unusually blunt. He had smiled as he always did, but his shiny little eyes had reinforced the message of his words. Moscow viewed the events at Uqba ben Nafi with the gravest concern. Neither Moscow nor its esteemed ally, the Libyan Jamahiriya, could be seen to be giving direct support to terrorist acts. Moscow suggested most strongly that Baruni take all possible steps to end the crisis and to take control of the hostages away from the Abu Salaam faction without *further* delay.

Baruni had agreed to try, though he did not voice his own serious misgivings about the limits of his influence over Abu Salaam. The Russian's second "suggestion" was perhaps more helpful, though certainly more ominous. Moscow "suggested" that the Soviet advisory team be given a direct role in "organizing" Libyan forces for the defense of Uqba ben Nafi against an assault from the American Sixth Fleet, to ensure, Ambassador Timkin insisted smoothly, that Soviet equipment was used to the best advantage.

They are threatening me! Baruni raged inwardly. The clear implication was that if he refused either "request," Soviet advisers would distance themselves from him during the hostage problem and would perhaps soon withdraw their support entirely. Baruni knew that more than half his tanks and armored vehicles were presently garaged because of lack of trained Libyans to run or maintain them, and all but his oldest aircraft were flown and maintained by Russians or Cubans or North Koreans. Clearly the whole arsenal would

deteriorate rapidly without direct and continuous Soviet support. Baruni wished blackly that Abu Salaam, his once-bril-
liant protégé, had never returned to Libya.

But now I must go to him, he thought, reason with him,
even beg him to let me have those hostages!

Baruni turned and strode back toward the tent and the
vehicles. He tilted his head back and smiled his handsome
smile. Imitating a gesture he had seen his tank commanders
use, he twirled his finger in the horizontal plane, signaling
his vehicles to crank up. He was gratified to hear the vehicles
cough and roar to life and to see his guards salute smartly
as he climbed aboard the lead BTR.

⇋6⇌
Tripoli, Libya, 1800 GMT (1900 Local)

General Koslov paced the floor in his narrow office on
the third floor of the Soviet Embassy. "Did you read this,
Kolya?" Koslov waved the decoded message at the colonel
seated in front of his desk.

Colonel Nikolai Ivanovich Zharkov nodded, while flicking
an invisible mote of dust from his tailored uniform trousers.
At thirty-six, Zharkov was young for a colonel in the Soviet
Army, and he was very wary of old Koslov, who had been
a sixteen-year-old corporal at the Battle of Stalingrad. Zharkov
accounted himself a good and thorough officer, but he knew
Koslov regarded him as an elitist puppy, rising on party
connections. Zharkov had party connections, but he believed
they would only see to it that his hard work and political
consistency were not overlooked. Zharkov was tall, slim, fair-
haired, and blue-eyed, indoctrinated from Komsomol days
in the image of the new Soviet man. He secretly despised
Koslov as a peasant, but he feared the peasant's cunning.
Any suggestion, any question from Koslov had to be looked
at for two or four or forty meanings. "Yes, Comrade General,
as you instructed."

The general barked once; a laugh. "And what do you

think of this directive, first, that we take over the black-asses' defense of their decaying base against the inevitable American assault, and second, that we set up a Spetznaz commando independent of the Libyans?"

Zharkov shrugged. He wanted a cigarette badly, but he knew the general had just quit smoking, under instructions from his doctor. "They are *orders* we can easily carry out, Comrade General." He let his sentence fall quietly.

"But not the mission, Colonel?"

Koslov could fence all day, and Zharkov knew it. He assumed the conversation was being taped and wondered by how many different listeners. "We can certainly improve on the haphazard plan the Libyans have for holding the air base, Comrade General. With as much firepower as the Libyans have in place, we may even be able to thwart an American raid designed to extract their hostages, *if we are sure that is what Moscow wants.*" Zharkov paused, watching the general, whose smile remained perfectly fixed. "And, of course, we can separate a Spetznaz commando, to await further orders. The problem, Comrade General, is that we don't really have any idea what the *mission* for that unit, and indeed for all of us, *really* is!"

Koslov smiled. The snot-nosed kid has more sense than I thought. "We understand the delicacy of our position, then, Colonel?"

Zharkov smiled. Maybe we can get through this thing together after all, he thought. "Of course, Comrade General. Cigarette?" Zharkov produced a packet of English Dunhills.

"Thank you, Colonel," said Koslov, taking the forbidden, gold-ringed cigarette. "Perhaps we should talk further over a glass of vodka?"

The colonel nodded. What the general was suggesting was a walk away from the office, away from the microphones of the Third Directorate, and Zharkov strongly agreed.

KGB Colonel Sergei Ilyich Ychengko finished decoding the long message from Chairman Nevsky, read it twice, and then placed it in a gray folder with a dark red diagonal stripe and the legend "Most Secret" printed front and back. He placed the folder in the bottom drawer of his desk and locked it. He closed his eyes and rubbed his temples, rumpling his thick gray hair. He leaned back, opened his eyes, shrugged, and pressed the buzzer under his desk, summoning his assistant. Captain Ludmilla Petrovna entered and closed the door silently behind her. She smiled at her superior and Ychengko tried to smile back, but he could not hide his concern.

Petrovna was a short, strongly built woman, with fine blond hair cut short and parted severely on the left side. She had clear blue eyes under nearly invisible blond brows, an aquiline nose, and thin lips. Her naturally pale skin was pinkish from her repeated attempts to get a tan in the hot Mediterranean sun. She was not pretty, but she was attentive to Ychengko's needs and fiercely protective of her boss. Since her arrival in Tripoli nine months before, she had done everything she could to become Ychengko's closest associate and confidante. It was widely rumored in the Soviet compound that they were lovers. When he first heard of the rumors, the colonel had frowned; then he had shrugged and asked Petrovna what she thought. She had simply smiled, and lovers they became, but their relationship continued to have its foundations in mutual comfort and complete trust in each other, reinforced by fear and distrust of everyone around them.

Comfort and trust, mused Ychengko, as Ludmilla took over the massaging of his temples, commodities far rarer and more valuable than love and sex. He reached up and touched her hands and smiled. "Ludchka, thank you. Your touch has completely cleared my aching head. Now sit; Moscow has given us a delicate little problem."

Captain Petrovna sat, completely attentive. "Tell me, Comrade Colonel, how I may help."

Ychengko smiled. Always formal, little Ludchka, always correct. Even in bed, she never addressed him by anything less formal than his name and patronymic. "Who is the KGB Third Directorate officer with the Spetznaz, Ludchka?"

Ludmilla frowned. "Captain Suslov. The *zampolit*, Comrade Colonel."

The zampolit was a political officer, nominally in the Army, but in fact an agent of the Communist party, charged with maintaining and enforcing ideological purity among the men of his unit. "The political officer, Ludchka? Isn't that an odd choice?"

"Normally, yes, Comrade, but at least a zampolit has a reason to receive communications through other than normal army channels. Also, these Spetznaz troops are highly trained and very close-knit. Any outsider would be noticed as soon as he was assigned."

Ychengko smiled. "Except, of course, a political officer."

"Yes, Comrade. They expect to have one, and they can't be too obvious about excluding him from goings-on."

Ychengko smiled more broadly and patted Ludmilla's hand. "Your choice, Captain?"

She giggled. It was a pleasant sound. "No, Comrade Colonel, *yours!* My, ah, suggestion."

"Is he reliable?"

"Completely!"

"I will need to see him, Ludchka."

Petrovna rose to attention. "I will summon him at once, Comrade Colonel."

"Ask him to meet us for coffee at the little Italian restaurant near the Defense Ministry, tomorrow morning at ten."

"At once, Comrade Colonel." Ludmilla turned and left the colonel's office, closing the door silently behind her. She telephoned the Spetznaz zampolit, Major Suslov, and repeated the colonel's request. They both knew the simple private code: the meeting would take place in a filthy Tunisian restaurant near the port at nine o'clock. There were so many listeners.

⇌DAY FOUR⇌

⇆1⇌

Tzafon may Eilat, 18 February, 0300 GMT (0500 Local)

Stuart peeled off his sodden, filthy uniform and threw it in the big hamper in the head. He showered for ten minutes in the lukewarm water, which made very little lather because of its high salt content. He washed his hair, rinsed it, and did it again. The stench of the mud from the bottom of the reservoir clung to his skin, and he scrubbed himself again. When he was as clean as he could get, he dried himself, wrapped a clean towel around his waist, and returned to his room. The air-conditioning made the cement cubicle cold and clammy, and he shivered slightly as he crawled under the thin blanket on the narrow, lumpy cot. He closed his eyes and waited for sleep. After a moment, he opened his eyes and stared at the low ceiling.

His body was sore and exhausted, but he was just too keyed up to sleep. As soon as darkness had fallen the previous evening, the SEALs had begun their full-scale drills. With the lights on in the mock-up buildings and around the tarmac apron, the team had checked and run their routes from the pond to the Ops Building, to the fighters in the revetments, and to the large apron where the two BTRs waited, manned by Israeli soldiers. The SEALs, plus Stuart and Leah Rabin, then made the first of three drops into the pond and ran the whole assault. The first two drops had been made from a hovering helicopter without the parachutes, the last from an Israeli Air Force C-130 that dropped them from three thousand feet.

Each time, the SEALs activated their scuba gear and got out of the body bags. Guided by touch and tiny underwater lights on the tops of their helmets, they assembled on the bottom of the reservoir and checked each other's equipment. Osborne then surfaced, very slowly, and checked the perimeter of the pond.

The Israelis in the BTRs, and some on foot, had been equipped with powerful flashlights, which they were to use to simulate weapons for the drill—illuminate a SEAL and he was "dead." The Israelis played the game well, but aggressively. The lieutenant commanding the BTRs seemed to enjoy lighting up the Americans and then laughing too loudly. Hooper was getting pissed off and said so to Feeney and Jones, who were assigned to take out the BTRs. The Israeli lieutenant kept the BTRs moving around the area, making it difficult to set charges. The SEALs didn't think the Libyans would do that, but they couldn't complain, since it was plainly the right thing to do.

The drills were tiring, and they continued to come up with new problems. Jumping through the glass windows of the Ops Building had proved much more difficult than anticipated. Goldstein had actually bounced off on his first try, failing to break the window and breaking instead his own nose against the inside of the plastic visor of his helmet. The next time, he ran faster and jumped higher and struck the window with the butt of his carbine before engaging his face.

Once inside the building, the men had to adjust from night vision to the bright indoors and shoot only the terrorist cutouts. They addressed this problem by looking through the windows for a minute before entering the building, even though they would then be blind to anyone coming from the darkness behind them.

The last drop, which Hooper called the dress rehearsal, began at 0330 local time. The group stayed well bunched on the drop and formed up quickly underwater, with the correct gear in each hand. Osborne surfaced carefully and checked the perimeter, then descended back into the black water to communicate the all clear to Hooper and the others. The SEALs surfaced slowly, breaking the surface of the water with no sound, and the teams crawled out and separated. Stuart went with the assault force while Leah accompanied Miller and Osborne to knock out the ready fighters. Hooper wanted the whole job done, with the fighters mined, the BTRs neutralized, the terrorists dead, and all the SEALs inside the Ops Building, less than forty minutes from the time the SEALs hit the reservoir. The last run-through had taken fifty-three minutes.

The moon was just setting as the teams left the water. Working the deep, crossing shadows on the paved apron was much improved as the men memorized the patterns and established a rhythm for their rush-and-freeze movements, sometimes standing, sometimes on their bellies in the lizard-walk the Americans had learned about the hard way from the North Vietnamese. Hooper and his team were under the windows, in the dark shadows of the Ops Building itself, twenty-two minutes into the drill, and the clicks in Hooper's helmet radio told him the others were also in position ahead of schedule.

Hooper's team, plus Stuart, pressed themselves against the Ops Building below the windows, waiting for a signal from Feeney that he was ready to take out the BTRs. Hooper watched as one of the two eight-wheeled vehicles rolled slowly out toward the runway, while its mate covered it from the shadows. Smart-ass Israeli asshole, he thought, grinding his teeth. I'll bet he wouldn't patrol his own home that hard unless he knew something was coming. Fucking hotdog.

Seated on top of the moving BTR, Sub-Lieutenant Avram Levi called down into the troop compartment as quietly as he could and still be heard above the rumble of the APC's two ninety-horsepower engines. "Yanni, give me the big light. I see the silly bastards moving toward the Operations Building."

Sergeant Yanni Galen poked his head out of the driver's hatch. "Avi, leave them to it. They know as well as you do that their operation depends on an element of surprise."

"I know, Yanni, but they look so silly. They should let Israelis do this job for them; we have the experience."

Sergeant Galen sighed and handed up the big flashlight. The lieutenant took it and aimed it carefully at the dark, still lump near the front doors of the Ops Building that he was sure was an American SEAL.

Lieutenant Levi was thrust forward, stunned, by a sharp

blow on the back of his neck. He fell across the side of the BTR, next to the machine gun. As he twisted to look back toward his attacker, he was blinded and deafened as Petty Officer Second Class Feeney, standing on the roof of the BTR, discharged a full clip of blanks into the air. Levi fell back further, hearing as he did the sharp explosions of the SEALs' stun grenades and the sound of breaking glass, followed by shouts and carbines firing single rounds.

Feeney lifted the CAR-15 and pointed his own small flashlight at Lieutenant Levi's crotch, which Levi already knew was soaked with warm piss. The shooting and the shouting behind him gradually subsided, and Levi sat up, grinning crookedly at Feeney. Feeney smiled back and quick-saluted. "Thanks for the realism, Lieutenant." He jumped off the back of the BTR and ran toward the Ops Building. Levi sat up on top of the machine gun turret and shouted after him. "Good luck, Yank!"

Feeney waved and dove through the broken window. Pink fingers of dawn colored the eastern sky.

Hooper showered, then crawled into his narrow bed. His forty-three-year-old body ached in every joint from the running, and the jumping and the crawling. God, I feel mortal, he thought, twisting and stretching his sore back and legs. I have no business leading this mission. I should have chosen one of the nauseatingly earnest young officers in Norfolk, one of the qualified SEAL team leaders. They had all volunteered, although the mission was never officially published. This jump requires men with legs with the bendy strength of young bamboo, not my old sticks.

Hooper had told himself that he would not have taken the team except the mission had called for a night water landing. A hard-site landing would have been riskier for his middle-aged legs and back. He had rationalized further that night water landings had their own risks, and he had the experience, the *combat* experience, his younger officers lacked. I bet they're cursing my name in Norfolk, he thought, massaging his screaming thighs through the thin blanket.

The truth, Hoop, old son, is that you have grown old without ever growing up. You want to be the cavalry, and you want to rescue the innocent settlers from the bad guys. You want the medal, and the parade, and the girl with the raven hair. You want to be the Catcher in the Rye.

He swung his legs down from the cot and stood. I need a whirlpool or a sauna. He dressed slowly, hopping painfully to get his ripstop trousers on. Maybe I will feel better when the day warms, like the old lizard I am.

I was a hero, once, he thought. I led a group of SEALs and a few unattached marines through the red-light district of Da Nang on the first night of Tet, in 1968. We stopped an attack by what proved to be an entire company of North Vietnamese regulars, and turned them into our artillery, my Sealies and I. The Navy gave me the Navy Cross on behalf of a grateful nation and a Purple Heart for my gallant wounds, and I took them, and pinned them on, and went home to my wife in San Francisco. The people of the grateful nation lifted their voices and called me killer and threw shit, *real human shit*, on me as I limped through the airport on crutches.

Hooper forced himself through slow knee bends and stretching exercises. He bent over, already feeling looser, and laced his jump boots. I am here because I could never accept that what I did in Nam did not make me a hero. I never got past that point, and now I am bitter and too old to be the cavalry anymore.

Hooper smiled. That bastard Stuart looks good, he thought. Four years younger than me, but he looks fresh. He is a successful executive, and it is easy to see that he never thinks of this shit. Of *the* Shit. Here to teach us method, my ass. He would jump himself if there was a place. As fine a man as ever I knew in Nam, and his wife wrote him a Dear John just before Tet. But he moved on, and grew up, while I froze myself in my youth image of the selfless, heroic commando, waiting for my country to recognize me and give me my triumph.

Hooper stepped out into the warming haze of dawn, still smiling. That bastard Stuart is going to get the raven-haired beauty, too.

I am good for this mission. I belong here, and I believe I have the right. One last bugle, one last plea for realization.

Stuart felt a warm presence against his back, then cold hands caressing his chest and his groin. He was so deeply asleep he thought he was dreaming, then he knew he wasn't, but he couldn't pull himself free of sleep. He rolled onto his back, unpinning his right arm, and touched her hair. Leah pulled herself onto his chest and covered his mouth with hers, probing deeply with her hard, moving tongue. She gently squeezed his scrotum and stroked his penis until it awakened and grew to fill her hand. Her mouth still locked on his, she straddled his legs and guided him into her. Stuart still did not feel completely awake, and his body seemed to become aware of the sensations of Leah deliciously slowly. She broke her lock on his lips and smiled, baring her teeth like a yawning cat. She looked wanton, abandoned. She licked his face, then closed her eyes and leaned back, digging her short-clipped nails into his chest as she rode him. She began to moan, softly through clenched teeth, then rose to a squat and increased her pace. Stuart finally felt himself fully awake and engaged. He gritted his teeth to hold himself in check as Leah collapsed on his chest, gasping, begging him to turn her over. They turned over without separating, and Stuart began thrusting deeply, gripping her tightly under her squirming hips.

"Oh, please!" Leah keened softly.

Stuart speeded his rhythm, his breath coming in gasps. Suddenly he felt her muscles contract on him, then release. She bit his shoulder to stifle a scream, and hugged him, and he felt his orgasm surge from him in multiple waves. Gradually their movements subsided together. Stuart kissed

Leah lightly, then buried his face in the pillow beside hers. They listened to each other's harsh breathing, then rolled facing each other, soaked with each other's sweat.

Leah smiled at him impishly. "Gee, William, I thought you would never ask."

Stuart grinned sheepishly. "Gee, Leah, it just didn't seem—"

"I know, you are just shy. Your friend Hooper told me that."

"When did he say that?"

"Right after he asked me to sleep with him. Within hours of his surly arrival." Stuart felt a pang of jealousy.

"I told him I fancied you instead. He promised to tell you, but told me I would be disappointed. I wasn't, by the way, once you finally woke up."

Stuart smiled, kissed her nose, then her mouth, deeply. Hooper, of course, had told him nothing. "Well, I am relieved to hear that. I may even improve with practice."

Leah pulled the damp sheet up around her shoulders and nestled against him. "I hope we have time, William. And I hope the SEALs have time; they need practice more than you do."

"It's getting better. Another day, maybe two, we'll be ready."

"But it is still very rough, especially the entry and assault on the Ops Building. This is a very tricky operation, even if the Libyans are as sleepy as we hope."

"You sound as though you would like to go along."

Leah raised herself on one elbow and looked at him. "I'd love to! Wouldn't you?"

Stuart thought about that. Yes, and no. The operation was difficult and exciting, but it had been too many years. Time had slowed his reflexes, and easy living had curbed his desire to take insane risks. Still. . . .

"I know you would," said Leah, probing his ear with her hot tongue. "We would be great together."

"Let's just stay right here and be great together." Stuart

felt her fingers lightly stroking his chest and stomach. When she reached his groin, his penis had stretched forth to meet her hand.

⇆2⇄

USS *America*, thirty-one miles northeast of Tripoli, 18 February, 0815 GMT (0915 Local)

The admiral's briefing had been under way for an hour when Lieutenant Colonel Loonfeather landed by navy helicopter. He was guided to the wardroom by a "yellow shirt," one of the sailors who directed aircraft on the flight deck. He sat in the back of the room and opened his briefcase. The briefing in progress was about rotating the various ships of the huge armada through the oilers and other supply ships for replenishment of fuel and stores and, in the case of the combatant ships, special ordnance that would be used against enemy vehicles and formations. When the supply corps lieutenant commander finished taking questions, the rear admiral who was running the brief rose and declared a ten-minute break for coffee. Loonfeather picked up his briefcase and moved down toward the front of the room, where he found Colonel Brimmer.

Brimmer grinned, shook Loonfeather's hand warmly, and pointed to a seat next to his own. "Good to see you, Colonel. Sit, and I'll get us some coffee. Black, as I recall from late nights in London?"

"Yes, sir. Thanks, Bob." Loonfeather sat.

Brimmer returned with two china mugs of very hot coffee. Loonfeather sipped his and found it good. Brimmer spoke softly, "Rufus, you won't be asked to brief this morning, although the admiral might ask you to say a few words about the status of your preparations. He wants you and me to get together first, define unit boundaries, signals, et cetera, then get with the N-3 Operations people on his staff to work out supporting arms. We will brief jointly either this afternoon or tomorrow. What *is* the status of your task force, by the way?"

Loonfeather handed Brimmer a single sheet of paper. It was a Table of Organization for Airborne Task Force 14b—"Task Force Bowie."

"Who is Bowie?"

"The light colonel who gets to take this lash-up to war, the lucky bastard! I'll go over the T/O with you later, but to answer your first question, we're in good shape. All the troops, an infantry company from the Five-Oh-Deuce, and my armor troops from the 3d of the 73rd are assembled at Fort Bragg. The gear, including the eight Sheridans we plan to drop, are positioned at Pope Air Force Base, next door to Bragg. Also at Pope are ten C-141s from the Twentieth and the Seventy-sixth Military Airlift Squadrons, Four-Thirty-Seventh Airlift Wing from Charleston AFB, fueled up and ready. The troops have been over it, have practiced the drop and assault on a mock-up we built at Pope, and are rarin' to go."

"How soon will you be moving to Europe?"

"I don't know. I'm not sure which of our gallant allies has volunteered to take us, but we could fly today if we had to."

"Good. Ah, Captain Adams, he's the Sixth Fleet N-2, is about to start briefing on the supporting arms plan. I think you'll find this interesting."

At 1015, the full admiral's briefing ended. Brimmer and Loonfeather found a quiet corner of the *America*'s wardroom lounge and sat. Several other small conferences were occurring in other parts of the room.

Brimmer accepted two cups of coffee from a passing steward as Loonfeather spread plans of Wheelus and recent recon photos in front of them on the small table. Brimmer spoke first. "What did you think of Captain Adams's rundown of this task force's firepower?"

"Awesome. I never dreamed the old battleships could throw so much metal," said Loonfeather, sipping coffee and trying to remember his last full night's sleep.

"Not to mention the cruisers and destroyers, plus the naval and marine aircraft, Rufus."

"Yeah. I hope they know how to shoot tanks. I could wish for some Warthogs or an AC-130 gunship."

"We may get them, if the Italians go along."

"Yeah, Bob, we will for sure hope, but if a pig could fly—"

Brimmer interrupted. "Rufus, if we have to, we'll handle it entirely from assets on these ships. That's why it's imperative that I fully understand your requirements and, therefore, what you plan to do."

Loonfeather grinned. "Good. Let's run it down. Bob, who do we work for in this operation?"

Colonel Brimmer smiled. "You work for me."

"OK," said Loonfeather.

"And I report to Fleet Marine Force, Sixth Fleet. Major General Morton."

Loonfeather detected the worry in Brimmer's voice and expanded his grin. "Good guy?"

Brimmer swallowed. "Nail-eating marine, Rufus. His radio call sign is 'Hammer.' And I have to tell you, he's no fan of your participation in this."

"Colonel Brimmer." The voice was gravel, slowly stirred.

Brimmer leapt to his feet. "General!"

Loonfeather got to his feet. General Morton was about five feet six inches tall, built like a fireplug. His complexion was red and his eyes were beady-black beneath bushy gray brows. His hair was gray and cut a quarter inch from his skull. "General," said Loonfeather, standing at rigid attention.

"This is Colonel Loonfeather, General. He'll control the Airborne."

General Morton gazed up at the tall Indian without apparent interest. "I hope you're comfortable here, Colonel."

"Yes, sir. Colonel Brimmer is taking good care."

"Just so there's no misunderstanding, Colonel, I want you to know that I see no use for your paratroopers in this operation."

"Sir," said Loonfeather, looking at a point ten inches above the marine general's head.

"Nor your tanks," continued General Morton.

"General," said Loonfeather carefully, "may I offer a comment?"

"By all means," said General Morton evenly.

"General, my paras can land faster than heliborne marines, and they are less vulnerable to ground fire while doing it."

"Go on, Colonel," said General Morton.

"The Sheridans are insurance, General. If the Libyans get close, the Sheridans will be worth their weight in gold. If not, I'll offer the general dinner at Bragg, at a time of his choosing." Loonfeather smiled his most winning smile.

General Morton allowed a shadow of a smile to tilt the corners of his mouth. "Very well, Colonel. You'll prove your point, and I'll acknowledge your necessity. Fair enough?"

"Done, General," said Loonfeather, stiffening to attention.

General Morton squeezed Colonel Brimmer's shoulder. Morton was unable to suppress a grin. "Watch this officer, Colonel."

"Aye, aye, sir," said Brimmer, trying to control his face.

"And make sure he gets our total support," said Morton. The general turned and marched out of the wardroom.

Brimmer looked at Loonfeather, who exhaled sharply, then smiled. Brimmer pressed Loonfeather back into his seat. "First, Rufus, let's discuss equipment. You mentioned earlier you intended to drop eight tanks—"

Loonfeather took a slow, deep breath. Hammer had taken his wind. His grin returned. "Not exactly tanks, Bob. Have you ever seen an M-Five-Five-One Sheridan?"

"No. I'm a verticle envelopment jarhead, man. Light weapons, only what a man can carry."

"OK. The Sheridan is a hybrid, not tank, not tank destroyer. It has two strengths: it's fast and it has a humongous 152mm gun. It also has two major weaknesses. It has very light armor; it will likely be damaged by concentrated fire from a .50-caliber machine gun and almost surely knocked out by a 23mm antiaircraft gun firing either armor-piercing or high explosive. A hit from any tank's main gun and the Sheridan is history." Loonfeather took another sip of coffee and looked at Brimmer.

"So what's the second weakness?" asked the marine colonel.

"The gun. It's so big, it has to have a naval screw-type breechblock. It's difficult to load and lock, and the rate of fire is not much over three rounds a minute."

"Doesn't it have a missile capability?"

"Yeah, but it's a missile called the Shillelagh, which has to be fired through the gun tube. Huge fucking missile, and very effective; indeed, one of the reasons why the screw-type breechblock is needed. We won't be carrying any Shillelaghs, however."

"Why not?"

"Well, look at the photos, Bob. We figure there's a battalion of tanks there, plus what may be an additional independent company. Forty-plus tanks. The Sheridans are going in *only* to waste the tanks that get very close to the hostages, and to the Sheridans themselves. Anything far enough away from a Sheridan to require a missile will be delegated to supporting arms, whether that means air, naval gunfire, helicopters, or all three."

"So what will the Sheridans be carrying?"

"Some Cannister anti-personnel rounds, but mostly HEAT rounds. High explosive antitank."

"I know. We even have those."

Loonfeather grinned. The Marine Corps always complained with pride that they got new equipment long after the Army, but HEAT rounds had been in both inventories since the 1960s. "The infantry company will be carrying extra Dragon antitank missiles, and a whole extra antitank section."

Brimmer was scribbling notes on a yellow pad. "What kind of vehicles does the enemy have?"

"The tanks in the photos are Russian T-72s. Good tank, 125mm smoothbore main gun, fires a very effective antitank round called a hypervelocity, fin-stabilized, armor-piercing sabot, also HEAT and HE rounds. Two machine guns, layered armor, good rate of fire with its automatic loader. An all-round excellent medium tank. The Libyans also have a variety of armored personnel carriers, including a dozen or so BMP-76s, which can fire SAGGER antitank missiles. Again, if we're working in close, the SAGGERS won't be of much use, since they need to fly about eight hundred meters before their guidance system picks the missile up. Vehicles or individual soldiers—the SAGGER can be carried in a man pack—firing SAGGERS at us will have to be dealt with by supporting arms."

Brimmer filled a page with notes and readied another. "So tell me how eight of these slow-firing, light-armored Sheridans will deal with forty tanks."

Loonfeather grinned. "That's the beauty of this operation, Bob! We don't, because we'll be landing inside of them. Most of the enemy tanks and APCs will be guarding the very long perimeter of the base, a long way from us, and therefore easy prey for naval gunfire and air-launched missiles. Look again at the photo. Our biggest problem will be these two platoons of tanks on the beach just on the western edge of the north end of runway 03/21. Six tanks. Our plan is to chew them up piecemeal as they come in. Believe me, Bob, as slow as that 152 mike-mike gun is, it *do* hit 'em to leave 'em!"

Brimmer looked at the date-time group on the photo. "This picture is eight hours old."

"Yeah, there's weather; low clouds and wind. Rough ride in here. We'll have clearer pictures tomorrow morning."

Brimmer set the photos down. "Tell me again, how you get this force into Wheelus."

"Uqba ben Nafi," grinned Loonfeather.

"Precisely, Colonel."

"We'd better get some more coffee, first. Are we bunking here on the *America*?"

"I'm over on *Inchon,* the helicopter carrier, with my battalion landing team. I can get you put up here, with the main staff, or with me."

"I better go with you. When this thing goes down, you and I should be in the same room."

⇆3⇌

Uqba ben Nafi, 0900 GMT (1000 Local)

Colonel N. I. Zharkov stood on the crest of a low sand hill overlooking the huge air base from the south. He had been driven slowly around the perimeter, stopping several times to look at features that would have a bearing on how he planned to defend the air base. Every time he stopped, he left the Military Advisory Group car, telling the driver to remain with the vehicle. Colonel Zharkov liked to talk to himself while he thought things through, and he didn't want to be overheard. The KGB tried very hard to recruit army drivers, for what they might overhear their officer-passengers discuss.

General Koslov had explained the rest of Moscow's instructions during their walk on the previous evening. He was to supervise the organization of an effective defense for the base and put Military Advisory Group officers into key command positions to "advise" the Libyans. He had also established a small maneuver force, under his personal command, which could act independently of the Libyan command. If Moscow's demands on Colonel Baruni to take control of the American hostages and end the crisis were not met, Zharkov might be ordered to seize the hostages from the terrorists. Zharkov knew without being told that the KGB had a major stake not only in Baruni but in the Abu Salaam faction, and that he must keep the mission of the special unit, if not its existence, secret from the KGB for as long as possible. That meant he had to do all the planning himself, since he didn't know the identity of the Third Directorate spy in his Spetznaz company, though he suspected the zampolit, Captain Suslov.

Zharkov had a plan of the air base on his clipboard. He had marked the positions of Libyan tanks and armored cars, as well as the SA-3 antiaircraft missile batteries and the S-60 57mm antiaircraft guns as he made his tour around the perimeter. He now looked at his marked-up plan and shook his head. Tanks and infantry in BTRs were deployed around the entire base and on the beach facing the sea. Security in the immediate area of the Operations Building was established around two BTRs in front of the building and another in the rear. The antiaircraft guns were placed near the ends of the two runways, and the four quad launchers for the SA-3 missiles were deployed in two clusters near the intersection of the two runways. SA-3 launchers were not mobile; they could be put on trucks and moved, but not quickly. Zharkov would have bet they had not been moved in months, and he was sure that American photoreconnaissance data on their positions, as well as positions of most of the tanks, were already in the fire-control computers of the navy ships he knew were waiting just beyond the horizon.

Zharkov frowned. "I don't expect much from these blackasses, but there are Russian officers assigned to these units," he said to himself. The defensive layout seemed designed to repel a perimeter assault by light forces from the desert, or perhaps beat back an unsupported landing on the beach. "The Americans will blast the shit out of the vehicles on the beach before sending a single boat!" said Zharkov. He looked across the base with his binoculars. Except the Americans won't be sending any boats, he thought. The beach along the entire north side of the base sloped steeply upward to a height of between ten and twelve meters. It would be too slow to come across that beach, and the soft sand would trap the vehicles. "The enemy will come in helicopters, clouds of them, following bombers and naval gunfire. And he will not be trying to take the whole base, just the center, where the hostages are. The only safe place to be will be right next to the hostages; any units on the perimeter will be destroyed." Zharkov smiled; it was an interesting problem. He knew where his enemy *had* to go. Because the enemy had naval artillery and would have complete superiority in the air, Zharkov did not have the wherewithal to prevent a landing, but if he used his tanks well, he could make sure that very few of the enemy soldiers, much less the hostages, ever left Uqba ben Nafi.

"The question is, Kolya," said Zharkov to himself, "is that what Moscow wants to happen?"

There was another way. He could set up the base to disrupt, even defeat the Americans' assault, yet preserve the option Moscow wanted, that he himself might get the hostages. He needed to position himself and his all-Spetznaz unit in a concealed place where he had a clear run into the Operations Building, without being obvious that that was what he wanted, then position the Libyans to wreck the American assault force if Moscow changed its mind. The colonel began sketching rapidly. He would concentrate the Libyan armor in two places—a few kilometers below the low sand ridge south of the air base upon which he now stood, and in the ruined golf course 300 meters to the west of the Operations Building. Tanks and armored personnel carriers south of the air base could move to fighting positions dug into the south side of the sand ridge as soon as any bombardment stopped before a landing, and would have a clear field of fire at any American helicopters and troops approaching the central apron of the base, at optimum range for their guns and missiles. Tanks dug into the sand face lower down the slope facing south could oppose, from excellent fighting positions, any attempt to break into the center of the base by heliborne or parachute troops landing in the fields. The tanks and infantry concentrated in the golf course would have some very good cover from aerial observation in the groves of palm trees the Americans had planted to give their playground some shade, and could move rapidly to block both runways and to surround the Operations Building.

He would place his own unit, a tank platoon and a BTR-mounted infantry platoon, in a group of supply warehouses east of the north end of runway 03/21. He could tell the Libyans he was a maneuver force to oppose a landing across the beach, while being in a good position to move to the Operations Building quickly if ordered to take control of the hostages.

Zharkov knew that the Americans could detect electronically the trucks that carried the SAM-3 radars, so it didn't much matter where he put them, other than far from his own position, for they were sure to get clobbered. He decided they ought to be moved anyway; at least make the bastards find them. Zharkov smiled slightly as his plan came together on his clipboard. He looked up at the low, wet clouds blowing in from the Mediterranean. We might even get this done before the American spy planes and satellites can see us moving. Zharkov covered the clipboard and walked briskly back to the waiting car.

⇌4⇌

USS *America*, 0930 GMT (1030 Local)

Lieutenant Colonel Loonfeather spread a chart on the coffee table in front of Colonel Brimmer. It was smaller scale than the plan of Uqba ben Nafi they had been studying, and showed the Libyan coast from Tripoli to El Asciar, and the Mediterranean out to a distance of twenty miles from the coast. "The whole concept of the Airborne Armor Raid, Bob, has never officially been written down. Too many people think it's a suicide mission, and the main problem is that we just cannot get enough Sheridans into a target, unless we commandeer the entire Military Airlift Command. But we've been playing with the concept for years, and I think it should work to take over an airfield and extract people.

What we cannot do is hold. We can do heavy damage to an enemy force, until we run out of resources."

"Resources?"

"Us, Bob."

"I see," said Colonel Brimmer, frowning.

"Anyway," continued Loonfeather cheerfully, "you wanted to know how we get in. We need ten C-141s. We orbit low out over the Med, maybe fifteen miles out. We'll have to get a positive signal from the SEAL team that they're in control of the hostages, then we come roaring in, right on the water, crossing the coast about halfway between the SAM sites at Wheelus and El Asciar," Loonfeather pointed to the spot on the map. "We head down far enough into the desert to line up on the long runway from about six miles out, flying N.O.E.—"

"Hold it, Rufus. What's N.O.E.?"

"Nap of the earth. Lower than low. Around trees, climb to clear a camel."

"In a C-141? That's a hell of a big aircraft!"

"In a C-141, Bob."

Brimmer grinned and shook his head. "Now *that* must be something to see!"

"If you see it from the jump seat behind the pilots, Bob, it's truly fucking terrifying."

"Jesus, I guess! Well, what next?"

Loonfeather pulled the plan of Wheelus from beneath the smaller-scale chart. "The first two aircraft will be carrying the infantry company; about 145 men, including the augmentations. They'll have to pop up to minimum 650 feet so the men can jump safely. All the grunts will un-ass from the two aircraft in the one pass. They'll land along here, the taxiway parallel to runway 11/29."

Brimmer nodded, tracing the taxiway. "What about any fighters in the revetments along the taxiway?"

"First order of business. Nasty wake-up for a sleepy fighter-jock," Loonfeather grinned. "But now comes the good part. The next eight aircraft, C-130s, *still* flying N.O.E.; roar down the runway, shaking the earth, and LAPES out the Sheridans. One Sheridan in each aircraft, so all are out in the first pass. All the vehicles should be down and cranked up inside of three minutes."

"What does LAPES mean, Rufus?"

"I think marines do it too, but only with lighter vehicles. LAPES is Low-Altitude, Parachute-Extraction System. Essentially, a progressive-opening chute is ejected out the back door of the aircraft, into the slipstream. As the chute opens, it drags the vehicle, on skids, right out the back, to land on the runway with a mighty thump."

"And you can drive it away after that?"

"Yeah. Not always, but yeah. We have to strip off a shell of laminated cardboard packing, but we should drive away at least five, which we figure is enough, and with any luck, six or more."

"And then you just sprint to the Operations Building?"

"Well, more or less. Depending on the latest recon we have, we have some choke points we want to hold. Any tanks on the apron directly in front of the Operations Building should have been knocked out by the SEALs or by the antitank sections of the infantry company. Our main function is to get any enemy vehicles who try to come in from their perimeter defenses, although our spotters in the ANGLICO detachment will be calling in all sorts of air, missile, and naval gunfire attacks on tanks south of the long runway as soon as we're clear of it, and the Navy will be able to spot-direct at the tanks dug in along the beach. I figure once we get in there, we have an excellent chance of driving the enemy away from the center of the base, and giving you heliborne gyrenes time to come and pick up the people."

Brimmer whistled and shook his head. He did not find it surprising that the army brass thought such an undertaking suicidal. "OK, Rufus, let's go see Captain Adams and work up the details of the close-support, both air and naval gun."

He looked at Loonfeather, who was still grinning. He looks a little crazy, thought Brimmer, as his own face cracked into a broad grin. "I have a few ideas I think might help."

"Lead on, Colonel," said Loonfeather, gathering his papers and stuffing them into his briefcase.

⇋5⇌

Tripoli, 0930 GMT (1030 Local)

Captain Suslov, Political Officer of the Second Independent Airborne Company (Spetznaz), Soviet Army, walked back and forth in the small plaza near the June 11 Monument. Colonel Ychengko's bitch had told him to be near the Tunisian restaurant next to the plaza at nine in the morning, to wait for instructions from "the highest levels." He knew that meant neither the Army nor the party, but the KGB. The prospect of a meeting, either with Colonel Ychengko or with his hatchet woman, Captain Petrovna, made him very nervous, and he was naturally a nervous man to begin with. The Soviet community in Tripoli was very small, and such a meeting, if noticed, would not be put down to chance. He much preferred receiving his instructions in code and by courier, or better yet, not at all. His main job for the Third Directorate was to file periodic reports on the reliability of officers of the Spetznaz, and he did this assiduously, without instruction or interference from Ychengko.

Suslov took shelter under a low palm tree as rain began falling lightly. He was dressed, per instructions, in civilian clothes, and somehow that made him feel more conspicuous than if he had been in uniform. Rain dripped on his broad-brimmed straw hat. He looked at his watch; his masters were late. He put a cigarette in his mouth and turned out of the damp wind to light it under the brim of his hat. As he turned, he came face to face with Colonel Ychengko, wearing an old-fashioned seersucker suit and a similar silly straw hat. Suslov's jaw dropped, and he almost lost the cigarette. He stifled the instinct to salute, and said quickly, "Good morning, Comrade Colonel."

"Let's walk, Suslov," said Ychengko, pointing toward the harbor.

Ychengko found a bench he liked, looked around carefully, and sat, patting the space beside him for Suslov. The rain lessened and became a heavy mist, but all the Arabs had taken shelter. Suslov felt even more conspicuous, but Colonel Ychengko seemed unconcerned. The older man leaned close to Suslov and spoke quietly. "Suslov, we have special instructions from Moscow concerning this American hostage business." The colonel paused. Suslov returned his gaze without expression. "Has the Spetznaz company received any new orders?"

"Just this morning, Comrade Colonel. Colonel Zharkov has set up a special commando, a platoon of tanks, plus a platoon of motorized infantry, to be placed under his personal command." Suslov paused, feeling the pull of his fragmented loyalties.

"Go on," barked Ychengko.

Suslov felt his nervousness increasing. "The commando is to be made up entirely of Spetznaz officers and men, handpicked by the colonel."

Ychengko nodded and waited for Suslov to continue. When he did not, the colonel looked up with evident annoyance. "Well, what else, Suslov? What is this commando supposed to do?"

Suslov shrugged. "Nothing has been said, Comrade Colonel. When I left to come here, the men and vehicles were being assigned and moved to supply warehouses at the northern end of the base."

"By any chance have you been *handpicked* for this commando, Captain?"

"No."

"Damn! How am I going to find out what they are doing?"

Suslov looked at the KGB colonel, pleased to see him agitated. "I am sure I could get into the commando, if it is *important,* Comrade Colonel."

Ychengko looked at Suslov skeptically. "How are you sure?"

Suslov smiled slightly. "I am a qualified Spetznaz officer, and qualified in armor. I am sure Colonel Zharkov will give me a place. We are . . . quite friendly."

Ychengko arched his bushy brows in a quizzical look. He knew the low regard in which zampolits were held by combat commanders. Suslov looked back, holding his slight smile, knowing exactly what Ychengko was thinking. Suslov was under no personal illusions about the depth of Colonel Zharkov's friendship, but he felt he could count on Zharkov to continue to treat him well. Zharkov was ambitious and had excellent party connections of his own, but the glowing reports Suslov wrote about his colonel could only help. Suslov nodded slightly at the still-smirking Ychengko. Zharkov would put him in a tank, if he asked.

"Well Suslov, by all means get on that commando if you can, and if you can, find out for me what its mission is. But Suslov, this thing could boil over at any minute, and you could find yourself in the midst of an American assault. If you do, you are to *ensure* that your *all-Russian* unit inflicts casualties *directly* upon the Americans, do you understand?"

Suslov didn't understand. "But, Comrade Colonel, our government has never acknowledged our military presence in this country, beyond embassy personnel!"

"Those orders, Suslov, come directly from Moscow. Do you understand *that?*"

Suslov nodded slowly. Ychengko got up curtly and strode away across the deserted park. Suslov finally lit his cigarette, turning the whole thing over in his mind. If Russians shoot Americans, Americans will shoot Russians. Why would the government want that? More precisely, why would the KGB want that?

⇌6⇌
Tripoli, 1015 GMT (1115 Local)

Ambassador Timkin, General Koslov, and Colonel Zharkov filed into the large audience room at the Defense Ministry. Colonel Baruni sat alone at a long wooden table in the otherwise empty room. He was in uniform—open-collared khaki shirt with red collar tabs, shoulder boards of rank, many rows of ribbons. He still wore his dark aviator-style sunglasses. Timkin thought he looked pale and distracted. Koslov thought he looked slightly comic. Without rising, Baruni waved the three Russians to chairs across the table. Timkin made a mental note of the uncharacteristic lack of courtesy. One of the elite guards entered, put tea and dates in front of each man, and departed. Zharkov noted that the top three buttons of her uniform blouse were unbuttoned.

"Good morning, Comrade Colonel," began Timkin pleasantly.

Baruni sat up and removed his glasses. He looks as though he hasn't slept in days, thought Timkin. "Thank you for coming, my Russian friends," said Baruni, gesturing with the sunglasses, ignoring the fact that the Russian's request for the meeting had been scarcely less than a demand. "I understand you wish to get my approval for your plan to defend our base at Uqba ben Nafi."

Timkin smiled despite himself. He had always admired the colonel's dramatic flare. "Yes, Comrade Colonel. And to ask for . . . progress in the matter of Abu Salaam and his hostages."

"Of course." Baruni smiled his famous smile. "Let me see the defense plans, first."

Colonel Zharkov unfolded a large plan of Uqba ben Nafi Air Base in front of Colonel Baruni, who continued to toy with his glasses. He pointed out the significant points of the redeployment of the Libyan forces. He confirmed his intention (by now, already fact) of forming a small Spetznaz unit for "tactical evaluation," but said nothing of its combat mission or present disposition. Baruni nodded, taking no apparent interest. Zharkov finished his briefing and left the marked plan in front of Baruni, who appeared to study it while chewing on one earpiece of his glasses.

"The only thing I question, Colonel Zharkov," said Baruni, smiling warmly, "is your recommendation that we remove most of our combat aircraft."

Zharkov looked at Koslov, who nodded. "Comrade Colonel, if the Americans come, they will come very quickly from just over the horizon. They will immediately establish air superiority over Uqba ben Nafi. It is unlikely that any aircraft could even get airborne; they would be bombed or strafed while still in their revetments."

Baruni frowned. "But surely *some* would get up?"

Zharkov pointed to the plan. "We suggest that two sections, four aircraft, be spotted, one section at the landward end of each runway, armed with antiship missiles. These planes must be manned, pilots strapped in, engines warmed

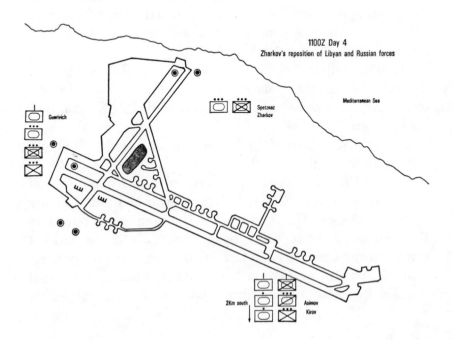

1100Z Day 4
Zharkov's reposition of Libyan and Russian forces

Mediterranean Sea

Guerivich

Spetznaz
Zharkov

2Km south

Asimov
Kirov

up, around the clock. There is no hope that four aircraft, no matter how bravely flown, can break the Americans' control of the skies, but they might be able to fly out low under the assault and strike a blow at the ships of the Imperialists."

Baruni smiled. The picture in his mind of an American ship sinking from a Libyan missile attack might make this whole mess worthwhile. The Russians smiled back, imagining the Americans' fury and embarrassment should that occur. Baruni looked back at the plan, and his smile faded. "But how will we defend the base without our fighter planes?"

"We suggest that the fighters be redeployed to your bases near Benghazi and Tobruk, with perhaps some of the longer-range attack aircraft and heavy-lift aircraft being sent to Al Kufrah and Jabal al Umaynat. The Americans will probably attack at least Benghazi and Tobruk, but at least you will have more time and more runways to get your aircraft airborne."

Baruni nodded. It made sense, dispersing his fighters. It made sense as well to get the transports and other noncombatant aircraft to Al Kufrah and Jabal al Umaynat, which were over by the Egyptian border and unlikely to be attacked by planes from the carriers. "I agree. Please continue, Comrade Colonel." He favored Colonel Zharkov with another brilliant smile.

Keep it simple and he will buy all of it, thought Zharkov, smiling in reply. "Comrade, the American air superiority will do them no good as long as we control the hostages. Therefore, we can win the battle on the ground by concentrating forces close to the hostages and making the Americans come to us. But to do that, to get really close, you must gain control of the hostages from the Palestinian fighters."

Baruni nodded again. "Abu Salaam has not allowed us to bring tanks to the apron in front of him. He says to put them out on the runways!"

"Where the enemy will have a clear shot at them," said General Koslov, smiling.

"Yes!" Baruni nodded more vigorously. "But you will

be very close to the Operations Building, once you have moved tanks to the old golf course, and the tanks dug in south of the air base will have a clear field of fire at the enemy assault force. I approve, my Russian friends. You may execute the movements of forces required!" Baruni stood, rubbing his hands, and his three Russian guests stood.

Those forces have been in their new positions for at least an hour, thought Koslov. "Thank you, Comrade Colonel," he said.

"May we then suggest that you go and talk to your protégé, Comrade Colonel?" asked Ambassador Timkin gently.

Baruni's good humor evaporated. When the Russian said "his protégé," he meant his *problem.* "Yes, I will go at once."

"Please allow Colonel Zharkov to accompany you, Comrade Colonel," smiled Koslov. "You and he can go over the defensive operation in detail."

"Of course. My pleasure, Colonel Zharkov. We will leave from here in half an hour."

"Thank you, Comrade Colonel. I will wait downstairs with your detail." Zharkov turned and followed the other Russians out of the room.

⇋7⇌
Uqba ben Nafi, 1115 GMT (1215 Local)

Abu Salaam grunted into the telephone. He scowled and covered his eyes with his hand. Ahmed sat across the table from him, tidying his notes from the naqib's conversations with the hostages. The naqib seemed to grow more agitated as he listened to the telephone; he spoke little, and his voice was muffled behind the hand that rubbed his eyes. Ahmed couldn't really overhear, yet he wondered if he should leave the room until the leader finished. Abu Salaam balled the hand on his head into a fist and banged it on the table in front of him, then said "yes, yes," several times in Arabic and slammed the phone down. He looked at Ahmed with his fierce, smoldering eyes and spoke softly. "That was Colonel

Baruni, Ahmed. He insists on coming here again. That can only mean trouble."

"Yes, Naqib?"

Abu Salaam got up and began to pace. "Yes! It means the Russians are pressuring him. We may have less time here than we thought, Ahmed."

"Yes, Naqib," said Ahmed, not really understanding.

"Well! Anyway, we have talked to each of our prisoners, eh? What did you think?"

Ahmed shrugged and smiled nervously. He did not like to be asked for an opinion by his captain. "They all seem very ordinary people, Naqib."

Abu Salaam scratched his beard. "Quite. And now we must choose the first to be executed. Any recommendations, Ahmed?"

Ahmed shook his head vigorously and swallowed.

"No?" Abu Salaam's tone was gentle. He liked the young fighter. "Then I must choose." He looked at his copy of the list. "Stevens, Craig G., Lance Corporal, USMC—Walid has recommended him, and I concur. Next, Cummins, Barbara B., Seaman, USN; then Boboski, Robert, NMI, Airman, USN. Tell Walid to separate them from the others, Ahmed. He can put them in the room next to this one."

Ahmed rose quickly, still studying his list. "Yes, Naqib." He turned toward the door.

Abu Salaam stopped him with a gesture. "You look puzzled, Ahmed."

"No, Naqib! It is just, well, there are several Jewish names on the list."

"And you think we should start with them?"

"Well—"

"Ahmed, the message we want to send, to Arabs, to Muslims who are not Arabs, to Jews, and especially to *Americans*, is that Zionism is the cancer destroying our homeland and our people, but the evil that makes Zionism possible, and therefore the greater enemy, is *America!*"

Ahmed looked at his papers clasped in his hands in front

of him. How the naqib's eyes burned! "Yes, Naqib," he said
helplessly.

"And so, Ahmed, we begin with Americans who are not
Jews. Americans with American names, from little towns.
Do you understand, my brave fighter?"

Ahmed stiffened to attention. "I think so, Naqib."

"Good," smiled Abu Salaam. "Tell Walid, and then ask
him to come to me."

"Yes, Naqib." Ahmed left the room.

Now what am I going to say to Colonel Baruni? mused
Abu Salaam.

Colonel Baruni's Mercedes limousine, preceded by one
troop-carrying BTR and followed by another, passed through
the western gate of Uqba ben Nafi. At Colonel Zharkov's
suggestion, the little convoy turned north, around the end
of runway 11/29, and into the now-dry golf course the Americans had built. Baruni could see groups of his tanks bunched
along the nearly dry watercourse, partially concealed by the
swaying palm trees. Most tanks were already covered by
nets, and soldiers in desert fatigues were gathering fallen
palm fronds to add to the camouflage. Soldiers had rigged
gas-engined pumps from the stagnant wadi and were spraying
the vehicles as they were set into their positions. Baruni
frowned. "Colonel Zharkov, why are those men washing down
my tanks?"

Zharkov smiled. "To cool their engines, Comrade Colonel.
To reduce their infrared signatures in reconnaissance photos."

Baruni nodded slowly. The Russians are working quickly,
he thought, as the convoy rolled slowly past the concealed
tanks and armored personnel carriers. Either that, or they
just presumed I would agree, and began hours ago. The
colonel counted thirteen tanks, a company, and an extra platoon, plus a platoon of BMPs and another platoon of dismounted infantry. He forced a smile and waved to his troops,
ignoring the salutes of the Russian officers and non-coms.
Even if this incident ends well, he thought bitterly, the Rus-

sians will have tightened their grip on me and my revolution. How I would like to be rid of them all, and then devote all of my energies to building the Arab nation!

Colonel Zharkov interrupted Baruni's train of thought. "Comrade Colonel, if you please, we could drive directly onto the taxiway, and you can see how easily the tanks positioned here can reach the Operations Building."

If you please, thought Baruni, with mounting irritation and despair. "Yes, Colonel," he smiled. "Let us see, and then I will explain things to Abu Salaam." Zharkov leaned forward and spoke in Russian to his aide, who was seated beside Baruni's driver. The aide pointed and relayed the instruction to the driver in Arabic. The limousine drove slowly across the rolling, hard-packed earth to the paved taxiway, then around the Operations Building, where it stopped. The BTRs followed, then stopped just behind the Mercedes. The guards jumped down, holding their weapons in front of them.

Ahmed dozed on a chair in the front of the main hall of the Operations Building, his feet up on the windowsill. His sleep was softly invaded by the low sound of heavy diesel engines. He jumped up with alarm as he saw the vehicles and the armed women suddenly appear on the apron in front of the building. "Naqib! Walid! Soldiers!" he shouted, picking up his AKS assault rifle and backing away from the window.

Walid and Abu Salaam ran back into the main hall from the office area. The hostages, seated in small groups in metal folding chairs or on the floor, began to whisper among themselves. Several in chairs quietly got down and lay flat on the floor, motioning others to do likewise.

Abu Salaam rushed to the edge of the window. His heart was pounding as he waited for the explosion that would blow the doors open. Walid took up his assigned position behind the group of hostages in the center of the room and chambered a round in his AKS. He had several fragmentation grenades clipped to his belt. Ahmed, once over his initial panic, took up his own position on the other side of the silent, wide-eyed hostages. Amin, the boy from Nablus, stood in the shadows to the rear, and Yusef was forty feet above them, in the control tower, watching the apron and the two Libyan air controllers, who had nothing to do since nearly all aircraft had departed two hours earlier.

Abu Salaam edged to the window and peered out. He saw Colonel Baruni step out of the limousine, straighten his tunic, and wave toward the building. Abu Salaam let out a long breath, his fear suddenly replaced by anger. He checked his Makarov pistol in its holster on his web belt, then took a fragmentation grenade from the leg pocket of his fatigue trousers and concealed it in his left hand, held behind his back. He unlocked the door with his right hand and stepped onto the tarmac, closing the door behind him.

Colonel Baruni stepped forward, smiling broadly, and held out his hand. Abu Salaam's face was set in a scowl of pure hatred, his teeth slightly bared. Baruni stopped four feet from the smaller man and dropped his hand. "Ali, my friend—"

"How dare you come sneaking around the side of the building with all of these soldiers?" hissed Abu Salaam through his clenched teeth.

"Ali! These are just my guards! Come, we must talk." Once again, Colonel Baruni extended his hand.

Abu Salaam brought his left hand from behind his back, showing the grenade. With his right hand, he pulled the pin, while holding the spoon tightly. He took a half step toward Baruni, who involuntarily took a half step backward. Several of Baruni's guards raised their carbines and pointed them at Abu Salaam.

"If your guards shoot me, Hassan, I will drop this grenade at your feet."

Without turning, Baruni made a downward gesture with both arms. Abu Salaam watched as the guards lowered their weapons. "Ali, what is the meaning of this?"

"Two of your armored cars are in front of this place all the time. Now four. I want them all removed."

"But Ali, they are here to defend you! If the Americans come, they must come this way! We should have more troops here, Ali, and tanks—"

"No! No troops, and no tanks! If the Americans come, shoot down their planes! Sink their ships! Troops and tanks so close threaten only us!"

"Ali, you have asked us to protect you. The Russians are helping—"

"Fuck the Russians! The Russians will sell the Palestinian people for American grain! The Russians want to take my prisoners!"

"Ali, it would be better if you turned over, ah, security, for your prisoners, to me. You and your fighters could rest—"

"There, Hassan! Oh, you were once a fighter, but now you work for the Russians! The filthy, oil-soaked, debauched Kuwaitis hold our brethren, and the Zionists piss on our homeland, while you, *you*, Colonel, would take a stand against true servants of Islam!" Abu Salaam waved behind him toward the Operations Building. His voice rose toward a scream. "Take your armored cars away, Ali! And your tanks! And keep them away!" Abu Salaam seemed to shrink. It is the tension, thought Baruni. Despite his fear of Abu Salaam and the grenade in his hand, he took a step forward and held out his arms. "Ali, please listen. I am your friend; we all are your friends."

"Send away the guards, and the armored cars." Abu Salaam's voice was a tiny whisper.

Baruni turned and waved his arms. Turn, go! the gestures said. His guard remounted the BTRs of the colonel's personal detail, all except the two women who always followed. The four BTRs revved up and slowly withdrew across the apron and out of sight.

In the back seat of the limousine, Colonel Zharkov thumbed the safety back on his own Makarov pistol. Glad to see those BTRs leave, he thought. They would have been in my way. He was now sure Moscow would tell him to take control of the American hostages.

When the BTRs were no longer visible, Baruni turned back to Abu Salaam. "There, Ali, you see? They are gone."

"They must be kept away. You must keep the Americans away."

Baruni took another tentative step forward. "Ali, let us look after your prisoners. You are tired."

Abu Salaam raised his head. His fierce eyes returned to focus on Baruni's. He raised his left hand and showed the grenade. Baruni thought Ali's thumb was loosening on the spoon. Baruni stepped back, his throat tightening. "Ali—"

Abu Salaam seemed to smile. His teeth were bare, but no longer clenched. His beard was slick with saliva. Baruni found him repulsive, yet fascinating. "Ali, my friend—"

"Stay where you are, Hassan," said Abu Salaam, backing away. "I will give you one hostage, as a token of my good faith." He opened the door and slid inside, closing it behind him.

Colonel Zharkov heard Baruni shout something to his driver and his guards. Colonel Baruni was smiling. "What is he saying, Captain?" he asked his aide.

"He says Abu Salaam is sending one hostage out, as a token of goodwill."

"Good," said Zharkov. I guess that is progress, he thought.

Abu Salaam leaned on the locked door and fought to control his trembling. He reinserted the pin in the grenade in his hand and returned it to his pocket. He drew his pistol and thumbed the safety lever to fire. "Walid!"

"Yes, Naqib!"

"Bring the prisoner Stevens here, at once!"

"Yes, Naqib!"

Walid prodded Lance Corporal Stevens to the door of the Operations Building. His arms were tied behind his back, but he twisted and looked Walid full in the face. Walid blushed, his face contorted with anger, and he prodded Stevens between the shoulder blades with the barrel of his AKS.

Without a word, Abu Salaam grasped him by his shirt collar, unlocked the door, and shoved him outside. "Walk," he said in English. Stevens walked, blinking in the glare of the sun just breaking through the clouds. He recognized Colonel Baruni from his visit two days before. The colonel smiled and beckoned with both arms.

Baruni held his hands out to receive the young American. He saw Abu Salaam emerge from the doorway, his pistol in his hand. When Lance Corporal Stevens was fifteen feet from the door of the Operations Building and ten feet from Colonel Baruni, Abu Salaam shot him twice. The first shot struck Stevens between the shoulder blades. His mouth opened in an O as his breath was knocked out. The second shot split the top of his skull and sprayed Colonel Baruni with blood and fine bits of bone. Lance Corporal Stevens fell face forward on the tarmac and did not move. Colonel Baruni stood rooted to the ground, his arms still outstretched to welcome the American boy. From the crack in the door of the Operations Building, Abu Salaam screamed his fury.

"There, Hassan! There is my good faith! Tell the Americans, tell the Jews, tell your friends, the motherfucking Russians! I want my people! I will send you a body every eight hours, or four, or two! Tell them, Hassan!" He slammed the door.

Baruni scrambled back into his limousine beside Colonel Zharkov. The Russian observed Baruni was white as a sheet and trembling as the limousine sped away.

⇌8⇌
USS *America,* 1220 GMT (1320 Local)

Lieutenant Colonel Loonfeather and Colonel Brimmer sat together in the vast wardroom of the *America,* eating lunch with Lieutenant Commander Wallace, who had been detailed from the admiral's staff to deal with the specifics of the paratroopers' air and naval gunfire support, and with Major Morgan, the Operations Officer of Marine Heavy Helicopter Squadron 144, embarked in *Inchon*. Loonfeather liked what he heard. The Navy had the thing well thought out, and since the men of the ANGLICO attached to Task Force Bowie were navy-marine types, they knew the communications and spotting procedures. The ANGLICO spotters would just have to be handed the day codes and the coded list and map coordinates of various points in and around the air base, which were already in the ships' computers and which would be used for references for precise spot.

Loonfeather watched idly as a naval officer in working khaki entered the wardroom and whispered to the ship's executive officer, who was seated at the table nearest the door of the wardroom. The XO's eyebrows shot up and he shook his head. The officer nodded vigorously and withdrew. The XO stood and tapped his water glass with a fork. The room fell silent as heads turned to look.

"Attention, please, gentlemen. Communications has just monitored a broadcast on Italian state radio. Their correspondent in Tripoli has reported that the terrorists have just executed one of our people."

The crowd buzzed for just a moment, then fell silent again. The XO continued. "There are no details, except the man was apparently a marine. For those of you directly involved in the rescue operation, the admiral's and subsidiary briefings scheduled to resume at 1400 will resume in ten minutes. That is all."

Officers all across the room stuffed a last few bites of lunch into their mouths and stood. Brimmer grabbed Loonfeather's arm. The big American Indian looked to be in shock. Brimmer shook him gently. "Christ, Rufus! We may have to go tonight! We'll have to plan to go without your people!"

"No fucking way, Bob," spat Loonfeather, his voice shaking with anger. "My boys can load up and leave in a matter of hours."

"But there's no way they can be staged and ready to attack tomorrow!"

"The Airborne will fly all night, refueling in the air, and

jump at dawn from the same aircraft." Brimmer looked skeptical, but sympathetic. "I intend to recommend we do just that, Colonel," said Loonfeather.

Lieutenant Commander Wallace caught up with them. He looked from Loonfeather to Brimmer and back. "Then, gentlemen, may we finish up our support plan?"

"Right," said Brimmer, pulling the rigid-faced Loonfeather along by the arm. "We have a lot to do."

Loonfeather marched along the passageway, muttering to himself. Suddenly he stopped and turned, colliding with Colonel Brimmer, who was following close behind. Brimmer pushed himself back. He thought Colonel Loonfeather looked shocked, his eyes wide, his mouth open.

"Damn!" shouted Loonfeather, slamming his fist into the bulkhead. "Damn!" he roared, oblivious to the startled glances of naval officers pressing past him.

"Rufus—" said Brimmer, placing a hand on the bigger man's shoulder.

"Bob! The *tanks!*"

"What about—"

"We can fly the airborne infantry here from Bragg nonstop, Bob. We have done that; hell, we once made a nonstop drop from Bragg to Egypt. But the Sheridans *have* to be staged in Europe, because we have to transfer them to C-130s for the LAPES."

"You can't LAPES from the 141?" asked Lieutenant Commander Wallace.

"Shit, we could, but the Air Force has never approved it! The 130 is much more agile near the ground, especially over small LAPES drop zones." Loonfeather resumed his march down the passageway, continuing to talk over his shoulder. "But we have here a large and unobstructed DZ, a whole fucking airfield." He stopped and turned. "The Air Force *has* to deliver my tanks!" He turned and once again marched along.

"Is there any other way to get them in?" asked Brimmer, hopping to keep pace with the Indian's long strides.

"The Air Force will want to heavy drop, from say 1500 feet, using eight huge parachutes. But the desert cools off rapidly this time of year, and we should have a strong land breeze even at dawn. Those tanks would be spread all over the air base, way outside any reasonable perimeter the paratroopers could establish." Once again Loonfeather came to an abrupt halt, and spun around. He caught Brimmer by his shoulders just before a second collision. "Bob, the only thing the Air Force needs to LAPES my tanks from the C-141s is a few pilots with large-caliber testicles!" Loonfeather held his large brown hands in front of him, fingers splayed as though supporting two imaginary basketballs. "Come on."

Brimmer resumed the chase as Loonfeather turned and loped off. "Where are we going?"

"To communications. We need to call Charleston and speak to the only colonel in the Military Airlift Command suitably equipped in the gonad department, and the man I originally talked into establishing a test program for LAPES from C-141s. An amiable Italian madman named Paul Squitiero."

⇆9⇄
Tzafon may Eilat, 1230 GMT (1430 Local)

The SEALs had been given the morning off after practicing all night. Hooper had told them they would have a drill on the penetration of the Operations Building at 1600, then go over problems until dinner, and then, once again, drill all night.

Stuart had spent an hour and a half on the secure radio link in the morning, talking with Lieutenant Colonel Loonfeather and Colonel Brimmer, reviewing just how the SEAL drop fitted into the larger operation. It was agreed that the Air Force would pick Stuart up the following morning and fly him to Catania, and that he would then be picked up by COD (carrier onboard delivery) aircraft to join Loonfeather and Brimmer on *America* and move with them to

Inchon to coordinate the three elements of the raid with them.

Stuart explained the updates and changes to the op plan to Hooper and Leah over a leisurely lunch. The rest of the team rested and looked after their equipment, except Goldstein, Feeney, and Cross, who had been invited to have lunch at the IDF Noncommissioned Officers' Mess, and had been told by Hooper to go ahead.

The secure radio link, capable of sending and receiving scrambled voice and teletype, was established in a small air-transportable trailer next to the Israeli command bunker. It was manned by four rated U.S. Navy radiomen working in two shifts. Radioman Third Class Meyer ran up to intercept Stuart as he walked toward the bunker with Hooper and Leah Rabin.

"Excuse me, Commander Stuart," said Meyer. "There's voice traffic for you from Sixth Fleet."

Stuart followed Meyer into the trailer and picked up the handset. "This is Commander Stuart, over."

"This is Rear Admiral Wilson, Commander. I have some very bad news."

Stuart sat down and listened to the very bad news. When he had it all, he returned to the command bunker on a dead run.

Sergeant Yanni Galen answered the phone in the NCOs' Mess on the second ring. He listened to Capt. Leah Rabin for fifteen seconds, then hung up. "Hey, Goldstein! Your lot are to get back over to your area at the double! You may be pulling out of here this afternoon!"

Goldstein, Cross, and Feeney were out of their chairs and immediately ready to move. "What's happened, Yanni?" asked Goldstein.

"Come on, David. I'll drive you in the pickup," answered Galen.

"What did they say?" persisted Cross.

"Captain Rabin said you may be picked up today and

flown to wherever it is that you'll be picked up by the bomber.
It seems the terrorists have shot at least one hostage, a marine."

"Holy shit," whispered Feeney. "It's a go, then."

"Let's get in the truck," said Goldstein.

Feeney jumped in the cab of the gray pickup next to
Sergeant Galen, while Goldstein and Cross climbed into the
cargo bed. Galen accelerated out of the vehicle park and
down the taxiway. He took the first corner so fast that Goldstein and Cross were thrown across the bed and rammed
into the side. "Shit," cursed Cross softly, rubbing a bruise
on his elbow. "It can't be that fucking urgent!"

On the open taxiway, Sergeant Galen drove even faster.
Feeney watched him, hoping Yanni knew what he was doing.
As the truck turned onto the crossing taxiway, its rear wheels
hit a patch of blown sand and began to slide. Galen corrected
for the skid, but then the right rear tire blew, and Yanni
lost control. The truck did a complete spin, then slid backwards off the taxiway and down an embankment into some
rough boulders. Galen and Feeney were slammed against
the backs of their seats. Goldstein and Cross were thrown
from the rear of the pickup into the rocks. Goldstein lay on
his back, with his right leg twisted under him at an impossible angle. Cross was facedown and unconscious, bleeding
from a deep head wound. Feeney climbed down to the
injured men while Yanni Galen radioed for the base ambulance.

The SEAL team assembled in the command bunker, minus Goldstein and Cross, who were on their way to the
hospital. Goldstein's leg was broken in two places, and Cross
had broken ribs in addition to his head wound. A tearful
Yanni Galen sat in the corner, explaining to Captain Rabin
what had happened.

Stuart and Hooper walked into the briefing room after
watching the ambulance speed away. "How are the guys,
sir?" asked Feeney, who still felt a little dizzy.

"They'll be all right; fine, in fact. But they won't be

jumping out of any airplanes for a while. Damn!" Hooper pounded his fist on the wooden table hard enough to hurt his hand.

Leah Rabin dismissed the Israeli sergeant and joined the SEALs. "How long to get replacements in?"

"Shit!" spat Hooper. "We could get a couple of divers down from Athens, but they probably wouldn't be parachute-qualified. Besides, we've been training on this for a day and a half, and we still have problems! Depending on what gets decided at Sixth Fleet and in Washington, we could be called on to drop tomorrow."

"You can't do this with six men, Hoop," said Stuart.

Hooper scowled at Stuart, then suddenly he smiled. "I see my seventh, Willie-Boy."

Stuart took a step back. "Oh, no! No way, Hoop. It's been a hundred years!"

"How's your Arabic, William?" asked Hooper sweetly.

"Hey, it's great, if the terrorists want to talk about oil-field equipment! Come on, Hoop, you'll have to get somebody qualified!"

"You would still be a man short, anyway," interjected Leah Rabin. The two American officers turned to look at the tiny Israeli officer. She tapped the parachute badge sewn to her fatigue shirt. "My Arabic is fluent," she said softly.

There was a moment of stunned silence, then Hooper exploded. "Hey, Leah, thanks, but no way are you coming!" He looked quickly at Stuart, then at the rest of the team for support. Nobody moved; nobody shook his head. Stuart smiled at Hooper and shrugged. Hooper slammed his hand again on the table. "William, Sixth Fleet will *never* go along with this!"

Stuart shrugged again. "They might. We don't have a lot of options, and she does know the drill."

"But she's a woman!" shouted Hooper, throwing his hands in the air.

"Dammit, Commander, I am qualified!" shouted Leah with equal vehemence.

"It may frankly be a bigger problem, politically, that you are Israeli, Leah," said Stuart.

"I will wear an American uniform. If I get killed, no one will ever know. If I don't, my participation need never be officially acknowledged."

Hooper stopped pacing and turned to face Stuart. "So, William?"

Stuart smiled broadly. "It's your call, Commander. You lead."

"Jesus! Well, all right! If Sixth Fleet agrees!" he jammed his finger into Stuart's chest. "You're number seven, and you," Hooper tapped Leah lightly on the shoulder, "are number eight!"

The SEALs applauded and crowded around the officers. Stuart shook Leah's hand and gave it an extra squeeze. I know she can do it, he thought, but I wish she didn't have to. He separated himself from the group and started for the door.

"Where do you think you're going, *Troop?*" asked Hooper sarcastically.

"To call Sixth Fleet, tell them our problem, and give them *your* recommendation that we include Capt. L. Rabin in the team."

"Come back quick. We had better walk you two through in your positions."

⇆10⇌
Washington, D.C., 1400 GMT (0900 Local)

The President listened carefully as the Chief of Naval Operations briefed for the Joint Chiefs. The operation was drawing together nicely, although the three elements of the ground-assault force, the most difficult and dangerous part of the problem, were far apart and had never worked together or even seen each other.

"Well, Arch, what's the bottom line? Can your people go in there and get our hostages away from those murderous lunatics?"

"Yes, Mr. President, I believe they can. One advantage we have is that the officers who designed the assault will be together to run it, embarked on *Inchon,* just offshore." Daniels was unaware of the accident in Israel and that, therefore, one of the three "assault coordinators" would not make it to the *Inchon.*

"Well, that should help, shouldn't it?" asked the President.

"Yes, sir," said Admiral Daniels, and sat down.

"So when can the rescue be carried out, Admiral?" asked the President, a hint of irritation in his voice.

Admiral Daniels stood again and looked around the cabinet room. That really wasn't his question. "We're looking at dawn, February 20, Mr. President. It's really a *political* question, sir. We don't have permission from either the Spanish or the Germans to launch the paratroopers from bases in their countries—"

"But I thought all the force we needed was on the ships of the Sixth Fleet!"

"Not really, sir. If we had one more carrier battle group, we wouldn't need the air force bombers from England, but the *Kennedy* and her group are still two days west of Gibraltar. Besides, although we could rely solely on the marines to run the assault and rescue, the enemy's large number of tanks pose a threat to the helicopters both in the air and on the ground. For that reason, we have built an important part of the assault around army infantry and armored airborne troops, which can get on the ground fast and which have a strong antitank and antivehicle capability."

"And where are those army units?"

"Fort Bragg, Mr. President," answered the Secretary of Defense. "Loading their gear aboard air force transports. They can go as soon as the Spanish or the Germans give us a place to land and stage for assault."

"Henry?" The President looked to the Secretary of State.

"I'm sure we'll have all the concurrences we need by tomorrow morning in Europe, Mr. President. It's Sunday, and because this is a complex political issue, our various allies want to collect enough opposition figures to develop united fronts in their several countries."

"But Henry, three hours ago these thugs shot an American serviceman in cold blood! Surely, the allies *have* to support us!" The President's voice had risen and his cheeks were getting red.

The Secretary of State squirmed. "We were assured by the Italians, Mr. President, that the terrorists would honor their own commitment not to harm the hostages until 8 A.M. in Europe on the twentieth. We believed we could buy some more time. This morning's shooting was, I'm sorry to say, a complete surprise."

"But the allies *will* support us?" demanded the President.

"I'm sure they will, Mr. President, as soon as they can."

"Christ!" The President struck the table hard with the palm of his hand. "They shot an American marine in cold blood. Two hours from now, they may very well shoot another one, and you're telling me that we cannot get in there for *another two days?*"

There was a painful silence as the President looked around the room. General Klim, the Chief of Staff of the Army, cleared his throat. "Mr. President—"

"Yes?"

"Ah, there is another, ah, way, sir. The commander of the Airborne Armored element, who is with the Sixth Fleet staff, recommends we fly the raid straight from Bragg, tonight, refueling the planes in flight over the Atlantic."

"Then we wouldn't need the Europeans' permission?"

"Well, the transports would have to land somewhere, probably Torrejon, Spain, after they dropped the paratroopers. The Spanish might be pissed, but by then. . . ." General Klim let his voice trail off.

"What does Sixth Fleet say?" asked the President.

"Admiral Bergeron sent the recommendation along without endorsement, sir," said Admiral Daniels.

"Meaning he doesn't like it?"

"Yes, sir," said Daniels. "He says it will be impossible to coordinate."

"General Klim?"

"Mr. President, Lt. Col. Rufus Loonfeather, who commands the Third of the Seventy-third Armor, sir, who thought this up, says it can work, and I'm inclined to agree with him, though it would of course be preferable to have everything at least begin in Europe."

"But not for two days."

"That's the choice, Mr. President," said Admiral Daniels. Others around the table nodded.

The President rose from his seat. The others stood. "Gentlemen, I'm going to consult briefly with members of the Congress. When I return, you'll have one hour to convince me *not* to try this Lieutenant Colonel Loonfeather's plan. General Klim, when would the paratroopers have to leave North Carolina if we want to go tonight?"

"By noon today at the latest, Mr. President."

"Make sure everything is ready. I'll return within the hour."

⇋11⇌
Pope Air Force Base, Fayetteville, N.C., 1530 GMT
(1030 Local)

Lieutenant Colonel James E. "Jim" Bowie, Infantry, commanding officer of 1st Battalion, 502d Parachute Infantry Regiment sat in the Air Operations office, on the third floor of the three-story, white brick-face Operations Building next to the green ramp. The teleprinter had been running at high speed for two hours, transferring the entire op-order, with codes, commo net designations, and call signs, and a host of other details direct from Sixth Fleet in the Med. The slower fax machines had given him maps and symbolic renderings of the mission TO&E.

The colonel looked out the window into the cool rain. All of the airborne infantry company's gear had been loaded into the first two C-141s in line on the apron, including a prodigious number of Dragon shoulder-fired antitank missiles in canisters.

The Sheridans were fully rigged for LAPES on the improved 42k pallets that allowed them to be dropped with full fuel and ammo loads and staged on the self-propelled K-loaders. The K-loaders would move them to eight more C-141s and align them with the aircraft ramps to be winched aboard. The tank on-load was on hold from Division, though no one had told Colonel Bowie why. The planes were fueled and ready to go, their aircrews briefed except for final weather. The soldiers, in full packs with weapons and full ammo loads, squatted in the hangar adjacent to the ramp, out of the rain.

The teleprinter finally stopped. Its last comment was a simple "message ends." Bowie yelled for his runner and told him to assemble officers and senior NCOs immediately.

Lieutenant Colonel Bowie passed out copies of the final op-order to the officers and non-coms who commanded units. He handed several copies of the Supporting Arms Plan to Jason Brown, the navy lieutenant who commanded the ANGLICO detachment. The Supporting Arms Plan included the plans of the air base with the gunfire and air spot references, plus the day codes of all units, the list of code names and gun calibers of the ships, and bomb and missile loads of the fixed- and rotary-wing aircraft units. The army unit commanders would have the plan as well, but the ANGLICO would carry it out as long as they were neither knocked out nor masked from targets.

First Lieutenant John Connelly, Armor, commanded the two armor platoons: eight M-551 Sheridans. He received, in addition to the rest of the briefing package, the latest satellite and SR-71 reconnaissance photos. He noted that they were twelve hours old. He turned to the 82d Airborne G-2 Intelligence officer, who was coordinating for the mission up until the time it left Bragg. "No new photos, Colonel Sullivan?"

"Not since early this morning in North Africa, Lieutenant. Heavy cloud cover."

Lieutenant Colonel Bowie concluded the briefing. "OK, men, look through and mark the changes; we'll have a final brief in here just before we fly. I want every piece of gear and every man in the aircraft at eleven-thirty."

"Do we have a go then, Jim?" asked Lt. Col. Paul Squitiero, USAF, commander of the 20th Military Airlift Squadron, who would fly the lead C-141.

"No," said Colonel Bowie. "JCS and everybody else in Washington are meeting with the President. I spoke to the Army Deputy Chief of Staff for Operations ten minutes ago. We'll lift off on time with or without final approval; if they turn it down, we come back."

"What's your sense of it, Jim?" asked Capt. William Schubert, Infantry, who commanded the airborne rifle company, A Company of the 1st of the 502d.

Lieutenant Colonel Bowie shoved his own stack of papers into a plastic briefcase. "My feeling is that we'll sleep in the skies tonight, gentlemen. And then we'll hold a rather sudden reveille at the old Wheelus Air Force Base, tomorrow most early."

Schubert gestured to his platoon leaders and senior sergeants. "Go! Get loaded!"

The officers and NCOs filed out of the room. Lieutenant Colonel Bowie called to the ANGLICO commander and motioned him to a seat. Bowie's task force XO, Maj. John Donahue, sat on the edge of the table next to the colonel. "Lieutenant Brown, we have barely met. You know Major Donahue?"

"We met yesterday afternoon, when I got here, Colonel."

"Good. Your team will jump with me, from the first aircraft. Has your team been together long, Lieutenant?"

Brown shook his head. "No, Colonel. My gunny sergeant and I have been together three months, in San Diego and then Long Beach. The other guys have been collected from Norfolk to Mayport."

Colonel Bowie frowned. "Why didn't the Navy send an intact team?"

"We don't have many people who are jump qualified and ANGLICO qualified, Colonel. We had to piece it together. But the gunny and I do the actual spotting; we will be fine."

"The two of you have done actual spotting together?" asked Major Donahue.

"Yes, sir. Gunfire, up to eight inch, at San Clemente Island, and aircraft at Twenty-nine Palms."

"California?" Bowie asked. Brown nodded. Bowie stood, turned his back, and looked thoughtfully at the large plan of Wheelus tacked to the wall. We'll be a long way from California, he thought. "Lieutenant, I hope you realize that the proficiency of your spotting team, and of naval air and gunfire, is absolutely critical to the success of this mission."

"I . . . knew it was important, sir." Lieutenant Brown had been flying so hard in the last twelve hours he hadn't fairly had time to think.

Bowie turned back toward Brown and the others. "Not *important*, Jason, critical. You've read the op plans, but you aren't really experienced in airborne operations, am I right?"

"Yes, sir, I surely am not. Gunnery Sergeant Bright and I have only jumped with marine Pathfinder units, sir. I hope you'll bring me up to speed, Colonel." Brown felt it was a lame response, but it would hardly do to conceal the fact that he and his team had no knowledge *whatever* of airborne operations.

"Lieutenant," continued Colonel Bowie, "you've followed the sequence of events. First, we drop in the infantry company, including your people. Then, we LAPES in the Sheridans. Then we unwrap them and assemble them to kill the enemy's tanks. Clear?"

"Yes, sir."

"Good. The problem, Jason, is the time it takes to do all that. The Airborne Armor Raid is designed to drop behind enemy lines, but not in the middle of an enemy perimeter. It takes time for the infantry to land, assemble into platoons, and disperse to their positions. It takes more time to LAPES the Sheridans, get them off the pallets, and get them moving. All that time, Lieutenant, the enemy has us under his tanks and whatever else he has."

Lieutenant Brown followed the colonel's pointer around the photographed Libyan tank positions. "How much time, Colonel, before the whole thing is working?"

"We've compressed it as much as we think we can, Lieutenant, mostly by *reducing* the force we'll drop. At the minimum, twenty minutes from the time the infantry hits the ground."

"Jesus, sir! Why so long?"

"You cannot parachute soldiers without hard landings, Lieutenant, even into a plowed field. We will be landing on paved runways and taxiways. We will have casualties, broken ankles and legs. Those men will have to be cleared from the runway before the vehicles are dropped. Units have to gather, then disperse. It's an imprecise process."

"It's a clusterfuck, Lieutenant," volunteered Major Donahue.

"Thanks, John, for the clarification," laughed Colonel Bowie. Major Donahue smiled.

"So where does that leave me and mine?" asked Lieutenant Brown.

"During the time when the infantry company is down, but not ready to move, as well as while we're LAPESing the vehicles, we'll have nothing to protect us from enemy tanks and vehicles except our own shoulder-fired Dragon missiles, and whatever naval air and gunfire you can bring in."

Lieutenant Brown nodded slowly. "I see, Colonel."

"Can you do it?"

"Yes, sir. You can believe we can."

Bowie smiled. "Better get packed then, Lieutenant."

"Aye, aye, sir!" Brown saluted. Funny, he thought, as he went to look for Gunnery Sergeant Bright. Up until now, the most important thing had seemed surviving the low-level jump.

"Atten-HUT," called a voice from the back of the room.

"As you were, men," said Major General Francis Xavier O'Brien, Commanding General of the 82nd Airborne Division, as he strode to the briefing podium, followed by three scurrying aides. "Colonel Bowie, Colonel Squitiero, and Lieutenant Connelly, I need the three of you briefly."

The last few men filed out of the room, glancing back at the general and murmuring questions to each other. General O'Brien sat at the head of the gray metal table and put on his half-glasses. A colonel in Class A green uniform laid a light blue folder in front of the general and stepped back.

General O'Brien was six feet tall, and lean as a greyhound. His iron-gray hair was cut high and tight in the tradition of the Airborne. He looked ten years younger than his fifty-four years. His Class A uniform displayed eight rows of ribbons, topped by the Distinguished Service Cross, with the Combat Infantryman's Badge and jump wings with a gold star in the suspension lines, signifying at least one combat parachute jump, above the ribbons. He opened the folder, and then studied the faces of the two colonels and the lieutenant who stood before him at attention with his light blue, almost colorless eyes. "Sit, please, gentlemen."

Lieutenant Colonels Bowie and Squitiero and First Lieutenant Connelly sat. The room, boisterous a minute before, was bleakly quiet. "Gentlemen," said the general, speaking slowly and softly, "given the change in plan, and given that we will be unable to stage in Europe and transfer the Sheridans to C-130s, I have to decide whether to delete the armor from the mission."

"Damn!" shouted Lieutenant Connelly, leaping to his feet. His expression flushed to anger, and then bled white to embarrassment.

"Steady, Lieutenant," said Colonel Bowie, sharply.

"It's all right, Colonel," said the general, evenly. "Let him speak his piece."

Connelly drew in his breath. "I beg the general's pardon. When the Eighty-second saddled up for Grenada, sir, the Third of the Seventy-third was the only unit left out of it. It was said then that there was no armor threat on Grenada. I wasn't even here, then, sir—"

"Neither was I, Lieutenant," said the general, softly.

"Yes, sir. But the senior NCOs in the battalion have never stopped talking about it, sir. And I recall that when the general took command of this division, you came and talked with us, and showed us the after-action evaluation, which said in part that not only was there Soviet-built light armor on Grenada, but also several strongpoints that could easily have been reduced by tank fire, and that perhaps we might have saved some lives."

"So I did, Lieutenant," said the general.

"And you told us, General, that if a similar operation came along in future, we would go." Connelly waited for the general to respond. The general looked back in silence. Connelly took a deep breath and plunged on. "Sir, on this mission, the *major* threat is enemy armor, *heavy* armor, sir. If there was no armor threat, the Marines would keep the whole mission for themselves."

"Anything else, Lieutenant?" A hint of a smile tickled the corner of the general's lips.

"No, sir," said Connelly, sitting down and feeling sheepish. I wish Colonel Loonfeather was here, he thought, helplessly. "But we are good to go, sir."

The general's smile broadened. "Colonel Bowie?"

"Sir," said the ground-force commander, stiffening to attention.

"Are you prepared to accomplish this mission without the armor? Won't the Dragons be enough?"

Bowie took a deep breath. "Sir, the Dragon is an excellent antitank missile. Fired by fully qualified people, it is a one-shot kill weapon against all enemy armor. It has, however, proved a difficult weapon for ordinary troops to guide."

"Go on," said the general, glancing at Lieutenant Connelly, who was looking hard at his boots.

"General, the Dragons will be within the perimeter. Oncoming tanks will present their most heavily armored surfaces, the turret face and the glacis, or front slope. A Dragon kill against the front of a T-72 is problematic at best. The tanks, on the other hand, can maneuver; get a shot at the enemy at his much more vulnerable tracks, or against his relatively unprotected ass-end."

"You concur with Lieutenant Connelly's analysis, then, Colonel Bowie?"

Bowie sat back and cleared his throat. "I do, sir. I want those tanks."

The general took off his glasses and set them on top of the blue folder. "So do I. Most definitely, so do I. My problem is—" the general turned and looked hard at Lieutenant Colonel Squitiero, "—that the Air Force has no proven capability to deliver Sheridans by LAPES from a C-141, and my good friend General Browning at Military Airlift Command cannot assure me that it can be done." Colonel Squitiero opened his mouth to speak, but the general held up his hand. "General Browning has left the decision to me, Colonel Squitiero, and now I would like to hear from you."

Colonel Squitiero concentrated on meeting the general's eyes. "It is true, General, that we have not established a LAPES capability with the 141. My squadron has been practicing, trying to perfect the technique, for four months now, at Charleston."

"With what results, Colonel?"

"Mixed, General. The 141 has a higher stall speed than the 130 by twenty knots. Also, the jets on the 141 cannot build power as quickly as the turboprops on the 130. But the LAPESs themselves have gone well with dummy loads, up to and exceeding the weight of the Sheridan, as long as we have a very shallow descent and climb-out, and a relatively long drop zone."

"General Browning tells me you have never actually dropped a Sheridan."

Squitiero smiled. "True enough, General, until yesterday. We dropped four here yesterday, and didn't bust even one."

The general leaned forward. "You did that here at Pope?"

"Yes, sir. Alfa Company let us have four, the riggers rigged them, and we dropped them."

The general leaned back, and allowed his slight smile to return. "Can you assure me, Colonel, that your crews—and how many trained crews do you have, by the way—can handle this mission?"

"We have eight crews in the test team, sir, and they all are here. They have extra loadmasters with LAPES experience in 130s riding with them. General, I am going to be perfectly candid. If the drop zone was an open field, or even a highway, or if there were trees around, or telephone poles, or built-up structures of any kind around the DZ, then no, we wouldn't be ready. But General, the DZ is an eleven-thousand foot runway, a paved parallel taxiway and the hard dirt in between. Better than that, it used to be a U.S. airbase. We dug all the old approach plates out of archives, and the crews have been drilling with them since they assembled here."

The general looked at the stocky Air Force colonel. He noticed Squitiero had Army jump wings sewn on his gray flight suit. That shouldn't influence me, he thought, but it does. "So the answer is yes?"

"Yes, sir. The Air Force is fully capable of supporting this mission."

"Your personal assurance?" asked the general, smiling more broadly.

"Better than that, sir. I am flying the lead bird."

"With the troops, though."

"Yes, sir, because I like to lead. But I will happily fly a tank in if you wish."

The general waved the thought away. "I am sure you know best how to assign your crews, Colonel." The general steepled his fingers in front of him, and thought in silence. He slowly nodded. "Lieutenant Connelly."

"Sir!" Connelly jumped to attention.

"You had better go and see to your onload. There is very little time."

"Yes, sir! All the way, sir!" Connelly saluted crisply.

"Airborne," said the general, returning the salute. Connelly ran from the room. The general turned back to Colonel Squitiero. "I had to hear that from you, Colonel."

"Yes, sir. Understood, sir."

"You should be told, Colonel, that this general officer will be very upset if, following your assurances, you leave my infantry on Wheelus without its much-needed armor."

Squitiero let loose a bark of laughter, and then tried vainly to suppress a second.

"Something amuses you, Colonel?" said General O'Brien, scowling.

"No, sir. It's just that I had a call some hours earlier, from a colonel in your command, Rufus Loonfeather."

"Go on," said the general, his scowl fading.

"Well, sir, he assured me that if we screwed the pooch on the tank delivery—pardon, sir, his words."

"I know Loonfeather well," said the general.

"Well, he described how the Dakota Indians rewarded braves who, ah, failed in battle."

"And so you fear him more than me?" General O'Brien chuckled.

"Well, he said he would find me first."

The general laughed and stood up. Bowie and Squitiero jumped to attention. "Well, that's all I have. Good mission, gentlemen. Bring all my troops back, if you can." The general handed the folder back to his aide. The two colonels saluted, and the general returned the courtesy. "Airborne."

⇆12⇄
Uqba ben Nafi, 1700 GMT (1800 Local)

"What time is it, Walid?" asked Abu Salaam, yawning.

"Just six o'clock, Naqib."

"How long since we executed the marine?"

"Just less than six hours, Naqib."

"And we have heard nothing of our brothers in Kuwait?"

"Aqid Baruni called twice. He says he is doing everything he can."

"I am sure he is," said Abu Salaam sarcastically. "It seems we are being ignored, Walid. Perhaps another lesson is required."

"Shoot another one, Naqib?"

"Yes. Who is next on the list?"

"A Navy seaman. Barbara Cummins."

"Very well. Have Ahmed bring her in here so we can explain the meaning of her sacrifice. Then you may do it, Walid."

Walid swallowed. I don't want to shoot that scared young girl, he thought.

"You must remember your hatred, Walid," said the Naqib, seeming to read Walid's mind.

⇋13⇌
Tripoli, 1700 GMT (1800 Local)

Colonel Baruni's secretary entered the colonel's office. Baruni was slumped in his chair, a wet cloth covering his eyes. "Colonel, I have finally got through to the Italian Prime Minister."

Baruni sprang to his feet, throwing away the cloth. "Good! Where can I take the call?"

"Here, my Colonel. The light will flash."

"Thank you. You may go, then." The secretary withdrew and closed the door. Baruni picked up the receiver as soon as the light flashed. "Nino, is that you?"

The connection with Rome was good. Prime Minister Nino Calvi sounded distant, but clear. "Good God, Colonel Baruni, what is going on down there?"

Colonel Baruni gripped the receiver in his left hand and gestured broadly with his right. "Nino, you have to help us! You have to tell the Americans that we do not control Abu Salaam! If they attack us, the situation can only grow worse!"

"I don't think they will listen, Hassan, especially to me. It was me who gave Abu Salaam *into your control.*"

"But, Nino! I had no idea he would defy me! He shot that boy practically in my arms!"

"And he still controls all the hostages?"

"Yes."

"When is his deadline to shoot another?"

"He said eight hours. I think he said eight hours, Nino."

"And there have been no more shootings, Hassan?"

"No, praise God! My men at the base tell me everything is very quiet."

"Well, Hassan, all I can say is to keep trying to get Abu Salaam to release at least some hostages. The Americans may hold off if they see you gaining some control."

"All right, yes, Nino, I will keep trying. Please talk to the Americans."

"I will, but if any more of those people are hurt, I doubt if anyone will be able to help you, Hassan."

"Tell them we will try everything."

There was a hollow click as Rome broke the connection.

Walid returned with the girl and Ahmed. Of the two, Abu Salaam thought Ahmed looked the more frightened. Maybe I should have Ahmed pull the trigger, thought Abu Salaam. But no, Walid truly deserves the honor.

"Do you understand what we must do?" asked Abu Salaam in Arabic. The girl waited while Ahmed translated.

She is pretty, thought Walid. She had very pale skin, almost translucent, and big brown eyes. Her hair was jet black, short, and parted in the middle. Her lips were full and sensuous. She was rather thinner than Walid liked a woman, but her breasts swelled nicely beneath her wrinkled uniform shirt.

Remember your hatred, thought Walid.

Ahmed's voice cracked as he translated the Naqib's words. He couldn't look at the woman.

Seaman Barbara Cummins turned to look at the chief terrorist slumped in his chair, his feet on the table. He looked filthy and truly evil, with his matted beard, damp around the mouth, and his burning eyes. "Am I next, then? Are you going to shoot me?"

"We must. Your government has ignored our just demands." The chief terrorist sounded sad, but Seaman Cum-

mins saw he was still smiling. The young one, who wouldn't
look at her, mumbled his translation.

Barbara Cummins understood. She was going to die. She
was at once terribly frightened and very angry. "You have
no right to take hostages! You are just pirates! Cowards who
shoot innocent people!"

Abu Salaam cut her off with an angry shout. Ahmed
cringed and translated as quickly as he could. Abu Salaam
whitened with anger and began to speak softly. The kid translated. It was a litany of all of the injustices inflicted upon
the defenseless Palestinians by the Zionists and the Great
Satan that was America.

Barbara interrupted Ahmed's halting translation. "Tell
him I don't want to hear this shit. Tell him to get on with
it." She was afraid her fear would soon overcome her anger
and that she would beg them to spare her. She wanted to
avoid that above anything, because she was sure it would
do no good.

The chief terrorist was clearly surprised when Ahmed
translated. "What do you think of that, Walid?" asked Abu
Salaam in Arabic.

"She reviles us, Naqib; she is brave."

"Brave, Walid?"

"Yes, Naqib," said Walid softly, "brave, and beautiful."

"Is she as beautiful as your youngest sister was, Walid,
when last you saw her?" Abu Salaam's voice was a hiss.

Walid remembered Fatimah, his youngest sister, the really pretty one. He remembered digging her headless body,
covered with fat black flies, from the rubble of their family's
home after the Israeli air raid. Bitterness rose in his throat,
and he choked and closed his eyes against the awful vision.
"I will do it, Naqib," he whispered.

Abu Salaam leaned forward and patted Walid's thigh.
"Brave fighter, Walid. Take her out; let the others see what
will happen and then shoot her, just outside."

The tall one took Barbara Cummins's arm. "Come," he

said in English. Oh God, let me be brave, she thought. He
guided her out of the small office and back into the main
room where the others sat in chairs or on the floor. She
forced herself to march, chin up, fighting back tears. Marching
was awkward with her knees shaking and her hands tied
behind her, but she marched. The civilian pilot who had
flown the aircraft stood up quickly, but one of the terrorists
moved in front of him and shoved him back. When he shouted,
the terrorist stabbed him in the stomach with his rifle. The
pilot doubled over, gasping.

When they reached the door, the young terrorist, who
was following, said something urgent in Arabic. The tall one
stopped, then pulled off his red and white checked headdress
and offered it to Barbara. "Blindfold?" the young one asked
softly.

She shook her head. "Why bother, you bastards are going
to shoot me in the back, anyway." She said it quickly, and
the young one looked confused.

"Not understand."

"No, goddamn you! Just get on with it!" She knew she
was going to cry. The tall one let go of her arm and gave
her a shove toward the open door. She walked out into the
cool evening, then turned quickly and looked back. Walid
stiffened, watching her fight against the tears that glistened
on her cheeks in the harsh lights of the apron. So brave, so
beautiful. He closed his eyes briefly and thought again of
his sister. Again the bile rose in his throat. He opened his
eyes and squeezed the trigger of his AKS. The weapon bucked
in his hands, and the girl spun around and fell face down.
Walid heard a gasp of anger and anguish from behind him
as he stepped out onto the tarmac and made sure the girl
was dead.

⇋14⇌
Tzafon may Eilat, 1730 GMT (1930 Local)

"Aren't you excited?" Leah clung to Stuart on the tangled
sheets of his cot, fragrant with the scent of their lovemaking.

She stroked the wet skin of his chest gently as she nipped his ear and kissed him. Stuart touched the soft damp curls on the nape of her neck, feeling passion for the woman he could not understand.

"Right now, I'm exhausted. But, Leah—"

"I mean about making the jump, tonight!"

Jesus, thought William, I'd put that out of my mind for a long moment. "Yes, I am." He frowned. I'm worried about her. I have plenty to worry about of my own, and Leah would think my protective feelings toward her absurd. "Maybe a little . . . nervous, but sure, excited." Stuart wondered if the word "nervous," used in like context, meant the same to Israeli soldiers as it did to Americans—scared shitless.

"Well, I think we'll be great." Leah stretched, and once again, William was reminded of a cat. "I can't wait to see those assholes' faces the moment before we send them straight to paradise."

William looked at her and forced himself to smile. "Bloodthirsty, aren't we?"

"Damn right."

"I, ah, was a little put off by your breezy 'if I get killed' speech of this afternoon, my sweet."

"Don't worry! We are well trained, we will have surprise, I just know it! We will get in, and we will get your people out."

"What about the Libyans?"

"They won't fight."

I hope you're right, he thought. She rolled on top of him, probing his ear with her tongue. His penis was stirring even before she found it with her hand.

"What time do we muster for the flight?" he said around her kisses.

"Twenty-thirty. Lots of time," she said, pressing her breasts onto his chest.

"You all packed?" he said, rolling onto his side and pushing himself away slightly.

She looked at him quizzically. "What's to pack? Your friend Hooper says everything I need will be waiting at Torrejon, even a special small-size body bag." She rolled beneath him and guided him into her. "Now stop talking and make me yours for a little time."

This is a little like Christmas, thought William as he moved inside her, watching her face. We wait anxiously for it to come, but then we're sad because it is so soon gone.

⇆15⇌
Moscow, 1800 GMT (2100 Local)

Doryatkin rode with Marshal Tikunin in the back of Tikunin's black Zil limousine. The glass separating the passenger compartment from the driver and guard in the front was closed. Nevertheless, the two ministers spoke with circumspection. "It is kind of you to give me a ride, Grigori Vladimirovich," said Doryatkin softly.

"Not at all," responded the Defense Minister. "Though I was surprised we have been called together . . . so soon."

"There have been developments."

Tikunin grunted. "Developments" these days meant changes in the precarious health of the General Secretary. "Will *he* be at the meeting?"

"He is at his dacha, with his favorite Jewish quack." Doctor Shamsky treated the General Secretary's emphysema with methods the doctors who normally treated very senior party officials found decidedly odd.

"It is worse, then."

"Yes."

The two ministers rode in silence for a while. Both were thinking about the power struggle that had already begun as to who would be the next General Secretary. The Politburo was badly divided. The younger men for the most part wanted a harder line against dissent at home, and a much harder line against the West. The leader of this faction was Nevsky, chairman of the KGB. Nevsky's group did not command a majority of the Politburo, but it was the strongest single faction. Doryatkin had gradually come to be regarded as the leader of a moderate, even progressive by Soviet standards, group of mostly older members, although Doryatkin himself at fifty-two was a year younger than Nevsky. Doryatkin believed that the most urgent problems of the Soviet Union were modernization of means of production and the elimination of the stifling effect of official waste and corruption, which paralyzed the economy. To effect such sweeping changes, he needed technology from the West, and therefore a relaxation of tensions.

The balance of power rested with several full members, who mistrusted both what they considered Nevsky's rashness and Doryatkin's naiveté. Most of these older men would probably have preferred that the current General Secretary, with his caution and reluctance to experiment either at home or abroad, live forever. This last group did not have a leader, and they did not seem to be individually ambitious, but the most influential among them was clearly the Defense Minister, Marshal of the Soviet Union, Grigori Vladimirovich Tikunin.

The Foreign Minister turned in his seat. The old marshal looked almost to be asleep. "You have heard, Comrade Marshal, that the terrorists in Libya shot another American?"

"Yes, I heard. Disgusting! They shot a woman, hardly more than a girl!"

Doryatkin felt the marshal's anger and was glad of it. "Surely the Soviet Union should no longer aid Baruni while this crisis continues?"

"I know what you are thinking, Doryatkin, but we just can't walk away. If he falls, even over something as fucked up as this, we shall be perceived as weak, especially in the Arab world."

"I agree," said Doryatkin, though he didn't. He had to proceed with extreme caution with the marshal. "But when the Americans attack, as surely they must, I hope there will not be any direct combat between Soviet and American forces."

"There won't be," answered the marshal firmly. "The Soviet advisers have done their jobs already. General Koslov has given the black-asses a pretty good defensive plan."

"And you have instructed Koslov about the Special Unit?"

"As we agreed. Colonel Zharkov commands it himself. His mission is to seize the hostages from the terrorists, should we order him to do so."

Doryatkin was pleased to hear the marshal describe Abu Salaam's "freedom fighters" as terrorists. "Do you think we should, Comrade Marshal?"

"Yes. After all, the Soviet Union does have forces on the ground there, Doryatkin. The world knows that, although we piously deny it. We cannot stand by while those black-asses murder women."

Good! thought Doryatkin. Yesterday the old man had insisted the Special Unit be held in reserve. "I agree, of course, Comrade Marshal, but I am worried—what will we say if our rescue effort results in heavy casualties among the hostages?"

The marshal turned and smiled broadly at the Foreign Minister. "My dear Doryatkin! Our Spetznaz forces are highly competent!"

Doryatkin couldn't see the humor. "Of course, Comrade Marshal, but it could happen, surely? A single dropped grenade?"

Tikunin laughed happily and slapped his thigh. "It is true, then, as some of my oldest friends say, that you are too young to understand the lessons of the founders of our revolution!"

Doryatkin smiled self-deprecatingly. He still didn't see the humor.

The marshal leaned close to the Foreign Minister. "Ilya Antonovich, think of Stalin, think of Khrushchev! If the rescue gets fucked up, we simply blame the Libyans!" Again the marshal laughed enormously.

Doryatkin felt chilled. This all could go so very wrong, he thought, watching the old marshal settle back into his seat, still chuckling.

⇋16⇌
Washington, 1920 GMT (1420 Local)

The President sat in a deep wing chair in the White House living quarters. He had just risen from a brief nap, and he waved at the Secretary of Defense to begin.

The President looks tired, thought the Secretary. He favors simple solutions to problems, but there are no easy answers to this problem. "Mr. President, we have identified the second executed hostage."

"Murdered," said the President, softly.

"Yes, sir, murdered, of course. She was a navy seaman, Barbara B. Cummins, from Zanesville, Ohio."

The President rubbed his eyes. "Jesus, Dave! How could they just go and shoot a young woman like that?"

Wasserstein sat on the edge of a chair opposite the President. "I don't know, sir, I just don't."

"Any progress on the diplomatic front, Dave?"

"Henry is in hourly contact with our allies. The Italians claim they were talking to Baruni just before the girl was shot. Henry says they are very embarrassed at having let Abu Salaam go."

"Embarrassed? Embarrassed! Christ, Dave!"

"Sir?"

"Go on, Dave."

"Well, the Kuwaitis insist they will not release the terrorists who attacked our embassy, and remind us that we have always supported them in that position. The issue as they see it is the very control of the Emirate in the face of a restive Shiite majority."

The President nodded. "We have told them that very thing."

"Henry is also talking to the Russians, but they seem preoccupied with their own problems."

"What?"

"The rumors persist, sir, that the General Secretary is gravely ill."

"Yes, I know. So no progress. Where are those paratroopers?"

Wasserstein looked at his watch. "They departed from Pope Air Force Base just over two hours ago. They should hit their refueling stations in four more hours."

"They'll be able to get in there at dawn tomorrow, then, Dave?"

The Secretary stood up. "Yes, sir."

"Sure, Dave?" For the first time, the President looked straight into his eyes.

"Yes, Mr. President. We still need, of course, your final approval to refuel and proceed into the Med."

"You have it, Dave, as of now."

"And to launch the operation itself, of course."

"Let's keep updating, Dave. Come back at four o'clock; bring Henry, Admiral Daniels, and General Elmendorf. I want to think this through."

"Yes, Mr. President." The Secretary of Defense picked up his papers and stood. As he strode across the room, he heard the President's voice, choked with rage, or grief.

"Sweet Jesus, they shot a twenty-year-old girl!"

David turned and saw the President, still seated, with his head in his hands. The Secretary left the room.

⇌17⇌
USS *Inchon*, 2030 GMT (2130 Local)

"Colonel Brimmer?" the third-class radioman turned from his console. "I have the Flag for you, Colonel; green handset."

Brimmer stubbed out his cigarette as he sat down. Loonfeather brought two cups of coffee and sat beside him. Brimmer picked up the green handset and pressed the flashing light. He could hear the hiss-click of the scramblers matching; when the line cleared, he said "Colonel Brimmer."

"It's Admiral Wilson, Colonel. How are things on your end?"

"Coming together nicely, Admiral. The marines have all been briefed, and the assault units have been divided between *Inchon* and *Saipan*, along with their assigned helicopters.

Colonel Loonfeather and I are settled in here; the commodore has graciously given us the whole of his Flag Plot to run the landing and extraction."

"Where are Loonfeather's soldiers?"

"They got off from Bragg at seventeen hundred zulu, sir, just three and a half hours ago. They should reach their refueling rendezvous two hundred miles west of Lisbon in less than ninety minutes."

"The tankers all set up?"

"Yes, Admiral. Five KC-10s from Keflavik on their way to the rendezvous in plenty of time."

"Well, it sounds good. I still wish we had all the command elements of this operation in one big room, Colonel."

"I agree, Admiral, but we don't have any rooms that big."

"Yeah, I know we had to do it this way, but shit! We have overall command here on *America,* and the tactical attack aircraft, but that got so big we had to give the Combat Air Patrol to Admiral Bellmon on *Nimitz.* Naval gunfire assignment is on *New Jersey,* and the ground assault is with General Morton here, and with you and Colonel Loonfeather. It's too spread out."

Colonel Brimmer shrugged and looked at Loonfeather, who was sitting at the adjacent console, who shrugged back. Brimmer keyed the handset. "Well, Admiral, as long as the commo plan holds up, the troops in the field will be able to talk to any embarked command or supply element they need, and all others will be able to monitor."

"OK, Bob, I know. I'm just blowing off steam. I guess I'm getting edgy."

"We all are, sir, but we'll get it done."

"Of course. How are you going to coordinate with the SEALs, now that Commander Stuart has become a rifleman?"

Brimmer and Loonfeather grinned at each other. They had taken great delight at Stuart's earlier protestations that he didn't really want to make the jump. "I'll take them, personally, Admiral," said Brimmer. "Stuart and I ran down

the entire coded sequence—which is very simple anyway—
and we'll talk again when the SEALs reach Torrejon to link
up with the B-52."

"When will that be?"

"The SEALs should land before twenty-three hundred
zulu. The bomber is already there."

"Good, OK. Anything for me?"

"Admiral, Lieutenant Colonel Loonfeather, sir," Loonfeather broke in. "Any new word from Tripoli, or from Washington?"

"Not in the last hour. We have a go from JCS for the
Airborne to refuel and to enter the Med. JCS expects to
have a full go for us shortly after that."

"OK," said Loonfeather.

"Apparently the President is really torn up about the
woman they shot."

"I guess. Well, I hope we get there before they shoot
any more."

"That the only thing you're worried about, Colonel?"

"Just about, Admiral, just about."

"Everybody stay on this net. Top Hat out."

"Aye, aye, sir. Thunder, out," said Brimmer, putting
down the handset.

⇋18⇌

Over the central Mediterranean, 2100 GMT

Stuart sat next to the window and listened to the pitch
of the engine noise change as the aircraft reached cruising
altitude. The air force C-140 Jetstar had picked the SEALs
up from the Israeli desert base half an hour ago, exactly on
schedule. Leah was curled up in the aisle seat next to him,
sleeping soundly. The rest of the SEALs were bunched in
seats in the front of the aircraft. Hooper had been in the
cockpit since takeoff, talking on the secure radio.

Stuart looked out the window into the rainy blackness.
The SEALs had been boisterous as they gathered their gear

and waited for the plane, and then Hooper had come out of the communications shack and announced that another hostage had been killed. Everyone on the team asked angry questions; Hooper had few answers. Stuart noticed that while Leah had shown anger at the terrorists and sympathy for the Americans in their shared loss, she showed no surprise and no particular outrage that the latest victim was a woman. The woman had been military, and as such, a more legitimate target than a civilian male, she said in a sharp, whispered response to Stuart's question as they boarded the aircraft. The people we go to *kill,* she added, do not play boys' games.

Stuart looked at Leah, as peaceful in sleep as a child. How quickly we Americans must grow up, he thought bitterly. These peoples, Arabs *and* Israelis, are more like each other than either is like us. Our codes of chivalry and just war, rooted in our northern European roots, are as alien to them as they would be to any other Asiatic people.

And maybe as absurd. Boys' games.

Stuart closed his eyes and slept.

⇆19⇌
Moscow, 2200 GMT (0100 Local)

The chairman of the KGB waited impatiently as the phone rang in the Soviet Embassy in Tripoli. When the duty officer answered, Nevsky barked at him, demanding that Colonel Ychengko be brought to the phone. By the time Nevsky had waited fifteen minutes, he was fully enraged.

"Yes, Comrade Chairman?" said the sleepy voice Nevsky recognized as Ychengko's.

"Ychengko, have you been able to get your man into the Spetznaz unit Koslov has set up on that air base?"

Ychengko reacted to the angry tone of the chairman's voice and shook himself fully awake. He had shared a bottle of vodka with Petrovna after dinner and fallen fast asleep an hour ago with his head in her lap. "Yes, Comrade Chairman. Captain Suslov commands one of the tanks."

Nevsky relaxed a bit. "Good. He has his orders to ensure that any action by that unit results in direct conflict with Americans? Casualties, if possible?"

"Yes, Comrade, I told him myself."

"Does he *understand* his orders, Ychengko?"

"Well, Comrade, he will carry them out. I am not sure that I myself understand why this must be done."

"Ychengko, even though this is a secure line, I cannot go into detail, but I will tell you that that Spetznaz unit has been ordered to wrest control of those hostages from those absurd Abu Salaam fighters. They may get away with it, and if so, our liberal colleagues in the Foreign Ministry propose handing the hostages over to the Americans as a gesture of our political responsibility and trustworthiness." Nevsky spat out the last three words.

Ychengko understood. The KGB wanted a hostile America to strengthen its hand in Moscow against the liberal faction. Ychengko wondered if the General Secretary's health had worsened again, but was afraid to ask. "How does that affect our plans for Comrade Suslov, Comrade Chairman?"

"Well, he will just have to see that Americans are killed when the hostages are taken, although the Army will probably try to make the Abu Salaam fighters look responsible for any casualties. His only real opportunity lies if the Americans mount an assault on the base while his unit is in control of the hostages, and before my brave Comrade Doryatkin can hand them over to the Americans. It is nothing we can control, Ychengko, but he must be ready, and he must strike when the opportunity presents itself!"

"Are the Americans ready to strike, Comrade Chairman?"

"There is no evidence of it in Europe, but their fleet is way over normal strength. They cannot wait much longer now that that fool terrorist has started shooting women."

"I will telephone the air base, Comrade Chairman. Perhaps I can remind Suslov of the importance of his mission."

"Good, Ychengko, but be careful. By now the Spetznaz unit will be getting into position to grab the Americans."

"When are they going to try it?"

"Marshal Tikunin has told Koslov to have them ready to attack at dawn today. Tomorrow, your time."

Ychengko looked at his watch. Tomorrow was thirty-five minutes away. "I will try to reach Suslov, Comrade Chairman."

"Good, Ychengko. A lot is riding on this." There was a cold menace in Nevsky's tone.

Ychengko put the phone down, then picked up the local scrambler phone and began dialing the number for the Soviet duty officer at Uqba ben Nafi.

⇌20⇌
Over the North Atlantic, 2220 GMT

Lieutenant Jason Brown, USN, shifted in the uncomfortable seat and reviewed the problem once again. He had been asleep earlier, but in the last several minutes the steady drone of the engines had been replaced by many changes in thrust, and therefore in level and pitch of sound, and he had awakened. Brown surmised the sound changes were the result of maneuvering the giant aircraft into station on the tanker, and of holding position. A few minutes later the word was passed from man to man that they were indeed refueling.

Brown was sitting in a row of red-webbing folding benches on the centerline of the C-141. There were four rows of benches—one on each side of the aircraft facing inboard, and the two rows back-to-back in the center, facing outboard. Brown and three of his unit's radiotelephone operators were seated near the forward end of the row, which meant that they would go toward the end of the jump. Gunnery Sergeant Billy Bright, USMC, and the other two RTOs sat right behind Brown in the other centerline row, so the whole team should leave the aircraft at approximately the same time.

Brown had been puzzled at the arrangement, because he would have thought the Army would have split his team into two sections, on separate aircraft, in case something went wrong. Just after takeoff from Pope, he had made his way aft to Lieutenant Colonel Bowie, who was aft of the ANGLICO in the same row, and asked about it.

"Lieutenant, airborne operations are by nature high-risk, and normally we do try to balance loads so that the loss of any one aircraft would not be catastrophic," answered Colonel Bowie. "The XO is on the other bird, with about half the signals people. But the nature of this operation is such that we just can't provide properly for losses, at least not until we get on the ground and get formed up."

"You're saying, in effect, Colonel, that we can't lose this aircraft."

"Basically, yes. In addition to your good people, half the Sheridan crews are on this bird, half with the XO. The tank crews will jump with the first elements, even though the Sheridans themselves won't come until the drop, some ten minutes after we and the troops on the second bird un-ass."

"Why is that, Colonel, if you don't mind so many questions?"

"Not at all! I want you to learn as much airborne as possible. Shit, Lieutenant, if this goes the way it usually does in drills, you may end up in command!" The colonel smiled at the thought, but Brown missed the humor.

"Surely it can't get that fucked up, sir?"

"Oh, it truly can, Lieutenant. You see, the infantry must immediately secure the area around the building where the hostages are, and prevent the Libyans from crashing in. If the infantry fails to do that, the mission fails. The Airborne Armor cowboys have to drop at the head of the stick, because they'll have to form up into crews and disperse along the runway to be ready to unpack the Sheridans and get them moving as quickly as possible. By that time we may expect to be under heavy fire, but those Sheridans will have to reach predetermined choke points to fight the enemy's tanks. One Libyan tank breaks through to the hostages, and once again, we fail."

"What happens if it works to there?"

"We'll have to knock out all enemy vehicles and all enemy concentrations near us. You, and the naval air and gunnery operating under its own control, will have to kill off tanks and vehicles farther away, or at least make them keep their heads down, because unless and until you do, the marines will not be able to get in to extract the hostages by helicopter. A helicopter landing or taking off is a mighty big target for a tank, or even a heavy machine gun. Some lucky Libyan pots a helicopter full of hostages fifty feet off the ground, and once again, we go home covered with shit and not with glory."

The colonel seemed amused by his litany of potential disasters. Brown shook his head. "Not much margin for error, sir."

"Very little. The people who planned this had to assume the Libyans would be taken by surprise, and wouldn't fight effectively once they woke up, and they had to assume that Supporting Arms from the fleet—we're back to you, Lieutenant—will be able to do away with the vast majority of the enemy's vehicles before they get anywhere near us."

"The ships will shell the tanks on the beach and the ones lined up south of the big runway just before we land," said Brown.

"Right, and then they'll have to lift fire so we can land. Navy and marine corps bombers armed with smart munitions will come in with us, and very shortly thereafter, helicopter gunships. Gunfire won't be able to come back in until all of our people have gotten off the runway and secured our position, but we'll have plenty of airborne firepower. If we can deal with the threat that's closest to us, we'll be all right."

"Doesn't the enemy have surface-to-air missiles, and fighter aircraft on the base?"

"The Navy has assured us that they'll be taken care of," said Colonel Bowie, still smiling.

⇋DAY FIVE⇌

Washington, 19 February, 0200 GMT (18 February, 2100 Local)

Admiral Daniels put the handset down and turned to the tall, broad-shouldered man seated in the shadows in the back of the White House basement situation room. "Mr. President, the paratroopers' aircraft are over the Med. They were all successfully refueled."

"Good, Arch."

"I recommend we shift command and control of the operation to Sixth Fleet, sir."

"We could get it back?"

"Of course, sir, at any stage. But the timing is tricky, and it will be better if Admiral Bergeron and his staff can get the feel of coordinating all the elements."

"OK, Arch. Give them the ball."

"Yes, Mr. President." Admiral Daniels turned to his radioman, who immediately fed the tape with the coded command into the teletype transmitter in front of him and pressed the high-speed transmission key. The signal, double-encrypted, was transmitted from the radio tower on the White House roof to a satellite in geosynchronous orbit over the Atlantic, and relayed instantaneously to the *America,* where it was unscrambled and decoded. The Communications Chief of the Watch took the short message into Flag Plot and handed it to Admiral Bergeron. The admiral read the message and handed it to his Chief of Staff. "Gentlemen," said Admiral Bergeron to his assembled staff officers, "in all but name, we are now at war."

The Chief of Staff held the tape up to a red night light and read it:

```
0219-0211Z
TOP SECRET LIMDIS OSCAR/FIRE ARROW
FLASH
FM: MILESTONE
TO: TOP HAT
PROCEED FIRE ARROW UNODIR EXECUTE
ENDS
```

⇌2⇌

United States Air Force Base, Torrejon, Spain, 0210 GMT

The black, blue, and green camouflage-painted B-52 bomber began its takeoff roll along the 13,000-foot main runway. The aircraft was light, with no weapons package aboard, and it used just over half the runway to get airborne. It circled, gaining altitude over the sea before heading nearly due south, crossing the coast of Morocco and flying deep into central Africa. The copilot logged the time of crossing the coast; it was the first of many sovereign airspaces the plane would violate. The top secret flight plan called for the bomber to pass from Moroccan to Algerian airspace deep in the Sahara, proceed east across Niger and finally north, crossing over Libyan territory near the disputed oasis town of Bi'r al Wa'r, and then to orbit over the desolate sandy desert of Sabra Marzug. When the final go command was received from the fleet, the aircraft would fly north to make the drop at Uqba ben Nafi and return to Spain flying over the Med. The Spanish government had been informed that the aircraft was on a routine training mission and that it carried no weapons. The Libyans would be looking for trouble to come from the north, it was reasoned, although no one believed the Libyan radars could acquire the bomber flying above 40,000 feet, especially since the aircraft would be using her electronic masking equipment.

The SEAL team sat in jump seats in a small compartment just aft of the flight deck. The compartment was pressurized, so they did not yet need their oxygen masks, but it was kept cold so they would not overheat in the thick "poopy-suit" immersion suits. Before making the drop, they would have to help each other into tanks, close the body bags, and belt on ammo and weapons packages and, finally, parachutes and the small chest-pack oxygen tanks. For now, they sat talking quietly, sometimes looking at the plan of the apron and the Operations Building of Uqba ben Nafi, which was covered with many different-colored lines.

There was a secure voice radio in the little compartment, and Stuart called Top Hat and then Thunder to check the frequency and the reception. Before the aircraft turned toward Libya, they would go radio-silent, communicating only by "breaking squelch" in agreed codes. Each time an operator pressed the talk key, the background hiss would be momentarily interrupted. It would be virtually impossible for anyone trying to locate the aircraft to home on a break squelch signal.

Stuart sat down next to Hooper. "Well, Hoop, we have a go from the President."

"Yeah. Like the old days." Hooper's fingers drummed on his carbine in a nervous rhythm.

"The very old days, Hoop."

"You know what I'm afraid of, old buddy? That they drop us in the soup, and then the President gets cold feet about the whole thing and calls the main operation off."

Stuart nodded. "It's happened to us before."

"Jesus, don't I remember! Operation Bear Trap, in 1968."

Stuart remembered. He and Hooper, in separate Pathfinder units, had crossed the Ben Hai River from South Vietnam into the North, to scout enemy positions immediately in advance of a multibattalion attack, partially from below the DMZ and partially by amphibious assault south of the North Vietnamese port of Dong Hoi. After the Pathfinders had crossed the river, forbidden to communicate by radio, President Johnson had decided that an invasion of North Vietnam was politically unacceptable, and the main assault was cancelled. Very few of the Pathfinders had returned.

"I don't think that will happen this time, Hoop," said Stuart softly.

Hooper shifted in the jump seat. For the first time since he had joined Stuart in the Negev, Hooper was genuinely worried. "William, you were in on the planning of this whole thing. Do you think it can work?"

Stuart realized he really had no idea, but he felt he had to sound reassuring. It surprised him that Hooper would voice doubts in front of his team at this late hour. "We'll need to get most of the breaks, but yes, I think we'll accomplish the mission."

"Hm," said Hooper. Stuart couldn't see his expression in the dim red light.

"Hoop, what I worry about is not so much getting the hostages; I really think we'll blow by the terrorists," said Stuart quietly. "I worry about the paratroops and marines. Once the shooting starts, they'll be much more exposed than us."

"Yeah. William, no matter how fucked up the Libyans are, there are going to be serious casualties. And then there could be pictures on Libyan television of American soldiers and marines held in a Libyan prison."

"You can't possibly leave anyone behind," interrupted Leah with some heat, "not even the dead!"

Hooper looked at her and at the other members of his team, all of whom were listening intently to the conversation. "Captain, of course we wouldn't leave anyone we could find, but do you have any idea how many people will be running around on that airstrip? Some will just flat get lost! Christ, in a *normal* paratroop *practice jump*, a fifth of the jumpers usually land outside the primary drop zone!"

Leah frowned. "At Entebbe—"

"Entebbe was a brilliant operation, Leah, but your people didn't jump in," said Stuart softly. "The aircraft landed. There was no significant Ugandan military support for the terrorists."

"And it's those goddamned Libyan tanks that make it impossible for the assault aircraft to land, then let the troops walk off the aircraft in nice organized bunches, with all their equipment intact," said Hooper. "Look, I'm not saying this to worry you. I just want all of you to remember that this is a very difficult operation, and that the plans could change many times before we're safely at sea with the Navy. All our training has been focused on getting into that air base and that building. Think contingencies for getting out."

Hooper fell silent, and the others gradually began to talk again, and to look at the base plan again. Stuart leaned close to Hooper and whispered, "Is this just to keep them alert?"

"I tell my people everything."

"OK, but are you really worried?"

"You bet your ass. Remember how we all felt before Bear Trap? We *knew* that Johnson would *never* let us invade the North; we *knew* the operation would be cancelled. We couldn't believe it when they dumped us in the DMZ and told us to start walking north!"

Stuart remembered. His unit had been ambushed twice, and when he had broken radio silence to call for medevac, there had been no response. The invasion had already been denied. "We have a different president, Hoop, with different ideas of what's politically possible."

Hooper slapped Stuart on the knee. "As brother Napoleon said, 'Always have two plans; leave something to chance.' "

The intercom phone buzzed and lit up. Hooper reached over and picked it up, grunted acknowledgment, and put it back. "AC has a coded signal from the fleet. Everything is still go."

⇌3⇌
Washington, 0245 GMT (2145 Local)

The large-screen computer display in the front of the White House situation room showed an outline of Western Europe, the Mediterranean, and Africa north of the equator. Different-colored arrowheads showed the position and direction of the various units; the Sixth Fleet thirty miles off the Libyan coast, the air force transports carrying the Airborne passing south of Sardinia en route to their orbit area east of the fleet, and the B-52 carrying the SEALs flying slowly east across southern Algeria. A light point in central England began to glow and pulse.

"What's that?" asked the President, pointing.

"That means the Air Force is about to launch the F-111s, Mr. President," answered Admiral Daniels.

"Shit!"

Heads turned toward the source of the expletive outburst, loud in the quiet room. "Mr. President, Admiral, we have a problem," said the Secretary of State, rising from his console and walking hurriedly across the room.

"What is it, Henry?" said the President.

"That was the French Ambassador. The French government has denied us permission to overfly France."

"Jesus!" said the President. "How in the hell can they do that?"

"Their position is that since there is no evidence of official Libyan involvement, Libya should not be attacked. Apparently the Libyan Ambassador has convinced them that Colonel Baruni is doing everything he can to gain control of the hostages."

"But surely they understand we're only attacking in order to free our hostages!"

"They do, Mr. President, and they wish us well, but they do not wish to be associated with bombing raids on two Libyan air bases far from Uqba ben Nafi."

The President looked a question at Admiral Daniels. The Chief of Naval Operations nodded. "That's the One-Elevens' mission, Mr. President."

"Do we *need* to attack those bases? Really need to?" asked the President.

"If we don't, sir, the Libyans will be able to launch massive air attacks on our fleet, and maybe penetrate the Combat Air Patrol and disrupt the assault and extraction itself." Admiral Daniels tapped his computer console and a new display came up, showing the Libyan air bases at Benghazi and Tobruk, with symbols denoting aircraft on the ground. "Our best intelligence is that both these bases have more fighter and attack aircraft on the ground than usual; we presume they have been redeployed from Uqba ben Nafi."

"So what can we do? Fly our F-111s around, through the Straits of Gibraltar?" There was an edge of sarcasm in the President's voice.

"That is in fact what the French suggest," said the Secretary of State softly.

"That isn't possible!" the President thundered, pounding his console. "Is it?"

General Vaughn broke away from his air force staff officers, all of whom were shaking their heads, and walked to the President's table. "Theoretically, it is, Mr. President. We would have to refuel them twice en route. The problem is we simply do not have nearly enough time, even if we had such an operation already planned, which we don't."

"So where does that leave us, gentlemen?" the President's voice was tight with frustration and fatigue.

"We can cancel and set it up tomorrow, with in-flight refueling," said General Vaughn.

"Or we could go without the Air Force, and hope the Navy CAP gets all the aircraft in the air," said General Elmendorf.

"Arch?" said the President, looking at the CNO, who was in hasty conversation with the naval staff officers.

"Mr. President," said Admiral Daniels, carefully weighing his words, "we can do without the Air Force, but we run a terrible risk of major losses, maybe even a capital ship. Even a poor pilot can get lucky with an antiship missile. The place to eliminate the threat of the Libyan Air Force is on the ground, and for that we need the air force F-111s."

"We all understand that, Arch," said the President, after waiting for the admiral to go on.

Admiral Daniels took a deep breath. He spread his large hands in front of him and spoke slowly. "I suggest, Mister President, that we simply notify the French we are overflying, sir. Just tell them. After the fact, we'll give them any kind of apology they want, or even put the word out that we did indeed fly all around the continent of Europe to avoid offending their delicate sensitivities."

"Nobody will believe that!" interjected General Elmendorf.

"Mr. President!" burst in the Secretary of Defense. "An overflight of French territory without their permission is an act of war!"

"Jesus, Mr. Secretary, the French aren't going to war

over this!" Admiral Daniels threw up his hands. The computer display had been returned to display the map of Europe and Africa. All eyes were drawn to the pulsing light in the center of England, which represented Upper Heyford.

The Secretary of Defense looked angrily at the Chief of Naval Operations. "The French, Admiral, are our oldest allies!"

"What have they done for us lately?" asked the President rhetorically. "How long can we hold the bombers while we talk to the French, General Vaughn?"

General Vaughn looked at the digital clock on the wall. "Not more than another half hour, Mr. President. May I make a suggestion?"

"Of course."

"The head of the French air defenses and I know each other pretty well. He used to be a test pilot, a good one, and he spent quite a bit of time at Edwards when I was commanding general there. He usually stayed at my quarters."

"Well?"

"Let me see if I can reach him. I don't think the French would shoot, but if he knew, there would be much less chance of an error."

"OK," said the President, weighing the choices.

"Then we could have the Secretary tell the French Ambassador about your decision, with the cover story Admiral Daniels suggests. Given it's the middle of the night in France, our aircraft would probably be out of French airspace before the government could even find its voice to protest."

"What about the return flight?" asked General Elmendorf.

"We can get those tankers from Keflavik back on station to the west of Portugal in plenty of time. They should be landing back in Iceland already. It will be tight, but doable," said General Vaughn. This time the group of air force officers behind him nodded, some enthusiastically.

The President sat silently, his chin in his hands, staring at the computer display. The officers and the two cabinet secretaries looked at each other and around the room. "Well, I think we're going to have to do it. I won't risk the loss of more of our people in what is already a dangerous operation to save Gallic pride, or faintheartedness, whichever it is. Make it so, Arch."

The President slumped back into the shadows as staff officers scurried to make the needed changes in the op-orders, and to arrange for the quick turnaround of the KC-10s at Keflavik. The Secretary of State grinned to himself in the dim light as he began making notes of what he would say to the French Ambassador. I'm the chief foreign policy officer of this administration, he thought, and as such I should have argued vigorously against this terrible insult to an old ally. But, God help me, I love it!

⇋4⇋
Uqba ben Nafi, 0330 GMT (0430 Local)

Sergeant Julio Cifuentes of the Cuban People's Army had been up all night and was getting cranky. That strutting *maricon* of a Russian captain had demanded that the ZSU-23-4 be made ready for duty without delay to defend the air base against the *yanqui* marines, who the smooth-looking Russian colonel insisted would soon be landing by helicopters. The ZSU was an especially effective weapon against helicopters, and since the Libyans by themselves had no hope of getting this one running, Sergeant Cifuentes, the head of the vehicle maintenance assistance team that the Maximum Leader, Fidel Castro, had sent to Libya, had been told to do it himself. And so far Sergeant Cifuentes had been unable to get the motherfucker to run.

The fact was, thought Cifuentes as he lay head down and sweating in the engine compartment, he rather liked the ZSU. It was an ugly machine, with a big, blocky turret mounted above tank tracks, but it was a self-contained antiaircraft system, with four water-cooled 23mm cannons that were capable of firing 800 rounds per minute each. (If you tried to do that, however, as the monkeys in Angola had done while Cifuentes watched in disgust, you would expend all the ammo in the vehicle in half a minute and melt the barrels; to do it right you fired in very short bursts.) The vehicle had its own fire-control radar, which could both acquire and track targets, as well as optical and infrared sights. Best of all, it was normally reliable and easy to maintain. The six-cylinder, 240-horsepower diesel was an old and proven design, and could drive the ZSU at fifty kilometers per hour over level ground, if Cifuentes could just get the damn thing to run.

Cifuentes removed the high-pressure second-stage fuel pump and handed it to Mohammed, his handsome, friendly, and very stupid "mechanic," who was in fact of little use other than as a helper. Cifuentes climbed out on the engine compartment and motioned Mohammed to take the pump to the bench, where he would tear it down yet again.

The Russians had sold the Libyans twelve of the ZSUs. They were supposed to be a forward defense weapon for leading elements of troops on the attack, and Cifuentes had heard that the four that were with the Libyan troops invading northern Chad had scared the shit out of the French jets that attacked them, although there had been no confirmed reports of aircraft actually downed. The rest of the ZSUs had been divided between Uqba ben Nafi and Benghazi air bases to provide point defense against low-flying aircraft. Of the four attached to Uqba ben Nafi, one was permanently detached to follow Colonel Baruni and his entourage around, one was dug in south of the intersection of the two runways, one was in the back of the bay where Cifuentes was working, with a cracked engine block (the fucking Libyans had forgotten to put lubricating oil in it, Cifuentes supposed), and the last was the one he was trying to fix. Cifuentes mopped the sweat from his brow and began to disassemble the delicate pump.

⇋5⇌
Paris, 0330 GMT (0430 Local)

General Henri Beneteau replaced the telephone in its cradle on his ornate antique desk. He dug a crumpled packet of Gitanes from the pocket of his robe and lit one of the strong cigarettes. What his old friend General Vaughn had just told him had made him both angry and sad. He had protested vehemently to Vaughn, while at the same time feeling ashamed at the gutlessness of France's socialist government. Nevertheless, he felt his beloved nation about to be violated by the American aircraft that would soon be streaking through French skies against the expressed wishes of her government.

General Beneteau unlocked a drawer of his desk and removed the list of secure telephone numbers of key French government and military installations. He knew he should telephone the President and the Premier, as he had threatened to do, but instead he dialed the number of the duty officer of the Air Defense Command, underground near Metz. He had a short and eventually heated conversation with the captain who was on duty. The captain had demanded that the general make his request a direct order, and Beneteau had shouted at him. The captain had signed off with a curt "oui, mon general," and hung up. Beneteau sighed and locked away the telephone list. He knew he should get dressed and go into his office in the Defense Ministry, but for the moment he just sat and smoked. How sad it is, he thought, that in our times the sleep of a soldier is more often disturbed by politics than by war.

⇋6⇌
Uqba ben Nafi, 0345 GMT (0445 Local)

Senior Lieutenant Kim Dong-Hoon of the North Korean People's Air Force sat in the cramped cockpit of his Mirage 5, parked in a large revetment off the taxiway at the southern end of runway 03/21. His wingman, Lt. Choi Kuen-Buk, was parked next to him. They had been driven down to the aircraft at 4 A.M., relieving two other North Korean officers, and would sit here until relieved at 8 A.M., turning up the engines once an hour.

Senior Lieutenant Kim was bored, but happy. He was eating kimchee from a plastic cup. His sister had sent it to him from Pyongyang, and he savored each pungent, crisp bite. His sister's letter had said the young cabbage had been harvested from their family's tiny garden two years ago, packed with others in an earthen jar, along with vinegar, red pepper, spices, and garlic, then buried in the garden, to be dug up the following summer.

Kim liked especially to eat kimchee in his aircraft, because the fragrance of the garlic and spices hung around him in the tiny space, and could be savored over and over. He smiled when he thought of the strutting Cuban captain who would relieve him in the morning, and how he would curse and bellow about the "stink" in the cockpit. Kim had decided he liked Cubans even less than Russians.

Kim glanced across at Choi's aircraft. His wingman's head was back, and he appeared to be asleep. The two Libyans manning the auxiliary power cart between the two aircraft were certainly asleep, stretched out on the tarmac.

Kim was happy at the thought of getting in some real flying, even though his commander had warned that flying a missile attack against the American Sixth Fleet had to be viewed as a high-risk mission. Kim was primarily a fighter pilot, but he had volunteered to stay behind when the rest of the aircraft had been flown out two days before, because he loved to fly the sleek, dart-shaped, elegant French aircraft. The Mirage felt so much lighter and more responsive to his touch than the heavier Soviet machines he was used to, and it could accelerate beyond Mach 2 at high altitude, or race along on the deck at 750 knots, as long as its pilot had the skill and the nerves. The Mirages had been modified by Russian technicians to carry the Soviet AS-7 antiship missile and its electronics package, originally designed for the Russian Yak-36 Forger aircraft.

Kim swallowed a tiny, well-chewed bite of his sister's kimchee and burped, filling the cockpit with the aroma of garlic. He stretched his cramped muscles and thought about guiding his missile into a great, fat aircraft carrier.

⇋7⇋
Over the central Mediterranean, 0330 GMT

Lieutenant Colonel Bowie dismissed the final briefing and sent the unit commanders back to discuss the plan with their troops. Most of the men were cleaning rifles and checking ammunition belts, grenades, and other equipment. The men had been fed before the briefing, and had been told that the mission was still a go and that the aircraft had almost reached their first assembly point over the southern end of the Adriatic Sea, where they would orbit at cruising altitude. Their second assembly point would be at very low altitude some forty miles off the Libyan coast near El Asciar.

Prior to the colonel's briefing, the men had had no official word that they would be jumping into Libya, but most had guessed. What they hadn't guessed was that they would be making a mass tactical jump from 650 feet up and landing mostly on paved runways. The men were reminded to make good parachute landing falls and to turn their MC-1 steerable parachutes into the wind and flare them by pushing the handles attached to the risers away from them as they landed.

The troops were also surprised that they were jumping right in the middle of an air base known to be ringed with Libyan tanks, but that explained the many extra cases of Dragon antitank missiles stacked in the front of the aircraft. Captain William Schubert, the infantry company commander, looked around at the faces of the men. Some looked scared; some grinned foolishly. Schubert knew there would be many casualties, and many more if he and the other officers and non-coms did not get the troops assembled into their units and dispersed to their areas of operation within minutes of the landing.

Captain Schubert found 1st Lt. John Connelly, commander of the two-platoon task force of M-551 Sheridans from the 3/73, briefing his four tank crews. The other four were with 2d Lt. Robert Baird on the second troop C-141. Both C-141s would off-load their troops on the same pass over the long runway, and the Sheridan crews would have to assemble in revetments alongside the runway, or in whatever other cover they could find, until the subsequent wave of aircraft came in and LAPESed out the vehicles. That couldn't happen until the infantry had cleared off the runway.

Captain Schubert joined the tankers' briefing. Navy Lieutenant Brown was there as well, listening carefully.

"I expect the first thing we'll want to do is to lay smoke along the southern end of runway 11/29," said Lieutenant Connelly. "Met reckons the wind will be light and offshore."

"Won't the Navy put smoke in there before we land?" asked a Spec 4 gunner named Harrigan, who was cleaning a 9mm pistol.

Connelly looked at Lieutenant Brown, who answered. "As soon as we have the Operation Execute Signal from Top Hat, the Navy will shell the tank positions in the recon photos south of runway 11/29 with very heavy H-E, and lighter VT frag rounds as well, to pin down any personnel in the open. Lighter ships will shell the positions you can see marked on the beachfront, without spot. The heavy should get at least an area spot from the SEALs in the control tower." Brown pointed to the Operations Building. "The tower is here."

"What's 'heavy H-E,' Lieutenant?" asked Captain Schubert.

"Battleship. Sixteen inch; shells weigh almost nineteen hundred pounds apiece."

"Jesus," whispered Sgt. Matthew Tucker, one of the Sheridan commanders.

"What's their rate of fire, Lieutenant?" asked Lieutenant Connelly.

"The *New Jersey* will be approximately fifteen miles off-shore, so as to deliver plunging shot. More accurate, and easier to correct. Best rate of fire, two rounds per minute per gun. Nine guns, so eighteen rounds a minute."

"And the light frag?" asked Captain Schubert.

"From destroyers, approaching the beach from the twelve-mile limit at flank speed as soon as we get the OES. They have a range of about fourteen miles, but will close right up to the beach to be able to knock out anything they can see, or that we or aircraft can spot them onto. Forty rounds per minute per gun; three destroyers, the *Adams*, the *King*, and the *Lawrence*, two guns each."

"Jesus *Christ*, that is *metal!* How long can they fire?" asked Sergeant Tucker.

"At least five minutes," replied Lieutenant Brown, "maybe a bit longer. As soon as the pilot of this aircraft signals that he has turned to final approach, some four miles from the end of the runway we'll drop on, the ships will raise and hold fire. They won't be able to fire again across the runway until the aircraft are clear. After that they'll fire on our spot, and once everybody and all the vehicles are clear, the battleship will crater the runway to prevent enemy tanks from crossing in any kind of order."

"So what about the smoke, sir?" asked the Spec 4, reloading the clip for his Beretta pistol.

"The last rounds out from the battleship will be smoke, but they should fall no closer than two hundred meters south of the runway."

"So we'll have to pop our own smoke at the runway's edge," said Lieutenant Connelly.

"Hell, sir, we might as well. We'll have to sprint up that runway anyhow, to get into the choke points around the Ops Building," said Sergeant Tucker.

Lieutenant Connelly looked at the two- by three-foot plan of "Wheelus Air Base" and tapped the center. "What we have to be prepared for is a genuine tank assault—from anywhere on the base. A tank anywhere in the area of this plan can hit the Ops Building or any of our forces from where he is. Assuming the navy and marine air get the bad guys that are at least five hundred meters away from us, we'll have to fight any that are close in, tank to tank."

"Practically every grunt makin' the jump gonna carry a Dragon, sir," said the sergeant tank commander of the number-four Sheridan, a hard black man named Dobbs.

"Which makes me think," said Connelly, tapping the plan, "we should sprint to the apron and hold until the infantry can establish strong fighting positions for the Dragons, then organize ourselves as a maneuver platoon to go after any *organized unit* of enemy tanks that shows up." Lieutenant Connelly turned and smiled at his men, then looked at Captain Schubert. "Captain?"

Captain Schubert gave a thumbs-up and smiled back. "Excellent. Maybe a light section covering the long runway, and a heavy to the western end of the base. That should let you move to oppose tank formations coming from the beach or from the south, while the infantry holds the fixed choke points." Schubert stood. "Let's get the colonel's OK. I feel better with you guys free to maneuver."

"So do we, Captain. We can run, and we can shoot, but we are too lightly armored by far to be pillboxes."

⇐8⇒

Uqba ben Nafi, 0345 GMT (0445 Local)

Praporshchik (Warrant Officer) Dmitri Sergeivich Tolkin gestured to the tank and BTR drivers, motioning them backwards into the supply hangars on the northern end of runway 03/21. The vehicles were maneuvered into place in the narrow spaces and shut down. The doors were closed, confining the sharp smell of diesel smoke. Tolkin stood with his back toward the hangar doors and lit a cigarette, avoiding the gaze of the officers, especially the zampolit, Captain Suslov, who strode back and forth shouting useless orders at the sweating Spetznaz troopers.

"A word, Tolkin?"

Tolkin whirled, dropping his cigarette, and saluted Colonel Zharkov. "Of course, Comrade Colonel."

"No need for all that courtesy, Tolkin. We enjoyed ten months in Afghanistan together, remember?"

Tolkin had always liked Colonel Zharkov, because he thought and acted like a soldier, despite his reputed party connections, yet he was wary of the colonel's confiding demeanor. "Of course, Comrade Colonel. Then, we had the black-asses on the right side of our guns."

That's a test, thought Zharkov, and smiled. "Do you trust me, Tolkin?" he asked abruptly.

Tolkin did, but he was surprised by the question. "Comrade Colonel?"

"Old Russian proverb, Tolkin: 'It is not always your enemies who put you into it.' "

" 'Nor your friends who pull you out of it.' Yes, my Colonel, I trust you."

"And I you. Captain Suslov will command your tank on the assault against the terrorists in the Operations Building."

"And I will gladly relinquish my commander's seat and take the morning off, Comrade Colonel."

"I would prefer you gave that leave to Gunner Potemkin instead, Tolkin, and stayed with your tank."

Tolkin chewed on this. He did not share the Russian passion for riddles. "Comrade Colonel?"

Colonel Zharkov placed his hand on the praporshchik's chest, with three fingers extended. Tolkin looked at the colonel's hand, then at his face. "The zampolit?"

"I fear so, Tolkin."

Tolkin was puzzled. The three fingers, from one *enlisted* man (or a warrant, who in the Soviet Army remained in spirit a senior enlisted man), meant Third Directorate; KGB. "My Colonel?"

"It is possible that the captain has orders that differ from ours, Tolkin. We are to take the American hostages intact, and hold them at the pleasure of our superiors in Moscow."

"Colonel—"

"It may be, Tolkin, that Captain Suslov has orders that are, shall we say, from another source, which might cause him to disobey, or *exceed,* an order of mine."

"But, Colonel, surely—"

"You, old friend, are to see that nothing like that happens."

Tolkin felt the itch of confusion on his brain. This was no decision for a warrant officer. "Comrade Colonel, what means should I use to stop the captain if he disobeys—"

"Any means, Tolkin," interrupted Zharkov, "all means, if it even looks like he might disobey my orders."

Tolkin was suddenly afraid. Eighteen years of soldiering had not prepared him to deal with a renegade officer, perhaps of the KGB, on the vaguest of instructions.

"We helped each other in Afghanistan, Tolkin," said the colonel very softly.

Tolkin remembered. They hadn't *helped* each other. Tolkin had gone down in a desolate valley with a leg wound, and his squad had been wiped out. Tolkin had seen the Afghan women moving toward him through the rocks with long knives in their hands. Colonel Zharkov had come back for him and carried him to safety. "Yes, my Colonel. I will look after Captain Suslov, with great care."

Zharkov smiled. "We must be ready to move by 0545 Local. We must capture the American hostages, intact, Comrade."

"Yes, Comrade Colonel. We will be ready." Tolkin saluted.

Colonel Zharkov returned the salute and walked over to chat with Captain Suslov, near the hangar doors.

⇆9⇄

Air Defense Command, Metz, France, 0410 GMT
(0510 Local)

Captain Henri du Clos sat at his command console, watching as the tight formations of American F-111 bombers appeared as bright dots in the northeast quadrant of the master radar repeater. At first, the crew of radar technicians had been very excited, until Captain du Clos told them to calm down, that they were to track the aircraft only, and that no alert was to be called. The men had looked at him for an explanation, but he gave them none, and they shrugged and went back to their consoles. Captain du Clos's own orders were to track the Americans through French airspace until they left it over the Mediterranean, and then to call General Beneteau and make his report. Captain du Clos intended that his first words to the general would be a profound apology for his earlier rudeness, but he was still seething that he had to preside over this massive violation of French sovereignty with all of his aircraft grounded.

⇋10⇌
First Airborne assembly point, over the southern Adriatic, 0410 GMT

The pitch of the engines of the C-141 rose as the pilot throttled up, and the nose of the aircraft dipped slightly. The word was quickly passed to the paratroopers to remove all rank insignia and to get into their gear, as the aircraft were descending to their final assembly point.

Each soldier seated on the left side of the aircraft clipped his M-16, enclosed in the soft black M-1950 weapons case, to the left side of his parachute harness, tying it down to his leg with a bootlace. Most of the troops on the right side of the aircraft carried a cased Dragon missile canister in the same left-side position, with their M-16s in the slip on the outside of the Dragon case. Because of the bulk of the missile pack, only jumpers exiting the right door could jump the Dragon; there was too much risk of getting it hung up in the static line for left-door jumpers.

The men grew bulkier and more awkward-looking as they donned the entire equipment package. MC-1 main parachutes went in back, with the T-10 reserves in front, low on the men's stomachs. Each man's rucksack, weighing anywhere from forty to sixty-five pounds, hung suspended from the front of the harness in front of the man's knees. When the

jumpers had descended to 200 feet above the DZ, the rucksacks and the weapons packages would be unclipped and
allowed to dangle ten feet below the trooper on yellow nylon
straps, leaving his legs free to flex and break his fall.

The paratroopers checked their own equipment, then
buddied up and checked each other, making liberal use of
the green vinyl "100 mph" tape to cover and secure anything
that might foul a static line or a parachute shroud.

Lieutenant Jason Brown checked his own gear, then he
checked that of his two radiomen while they checked each
other's and his. He turned around in his seat and had a
final word with Sergeant Bright. Lieutenant Brown felt a
strange exhilaration and, to his surprise, no fear. Something
about the atmosphere in the aircraft as the paratroopers exchanged soft punches and hand slaps seemed to lift everyone's
spirits. It felt like a football locker room before a very big
game.

Jumpmaster-qualified personnel worked their way down
the lines, hanging on to the static-line wires above them
and walking over the seated troopers' rucksacks. They checked
each man's equipment, making sure that nothing was loose
or protruded, and that everything was clipped on, buttoned
up, or taped flat. They reminded a man here and there to
make sure his static line, once hooked up, was behind his
shoulder.

One of the safety NCOs came behind the jumpmasters,
carrying two Dragon packs. He stopped in front of Lieutenant
Brown. "Care to jump one of these Dragons for us, sir?
We're asking everyone jumping right door who doesn't have
an extra load to take one more for the grunts."

Jason Brown looked at the bulky Dragon launcher. What
the hell, he thought, and grinned. "Will do, Sergeant."

The jumpmaster helped him hook up the strap and tape
the heavy weapon to his left leg. "Don't forget to let that
drop below you as soon as you check your canopy, sir."
The jumpmaster passed on.

Now that the paratroopers had all their gear on including
the parachutes, they looked more crowded and uncomfortable

than ever. Unaccountably, thought Lieutenant Brown, they looked much more cheerful. Brown heard an insistent humming, soft at first but then growing as more troopers joined in. He recognized the tune and smiled. It was the chorus of the "Battle Hymn of the Republic." Connelly was a religious man, and he crossed himself as the humming swelled. How strange, he thought, and yet how fitting, that these bone-hard, foul-mouthed, tobacco-chewing paratroops should want to join one another in a hymn, and for them, what better hymn.

"Sing it, Reilly," said a fierce-looking black sergeant directly across the row from Connelly.

"Yeah, Reilly, sing it," chorused several others.

A fresh-faced redheaded trooper whose cheeks looked never to have seen a razor flushed red to his freckles and shook his head.

"Stand him up," said a company first sergeant, four down the bench from Connelly. The troopers on either side of Reilly lifted him to a standing position and pushed their shoulders together under his hips so he couldn't sit back down.

Reilly smiled. He looked like an altar boy. The humming grew louder as more troopers joined in. At the end of the chorus, Reilly began to sing, in a clear, trilling tenor:

"There was blood upon the risers
    There were brains upon the chute
Intestines were a-dangling
    from his paratroopers' boots.
They picked him up, still in his chute
    and poured him from his boots,
And he ain't gonna jump no more!"

The troops thundered:

"GORY, GORY, WHAT A HELL OF A WAY TO DIE!
GORY, GORY, WHAT A HELL OF A WAY TO DIE!
GORY, GORY, WHAT A HELL OF A WAY TO DIE,
AND HE AIN'T GONNA JUMP NO MORE!"

Connelly shook his head in amazement as Reilly cheerfully sang out a new verse even more gruesome than the last.

A horn in the center of the cabin blew, and the red

jump lights flashed. The men fell silent. Lieutenant Colonel Bowie spoke into a portable bullhorn. "Men, we have a signal from Thunder. The SEALs are jumping *now*. We will be un-assing in Colonel Baruni's face in thirty to forty-five minutes. I want to see every one of you safely on the ground!"

Lieutenant Brown joined the unrestrained, almost savage cheering that filled the cabin of the aircraft. The cheering gradually coalesced into a two-syllable drumbeat, such as might have driven Roman oarsmen on the waters below two thousand years before:

Air-BORNE!
Air-BORNE!
Air-BORNE!

⇋11⇌
Uqba ben Nafi, 0430 GMT (0530 Local)

The eight-member SEAL team dropped from the cavernous bomb bay of the B-52 in a tight cluster. Hooper and Osborne had been on the bottom of the pile inside the aircraft, with Feeney, Ricardo, Stuart, and Leah Rabin above them and Miller and Jones on top. They had hung suspended in a nylon web net above the bomb bay, each person gripping the harness of the person or persons below him. When the bomber's crew and computers agreed they were on target, the light net with the team in it was dropped from the aircraft.

After they bounced through the bomber's slipstream, the net, which was heavily weighted in its center, collapsed and fell away behind them. They released their grips on each others' gear, held their arms tightly against their sides, and drifted slightly apart. Using just their hands to deflect the air rushing past them, they were able to maintain station close enough to land in a tight group, but far enough apart to avoid fouling each other's parachutes when they opened. Stuart found he had to fight at first to maintain the proper slightly head-down attitude, but he relaxed and concentrated on keeping station on the tiny blue light on the top of Hooper's helmet. Hooper extended his arms and did a slow half somersault, and looked back up at each member of the team. Satisfied, he gave a thumbs-up sign with his glove, which had been treated with phosphorescent paint, then half somersaulted back to his original face-down position. Below them the brightly lighted apron of the air base and the dark sheen of the pond were clearly visible.

The automatic releases for their main parachutes were set to open at two thousand feet above sea level, but Hooper would pop his as soon as the altimeter on his wrist showed twenty-five hundred. When they saw Hooper's canopy deploy, all the other SEALs were to pull their manual releases. The slight difference in time would shift Hooper's position from in front of and below the team to behind and above, and the team would thereafter fly formation on Osborne's green helmet light by maneuvering the steerable midnight blue airfoil-shaped parachutes.

The ground seemed to come up impossibly quickly, though there was little sense of motion. The only sound was the rush of wind past Stuart's helmet as he turned to look at Leah, twenty feet to his left as they dropped. Her visor was turned in his direction; she was looking at him, too.

Hooper extended his arms in a swimming motion and tilted his head up. The air deflected by his chest turned his body so his feet were now below him. The team members followed his actions and grasped their main chute release handles in their right hands. Hooper's first-stage chute popped suddenly, and he appeared to shoot upward. Stuart pulled his release and felt the chute deploy behind his head. There was a jerk, a sense of being pulled upward, then a stronger jerk as the main canopy opened and the drogue fell away. Stuart looked up to check his canopy, surprised to find it clearly visible despite the inky darkness. He checked the shrouds, then he pulled his tape and felt his radio and equipment pack drop below him and tug at the end of its strap. Quickly he grasped the handles attached to the risers on either side of him and rotated the parachute slowly. He saw Leah struggling to release her gear, and felt a pang of guilt that she was here. He was relieved when she loosed her ammo and grenade pack and gripped her riser handles to steer the chute.

Hooper floated above, watching the jumpers below him maneuvering closer together now that their parachutes were fully deployed. What a team, he marveled. They could all land in a ten-meter circle if they had to.

The pond sped up, growing larger. The SEALs fell in almost perfect silence, the only sound the soft rush of air through the vents in the parachute canopies. Hooper watched as the SEALs unsnapped the oxygen tanks and masks and dropped them, and he pitched his own. He unzipped his body bag enough to reach his scuba air supply behind his neck, and turned it to full on. He looked down at Osborne, who was sideslipping his chute to the very middle of the fire-fighting reservoir. Osborne pulled both shroud handles outward and down, flaring the chute and slowing his descent. Hooper watched the others flare, waiting a second longer himself to catch up with them. Hooper held his scuba mouthpiece in front of his lips and pressed the purge button. He felt the air from his tank brush against his cheek; then he put the mouthpiece in his mouth.

The eight SEALs landed in the water in an almost perfect octagon, less than twelve meters from side to side.

⇆12⇄
USS *America*, 0410 GMT (0510 Local)

Admiral Bergeron sipped strong coffee from a china mug and looked at the status boards in Flag Plot. The fleet status board showed the disposition of the two battle groups he now commanded. Both the *America* and the *Nimitz* were at flight quarters, steaming into the light southerly breeze and launching aircraft. First up were the E-2C Hawkeyes, two for overall air control and two more for communications relay with the landing force. Next the A-6 Intruder attack aircraft, armed with Shrike antiradar missiles, and the A-7 Corsairs armed with bombs and rockets for close air support. Once the first attack wave was off and orbiting in assigned areas, the normal four-plane Combat Air Patrol would be recovered and replaced with eight fully fueled F-14 Tomcat fighters, armed with Phoenix and Sidewinder air-to-air missiles. Two more Tomcats would then be spotted on the forward catapults of each carrier, fueled and armed and with crews strapped in. Eight Tomcats had been launched from *Nimitz* an hour before to give fighter cover to the air force F-111s, which awaited their attack signal in assembly areas sixty miles north of eastern Libya.

All of this information was displayed on the air status display and continuously updated by technical ratings at computer consoles, some in this room but most far away in the ship's Combat Information, Flight Operation, and Attack Direction Centers.

While the carriers and their screening vessels steamed toward the Libyan coast, some thirty miles out, the Shore Bombardment Group clung to the edge of the twelve-mile limit. Most of the firepower was on the refurbished World War II battleship *New Jersey,* with her nine sixteen-inch and twenty-five-inch guns. The three destroyers that would work in close were built in the 1960s and had two five-inch guns each, plus Tartar antiaircraft missiles that would be used to provide point air defense for themselves and the battleship.

The battle area status display showed the air force units as well as all the Navy and marines. The ten C-141s carrying the paratroopers were descending to their final assembly area forty miles off the Libyan coast and ten miles east of the fleet. East of them were the sixteen F-111s from Upper Heyford, ready to attack their targets at Benghazi and Tobruk, which were, respectively, 360 and 520 miles from Uqba ben Nafi. The admiral was very glad he could leave the Libyan Air Force to the F-111s.

The amphibious squadrons, centered on *Saipan* and *Inchon* and protected by their own screen of destroyers and air-defense cruisers, sailed just outside the Libyans' twelve-mile limit, under the overall command of Rear Admiral Kinnock in *Saipan*. Both ships had reported they had AH-1T marine Sea Cobra gunships, armed with 20mm cannons, antitank and antipersonnel rockets, and TOW antitank missiles, spotted and ready for takeoff. They would take off and orbit once the SEAL team reported they were ready to assault the Operations Building, and then CH-53 Sea Stallion helicopters would be spotted to take the marine rifle company ashore, and then to bring everyone back.

It could just work that way, thought Admiral Bergeron, sipping cold coffee. It *should*.

A telephone buzzed next to the admiral, and the sailor seated next to him picked it up. He listened, then passed the phone to the admiral, who pressed the transmit key and spoke. "Admiral Bergeron."

"Admiral, Colonel Brimmer. We have a signal from the SEALs. They are out of the pond, not detected, no casualties."

The admiral frowned. "I thought they were radio silent."

Colonel Brimmer laughed. It sounded like paper crackling through the scrambler. "They are, Admiral. They broke squelch, three shorts and a long."

"I see. When will they signal again?"

"If nothing goes wrong, just before they break in to take the hostages."

"Good. Everything holding up on your end?"

"Yes, sir. As soon as they tell us they're in control of the hostages, we'll begin the assault."

"Very well. Keep me informed, Bob."

"Aye, aye, sir. Thunder out."

Admiral Bergeron handed the telephone back to the sailor on watch. It could work, he thought to himself.

⇆13⇌
Uqba ben Nafi, 0422 GMT (0522 Local)

Stuart put the radio handset back in its holder after sending his three shorts and a long to the fleet. The signal had been acknowledged by a single click. His nylon poopy-suit was already drying in the soft onshore breeze, and he was getting warm. The SEALs would keep the immersion suits on until they were through the windows, as protection from broken glass.

Osborne and Miller had gone after the revetments to the east, and the rest of the team clustered in the deep shadow at the top of the berm around the reservoir, silently watching and listening. Feeney low-crawled to Hooper and Stuart and whispered.

"Commander, I can't see them BTRs anywhere."

"No, they sure as hell aren't where they were. I looked for vehicles as we were coming down; I didn't see any." Hooper handed his night binoculars to Stuart, who swept the apron and the shadows by the buildings but saw nothing.

"What do we do, sir?" asked Feeney.

"We go by the numbers. I don't see any people, either, and the windows of the Operations Building are dark, or nearly dark. Probably one small light, for the terrorists."

"Do me and Jones follow you across?" asked Feeney.

"Negative. Follow the path you've rehearsed, and try to find any vehicles in the deep shadow between the Maintenance and Ops Buildings. Meet us by the front door if you can in—" he looked at his watch, "fifteen minutes, if there's nothing. If you find something major, use your helmet radio." Each man had a tiny two-way radio in his helmet, ultra-high frequency and low power, with a range of two hundred meters or less. "Let's move out."

⇋14⇌
Uqba ben Nafi 0437 GMT (0537 Local)

Captain Suslov yawned as he climbed into the commander's seat of Praporshchik Tolkin's T-72. He was surprised that the warrant officer had elected to go along in place of his gunner. Normally, tank commanders resented having an officer replace them in the right seat in the turret, and left them to deal with an equally resentful crew, but Tolkin seemed quite cheerful about it and said he didn't want to miss the fun. So Tolkin stood in the gunner's hatch on the left side of the turret as the driver, a mean-looking Kazakh named Berezin, started the tank's 780-horsepower V-12 diesel engine. Soon all the vehicles were running at idle, and the doors of the supply warehouse had to be opened partially to let out the acrid blue smoke.

Colonel Zharkov walked past Suslov's tank and waved to the zampolit. Suslov waved back and watched as Zharkov climbed into the commander's hatch of the end tank and put on his helmet with its integral radio/intercom headset. Zharkov planned to lead the column in his T-72, followed by Sergeant Mishkin in the second tank and Suslov in the third. The three BTRs, each with a crew of three and carrying an eight-man rifle squad, would follow. The column would leave the supply warehouse and proceed south across the northeast-southwest runway to the area in front of the Maintenance Building, where the infantry would dismount. The three tanks would then advance to the Operations Building, smash the windows with their main guns, and present the terrorists with a fait accompli. The tank commanders would have a clear view from their hatches high above the turrets and, with the 12.7mm machine gun mounted at the commander's position, could deal with any terrorists who did not immediately surrender.

It was not a subtle plan, nor was it intended to be. Zharkov did not think the terrorists would try to fight three main battle tanks; if they did they would be killed. The tank crews would be protected from the terrorists' automatic weapons and grenades. The greatest danger was that the terrorists would detonate fragmentation grenades before the tanks could reach the building, resulting in death and injury to large numbers of hostages and probably to the terrorists as well. If the rescue mission turned into a bloodbath, the Soviets would claim they had intervened only after the grenading started, and only with intent to save American lives.

Suslov mulled over his secret orders from the KGB as

he waited for the order to move out. Zharkov had made a special point to the tank commanders and gunners that machine gun fire, if needed, should be tightly controlled, so that no American ended up with a Russian slug in him. The colonel stressed that the tank crewmen had plenty of protection and should aim carefully. Suslov doubted that he could get away with a deliberate "accident" with his machine gun unless the terrorists put up a genuinely heavy resistance. He would have to wait and see.

Stuart, Hooper, and Leah Rabin reached the deep shadows to the left of the large windows of the Operations Building without seeing any sign of activity. Ricardo had slipped around to the back door and reported in position by keying his helmet radio. Feeney and Jones had rejoined, slipping silently directly beneath the windows, and Osborne and Miller had come in at almost the same moment, crossing the lighted tarmac by a more southerly route, behind the revetments along runway 11/29. They reported in a whisper that they had found no aircraft in any of the revetments they had checked.

"OK," whispered Hooper. "We have everybody together, so let's make a few changes. Osborne, go around back and come in with Ricardo; remind him to tune his radio to command, then you stay downstairs when he goes up. Give us a key click when you're on station." Osborne nodded and glided away into the darkness. "Leah, you come in behind me, left side window; you look right, I'll look left. William, hit the right window behind Miller, same drill. Feeney and Jones, establish security ten meters back, facing outward, prone on the tarmac. Protect your night vision. After we crash in, give us a count of three, longer if you see lead or grenade fragments coming out at you, then hit the window to the left of the main door." Hooper paused. Everyone heard the sharp click in his radio, which indicated Osborne was on station behind the building. "OK, we're three minutes early, but there's no point waiting to get discovered. Let me see your grenades." Hooper looked at the cylindrical concussion grenades in each person's left hand, checking that none had selected a round fragmentation grenade by mistake. "Good. William, tell Thunder we're going in."

Stuart's heart was pounding with excitement. He made himself concentrate to get the cadence right, then pressed the transmit key. Three long, two short. He got the single click of acknowledgment back, tucked away the handset, and nodded to Hooper.

"OK," Hooper took a deep, slow breath. "Sonic valves in ears." Each SEAL inserted the rubber and metal earplugs that would protect their hearing from the blast of the concussion grenades. They could still hear normal speech. "Weapons on single fire." He waited while they checked. "Pull and discard the grenade safety pin." They did. Hooper pressed his helmet mike twice to signal Osborne and Ricardo. Then he began a slow count of ten while moving toward the windows, the others close behind him, fanning out across the front of the building. They began to jog, watching each other, keeping pace. Hooper finished his ten count and shouted "Go!" as he jumped for the window, his carbine held out butt first.

Sergeant Cifuentes finished reinstalling the fuel pump and bled the fuel system of air. He pulled his head from the engine compartment and shouted at Mohammed to try the starter. The engine ground through slowly, then roared to life. Cifuentes thought he heard a couple of extra loud pops, but then the engine ran smoothly. Good, he thought, wiping his hands. We will let it warm up a bit, then take it out for a test, then deliver it to its waiting Libyan crew.

Ahmed stood by the window next to the front door of the big room, staring out at the lights and shadows of the apron. Amin and Yusef had the watch, but Ahmed had been unable to sleep. Yusef was dozing in a chair behind the sleeping hostages, and Amin was upstairs in the control tower with the three controllers, two Libyans and a North Korean. Walid was asleep in one of the small rooms off to the right, and a faint light came from the room the naqib used as his office.

Ahmed picked up his AKS assault rifle and rubbed a bit of rust with a thumbnail. Where would it end? he wondered. How many would the naqib kill before the Kuwaitis gave in or the Americans came? Would he, Ahmed, have the courage to turn his weapon on the sleeping hostages before accepting martyrdom? Would he really see paradise if he did?

Ahmed heard a shout behind him, and turned. He saw the window in front of him burst inward, the glass catching the light from the apron in a million tiny shards. An enormous figure, all in black and with no face, emerged from the falling glass, and then Ahmed was deafened by the loudest sound he had ever known. It swept his hearing away, and with it his breath. Ahmed dropped his rifle and reached for his roaring ears. The black djinn shot him three times in the chest.

Hooper landed on the floor of the operations ready room, bits of glass streaming from his body. He was glad for the poopy-suit, the helmet, and the heavy gloves. The first thing he saw in the dim light was a slim man with a folded-stock assault rifle, barely three feet away. Hooper shot the man without hesitation. Toward the back of the room, another man with a rifle across his knees started to rise from his chair. Before Hooper could bring his rifle to bear, he heard a sharp crack to his right and saw Miller's CAR-15 flare. The man and his chair fell over and stayed down. "Osborne!"

"Here, sir. Nothing back here!"

They heard shouts from above, then heard the dull crump of a fragmentation grenade. Large chunks of plaster and dust came from the ceiling above them. Good, thought Hooper. Ricardo has taken the control tower. Hooper raised the plastic visor of his helmet and shouted to the hostages, lying on the floor and staring about like frightened nocturnal animals caught in a strong light. "Stay down, stay down! We are U.S. Navy SEALs!" Hooper saw Leah, her carbine hanging from her neck by its sling, motioning downward with her hands as she moved to the right. Of course, thought Hooper, these people are temporarily deaf from the grenades. Still clutching his carbine by the pistol grip, he motioned downward with his free hand as Stuart and Miller ran across the room toward the corridor, from which a light glowed. Stuart unslung the radio and set it down before following Miller into the corridor.

A navy chief petty officer pushed himself to a sitting position, holding his ears. "There are two of them down that hall, Navy! The leader and the one that murdered the girl!" He spoke with the unintentional loudness of one who could not hear. Hooper looked at Stuart, who nodded. Miller had disappeared into the corridor.

Miller reached the lighted doorway and waited for Stuart. Miller stepped past the door, and Stuart kicked it off its hinges. Abu Salaam crouched in the corner, teeth bared like an animal, trying to work the action of his Makarov pistol. Stuart shot him through the forearm and the pistol skipped away. Stuart reached in and dragged the gasping man from the small room into the corridor, then went after Miller.

Walid was awakened by the boom of the grenades, dulled by the intervening walls. He knew instantly what had happened—that the Americans had come—but he felt paralyzed in his cot. He heard shots, then a door being kicked in, then a single shot, close by, and then the sound of the naqib's voice, cursing and protesting. Walid crawled from the bed to the floor. I must be brave now, for my family, he thought. I must remember my anger.

The door to his sleeping room was kicked open. There was no light from the passageway, but Walid felt the presence of the American. "Wait," Walid said in English, "I want to come out, surrender!" It was too far across the room to his AKS, but Walid could just reach the fragmentation grenade in his jacket pocket. A few seconds—

"Take your time," said Miller, pulling the pin from a fragmentation grenade and removing the spoon before it could fall. He held the grenade two seconds, then tossed it into Walid's room, pulled the heavy door shut, and backed away. The blast followed almost at once.

Stuart emerged from the corridor, dragging Abu Salaam. Miller was out a second later. "I checked all the rooms, Commander. One guy, wasted."

Stuart picked up the handset on the tactical radio. "Call it in, Hoop?"

"Wait one. Let's be sure." He pressed his helmet mike. "Ricardo?"

"OK up here, Hoop. Three down, just me."

"OK, Ricardo," said Hooper. "I'm going to send Osborne out back. I want you to go out onto the roof and just listen; see if anyone is moving, and mark them. Don't be gone over two minutes." Hooper pointed to Osborne, who nodded and slipped out the back door.

"Roger, Commander," answered Ricardo. "I'm leaving the field radio. I'll call in on my helmet."

Hooper clicked the mike, signing OK. "Feeney, see to our prisoner."

Feeney moved behind Abu Salaam and cinched his wrists with plastic pull-through riot handcuffs, then pulled a field dressing from his pack. The little man struggled and poured forth a stream of shouted, angry Arabic. Leah leaned toward him and asked him a question in the same language. Abu Salaam sneered and barked a phrase at the Israeli officer. Leah pointed her finger at his face and spoke in a gentle, almost seductive tone. All color drained from Abu Salaam's face, and his eyes and mouth opened wide in shock.

"Jesus, Feeney, gag the bastard," said Hooper. Feeney took the red and white kaffiyia from around the terrorist's neck and tied it tightly around his mouth. The eyes above the gag remained wide and staring. "What was he shouting, Leah?"

"He says we are cowards. Says we will be defeated because we are sentimental about a few hostages."

"What did you say?"

"I asked him if he wished his remarks translated. He cursed me for a filthy Jewish whore."

"So what did you say to him? He shut up quick enough."

Leah reddened slightly. "I compared his beard to his sister's cunt."

Hooper's eyebrows shot up, and a smile played at the corners of his mouth. Stuart started to laugh. "Jesus, you sure did!"

Leah flushed a deeper red. "You understood that?"

"Most of it. God, the look on his face!"

"Well, come on, tell the rest of it!" said Hooper, grinning.

"It is a fairly common Arab curse," protested Leah.

Stuart fought to control his laughter. "Let's see. No translation can really match the Arabic, but she compared the two, ah, *features,* in terms of texture, smell, and usual employment." Stuart began to laugh so hard he had to bend over, and he sat on the step next to Abu Salaam. Hooper's big booming laugh joined in.

Leah turned away. Miller and Jones stared at her. Both looked embarrassed. "Come on, Miller," said Leah firmly. "Help me untie these people. Jones, try to find some drinking water." Leah moved swiftly among the hostages, cutting their bonds with her shroud-cutter knife, touching them gently. Macho pigs, she thought, the heat returning to her cheeks. She turned to look at Hooper and Stuart. Hooper squatted in front of Abu Salaam while Stuart sat next to him, holding onto the terrorist's shoulder. They are not mocking me, she realized. They are laughing at him, because we have beaten him. She watched Abu Salaam squirm and writhe against his bonds as the men's laughter lashed him like whips.

Hooper looked at the hostages. Leah was walking among them, helping them up into chairs. None were hurt, but all were rubbing their painful ears. Mostly the people were smiling at Leah, and some were hugging each other. Ricardo's voice crackled in Hooper's helmet radio. "Real quiet, Hoop."

"Good. Osborne?"

"Made a quick recon back here, Hoop. Nothing moving."

"OK, Osborne, get back inside."

"Roger, comin' in, Hoop."

Hooper looked back at Stuart. "Hey, Hoop! Told you getting *in* would be easy!" Stuart was smiling, but Hooper felt the fear. From now on, we depend on others to get us out, and for them, we *wait*. "Call us in, William."

Stuart pressed the transmit key, and for the first time spoke into the handset. "Top Hat, Thunder, this is Black Widow. Station, I say again, station."

⇋15⇌
Washington, 0451 GMT (2351 Local)

The President looked at the copy of the message that had just been transmitted from commander, Sixth Fleet to all units involved in the hostage rescue mission:

IMMEDIATE EXECUTE OPERATION FIRE ARROW IMMEDIATE EXECUTE 0450z

"Inform the Russians, Henry."

"Yes, Mr. President," said the Secretary of State.

FIRE ARROW

⇋1⇌

Uqba ben Nafi, 19 February, 0451 GMT (0551 Local)

Sergeant Cifuentes watched as Mohammed opened the doors of the Maintenance Building, then jumped up onto the turret and sat in the commander's seat. Mohammed was thrilled to be taking a ride.

The Russian lieutenant who was the duty officer stepped from his tiny office and held up his hand. His uniform was rumpled, and he looked angry. Probably woke the bastard up, thought Cifuentes.

"Where do you think you are going, Sergeant?" asked the Russian.

"Finished repairs. Test engine," replied Cifuentes in his heavily accented Russian.

"Call the vehicle's proper crew, Sergeant," said the lieutenant brusquely.

"Crew come half hour. Now just make test run."

"Sergeant, I want that vehicle deployed now. The crew can test it on their way to their assigned station."

Cifuentes smiled and shook his head, as though he didn't understand. He of course understood perfectly; he had had four years of Russian in school, and he had to keep it up to read the maintenance and technical manuals that allowed him to work on the Russian equipment. But he wanted his test drive after sweating over the balky engine all night. He eased the vehicle into first gear and let in the clutch. The ZSU started forward with a lurch. Cifuentes was amused to see the Russian leap clear as he pulled the steering bar to the right and drove the vehicle through the open doorway.

"Sergeant, I order you to stop that vehicle!" screamed the lieutenant in his high-pitched voice.

"*Chinga tu madre!*" called Cifuentes amiably, shifting into second gear and turning right again.

All vehicles and personnel had been ordered to keep clear of the front of the Operations Building, so Cifuentes drove into the alley next to Maintenance that would take

211

him around behind Operations and to the end of runway 11/29.

⇋2⇋

Four A-6s from VA-12 on *America* turned out of their low orbits near the twelve-mile limit and accelerated toward shore, climbing rapidly. The fire-control radars on the aircraft were slaved to the radar emissions from the truck-mounted Flat Face target-acquisition radars, which controlled the SA-3 GOA antiaircraft missiles. The Shrike missiles hanging beneath the A-6s' wings were locked on as well. The flight leader had assigned each of the other planes a target, and he pulled his own aircraft above the others and watched them fire, two missiles each. He withheld his own two missiles in case any radar emissions continued after the first strike. The GOA missiles themselves would not be destroyed unless the Libyans had been foolish enough to locate them near the radar trucks, but they would be blind and useless. The flight leader watched the time-of-flight display clock run down, then saw all three target blips disappear in rapid succession. He radioed his flight to turn home to *America*, to land and rearm. He would remain on station, in case another radar source should come up on the screen.

⇋3⇋
Benghazi and Tobruk, Libya

The sixteen air force F-111Es from the 20th Tactical Fighter Wing at Upper Heyford turned inshore on receipt of the "Execute Fire Arrow" signal, rotated their wings back to full sweep of 72.5 degrees, and accelerated toward the coast at best sea-level speed of 915 knots. All the aircraft carried mixed ordnance loads. The two lead aircraft carried Shrike antiradar missiles on outer external underwing hard points, with the missile electronics package in their internal bomb bays. All aircraft carried Walleye II television-guided bombs, and 750- and 1,000-pound iron bombs. Four aircraft in each attack force carried suspended underwing units (SUUs) of Sadeye cluster bombs. Each aircraft carried as well a pod containing the AN/ALQ-131 defensive jamming electronic countermeasures. For the F-111 aircraft, this was a light load.

The bombers began their attacks with Shrike missiles, as the lead aircraft gained altitude rapidly to draw the missile guidance radars. As soon as the radars had been reported destroyed, Colonel Wight, with the Benghazi flight, ordered the general attacks on both bases.

The attacks on Benghazi and Tobruk were identical in concept, differing only as required by the different arrangement of the two bases. Aerial and satellite reconnaissance of both bases had been heavy, and showed their revetments and taxiways packed with fighter and attack aircraft of all types in the Libyan inventory. The mission of the eight aircraft attacking each base was threefold. First, eliminate the surface-to-air missile defenses. Second, crater the runways and eradicate the control and support facilities of each air base to prevent the launching of any effective counterattack against the Air Force or the fleet. Finally, destroy as many aircraft as possible on the ground. The first part of the mission was accomplished by the Shrike missiles. The second part was effected by attacks using Walleye II bombs, which were given targets by the pilots before they were dropped and then guided themselves until impact. Eighteen of these bombs were dropped at Benghazi and fifteen at Tobruk, aimed at control towers, ground-control approach radars, mobile anti-aircraft guns, repair facilities, ordnance depots, and POL (petroleum, oil, and lubricants) tank farms. Following the Walleye II drops, each flight made runs dropping 750- and 1,000-pound bombs, many with armor-piercing cases and base-detonating fuses, which blew gaping craters in the runways, concentrated around intersections and taxi-access points.

The final wave of four aircraft at each target flew low over revetments and parking areas, dropping Sadeye one-pound cluster bomb units from the cylindrical containers suspended under the wings. Each SUU held over six hundred bomblets, and each aircraft carried two containers. When the containers popped open, the bomblets were strewn in a cloud 150 meters long and 60 meters wide.

Each Sadeye bomblet was a steel shell filled with three-quarters of a pound of TNT into which 600 steel shards had been embedded. Some of the bomblets were fused to explode thirty feet above the ground, others to detonate on impact. Originally conceived as an antipersonnel weapon, the Sadeye fragmentation bomb had been found to be especially effective against parked aircraft. Aircraft that had been disarmed and drained of fuel simply collapsed like wilted butterflies as the steel shards shredded their thin aluminum skins and cut away landing gear beneath them. The ready aircraft burned and exploded as the hot steel splinters sliced through fuel cells and weapons packages. If maximum casualties had been wanted, some of the bomblets would have been fused to explode from ten to thirty minutes after impact, to destroy fire-fighting crews and equipment, but the mission was directed against the aircraft alone.

The last F-111s completed their bombing runs, then raced out over the Mediterranean at low level. The Tobruk raid had taken four minutes; the raid on Benghazi, a somewhat larger base, had taken just under five. The aircraft reformed in two groups twenty-five miles at sea. All sixteen reported normal weapons function and no damage to themselves. Colonel Wight ordered a course for the Strait of Gibraltar and a slow climb to economic cruising altitude, giving the Tobruk bombers a higher airspeed so they could catch up to the Benghazi flight.

The eight navy F-14 Tomcats that had flown fighter cover for the F-111s waited on station until the navy RA-5C photoreconnaissance aircraft from *Nimitz* photographed both bases, then followed them back to the carriers. Not a single Libyan fighter had risen to challenge the bombers, and the Tomcat jocks voiced their disappointment in muted chatter on the fighter net.

⇋4⇌
Airborne final assembly point, eighteen miles north of El Asciar, Libya

The lead C-141 and the other carrying the remainder of the infantry company left the low-level orbit, descended even lower, and headed for the coast. Lieutenant Colonel Squitiero, flying the lead aircraft, watched the second aircraft form on him, thirty meters higher and fifty meters behind. He spoke briefly into his lip mike, and both aircraft descended further, the leader flying in the ground effect, barely forty meters above the calm sea. Lieutenant Colonel Squitiero flexed his hands on the yoke. Nap-of-the-earth flying was even harder over land, and he could see the low bluff of the Libyan coast coming up fast ahead of his aircraft.

⇋5⇌
USS *New Jersey,* twelve miles north of Uqba ben Nafi

The battleship was moving at five knots, barely rolling in the light swells. Her two anti-submarine pickets, the frigates *Capodanno* and *Truett* shadowed her, one four thousand yards ahead, and the other four thousand yards off the battleship's starboard quarter, out of the sound shadow of *New Jersey's* mammoth screws. The battleship's fire-control computer aimed the guns, which pointed upward into the gradually lightening sky. When the Operation Execute signal was received, the captain turned to the gunnery officer on the bridge and nodded. The gunnery officer spoke into the headset he wore under his helmet. "Main battery, commence fire." Nine jets of flame gushed from the sixteen-inch guns, each sixty-seven feet long, hurling nineteen hundred–pound shells at targets preset into the gunfire-control computer. The first targets were the fighter revetments and antiaircraft gun positions at the southern ends of the two runways. After enough shells had been spread over these to assure destruction, the computer shifted the fire to the tank positions south of runway 11/29. The noise was deadened by the protective headgear worn by every exposed man, but it lasted and resonated through the ship's steel structure, unlike the sharp, short crack of smaller naval guns.

With a low, clattering roar of a thousand freight trains, the shells fell through the air over Uqba ben Nafi and landed at the distant ends of the runways, and then at fifty-meter intervals in the grassy scrublands south of the long runway. Ricardo, in the control tower, heard the shells overhead and turned to watch the bright orange bursts and feel the concussion. He keyed his radio handset. "Devastation, this is Black Widow. No spot, you're right on target, out."

The *New Jersey* would fire two broadsides a minute, until the C-141s crossed their final phase line four miles east of the runway. The computer would make adjustments to each salvo to ensure that the entire length of the area of the tank fighting positions was bombarded. The huge shells dug overlapping craters fifty meters across in the hard earth and collapsed the fighting positions that had been bulldozed out for the tanks three days before. The tanks would have been destroyed and buried in their own holes if they had been where they had shown up on the reconnaissance photos, but they were gone.

Closer to shore, the destroyers *Adams, King,* and *Lawrence* approached the beach on an angle so that both forward and aft guns could engage. Each ship could fire automatically at forty rounds per minute per gun until the magazines were empty. Their targets were the antiaircraft guns at the northern end of runway 03/21, the tanks believed to be dug in on the low bluff overlooking the beach, and a low hill behind the beach some thousand meters to the east of the northern end of runway 03/21, where yesterday's photos had shown two platoons of tanks.

The destroyers didn't get a spot from the SEALs, but their gunnery was excellent. Three 57mm guns and their crews were destroyed at the end of the runway by the first salvos, sending up a series of secondary explosions easily visible from ten miles at sea. The rain of shellfire collapsed the empty depressions the tanks had dug for themselves in the sand.

⇌6⇌
Uqba ben Nafi

Senior Lieutenant Kim sat up quickly. He had seen a bright flash in the window of the distant control tower, and then the tower's lights had gone out. He pressed the microphone switch on the stick of his aircraft. "Chosun Flight Leader to tower, over!" He got no answer and tried again. The Libyans might be asleep, but there was always a North Korean Air Force officer in the tower when Korean pilots were operating.

"What is it, Chosun Leader?" Lieutenant Choi's voice came in loudly in Kim's ear. Kim was glad to hear him awake and alert.

"I saw what might have been an explosion in the tower window, Choi, and now I can't raise the tower."

"Do you think it could be an attack?"

"I don't know. Wake the ground crew; it is nearly time to warm up the engines again, anyway."

In thirty seconds they had the turbines started and the auxiliary power cart disconnected. There was still no response from the tower. Kim ran down the aircraft and missile checklists with Choi over the radio as the two aircraft taxied onto the runway and rolled slowly north. What to do? He wondered. Go? We should go.

Kim saw the yellow tracks of two missiles flash in from the sea, and saw the bright bursts of their detonation on targets. He pushed his throttle forward and raced through the rest of his takeoff checklist. He heard a low rumble growing beneath the high-pitched whine of the jet, and then a terrific explosion behind him shook the aircraft violently.

"What was that, Leader?" screamed Choi.

"Bombs, or shells. We go, Choi, roll in my wake!" Kim

increased the thrust to takeoff power and accelerated toward the darkened control tower.

⇋7⇌

USS *Inchon*

The Flag Plot was busy, but controlled. Lieutenant Colonel Loonfeather lit a cigarette from the butt of one just finished as a sailor dropped an envelope in front of him. "What's this?" he asked.

"Latest satellite photo, sir, in from the ground-control station in California. The Chief of the Watch in Combat told me to bring it right up."

"Good. Thanks, and thank the chief."

"Yes, sir." The sailor moved on.

Loonfeather looked at the date-time group. The photo had been shot only an hour before and was an infrared image. He glanced at it, his mind with the paratroopers now flying toward the Libyan coast at 300 knots. His attention was suddenly engaged as he looked at the photo. "Shit! Bob, look at this!"

Colonel Brimmer looked at the photo. Infrared images were hard to read unless you were used to them. "What is it, Rufus?"

"The defensive setup! It's totally different! Look, the tanks on the beach are gone, and the ones on the edge of runway 11/29 have been pulled back and concentrated two kilometers south of the airfield!"

"Where are the rest? It looks like maybe a dozen shapes to the south," said Brimmer uncertainly.

"You can't tell," said Loonfeather, his fingers tracing the images on the photograph. "They could be close together. Their heat signatures could merge, especially if they had been run recently. Shit! They had to have been run recently!"

"But that couldn't be forty tanks."

"No, Bob, no more than twenty." His finger traced the photograph. "Where would the rest be?"

"Where would you put them, Rufus?"

Loonfeather held his chin in his hand, concentrating. Ancient memories teased his mind as he stroked the photo with his fingertips. A place of concealment. In a deep draw, under the cottonwoods. Loonfeather's fingers stopped in the area west of the runways, marked "golf course" on the old plans of Wheelus. He spread his fingers and examined the area, but there were no heat signatures.

"There. Along the stream in the old golf course. But there's nothing there."

"Could they be concealed from the satellite, by trees or other camouflage?" Brimmer stared at the photograph, willing a sign.

"Ordinary camouflage shouldn't hide the heat of tank engines. They had to have been moved after that last photograph, and should still be plenty warm. But it could be," said Loonfeather. "Dammit! *Must* be!"

"Christ, Rufus! That area is practically on top of the Operations Building! Much closer than the Airborne, after they land! Can we warn Colonel Bowie?"

"We'll try, Bob. Right now Colonel Bowie is about as busy as a man can be."

⇆8⇆

Uqba ben Nafi

Hooper took off his helmet and his earplugs. He moved in front of the hostages and tried to smile some encouragement into their frightened faces. The shells from the battleship were very loud and the building shuddered, even though the nearest shells were landing more than half a mile away. These people realize this nightmare is far from over, he thought.

"Commander Hooper," said Leah, at his side.

Hooper felt her animal energy, and envied Stuart. "Yes, Captain?"

"We should dispose of this Abu Salaam."

"We'll take him back with us."

"To America? Why? He will get a trial; he will embarrass you, and you will lock him up until the Palestinians take enough hostages to make you exchange him."

"We don't exchange criminals for hostages."

"Bullshit!" Leah spat. "You have, and you will! Kill him, now!"

Hooper sighed. She was probably right. "We don't kill prisoners, Leah."

"I will do it for you."

"Leah, look. We have a deal, remember? You are here in American uniform, ostensibly an American SEAL. You *will* follow my orders, OK?"

"Hey, Hoop!" called Osborne from across the room. "Ricardo says he hears noises, a heavy diesel engine."

Hooper listened and heard a faint drumming, accompanied by the squeaking clank of a tracked vehicle. He snatched his helmet off the floor and put it on. "What can you see, Ricardo?"

"Just turned into the alley, Hoop, next to the Maintenance Building. Funny-looking thing; looked like it has four light cannons on top of a light tank chassis."

"That is a ZSU, Hooper," said Leah, listening in her own helmet radio. "The Syrians have them. Antiaircraft cannons; very high rate of fire."

"Jesus!" said Hooper. "Ricardo, can we get a shot with a Dragon from up there?"

"Negative, Hoop; it's too close. The Dragon won't arm until it has flown at least two hundred meters."

Hooper ran to the radio and picked up the handset. "Thunder, this is Black Widow. Can you hold things up a minute? We have a new threat, over."

"Jesus CHRIST!" yelled Ricardo into his helmet mike. "Commander, there are two fighter aircraft taking off, straight at us!"

"Call it into Top Hat, Ricardo," said Hooper, rushing to the front window. He heard the scream of jet engines and saw the two aircraft as a blur passing in front of the Ops Building.

A ZSU, and now fighters have gotten past the naval shelling! thought Hooper, shaking his head. If the fighters come in with the C-141s, we could have a disaster.

⇋9⇌

Colonel Zharkov's lead tank was a third of the way along runway 03/21 when the missile-radar truck parked next to the supply warehouse exploded. Moments later the first shells from the ships offshore began lighting up the night and causing his tank to sway as the ground rolled beneath it. Zharkov smiled as he was able to figure out the Americans' artillery plan. If I hadn't moved the tanks from the ridiculously exposed positions the Libyans had established, he thought, they would be gone.

It was clear that his own mission had to be aborted. Somehow, the Americans had gotten in and taken control of the hostages. "What I need," he said to himself, "is a safe place to hide until they are gone."

"Over there, sir," said Grishkin, his gunner, pointing. Zharkov hadn't realized he had keyed the intercom mike.

Grishkin had pointed to the Maintenance Building, across the open apron. One of the large bay doors stood open and light streamed out. The hangar looked large enough to hold his six vehicles, and it was too close to the Operations Building to be shelled from the sea. "Good, Grishkin. Driver, head for that open door, and speed it up, please."

Zharkov switched from intercom to radio as his driver turned the tank onto the angled turnoff and sped toward the Maintenance Building. Zharkov instructed the vehicles to follow him and for the BTRs to back in first, then the tanks. And then, thought Zharkov, we will close the doors and wait to see what happens next.

Zharkov looked back toward the runway and was amazed to see two jet aircraft roar aloft. Mother of God, he thought, those must be the ship-killers. I never thought they would get up!

Sergeant Cifuentes heard three sharp explosions and saw the result of one of them. A radar truck at the edge of the golf course just ahead of him disappeared in a white-hot flash. Then the heavy explosions started south of his position, masked from him by three-story buildings. The blasts looked like heat lightning, but the swaying of the ZSU told Cifuentes they were either bombs or shells.

The sergeant was suddenly afraid. The Americans will shell, and then the clouds of helicopters the Russian colonel had spoken of would really come. Fixing vehicles for these Libyan *boludos* was bad enough, but dying for them was crazy. Cifuentes forced himself to go on, and he turned left and drove quickly to the end of the runway, then backed into the deep shadow of a small shed topped by a light tower. A quick burst from Cifuentes's AK-47 extinguished the light at the top of the tower.

Hooper held the handset away from his face. Loonfeather was still talking, shouting, really, on the other end. He spoke carefully to his SEALs on the helmet radio. "Loonfeather says the C-141s are so low they can't turn without climbing, and if they do that, it will take them twenty minutes or more to regroup. Unless we want to play Fort Apache for twenty minutes against Libyan tanks, we have to knock that ZSU out."

"What about the fighters?" asked Stuart.

"Top Hat says they got 'em on radar from the E-2s. They're staying low and heading straight out."

"After the ships?"

"Apparently. Anyway, that's someone else's problem. Feeney, Jones, load up your Dragons and get going."

"Aye, aye, Hoop," said Feeney, picking up the bulky canister.

"Feeney," said Hooper. "You go out the front and work down to the runway. Jones, you go out the back."

"What if we find it too close to use the Dragons?" asked Jones.

Stuart was prying the lid off a wooden box he had found in the office used by Abu Salaam. "Hoop, the very thing!" He held up a Russian RPG-7 grenade launcher and grinned. "No self-respecting terrorist would leave home without one!"

"Yeah, OK. Take it and go with Jones; Feeney will probably see the thing far enough away if it continued south."

Stuart slung his carbine over his right shoulder and picked two of the bulbous-ended rocket-propelled grenades from the box. He seated one of the grenades in the launcher and stuffed the other inside the zipper of his jumpsuit.

"William, you *do* remember how to fire that thing, don't you?" asked Hooper.

"Like riding a bicycle, Hoop; one never forgets."

"Well, just remember first to look behind you, and don't forget to arm the grenade."

"No sweat, Hoop. Let's go, Jones," said Stuart, moving quickly toward the back door.

"Be careful, but get that thing before the Air Force arrives," said Hooper. Feeney shouldered the launcher and opened the front door. Hooper turned to Osborne, speaking softly. "Osborne, go cover Feeney with your 'Fifteen. Move out, and get back quick!"

"I should go with Jones and Stuart, to give them small-arms cover," said Leah to Hooper with quiet urgency.

"Thanks, Leah, but that would leave me just too thin here. But don't worry; there's no one in my knowledge who can get a slung carbine into action faster than Jones, unless it's Stuart."

⇋10⇋

"Stand up!" shouted the jumpmasters. "Check static lines!"

Jason Brown ran his hands over his reserve chute in front of him and patted down the M-16 and the Dragon tied and taped to his left side. He could feel the aircraft banking, making a very shallow turn. He had felt a sharp bump approximately three minutes earlier when the C-141 had crossed over the coast and been lifted by the ground effect of the coastal bluff. As he shuffled aft, closing up with Links, his nearest RTO, he felt the aircraft straighten up and begin to climb. There was a rush of noise and a swirling wind inside the aircraft as the jump doors aft on both sides were opened.

"Anything yet?" said Hooper into his helmet radio. The naval shelling had abruptly ceased, the last rounds to the south swirling out heavy, low-hanging clouds of gray smoke. The Airborne would be along any minute.

"Nothing," Feeney's voice whispered in the helmet radio. "We're nearly down to the intersection of the runways."

"It's down here somewhere, Hoop," said Stuart. "We're near the long runway, one hundred meters from the west end. We can hear the engine, but no track noises. We can't see it yet."

Shit! thought Hooper. "Ricardo, you see anything?"

"No, Hoop, but I reckon I'm going to see big, slow airplanes very soon."

"Stuart, find the fucking thing!" said Hooper, hearing the fear in his own voice.

"We're working west," said Stuart. "The engine sounds seem louder."

⇋11⇌

Senior Lieutenant Kim accelerated his aircraft at full takeoff power off the runway just as a huge explosion erupted at the northern end. The blast lifted his Mirage V and caused it to pitch upward, nearly causing a stall. Kim fought for control, bringing the sleek aircraft back down toward the surface of the sea as he headed north. He turned and looked up and saw Lieutenant Choi's Mirage behind him, twenty meters higher. "Get down, Choi," he barked. "Get lower;

the Americans will find you easily so high above the sea return."

"Leader," said Choi's voice, trembling in Kim's ear. "You are right on the waves!"

Kim had never flown with Choi before, except in the parade formations that so delighted Colonel Baruni. It was likely Choi had never had the rigorous and frightening training needed to skim along in the bumpy ground effect made by the choppy swells. "Be calm, Choi. What does your radar show?"

"Many large and small contacts, out some fifty kilometers. Very large, diffuse contact dead ahead, two kilometers, Leader."

"Take a major contact to the left of the distant formation, Choi; break off. I will go right. Look for an American carrier!"

"Yes, Leader. Look, in front of you!"

Kim barely had time to climb and pivot his Mirage as the huge battleship underneath him belched an enormous gush of flame. The aircraft rocked and shook him to his teeth. Kim checked his controls as the Mirage settled once more toward the sea. "Break off, Choi! No sense both of us being caught in one net! Good luck!"

"Good luck to you, Leader. Two out." Choi's voice sounded final and sad.

⇋12⇋
Navy F-14 Tomcat "Rodeo 202," six kilometers north of the coast of Uqba ben Nafi at 20,000 feet of altitude

"Rodeo Two-Oh-Two, this is CAP Control. We have two bandits outbound from runway 03/21. Find them and engage, over."

"Rodeo Two-Oh-Two, roger, over," replied Lt. Bill Bruce as he pushed his stick and throttles forward abruptly. The F-14 Tomcat sucked in her wings and kicked up to Mach 2 as its computer received target information directly from the huge tactical data computer on *America*. Bruce felt the computer take control, bending the aircraft toward the target aircraft. Fucking magic, thought Bruce as he checked the up-status of his missiles and guns. "You with me, Two-Oh-Four?" he asked his wingman, Lt. Cal Coolidge.

"Roge, Leader, right with you."

"Just get me close," whispered Bruce to the computer. "I want to use the gun."

⇆13⇄

Chosun Two, twenty kilometers north of Uqba ben Nafi

Lieutenant Choi flew as close to the sea as he dared, though he knew Senior Lieutenant Kim would be lower. Lieutenant Choi was very scared as he forced himself to go through the arming sequence for the AS-7 missile hanging beneath his aircraft. He checked the target acquisition radar and saw the big blip he had selected as his target fade and grow strong again as the radar signal was periodically interrupted by wave tops. Range to the target was down to thirty kilometers when the wailing tone of the radar-incoming alarm told Choi he had been acquired by an enemy fire-control radar.

Choi twisted in his seat, frantically looking above and behind himself for the enemy. He knew he couldn't attempt evasive action so close to the sea; a tight turn would put a wing tip into the water and drag the Mirage down instantly. If only I could get rid of this heavy missile, he thought desperately. He checked the range to the target again—twenty-four kilometers. The maximum range of the AS-7 was ten kilometers. Lieutenant Choi thought fleetingly of dropping the missile into the sea and turning back for Libya, but he put the thought out of his mind. Choi was scared, but he was no coward.

The wailing of the alarm rose abruptly in pitch and became steady. The enemy's fire-control radar had locked onto the Mirage.

⇌14⇌
Rodeo Two-Oh-Four, thirty-one kilometers north of Uqba ben Nafi

"I have both aircraft, Bill," said Lieutenant Coolidge. "Both on the deck. They're separating."

"Roger, Two-Oh-Four," said Lieutenant Bruce into his lip mike. "They must be going for a ship."

"Right. We better get them on the first pass. Which do you want?"

"My radar is painting better on the one to the left. You?"

"The same. The fucker on the right must be *really* low."

"I'll take the one on the right. OK, Cal, break and get on the other guy. Sidewinder at three thousand yards, then in with the gun."

"Roger, Two-Oh-Two. Good shooting." Coolidge dipped his port wing to swing around behind the target aircraft, which was passing under him at four hundred knots. He slowed from the eight hundred knots he was indicating as the range to the target dropped to under five thousand yards, noting that the fire-control system for the Phoenix missiles had locked on. He shifted the weapons selector from the long-range Phoenix to the short-range heat-seeking Sidewinder, and powered up the 20mm Vulcan cannon. The target aircraft flew on in steady course, and suddenly Coolidge saw it in front of him. "Charlie, kill the radar," he said to his radar intercept officer seated behind him. The RIO pulled a toggle on the fire-control panel, halting the emissions from the radar. The Sidewinders didn't need the radar, and neither would the cannon. No point announcing myself, thought Coolidge as he spread the Tomcat's wings and slowed further. The enemy continued on, straight and level. "Rodeo Two-Oh-Two, this is Two-Oh-Four. I am engaging, over."

"Roger, Two-Oh-Four," said Bill Bruce. He was having trouble keeping the second target in his radarscope because the Libyan was so close to the water as to mask his aircraft in the sea return. The fire-control radar refused to lock on automatically or manually.

Bruce looked frantically ahead and below as he descended below three hundred feet. What information his radar was giving him indicated the enemy to be no more than six thousand yards ahead. Suddenly he saw the target, ahead of and below him. At the speed he was going, he knew he would pass over the target before he could fire or launch a missile. With a curse, Lieutenant Bruce kicked in his afterburner and climbed into a tight turn, pulling his wings back into maximum sweep. I'll have to go around, he thought, and I had better hurry. The outer screen of the *America* battle group was barely twenty thousand yards ahead. Jesus, that bastard is *low,* he thought, admiring the pilot's skill and guts.

⇌15⇌

Chosun Two, thirty-eight kilometers north of Uqba ben Nafi

Lieutenant Choi checked his missile-control radar again. In the last twenty-five seconds he had closed the distance to his target to thirteen kilometers. His left hand hovered near the missile release toggle, while his right hand gripped the stick, ready to pull his aircraft up to sixty meters, the minimum altitude for a safe missile launch. Suddenly the radar-incoming alarm fell silent. I have lost him! thought Choi with immense relief. I will take the missile a little closer. The range fell below ten kilometers, and Choi began his climb. He saw his target for the first time; it looked like a cruiser. Choi steadied the aircraft and reached for the release toggle. He heard a roar below his Mirage and felt himself propelled upward as the nose dropped violently toward the sea. Choi pulled back on the stick, but felt no response. The stick was completely loose. The Mirage struck the sea at four hundred knots and disintegrated.

⇋16⇌
USS *America*

"Where are those bandits, Combat?" asked Lieutenant Allen, the general quarters Officer of the Deck on the bridge, holding down the communicator switch marked "Combat Information Center."

"One is down, Conn," answered the squawk box. "The other is twenty-eight thousand and closing."

Twenty-eight thousand yards! "Conn aye." Allen depressed the switch labeled "Primary Flight Control." "Prifly, Conn. I'm taking the deck. Sorry, but we have a bandit inbound." The Junior Officer of the Deck overheard, and reached up to the rear bulkhead and switched the deck status light display from green to red. The display had a repeater in Prifly, the aircraft carrier's control tower, on the same level as the bridge on the port side of the island superstructure. "Red Deck" meant all flight operations were suspended so that the giant carrier could maneuver.

"Combat, Conn. We have all jammers on?"

"Roger, just went up."

Another switch. "Main Control, Conn. Stand by for maneuvering combination."

"Main Control, aye. What's happening?"

"Maybe a missile. Tell Damage Control Central for me, will you, Commander?"

"Main Control aye."

USS *Ticonderoga*

"All engines ahead flank!" called the Officer of the Deck, Lt. Frank Decker. The Aegis cruiser's four giant gas turbines accelerated the 9,000-ton ship from eighteen to thirty knots in less than half a minute. Decker spoke to the captain at his general quarters station in the Combat Information Center. "We're going to cut off the *America*, Captain?"

"That's our job, Frank. Call the Tomcat; get him off. Is the missile locked on?"

"Yes, sir. I'll try to raise the fighter."

"Good." Captain Michael Conroy watched the computer terminal in front of his chair. He pressed a button on his squawk box marked "Weapons Control," the general quarters station of the weapons officer. "Weapons, Conn. Weapons free."

"Roger, Skipper," said Commander Phipps.

"Rodeo Two-Oh-Two, this is Archer—cruiser *Ticonderoga*," said Lieutenant Decker over the tactical fighter net. "We're launching missiles at your target. We have you separate, but break off; if you're close, the missile blast will bring you down with the target, over."

"Archer, Rodeo Two-Oh-Two. Do you have two distinct paints, over?"

Decker frowned and looked at the bridge repeater. "We have you identified, and a light paint below you, over."

"Then you're locked on me. This bandit is practically in the water. I know you have to fire, but wait as long as you can; I'm staying with this guy."

Captain Conroy picked up his radio handset. "Rodeo, you are ordered to break off and clear the area!"

"Rodeo Two-Oh-Two out," said Lieutenant Bruce, firing the first Sidewinder and then the second.

USS *America*

The deck under the consoles in Flag Plot tilted gradually to twenty degrees of heel as *America* turned out of the southerly wind and raced north, away from the approaching bandit. The ship's massive steam turbines pushed 280,000 horsepower through four propellors, driving the carrier up to thirty knots. As the angle of heel increased, Admiral Bergeron looked across the strained faces of the officers and men in the nearly silent compartment. "Gentlemen," said the admiral softly, but in a voice that carried, "we have an operation to run."

Plotters at the status boards and console operators picked

up their rhythm. Radio telephone operators checked circuits with each other, verifying frequencies that were assigned to nets not yet active. The heel of the deck decreased as *America* steadied on her new course.

Senior Lieutenant Kim let the Mirage rise another four meters above the gray, choppy sea and put the aircraft into a shallow turn to the right. He passed down the side of an American destroyer and under her stern, so low the ship couldn't fire. He was now flying just north of east, approaching his target, which had altered course to the north. As he cleared the destroyer's stern, he could see his target—a huge aircraft carrier. He checked the range: twelve kilometers. He checked to see the missile-arm light was lit. The missile would arm itself as it dropped free of the aircraft. Kim lowered his aircraft back toward the waves.

Lieutenant Bruce watched with horror as the first of his Sidewinders curved away from the bandit's tail and exploded over the aft stack of the picket destroyer. He imagined the pieces of white-hot shrapnel from the warhead sweeping the afterdecks, and winced with pain in his tight gut. He rolled his Tomcat past the destroyer and back onto the path of the enemy. The red ball of the sun was huge on the horizon, and the second Sidewinder rose from its track and curved away to seek the sun.

It's me and the gun now, thought Bruce, switching off his fire-control radar. He kicked in his afterburners and pulled the aircraft up, to get a downward shot with the cannon. One second, maybe two, and I'll have him.

Kim's radar range read ninety-five hundred meters to the carrier. He listened to the enemy's radar alternately squeal and then fade in his radar-incoming alarm. The American cannot lock on, thought Kim, feeling a rush of satisfaction at his skill at nap-of-the-earth flying, but he is still with me.

If I climb to release my missile, the American will blow me away with a missile, he thought smiling. I must at least make his shot difficult.

Kim held his Mirage on the wave tops, then executed a snap roll. As the aircraft inverted, he released the missile, which rose seventy meters from the centrifugal force of the rolling aircraft. Kim completed the roll barely above the sea surface.

Bruce watched in wonder as the enemy aircraft flipped his missile and descended back into the sea return. Fuck you, Libyan, thought Bruce, and maybe fuck me, too, but you're going down. Bruce pointed the nose of his fighter toward the dappled sea surface and fired the Vulcan cannon.

Kim saw tracers passing over the Mirage, and he threw the aircraft into a tight turn despite his unsafe altitude of twenty meters above the sea. He heard the sound of tearing metal and saw his port wing tip chopped to pieces. He fought to steady the aircraft, but he could no longer turn. I nearly made it, he thought. The next burst will tear me to pieces. Kim smiled and pulled back on the stick to take a last good look at his aircraft carrier, and then died as the cannon shells tore into him and his Mirage.

USS *Ticonderoga*

"Standard missile launched and tracking!" said the missile officer.

"Is that Tomcat still in the middle of it?" asked the captain.

"He's above– he's climbing. Sir! I think the bandit is down!"

"You *think?*" shouted the captain.

"He was flying so low—"

Lieutenant Bruce saw the bandit break apart, and immediately pulled maximum power, pointing the nose of his aircraft straight up. "Archer, Rodeo Two-Oh-Two. I got him! I am going ballistic! Kill your missile!"

USS *Ticonderoga*

"Kill it," said Captain Conroy.

The missile officer, Lieutenant Commander Tarter, pressed the "Destruct" button and saw the missile-tracing screen go blank. "Killed, Captain," he said into his headset.

"Combat, Air Defense," barked the squawk box. "The bandit launched his sea skimmer. We have it."

"Shoot it!" said Captain Conroy.

"Too close for a missile, Captain. We'll have to rely on the CIWS."*

"Will we interpose our hull between the missile and the *America?*"

"Maybe just, Captain," said Decker. "Close."

"Kill the missile jammers," said Captain Conroy.

"Sir?" said the ECM officer, Lieutenant Moore.

"We have to pull the missile away from the carrier."

"Aye, aye, sir," said Lieutenant Moore, stabbing a switch. "Here she comes."

The missile curved in toward the cruiser, flying ten meters above the sea surface. When it closed to under eight hundred meters, flying at Mach 1, the CIWS activated automatically. The six-barreled Vulcan cannon spewed out three hundred shells in three seconds. The missile disintegrated five hundred meters from the ship. The CIWS itself shut down automatically, its fire-control radar waiting passively for another alarm from the ship's central computer.

$$\leftrightharpoons 17 \rightleftharpoons$$

Sergeant Cifuentes stiffened in the sudden silence that marked the end of the shelling. *Dios mio,* they will come now, he thought. He climbed up onto the turret, lowered himself into the gunner's seat, and lit off the hydraulics that

---

*Close-In Weapons System—a totally automatic defensive system capable of shooting down missiles, or even naval gunfire projectiles, based on the 20mm Vulcan cannon.

moved the turret and elevated the guns. Mohammed stood on the back of the vehicle and watched.

The turret bucked and shifted as the hydraulic pump motors wound up to constant speed. Since he didn't have a radar operator, Cifuentes would have to use the optical sights. But against massed helicopters, the optics were better anyway because the gunner could shift targets faster.

The sky was lightening rapidly and Cifuentes looked east to see the first pinkish fingers of dawn. His eyes snapped open and his jaw dropped. Clearly silhouetted against the sky were two enormous black airplanes. As they crossed over the far end of the runway, Cifuentes could see parachutes. "*Santa Maria, Madre de Dios,*" whispered Cifuentes as he armed the guns. When those planes are halfway to me, he thought, I will fire. The maximum range of the cannons was twenty-five hundred meters. Cifuentes had the lead aircraft in the optical sight and the guns elevated as he held the image. One burst for each aircraft, he thought, but I will be sure to get the first one.

"Go! Go! Go!" chorused the jumpmasters, tapping each man on the shoulder as he stepped into the slipstream. Lieutenant Brown was about ten men from the door, pulling his static line along the wire over his head. He felt the adrenaline coursing through his body as his heart pounded in sync with the "Go, go, go!"

The aircraft were over the middle of the runway now, and their engines were very loud. Cifuentes mentally crossed himself and squeezed the firing handle. The ZSU bucked and quivered as a thick stream of green tracers surged toward the lead aircraft.

"Jesus CHRIST!" screamed Jones, falling flat on the pavement. The ZSU's cannons had fired from the shadow of a shed not forty meters away. Stuart dropped beside him, the RPG-7 launcher already resting on his shoulder. Stuart reached forward with his left hand, pulled the arming pin on the grenade, and aimed at the base of the four guns as they fired a second burst. The vehicle filled the entire field of the night optical sight. Stuart squeezed the trigger and the grenade's rocket motor drew an orange line behind it as it streaked to the target.

The grenade detonated in front of the turret and the cannons abruptly stopped. Stuart saw the bodies of two men on the runway next to the smoking vehicle. He stood and grabbed Jones by the shoulder. "Let's get the fuck out of here."

Jones nodded and scrambled to his feet. Both men whirled as they heard the roar of multiple cannon fire from the south. They could see green tracers rising from another ZSU south of the runway intersection. Jones sat on the runway, resting the Dragon launcher on his shoulder and bracing the forward rest with his feet. He saw a streak of missile exhaust race across the runway, and then the turret of the ZSU disappeared in an almost flashless explosion.

"Feeney got him," said Stuart, again pulling Jones to his feet. "Not your day, Jones."

"I have a feeling I'll get another chance," said Jones. "Let's go."

They sprinted down the runway as parachutes continued to fall from both aircraft.

Lieutenant Brown heard a tearing, booming sound behind him, and saw colored balls of fire shoot through the aircraft. Several soldiers in front of him fell down. Brown could see the back of one man's head split open, gushing blood.

The jumpmaster on Brown's side of the aircraft was bleeding from a cut on his scalp.

"Keep moving, keep moving, go!"

Brown tripped and fell on top of a dead man in front of him, his foot caught. Troopers behind him climbed over his back. Brown could see his static line hook tangled with those of the dead men, as well as with hooks of men behind him who had cut their lines. The right door jumpmaster grasped the back of Brown's harness and pulled him over the dead men, then cut his static line near the main chute. "Get moving, Troop!" yelled the jumpmaster, pushing him toward the door. "Jump your reserve! *Move!*"

Lieutenant Colonel Squitiero pressed the mike button on the yoke as he fought to keep the aircraft level. "Thunder, Carousel Leader. We're taking heavy ground fire. We're hit. Out."

The C-141 was pulling to the right and losing altitude slowly. A warning light over the rpm gauges told him the right inboard engine was on fire and the right outboard was losing power. We're going in, he said to himself, but if I can keep this thing flying, the rest of those boys in the back could get out. Squitiero looked at his copilot, young First Lieutenant Harkins. "Get out, Harkins," he said calmly.

"Colonel, I should stay—"

"Go, Harkins. I can do this by myself. Get as many people out as you can."

Harkins unclipped his harness and rose from his seat, his parachute dragging behind him in its seat pack. "Good luck, Colonel."

The aircraft began to shake violently and bank to the right, heading for the Mediterranean despite Squitiero's turning the yoke hard left.

As Harkins entered the troop compartment and headed aft, the aircraft banked nearly forty-five degrees, and the copilot found himself walking on the bulkhead as much as on the steel flooring. Harkins could see two jumpmasters and the infantry colonel guide the last few soldiers out the right side door, including one who was still hooked up to the left side wire. The aircraft was settling fast, and Harkins was climbing, dragging his parachute behind him. He made the door with the help of the colonel, and they went out together. Harkins felt the heat of the fire on the right wing singe his face, and then his parachute opened with a snap.

He saw that he and the colonel were going to land in the sea, although the colonel was working the risers of his parachute to swing him back toward the beach. Harkins's big emergency chute wasn't really maneuverable, so he just floated down. He turned and watched the C-141 roll over gracefully, burning all along the right side, and plunge into the sea. He watched in vain for a final parachute.

⇋18⇋

USS *Inchon*, 0510 GMT (0610 Local)

Lieutenant Colonel Loonfeather put the handset down and looked at the clear plastic status board in front of him. The board had a large plan of Uqba ben Nafi Air Base on it. Information received from the various elements of the airborne assault as to their location and situation was plotted by sailors monitoring the various radio nets. The sailors wrote backwards from behind the board, or represented different units with self-adhering plastic symbols.

"How does it look, Rufus?" asked Colonel Brimmer quietly.

"Well, it's fucked up, Bob, but fortunately the Libyans seem to be waking up slowly. We've lost one aircraft, and I'm afraid we may have lost the task force commander. Major Donahue thinks maybe the last ten or fifteen troops in the lead aircraft landed beyond the drop zone, but he has no communication with them. Unfortunately, that group seems to include the naval gunfire spotting officer, though we've collected his sergeant. We've relayed to him the information about the one- or two-company tank force we saw in the satellite photos, and he's talking to the battleship."

"We've sent two flights of Cobras to check that out," said Colonel Brimmer.

"Pray they don't have another fucking ZSU," barked Loonfeather.

"How come we didn't know about those?" asked Brimmer.

"We never saw them in any of the photographs. Damn!"

Loonfeather pushed the charts and photographs off his console. "We're lucky, in retrospect, that the SEALs spotted the first one and ended up in position to get both."

"Well, if the Cobras get shot at, they can back off and spot for the battleship."

"Yeah, if the Libyans don't reach the runway before I get my Sheridans down and moving."

"How long for that?"

"The aircraft just crossed the final phase line. The first vehicle should be on the ground in less than two minutes."

Lieutenant Brown hit the ground hard, and he was pretty sure his left ankle was broken. It had seemed that his reserve parachute had barely deployed before he bounced off the side of a tall palm tree and crashed into dense bushes. He could see straight up, but not to the sides. To the south of him he could hear voices shouting in a language he assumed to be Arabic, and the roar of many heavy diesel engines.

I'm in the middle of the old golf course, he thought, and in the middle of a major formation of tanks. I've got to find someone with a radio and call for fire before those tanks can move out.

He untaped and unclipped the Dragon and set it in front of him. He never had an opportunity to release it to dangle beneath him during his rapid descent, and that had assured his broken ankle. He worked the bolt of his M-16, chambering a round. He heard movement in the bushes to his left and pressed himself against the bole of the palm tree.

"Hey, Lieutenant! Lieutenant Brown! It's Links!"

Links! Links had a radio! "Over here, Links, by the tree!"

Links slipped into the brush and sat beside Brown. He was panting from exertion. "Jesus, Lieutenant, I saw you come down. I landed about fifty meters east, practically on top of a camouflaged tent!"

"Is your radio working?"

"Yeah. I got a quick radio check with Sergeant Bright.

He's over on the other side of the airfield, where we were supposed to land."

Brown spread the plan of the air base on the ground. It had a fine grid overlay for precise spotting. A warship's inertial navigation computer could calculate the ship's position relative to any point on the plan, and relay that information directly to the gunfire-control computer. Brown motioned Links closer. "Show me exactly where we are."

"OK. See this road that curves off to the south? We're in a depression—that should be it." Links pointed to a rough oval of contour lines. "All this immediate area is overgrown, and it's crawling with tanks."

"What are the tanks doing?"

"They're mostly just starting up. Some have formed up alongside the road. There are a lot of people running around, waving their arms and yelling, sir. Looks like a regular army early reveille clusterfuck, sir."

Lieutenant Brown smiled despite his pain. "Their officers probably slept in some nice dry quarters. OK, call Sergeant Bright on the company command net and tell him where we are. Make it point three-four-niner-slash-one-four-one. Then shift over to spot net and call Big Bang for me."

"We goin' to work right here, sir?"

"Yeah. We got to bust up these tanks before they move out."

"We're kind of in the middle of their AO, sir."

"I know, Links, and I have a broken ankle. Call us in, then help me get out to where I can see."

"Aye, aye, sir." Links began talking into the radio.

Brown stood slowly. His ankle hurt like hell; he felt he could walk on it, but not far. As soon as he could reach a vantage point, he would take Links's radio and tell the RTO to take off.

"OK, Lieutenant. The sergeant's doing a prespot for some tanks south of the airfield. Big Bang is on."

Big Bang was Naval Gunfire Control on *New Jersey*. Brown

took the handset. "Big Bang, this is Flashlight Six. Request immediate fire on point three-four-niner-slash-one-four-one. Target is concentration of tanks, over."

"This is Big Bang. I'm giving you Stonewall and Steel Gage. Talk to them, out."

Links led Brown through a hole in the brush and up out of the depression. Lying in dry grass, they could see tanks and smaller vehicles crawling out of camouflaged positions and forming up on both sides of the road. Officers, both Russian and Libyan, gestured and shouted. The shouting was clearly audible. Brown estimated the nearest tanks were roughly fifty meters away.

"OK, Links, give me the radio and take off."

"What the fuck, sir?"

"Links, I'm calling for fire on this position. I can't run; you can. Try to make the beach; you'll be spotted."

"I ain't gonna di-di and leave you here, sir."

"There's no sense both of us getting killed. Anyway, that's an order, Marine."

Links took off the radio pack and set it beside the officer. "Good luck, sir," he said, backing away slowly. The lieutenant was already talking on the radio.

Brown called the two destroyers, *Adams* (Stonewall) and *King* (Steel Gage), and set up the shoot. Both were in position. Brown asked for immediate fire.

"Flashlight, Stonewall. Be advised that we are under a lift-fire order. The Air Force has eight aircraft inside controlled airspace dropping cargo."

Damn! Brown felt himself near panic. "Stonewall, I need that fire! These tanks are about ready to roll!"

Captain Maxwell "Blue Max" Blumenthal, USAF, had his aircraft commander's seat reclined as far as it would go, so he could sight over the top of the instrument panel of the C-141 at the rapidly approaching airfield. His co-pilot, First Lieutenant Horace Wiley, leaned forward and watched the ground hurtling by forty feet below the aircraft with increasing anxiety. Blumenthal held the yoke lightly in both hands, adjusting to the tiny but sickening bumps caused by the unevenness of the ground effect. He had his dark visor down and locked, and was trying not to think of crashing. A lazy grin split his face below the visor. "Airspeed," he said, not wanting to look at the gauges for even a second.

"One hundred knots," said Wiley, his voice constricted. "Jesus, Max, we are practically in the scrub."

"Don't look out, Ace, if it bothers you. Is the one-eight bird still on us?"

"Tight formation," said Wiley. "Twenty meters off the right wing."

Blumenthal gave the yoke a tiny twist to the right. The runway slid away to the left as he lined the bird up on the taxiway to the north of it. "Everything ready in the back?"

"Sergeant Gaynor says ramp is down, drogue chute deployed."

"OK. Stay on the intercom with him. As soon as we cross the airfield endline, tell him to punch it out."

"Jesus, Max, why can't we just lay it down on the runway?" Wiley's voice whined, which irritated Blue Max despite his concentration.

"We the first, because we the best, Ace. Each later bird has a LAPES lane further south, easier." Max could see people running around on the runway, and tall palm trees at the far end. Steady, Max, he thought, grinding his teeth behind the smile. Steady.

The numbers "29" were clearly visible at the end of the runway. Max eased the yoke forward, and the giant aircraft descended. "Ninety knots. Jesus, Max!" whispered Wiley.

"Relax. Blue Max can fly. Just be ready to give me take-off power when I call for it, and then to suck the wheels and flaps."

"Right, Max." Ace's voice was a harsh croak.

The end of the taxiway rushed up and under the aircraft. Max flared as if to land. "Now, Ace!"

"Cut it loose!" screamed the co-pilot into the intercom.

The aircraft's nose lurched suddenly upward, and the stall-warning horn bleated loudly. Max pushed the yoke forward, forcing the nose down toward the runway. "Takeoff power!"

Wiley pushed the four throttles forward as hard as he could. The engine noise behind him rose to a scream, but painfully slowly. "Loadmaster says clean away!"

"Airspeed!"

"One-fifteen! Coming up!" Wiley watched buildings flash by above the right wing. "One twenty-five."

Should be enough, thought Blumenthal, pulling the sluggish yoke slowly toward his chest. Come *on*, big girl!

"Positive rate of climb. Trees, Max!"

"No-o-o problem. Suck the wheels! Reduce flaps to forty percent!"

Wiley retraced the landing gear and reset the flaps. "Gear up, flaps forty percent!"

"Where is the one-eight bird?"

Wiley craned his neck right and aft. "Higher than us, and turning away north. He's OK."

Max nodded, babying the yoke, feeling the full power of the jet engines push them higher and faster, away from the awful airstrip. The bird climbed steadily and turned toward the Mediterranean. Max eased the throttles, let out his breath, and switched his headset to intercom. "Sergeant Gaynor! You get that tank out good?"

"Slicker than shit off a shiny shovel, Cap. The one-eight bird dropped his right next to ours. The tankers are already swarming all over them."

"Good. Close the ramp. Retract the flaps, Ace. I got me a taste for some Spanish brandy." Blue Max raised his visor and looked across at his copilot. "Think you can climb us back to economical cruise and fly us to Torrejon, Lieutenant?"

"I got her, Max." Wiley tried to relax his fingers on the yoke.

"Good. I am going to take a little nap, so you fly nice and smooth, Ace."

"Yes, sir."

Blumenthal closed his eyes, still smiling. Blue Max could fly.

"Flashlight, Stonewall. The first aircraft have made their drop. There will be three more groups of two. Hang on four to six minutes, Flashlight."

Brown looked at the tanks through the grass. A Russian officer was standing on the turret of the lead T-72, his hands on his waist. He pointed, and tanks formed behind him and moved to the road. I have to hold these guys up, thought Brown. He picked up the Dragon as two air force C-141s screamed overhead at full power, climbing and banking steeply over the sea. The tank crews simply stared at them in wonder. They'll shoot at the next planes, thought Brown. He stared at the Dragon canister, hoping to find instructions as to how to fire the thing.

"You don't know how to fire that, do you, sir?"

Brown turned to find Links kneeling beside him. "Do you, Links?"

"Jeez, sir, I am a fucking *marine*."

Links looked so offended Brown laughed. "All right, if you can't take orders like a marine, let's see you fight like one. Hit that tank with the officer standing on the turret."

"It's too close, sir. The Dragon has to run a couple hundred meters before it will arm." Links picked up his radio and the Dragon, then grabbed Lieutenant Brown's pack harness and pulled him upright. "I found a spot, sir, just across this holler. We'll be able to correct fire, and we'll be far enough away to pot that lead tank."

Two more C-141s climbed out over the golf course. Tank machine guns opened up, and Brown saw the flash and smoke trail of a SA-7 missile, but the aircraft flew on.

"We got time, sir, so let's go." Brown nodded and leaned on Links's shoulder, fighting the pain as they hobbled together back down into the depression and up the other side.

Major Donahue could see order coming out of the confusion of the jump. From his temporary command post in a revetment just to the west of the diagonal taxiway that connected the two runways, he watched as squad sergeants popped colored smoke grenades and blew whistles, and squads formed. Soldiers stripped off parachutes and ran back onto the runway to assist injured comrades. Serious casualties were taken to medics assembled in a revetment 100 meters east of the CP, already marked with a red cross.

Squads formed into platoons and checked numbers and equipment. Major Donahue wished for a jeep, but none had been provided, so he got all his information, other than what he could see, by radio. The company command net crackled. Major Donahue watched as one of the tank commander sergeants helped Lieutenant Baird, hopping and favoring an ankle, to a revetment east of the diagonal taxiway, where the Sheridan crews had agreed to assemble. Good thing he'll be riding, thought the major. Blue smoke curled from a grenade, and Donahue could see the tankers gathering, but the cavalry was the cavalry, so Donahue wasn't surprised when Sgt. Matthew Tucker pulled a battered bugle from his pack and blew the call for assembly.

All eight Sheridan crews rushed from their assembly point in the revetment to the two tanks which had skidded to a stop, shrouded by dust, not fifteen meters apart but further back on the runway than planned. The second pair of C-141s was fast approaching, seeming to crawl through the dirt and scrub rather than fly over it. Spec 4 Calandra reached the near tank and began cutting away the nylon lashings. The straps were so tight that they yielded instantly to the sharp shroud-cutter knives. First Lieutenant Connelly climbed over the track and began cutting away and throwing off the cardboard around the gun and the tank commander's hatch. Private Huckins dropped through the driver's hatch and started the engine. Private Morrow climbed on top of the tank and opened his loader's hatch, then dropped below to pull the heavy HEAT rounds out of their storage rings and stack them around his feet. Connelly unstrapped the fifty caliber machine gun and pinned it into its mounting at the tank commander's position. Calandra climbed up and stepped all over Morrow to get into his gunner's seat. Calandra unshipped the nine-foot and the twelve-foot radio antennas and passed them up to Lieutenant Connelly, who crawled out and fixed them in their mountings on the left upper surface of the turret. Calandra powered up the turret and the radios as Connelly slid back into his tank commander's cupola.

Sergeant Burnside yelled up from the runway. "You are all cut loose, Lieutenant, you are good to go."

"Drive it, Huckins. Along the taxiway and down to the far end," said Connelly into his helmet mike.

The tank lurched, then moved off steadily from the aluminum and cardboard pallet. "Kick it, Huckins," said Lieutenant Connelly, feeling the adrenalin rise as the Sheridan picked up speed. To his right, he saw Lieutenant Baird's tank belch blue smoke and drive off toward the revetments to the north.

"Major! I have Black Widow on Tactical! The SEALs in the control tower report tanks emerging from trees in the golf course," said Stevens, one of the major's four RTOs.

"Estimate of strength?"

Stevens's reply was drowned by the third pair of C-141s LAPESing out Sheridans. One of the vehicles released much too high by a nervous pilot, landed nose down and flipped over. Donahue winced. The first four had come out cleanly, and their crews were already cutting the nylon straps and stripping off the heavy cardboard padding, ignoring the danger of having the next Sheridan dropped on top of them.

"He says he can only see the front of the column, sir. T-72s."

"Calloway!" the major bellowed at the big lieutenant who had first platoon.

"Sir!" said Calloway, running across the apron.

"You about formed up?"

"One missing, sir. I think he's in the aid station."

"OK. Take your people and secure the area around the Operations Building. Get some men up into that control tower with Dragons and machine guns. Lots of Dragons; the Navy sees tanks approaching from the west."

"Yes, sir!" Calloway sprinted across the apron, gesturing for his men to follow.

Where the fuck are the tanks from the south? wondered Donahue, looking across runway 11/29, where thick smoke from the battleship shells continued to blow inland.

Hooper opened the doors of the Operations Building and stepped onto the tarmac. Soldiers in small groups were approaching the building, moving in short rushes. I hope these hyped-up paratroops don't shoot *me*, he thought, a little queasy, thinking it a distinct possibility. I hope these guys were told SEALs wear black uniforms in night operations.

Hooper stood in the doorway, visor up, hands on hips and carbine slung from his shoulder, muzzle down. Soldiers stopped three meters away, not really covering him with their weapons, but not far from it. "Hi, guys! What kept you?" said Hooper smiling.

"Hey, Lieutenant!" called the nearest soldier, a thin black man who looked both mean and scared.

A much larger black man with "Calloway" over his pocket and no rank devices ran up and stopped in front of Hooper. "You Black Widow?"

"Yes. Actually, I'm Commander Philip Hooper, U.S. Navy."

"Good," the man smiled a little. "I'm Kestrel—er, Lieutenant Calloway, sir. Is this building secure?"

"It is. Please remind your men that everyone in the building is either a friend or a prisoner."

"Yeah. Chill out, guys. We need to get up to the tower. There's a tank column coming."

Hooper felt himself reddening at the man's abruptness. We told you about those tanks, asshole, he thought, but suppressed it. "The only access is through the building and up an iron staircase on the outside of the back wall."

"Good. First squad, second squad! Through the building, then up the stairs outside! Set up Dragon and machine gun positions!" Now the lieutenant smiled a little more. "We'll have you out of here in no time, Commander!"

Hooper turned and walked back into the main room. The progress of First Squad had been arrested by the soldiers gawking at the trim, obviously female form of Leah Rabin. "Right on through and out the back, boys," said Hooper evenly.

"We in the wrong service," commented a Hispanic-looking sergeant as he resumed trotting toward the rear of the building.

"Stuart?" said Hooper, pressing his helmet mike key.

"Yes, Hoop," said Stuart from his spot point on the roof.

"There's an army on its way up to you. I think it's ours."

Stuart laughed. "Hey, Hoop? The ANGLICO officer just blew away the lead tank with a Dragon. He has two 'cans' for fire as soon as the Air Force is clear."

The building shook as the last two aircraft climbed out overhead. Hooper chuckled. "William, please make sure our dog-faced *guests* have a good view of the *righteous* way to break up a tank column."

"Aye, Hoop!"

Hooper grinned broadly. We'll have you out of here in no time, Commander, indeed. Shee-ut.

Jason Brown had watched the Dragon all the way from the launcher on Links's shoulder to its target. It looked like a tiny yellow fireball, whiffling like a badminton shuttlecock as Links held the launcher sight on the target. When it hit the tank at the base of its turret, there was a bright flash as the round detonated; then the tank seemed to explode from pressure within. The Russian officer was thrown, cartwheeling, sixty feet in the air. The T-72 slumped on a broken track, and the place where the turret had been boiled with red flame and black smoke.

Brown keyed the handset for the destroyers. *Adams* had spot communications for both ships. "Stonewall, Flashlight Six. We have just kicked over the hornet's nest. How long for fire?"

"The last two aircraft should be pushing out their cargo about now, Flashlight. What can you see of the target?"

"My RTO just bounced the lead tank with a Dragon. Two of the tanks are pointing their guns in this general direction—shit!" Brown pushed his face into the dirt as the number two tank fired a cannon shell over his head. "They're shooting at us now, Stonewall." Brown fought for control of his voice, which seemed to have gone up a full octave.

"Stand by," said Stonewall. The final pair of C-141s climbed out overhead. The tank that had fired and a smaller vehicle that Brown identified as a BMP-76 turned and started toward Brown and Links's position. The tank fired again, the shell screaming overhead.

"Time to di-di-mau, as in fuck *off*, sir!" shouted Links urgently.

"Flashlight, Stonewall. Shots in the air, one H-E and one smoke from each ship. Spot if you can, over."

"Roger, over." Brown turned to Links, "Take off, man! I can't run. You have done well; get back to the beach!"

"Shit," said Links. The word sounded strangely final.

Brown heard the fluttering, low-pitched roar of the incoming shells. He looked quickly through the spotting binoculars. "A flash of H-E and a red smoke is long, Stonewall. Drop two hundred, line is good. Yellow, drop fifty, right fifty for center spot. Shoot the box around that."

"Roger, Flashlight, spot is in. Stand by."

"Negative stand by, Stonewall. Fire for effect. We'll be moving, or dead. Flashlight out."

Links slung the radio and pulled Lieutenant Brown to his feet. The BMP fired its 73mm cannon into the trees to their left. Brown found he could run pretty well after all.

⇋19⇋
Hill 10, two kilometers south of Uqba ben Nafi

Colonel Asimov shouted and cursed and even kicked one sleepy Libyan trooper, trying to get his task force moving. The Libyan officers and non-coms did little to help. These black-asses are scared shitless from the shelling, he thought, and those shells were landing at least fifteen hundred meters away. Nonetheless, Asimov and his four junior officers had most of the vehicles running and the troops assembled and mounted in the vehicles and nearly ready to move. The camp would just be left; there wasn't time to strike it.

Asimov gave his final instructions to the Libyan company and platoon commanders, who nodded without enthusiasm and returned to their units. Asimov surmised from their sullen expressions that if he and his Russian advisory team were not here, the whole force would soon be heading due south and wouldn't stop until they reached the desert base at Gharyan, eighty kilometers away.

Asimov had command of the largest of the task forces Colonel Zharkov had established. He had three full companies of T-72 tanks, thirty in all, two platoons of BMPs equipped as scout vehicles, and a company of motorized infantry riding in open trucks and BTRs. His location, at the intersection of two tracks, one leading almost directly to the air base perimeter fence and the other leading toward Tripoli to the west, had been selected by Zharkov so that the force could attack any American force that landed directly on the base, or could interpose itself between the base and an airborne landing in the open country to the south.

The reports he had been getting from Russian officers on the base were confused and conflicting, but what was emerging was that a fairly large airborne landing was taking place on the airfield itself, and that he would have to get his task force onto the base as soon as possible to engage the Americans. He had to get into close contact before his task force was located in the open by American attack aircraft.

Asimov watched with something approaching satisfaction as two companies of tanks, a squad of three BMPs, and the infantry company moved off west, traveling on the track and through the barley stubble in the fields on either side of it. Rows of tall date palms lined the track and divided the fields, offering some concealment from aircraft. The southernmost column of tanks began making smoke, which drifted over the whole formation in the offshore breeze. Major Kirov rode in his command tank near the middle of the formation, and reminded the Libyan commanders via the command net to keep the vehicles spread out at proper intervals.

Kirov was to move west, then attack from a broad front along the base of runway 03/21. His orders were to suppress American fire, prevent the Americans from evacuating their hostages, and then await instructions.

Asimov would command the second element, which, though smaller, would be more maneuverable without infantry. With one company of tanks and the second BMP platoon, Asimov would proceed along the northerly track, breaching the base perimeter near the eastern end of runway 11/29, then attack in a northwesterly direction, giving heavy suppressive supporting fire to Kirov's tanks and infantry, should they need to advance. Even with the poor quality of the Libyan officers, the overwhelming superiority of Asimov's task force should quickly overwhelm any force the Americans could possibly have parachuted in. The troops themselves were from the elite Jihad Regiment, and their fighting spirit, at least, was quite good.

Asimov climbed into the commander's hatch and gave the signal to move out. The group, in spread formation, started north at twenty kilometers an hour. They would be in position to attack in six minutes. Asimov hoped that Major Gurevich and his reinforced tank company, coming in from the ruined golf course, wouldn't finish the battle before Asimov could bring his power to bear.

⇋20⇌
Washington, 0513 GMT (0013 Local)

The telephone on the console in front of the Secretary of State buzzed and lit up. Henry Holt listened to the White House operator, one subbasement below the situation room. "Mr. Secretary, we have Ambassador Dobrynin."

The Secretary frowned. He had been caught up in the reports coming in from the battle area, and forgot that he had put in a call to give the Soviet Ambassador formal notification of the commencement of military action. He placed that call fifteen minutes ago, and at this hour, he expected Dobrynin to be in his residence and immediately available to the American Secretary of State. "Put him through, please, operator." There was a series of electronic tones and the Russian Ambassador came on the line.

"Good evening, Henry," said the Ambassador.

His voice sounds tense, thought Holt. Might as well make this formal. "Good evening, Mr. Ambassador. The President wishes you to inform your government that the United States has begun a limited military action in Libya. The sole purpose of the action is to effect the freedom of United States citizens held on the air base at Uqba ben Nafi, and will be confined to the area of the air base, although limited strikes may occur against other military targets in Libya to assure the safe withdrawal of our forces."

"Oh, God, Henry!"

The Secretary surged on, ignoring the Russian's outcry. "The President wishes to emphasize that the United States recognizes Soviet interests in Libya and that our limited operation is not intended to threaten them in any way."

The Ambassador, seated at his desk in the small study next to his bedroom, took off his glasses and polished them on the lapel of his silk dressing gown. How to say this, he thought. "Henry, the General Secretary has died. Minutes ago, in his dacha."

"My God, Anatoli! You have our deepest sympathies, of course."

"Henry, how you handle your operation in Libya could cast a *strong* influence on the makeup of the new leadership of the party and the government!"

Holt let his breath out slowly. "I think I understand, Anatoli."

"Henry, you *must* understand! Pictures of dead Russian soldiers, or Russian prisoners guarded by grinning American soldiers appearing on Soviet TV could—encourage—certain elements who do not favor the improvement of relations between our two governments."

"Are you telling me there are significant *Soviet* units on that air base, Anatoli?"

How much can I tell him? thought the Russian. He knew Doryatkin's plan to rescue the hostages with a Russian unit, and he suspected Nevsky's intent to provoke a confrontation, but he had no idea just how. "Henry, it's difficult—"

"Anatoli, we are right now running a very complex operation in Libya, an operation made all the more dangerous because you have set Baruni up with so many sophisticated weapons! Surely you realize that American casualties inflicted by Russians will make it even harder for us to move toward accommodation with the Soviet Union."

"Of course. Henry, there may be—and I really don't know for sure, yet—a Soviet unit, a small one, somewhere on that base, which was going to try to rescue your hostages from the Abu Salaam faction."

"Will they fight alongside the Libyans?"

Dobrynin winced. What was Nevsky's plan? "Not unless they are attacked, Henry. Maybe the Libyans won't fight, anyway."

"They are fighting, Anatoli. With Russian weapons and, we believe, Russian officers."

"Henry, please counsel restraint. You and I have worked hard together to bring our two peoples closer!" The Russian's voice carried uncharacteristic emotion.

Mother of God, thought the Secretary. "Try to communicate with your soldiers in Libya, Anatoli. Try to get us some more information."

"I will try, Henry."

"There is very little time."

"I know. Good-bye, Henry."

"Good-bye." Holt put the phone down quickly and stood up. "Mr. President, there is a new problem."

⇋21⇌

Uqba ben Nafi, 0515 GMT (0615 Local)

Stuart watched from the roof of the Operations Building as the gunfire from *Adams* and *King* chewed up the armored column forming on the road from the golf course. He had been monitoring spot net and had taken the spot when he heard Flashlight Six go off the air. I hope that brave man got out, he thought.

The three-minute hailstorm of high-explosive shells, spread by the destroyers' computers over an area two hundred meters along the road and fifty meters on either side of it, had destroyed or disabled every vehicle in Stuart's view, including two that had tried to move off to the south. Stuart's only spot had turned both the latter vehicles into boiling cauldrons of flame and greasy smoke. The overpressure from the gunfire had also blown out every unbroken window in the Operations Building, and several soldiers who had not heeded warnings to get down and cover up had been cut.

"Stonewall, Black Widow. Cease fire, clear your guns, and stand by, over."

Four more rounds exploded among the ruined hulks and scorched bodies. "Black Widow, Stonewall. My guns are clear, standing by."

"Roger. Good shooting. Black Widow, out." Stuart stood and stretched. After a moment's hesitation, Lieutenant Calloway got up and looked out at the burning vehicles. "Shit, man, I climbed all those stairs for nothing." He sounded pissed off, but he was smiling.

Stuart smiled. "You going down to take a look? That column came from north, where we couldn't see them."

"Yeah, we'll send out a recon patrol. I just squared that with Major Donahue."

"OK," said Stuart. "Good luck, and be careful."

"Yo. See you later, Navy."

Two vehicles, the tank and the BMP who had gone after Lieutenant Brown and Corporal Links, had escaped the gunfire. They were now moving slowly east on a narrow lane between rows of barracks north of the battle, stared at as they went by Libyan civilians and military personnel who normally worked on the base. The sergeant commanding the tank, Abdul Hasaffi, was scared, and ashamed, and angry. Give me another shot at these American murderers, he prayed.

Eight AH-1T Sea Cobra gunships, from Marine Attack Helicopter Squadron 143 (HMA-143), launched from *Saipan,* crossed the coast at a thousand feet of altitude and headed south. They stayed above the flight path of the air force transports until they were well south of the air base, then broke into flights of two and gained more altitude to look for the Libyan tank formation, which had been seen in the satellite photos taken before dawn. The sun was now red and huge on the horizon, and shadows thrown by date palms and citrus groves seemed miles long and very deep.

First contact with the Libyans was made by 1st Lt. Billy Dynan, flying tail number 103. His gunner, seated in front of him down in the nose, had spotted dust trails, pinkish in the morning sun. Billy Dynan made a wide circle to the south and counted eight black tracked vehicles moving north in the shadows of a row of date palms. He pressed the white button on the control stick of the Cobra, which keyed the radio microphone.

"Viper Flight, this is Viper One-Oh-Three. Eight tanks moving north on the road near intersections of grids one-zero and one-two. Tall row of date palms to the east. Converge on me, over."

Each Cobra was armed with one three-barreled 20mm Vulcan cannon, two pods, each carrying seven 2.75-inch rockets, and four TOW antitank missiles. The patrol order gave the flight commanders the option of either attacking or standing off and calling in naval gunfire. The pilots preferred to attack. The attack plan called for two Cobras to position themselves on either flank of the tank column to engage specific vehicles with the wire-guided TOW missiles, while four more conducted rocket attacks from the rear of the formation. The rocket attacks, destructive in themselves, were also intended to protect the TOW-firing Cobras, since they had to stay relatively still while the gunner guided each missile to its target.

Colonel Asimov felt the beat of the helicopter rotors through the noise of the tank engines. He shouted into his microphone for the tank commanders to man their antiaircraft machine guns, and for each BMP to get a man ready with an SA-7 missile. Asimov had flown in helicopters in Afghanistan, as had Lieutenant Malenkov, who commanded the BMPs, and neither had any illusions about the vulnerability of helicopters to ground fire.

Viper 103 and 100 dove toward the tanks from the west. 103's gunner fired the first TOW while the Cobra was still descending. The missile roared away from its tube, rose a little, then streaked toward its target, a medium tank. The gunner adjusted the optical sight attached to his helmet and centered the tank in the cross hairs. The missile pulled two coils of fine wire behind it as it flew, connected to the helicopter and its computer. When the gunner moved his head to keep the target centered in the sight, the movement was transmitted to the computer by cables running from his hel-

met. The computer sent these movements as corrections to
the missile along the fine wires.

Asimov saw the helicopters hovering out to the left of
the column, 3,000 meters away and out of machine gun range.
They wouldn't hover like that unless they were firing wire-
guided missiles, he thought. He trained the turret of his
tank out left and ordered his gunner to put H-E frag shells
in the loading tray. He shouted into his microphone for other
tanks to do the same, then squeezed the green trigger that
loaded the gun and immediately the red trigger that fired
it.

Lieutenant Malenkov's BMP driver slewed his vehicle
out of line and reversed it into a deep shadow beneath a
clump of date palms. Malenkov ordered his other two scouts
to speed up and spread out in front of the tanks. The rear
hatch of Malenkov's BMP opened and a Libyan soldier
emerged, carrying an SA-7 antiaircraft missile and its gripstock. "Give me that," said Malenkov. The soldier disappeared inside the vehicle to get another missile. Malenkov
checked that the missile's canister was correctly attached to
the gripstock. He heard the American helicopters approaching
rapidly from the south.

Swinging around to attack the targets from the south,
Viper 106 and 108 flew thirty meters off the ground as they
chased the rapidly dispersing tanks. The two Cobras flew
in formation, with Six above and slightly behind Eight. The
gunners fired the 2.75-inch rockets, alternating HEAT and
fléchette antipersonnel rounds at the tanks as they passed,
then firing the cannons. Gomez, the gunner on Viper 106,
watched as his cannon, firing thirteen rounds per second,
opened up one of the smaller tanks like a zipper. Then he
saw two rockets strike a larger tank, sending the turret spinning into the air as the tank erupted with flame.

Viper 106 and 108 stayed low, circling wide over the

brown fields, waiting for Viper 101 and 105 to make their first run at the still-dispersing targets.

Second Lieutenant Matt Jaeger, flying Viper 101, hovered in the ground effect as his gunner fired the TOW. They were east of the tanks, and Jaeger hoped that the sun rising behind them would make them difficult to see. Viper 105, fifty meters away, had fired a TOW also. Jaeger could not make out any tanks in the long morning shadows, but the gunner kept saying he was locked on. Just hurry up, thought Jaeger, feeling horribly exposed, hanging like a Christmas-tree ball, waiting for a stream of bullets or a missile to shatter his helicopter.

Viper 100 thumbed his mike switch. He was lower and closer to the tanks, and he was watching as they aligned their guns on him and 103. "Three, this is One-Double-Zero. My TOW won't release. I'm pulling up and out; I'll drop back and cover you, over."

"Roger, One-Oh-Oh. Stay close, over." Billy Dynan shifted to intercom and shouted into his microphone. "Shit, Dave! Those tanks are shooting at us!" He saw the flashes of the tanks' cannons as they fired.

Dave Tolliver had his eye stuck into the rubber-protected optic. "Steady, Billy, steady; five seconds!"

A cannon shell burst on the ground in front of the helo, throwing a shower of dirt and metal fragments over the Cobra and throwing the aircraft up and twisting it to the left. The TOW missile, following the movement of the gunner's head, turned left and flew up and then down as Billy pulled collective and tilted the nose forward to gain speed. The TOW exploded in the barley field. "Aw, damn, Billy, you fucked up my shoot!" said the gunner into the intercom.

"Fuck this, man," said Billy, pulling the helo up sharply. "Let's give this to the Fast Movers! These assholes aren't the easy targets we were told about!"

Lieutenant Malenkov set the SA-7 missile on his shoulder and followed the strafing helicopters as they flew overhead. He squeezed the trigger to the first stop and held the helicopter in the optical sight, watching the red light in the center. When the light turned green, the infrared sensor in the missile was locked onto the target, and Malenkov pulled the trigger through to the final stop. The missile roared from the launcher, singeing the back of Malenkov's neck. Malenkov lowered the gripstock and watched as the *Strela* raced toward its slow-moving target. The helicopter disappeared in a flash, and Malenkov watched as the rotor, spinning slowly, fell by itself to the ground.

Matt Jaeger's gunner reported a hit, and Matt saw a bright orange flash between the date palms. Viper 107 reported their missile had impacted a tree. Both helos saw machine gun tracers arcing toward them and agreed to break off and return to the ships, having given the position of the tank formation to High Tor, controller of attack aircraft aboard *Nimitz*. The Viper flight reassembled to the east of the tanks, one helo down and one damaged by machine gun fire, and flew north. The damaged helo crash-landed on the eastern end of the air base as the rest of the flight heard High Tor direct two flights of A-7s to their target.

Colonel Asimov received his damage reports while still on the move. One T-72 destroyed and one crippled by rockets, another lost to a wire-guided missile. One BMP split open by cannon fire. Heavy losses, but the helicopters had been driven off. The Libyans fought rather well, he thought. *I hope the Americans haven't found Kirov.*

"Colonel, this is Malenkov, over."
"Yes, Lieutenant."
"We are sure to be hit again. Suggest we spread out more and speed up, over."

"You go ahead, Malenkov. Find a hull-down position short of the runway, and tell me what you see."

⇋18⇌
USS *Inchon*

Lieutenant Colonel Loonfeather stared at the status board in frustration. The Libyan defense of Uqba ben Nafi was far better organized than he had anticipated, and the reports coming in suggested major Russian involvement in the combat. A patrol sent out by the infantry into the golf course had brought back the papers of a Major Gurevich, and reported several other bodies in Russian uniforms.

One of the RTOs was monitoring the chatter of the helicopter pilots attacking the tank formation south of the base. They heard the pilots estimate the strength of the force at between eight and twenty tanks. That could be the entire force photographed earlier by the reconnaissance satellite, or only a part of it. Since Loonfeather found that pilots tended to exaggerate, he suspected that there was another force out there somewhere among the fields and date palms and citrus orchards, prepared to attack, in *minutes.*

He heard the RTO listening to the helicopters announce that they were breaking off, that they had damaged the column but not stopped it. A flight of A-7s was on its way, warned about the missile threat. Loonfeather made his decision. "Bob, I've got to get in there."

"I know what you're thinking, Rufus, but we need you here. This operation is about to reach its most critical phase."

"Yeah, I know, but this isn't the operation we planned. The Libyans are well set up and reacting better than we expected. We've already been lucky twice, once finding out about the ZSUs before they could have done much more damage, and once by having that gunfire-spotting team end up in the wrong place at the right time to call in the naval gunfire on the tanks coming from the golf course. But everybody is wide awake now, and the tank force approaching from the south could reach the airfield any time. And, as much as I like Major Donahue, he has never commanded anything larger than a company, he's new to the Five-Oh-Deuce, and he has never been in combat."

Brimmer frowned and then shrugged. "Well, Colonel, it's your call. I think we should land the marines without further delay, before those tanks are in a position to shoot at the helos."

"I want to go in in the first wave, and I think you had better have a second company ready, on call." Loonfeather unclipped his lieutenant colonel's oak leaves from the collar of his khaki TW shirt.

"You're going to be a bit conspicuous in that uniform, Rufus."

"I don't have time to change, or at least I hope I don't. I want to go *now*, Bob."

"OK. I'll square it with Flight Ops. At least let us provide you with a flak jacket and a helmet."

"And a weapon, my friend, please."

"Good luck, Rufus. You'll beat them."

"Thanks. I leave you to carry on the more important work here." A wolfish grin split his dark, sharp features.

Brimmer grinned in return. "You lucky bastard!"

⇌23⇌

The first four A-7s from *Nimitz* spotted the Russian-built tanks as the attack aircraft made their run in from the sea. They continued south, to deliver their attack from behind the tanks, hoping to hit lightly armored engine grill doors and fuel cells rather than the heavily protected front slopes and turret faces.

"Stallion Leader to Stallion Flight. Three-Oh-Two and I'll make the first run, Three-Oh-Three and Four to follow."

"Hit 'em hard, Chief," answered Three.

Lieutenant Commander Bruce "Brute" Bowman turned

the A-7 north, checked to see his wingman was in position, and started a shallow dive toward the tanks from an altitude of three thousand feet. The tanks were well spread out, tossing dust plumes behind themselves as they ran away from the center of their maneuver formation. "Two, Leader."

"Right here, Brute."

"I'm going to rocket the two big ones near the tree line on the right. Pick a couple farther left."

"Roger, I have two."

"Let's blast 'em, then drop the CBUs."

Lieutenant Commander Bowman lined up his first target and fired five HEAT-tipped rockets from each underwing pod, feeling the aircraft shudder as they departed. He then raised the nose of the A-7, turned it left, and fired the rest of his rockets at a second tank, watching tracer rounds from the tank's machine gun coming back to him like a cone of red sparks. Brave gunner, thought Bowman as he pulled up over the approximate center of the tank formation and dropped the five hundred–pound Rockeye cluster bomb unit from beneath the right wing, and a split second later, the other CBU from the left. This staggered drop caused the aircraft to yaw and rise as the weight fell away unevenly, but Bowman wanted maximum dispersion, and controlled the aircraft easily.

The CBUs blew apart five hundred feet above the ground, releasing 247 bomblets each, dispersed in an oval cloud fifty meters wide by one hundred meters long. The Rockeye was the antivehicle version of the CBU, and the bomblets were heavy-density steel cases filled with 1.1 pounds of high explosive. On detonation, the bombs would produce steel fragments moving at up to four thousand feet per second, and of sufficient density to penetrate six inches of armor plate. The effect on even heavily armored vehicles was devastating, either blowing off chunks of metal within the tank, which would ricochet through the crew compartment like shrapnel, or by blowing through the hull of the tank and shredding hydraulics, electrical systems, and crew members.

As Bowman and his wingman finished their bombing run, each released two parachute-stabilized magnesium night-illumination flares. These were sometimes effective in decoying heat-seeking SAMs. "Three and Four, this is Leader," said Bowman, savoring his run. "Concentrate on the lead elements, over."

"Roger, Leader. Three and Four coming down."

Asimov watched with a bitter taste in his mouth as the last two American aircraft streaked away, dropping flares behind them. At least they waste their flares, he thought. Asimov's only SAMs were in his armored personnel carriers, and Malenkov was now far in front of the tanks.

This attack had been far more devastating than the last, costing him four tanks destroyed and one stopped with a broken track. Only the rapid dispersal of his force had prevented its total destruction. Asimov's own tank, well back in the formation and close to the tree line, had escaped damage, and he had had a front row seat of the carnage as first rockets and then the diabolical bomblets had rained upon the tanks. He stopped long enough to direct a Libyan captain with a deep gash in his scalp to assemble the surviving crew members to separate and await assistance, then directed his driver and the one other undamaged T-72 to continue up the track to the edge of the long runway, half a kilometer away. He then called Major Kirov. "Kirov, where are you, over?"

"Colonel, we are digging in just south of runway 03/21. The perimeter fence was shredded by the American shelling, and there are many huge craters we can use for fighting positions. Leading elements are in place; some have camouflage nets over them already."

"You haven't been attacked by aircraft?"

"No, Colonel. The helicopters and the fixed-wing aircraft are searching, but mainly to the south of us. We made very good time."

Asimov smiled for the first time since the attacks began. At least *I have got the main body into position.* His own task force had served as a decoy. "Will your positions overlook the airfield, Kirov?"

"Yes, Comrade Colonel. The terrain is ideal, sloping gradually down from the runways and graded areas. We can get our guns to bear, at maximum depression, and still be hull-down."

"Good, Major Kirov, excellent. Continue to improve your position. The main attack will be entirely yours, although we will try to harass the enemy's flank. Have you heard from Major Gurevich's force?"

"Not from him. We heard from one tank, who told us that he and a BTR are the sole survivors."

"Damn! What happened?"

"The tank commander thought naval gunfire."

Shit, thought Asimov, *that will be the next gauntlet we have to run, but we must get* close, *so close to the Americans that they cannot use bombs and naval guns. Then my tanks and infantry will defeat the lightly armed paratroopers and marines. They won't stand a chance against Kirov's twenty tanks!* "Kirov, you cannot wait and shoot; the Americans have landed paratroopers ahead of their marines! You will soon come under attack from aircraft such as have attacked my force. You will have to advance; close with the Americans!"

"Now, Comrade Colonel?" asked Kirov.

"Wait for us, Kirov, if you can, but if you are detected, attack immediately. Your safety lies in closing with the enemy as quickly as possible."

"I understand, Comrade Colonel. We are confident of victory!"

Just get bloody close, thought Asimov grimly. He looked up as the tank slowed and bucked. They were entering the moonscape created by the American naval shelling that had awakened them just before dawn. They were finally on the air base.

⇋24⇌
Uqba ben Nafi, 0525 GMT (0625 Local)

Lieutenant Colonel Loonfeather jumped from the side door of the marine CH-53D Sea Stallion helicopter as it landed in front of the Operations Building. He carried an M-16 in one hand and a map case in the other. Twenty-eight marine riflemen, most carrying Dragons, LAWs, or machine gun belts in addition to their rifles and light packs, filed out after him, running as they landed to positions marked by gesturing, whistle-blowing army Pathfinders. Three more Sea Stallions landed on the apron, disgorging the rest of B Company, 1st of the 6th Marines. Major Donahue met Lieutenant Colonel Loonfeather at the doors of the Operations Building.

"I want you to understand, John, that my being here is in no way a reflection on you," began Colonel Loonfeather. "The situation has changed a hell of a lot since we last went over it."

"Not at all, Colonel. I'm glad to see you," said Major Donahue, smiling stiffly.

Loonfeather looked around quickly, noting machine gun emplacements and riflemen with Dragons dug in or digging in in unpaved areas off the apron, and others filling sandbags to reinforce positions on the tarmac. He could see other positions on the roof of the Operations and other nearby buildings. "Where are the Sheridans, John?"

"Five are spread out in a natural depression at the western end of runway 11/29. Colonel Bowie intended them to be a maneuver force, to oppose any enemy armor breaking through across the runway. Two are set up east, to cover that flank. They're in empty revetments on the north side of runway 11/29, along with mortar squads and Dragons. One flipped over on landing and broke its main gun."

Loonfeather nodded. Seven of eight intact was better than he expected.

"Just how many Libyans do you expect from the south, Colonel?" asked Major Donahue.

He means there had better be a real emergency for me to come loping in and take his command, thought Loonfeather. He resented the question and understood the feeling. "Major, we originally believed we had photographed forty T-72s and twenty-one smaller vehicles, mostly BTRs and a few BMPs. Navy photo recon and your own patrol have counted twenty-two tanks killed and five APCs of all types knocked out, so there's still a major force out there somewhere, redeployed after yesterday's photos were taken and not yet found by aircraft. I can't believe they can be anywhere but south of here."

"Perhaps they have withdrawn. The Navy and marines claim to have given one group to the south a thorough pounding."

"That's possible," conceded Loonfeather. "It's also possible that the shelling from the *New Jersey* and her destroyers buried some of them, in which case we might very well get out of here and never see another enemy tank." But I doubt it, he thought. The clever Russian son of a bitch who hid a tank company and a half in the underbrush of the golf course where we never should have found it would have a maneuver force somewhere. "What are your plans for evacuating, John?"

"The bird you came in on will hop down to the aid station and load up with the injured troopers," replied Major Donahue, pointedly ignoring the notes on his clipboard. "We'll divide the hostages into three groups and put them on the other birds. Once they're clear, we'll assemble all of our forces within this perimeter, and then try to lift them all out in one go. Ten H-53s."

"Good, Major, very good. You carry on with your plan. I want to walk around, get a feel for the place."

⇋25⇌

Leah Rabin kept most of the hostages on the floor of the Operations ready room, while allowing as many as possible to get food and water from the army medics and to make bathroom visits. She moved among the people, encouraging them, telling them they would be leaving soon. She helped organize splinter barricades, made of metal furniture, covered where possible with heavy overcoats. She told each family group to remain together, and had individuals buddy into teams, each member charged with knowing the whereabouts of all his team companions. She lectured, she cajoled, but mostly she just talked, very calmly, smiling often, touching often.

There was a mother with two daughters, one fifteen and the other thirteen. Their father was a chief radar technician on board the destroyer *Adams*. The thirteen-year-old, whose name was Angela, seemed fascinated by Leah and followed her constantly as she continued to organize.

Leah finished moving family groups to positions closer to the foundations of the building, which were made of cinder block and concrete and might afford some protection from small-arms fire. Leah stood back and looked at the tight groups of people, all of whom looked back at her. They seemed cheerful and confident. God, I hope we can get on those helicopters soon, thought Leah as she sat down on the metal desk near the bound form of Abu Salaam.

Little Angela approached the desk, on the side away from the terrorist. Leah smiled and stroked the child's curly blond hair. "Are you and your mother and sister ready to leave in the helicopter, Angela?"

"Yes, Leah. Will you go with us?"

"The officers will tell who goes in which helicopter, Angela."

"What if the Marines and the Army can't get us out?"

"They will get us out, Angela. The helicopters have already landed. Very soon you must join your mother and sister. I am counting on you to make sure they get to the helicopter safely."

"I will. But what if the Libyans come first? I heard a soldier say the Libyans have tanks."

"We will fight. We will defeat them, Angela, and then we will leave."

"We have to fight, too? Not just the men?"

Leah looked at the pretty child, her earnest expression and her innocent blue eyes. How unlike Israeli children, schooled on the never-ending need to defend themselves and their land. "Yes, Angela, if we have to. Women must fight: it is our freedom, our duty, just like the men."

"Will you be here to show us how, Leah?" The child's eyes shone with fear, and with courage overcoming it.

"Yes, Angela. Now, please join your family. We will surely be leaving in a few minutes."

⇋26⇋

Lieutenant Malenkov watched as the four helicopters landed by the cluster of buildings across the runway from his position. His BMP was dug into the face of a shell crater, its 73mm main gun barely a foot above the surface of the runway. Malenkov radioed Colonel Asimov for instructions, but he received no answer. Malenkov had seen the smoke and felt the concussions of the Americans' second attack, and watched as the attack aircraft had turned toward the sea, out of range of his two remaining SAMs. He wondered if Colonel Asimov was even alive.

The third and last BMP of Malenkov's platoon had broken down soon after the two vehicles had left the tanks. Its radiator had been shredded by the American antipersonnel rockets, and the engine had overheated and seized. Malenkov had sent its crew, on foot, to find Major Kirov's force, which also didn't answer the radio.

So it's mine to decide, thought Malenkov, watching the helicopter rotors spinning through the periscope sight of the 73mm cannon. I could be the only force left.

Malenkov looked up at the six Libyan soldiers sprawled in shallow dug-out positions to the left of the vehicle. "Sergeant Hamidi!" he shouted. "Are you ready with the *Strela?*"

Hamidi grinned, showing white teeth against his brown Berber face. He held the SAM-7 over his head and nodded. "Wait for my signal, Hamidi!"

Malenkov ducked down inside the turret, checked that the SAGGER missile was ready, then returned to the periscope. The first of the big helicopters rose from its position near the buildings and flew the short distance to the revetment marked with the red cross, where it hovered. Malenkov took a deep breath and fired the cannon. The BMP bucked. The rocket-assisted, fin-stabilized HEAT round struck the rotor head of the helicopter just as it was about to land. The helicopter fell to earth, twisting violently, and crashed over on its side. Malenkov wouldn't fire again until another lifted off. He hoped to remain undetected.

"Jesus! The helo down by the aid station just got hit!" said Stuart into his helmet radio. He looked below him. Hostages, running crouched over, were being guided to the three turning-up CH-53s on the tarmac. The loud report of the shell striking the helo, followed by the tearing sound of the aircraft crashing, caused all movement to freeze. The marine crew chiefs guiding the hostages quickly turned their charges back toward the Ops Building, then ran for their aircraft.

Loonfeather, who had been halfway up the stairway to the roof of the Ops Building, sprinted the rest of the way to the top, where he flopped beside Stuart. "Hey, my bad medicine pal! Where did that come from?"

Stuart was startled to see Loonfeather, in his khaki shirt and green uniform trousers and tie, but there was no time to question. "No, Colonel. South. I saw nothing, so I guess cannon, rather than missile."

Below them, the three helicopters, without passengers, lifted into the ground effect, wheels barely clear of the runway, pivoted around the axes of their rotors, and headed back out to sea, flying as low as they could.

"Sergeant Hamidi! Fire the missile!" shouted Lieutenant Malenkov.

"Commander Stuart!" said Ricardo, holding the radio handset. "One of the Sheridans says he's spotted a tank on the other side of the runway!"

"Did Major Donahue hear that?" asked Lieutenant Colonel Loonfeather.

"Yes, sir! He's on the net himself. He just said, 'charge!' "

Damn! thought Loonfeather. We need to save the Sheridans for close work. That tank should be given to the naval guns. I'm sorry, John Donahue. Loonfeather motioned urgently to a soldier with a radio on his pack to come to him. "Major Donahue, this is Colonel Loonfeather. I'm going to take command now, John. I want you to manage the perimeter defense."

"Yes, sir," said Major Donahue. He resented being relieved, but at the same time he knew Loonfeather had more experience and knew the plan better. He keyed into the company net. "This is Raptor Six. Colonel Loonfeather has assumed overall command. Colonel Loonfeather is now Raptor Six, out."

Loonfeather switched the radio to the armor net and thumbed his transmit key. "This is Raptor Six. Falcon Blue Leader, fire a round at the enemy tank to mark it, then withdraw pronto. We're calling naval gun."

"Falcon Blue Leader to Raptor Six. Wilco. Blue Two reports the enemy vehicle just fired a SAM."

"Shit. OK, tell him to shoot something at the target that we can see, and get back. I want to call naval gunfire to crater the runway."

"Roger. Blue Leader out."

Loonfeather twisted the selector back to company net. "Donahue, did any hostages board those helos?"

"No, sir, I thought it was too dangerous."

"I concur."

Loonfeather put down the handset. Stuart was talking

on Ricardo's radio. "Stand by, Devastation, over," said Stuart, his face taut. "Colonel, I want to lay some heavy H-E down beyond the end of runway 03/21, back about a klick. Walk it around; see what we scare up."

"I'm not sure how much we want to scare anything up, but do it. I feel a major assault coming, William."

"Yeah. I know." Stuart picked up the handset. "Devastation, this is Black Widow. For effect, now, over."

The three marine CH-53s skimmed along in the ground effect, flying single file directly over the runway. The SA-7 fired by Sergeant Hamidi was guiding on the twin turbines of the helicopter last in line. The helicopters fled toward the safety of their carriers at 180 knots; the missile pursued at close to 900 knots. The missile struck the big helicopter just as it passed over the coast, and the helicopter hit the sea in a burst of spray and then settled on its floats. The aircraft commander and the copilot were killed by metal splinters from the missile's warhead, which showered them from above. The crew chief and both door-gunners got out into the water and inflated their raft.

Sergeant Matthew Tucker sat in the commander's hatch as the Sheridan slowed from forty miles an hour. He pressed the button that activated the stabilizing system for the main gun. "You got him, Tommy?" he spoke into his helmet mike on intercom.

The gunner, Spec 4 Tommy Evans, answered at once. "Yo, Sarge. Got him in the twelve-power setting. Tough shoot, though; he's really low."

"You make the shoot, Tommy. Driver, stop." The Sheridan lurched as Pvt. Marty Grossman, the driver, brought it to an abrupt halt.

"Here goes, everybody." Tommy pressed the trigger. The Sheridan reared up like a colt as the forty-nine-pound HEAT round roared from the barrel.

Sergeant Tucker watched the round explode just short

of the black smudge protruding above the whitish soil. He saw a jet of flame spring from the top of the enemy vehicle and a dark object take flight. Below him he heard the bore evacuator blow like a foghorn. Henry, the loader, struggled to chamber the next round in the awkward screw breech. "Better hurry, guys. I think he launched a SAGGER." Tucker pressed the twin triggers of the .50-caliber M2 machine gun, and guided the tracers onto the tiny target.

"Colonel, this is Kirov. Heavy shellfire is falling in behind me, and there are two light tanks crossing the runway, heading diagonally away from the Operations Building."

They must be looking for Malenkov, with his dead radio, thought Asimov. Kirov had reported the downing of the first helicopter. "Kirov, I am hull-down, east of the two light tanks. I will deal with them. We must close with the Americans, or they will finish us with artillery and air strikes. Launch your attack."

"We are rolling, Comrade Colonel." Kirov switched frequencies and gave the attack order. In case any radios were malfunctioning, he fired two orange smoke grenades as his tank began to move.

Lieutenant Malenkov winced as the machine gun bullets rattled and screamed off the face of the BMP's turret. The turret was about the only part of the vehicle with sufficient armor to resist .50-caliber rounds. The SAGGER missile he had fired had overflown the target before the gunner could control it, and the American light tank was still coming. Because the BMP was tilted up in the crater, he couldn't depress his main gun sufficiently to shoot the American.

I have two choices, he thought bleakly. Back up out of sight and wait for a mortar shell or artillery round to find me, or drive up over the lip of the crater and face the bastard gun to gun. He smiled and pushed the intercom button. "Forward, Ali. Climb us out."

"Blue Two, this is Blue Leader. Break off and return to the revetment, over."

"Hey, Lieutenant, we got this guy!" protested Sergeant Tucker.

"Leave it, Tucker. Naval gunfire incoming," said Lieutenant Baird.

Shit, thought Tucker. "Blue Two, roger," he said into the microphone, then switched to intercom. "We're pulling back. Take a shot if you got one, Tommy."

"He's moving, Matt! He's coming up!"

"Up Tommy," said Henry, signifying that he had loaded the round, closed the breech, and got out of the way of the recoil of the gun.

Tommy watched as the enemy's turret emerged and tilted steeply upward. Then he saw the tracks churning sand. He pressed the trigger on the control stick. "On the way, motherfucker," he breathed. The enemy vehicle erupted in an orange-yellow burst of flame, which gathered itself into a black puff of smoke and was gone.

Private Marty Grossman floored the throttle and pulled the steering bar for a tight left turn. Heavy shells from the ships offshore were already raising clouds of smoke and dust to the south and east. Grossman looked through the periscope as he turned the Sheridan, watching the shell flashes near the end of the runway. He saw two low black silhouettes against the smoke. He thumbed his intercom button. "Sarge! Two tanks, on the runway, to your right!"

Sergeant Tucker pressed the palm switch on his control handle to take control of the turret and gun away from the gunner, and traversed the gun out to the right. He saw the tanks immediately, speeding toward him on the runway. He laid the gun by eye on the right-hand target, released the palm switch, and spoke into the intercom. "Take it, Tommy. Get the right-hand vehicle in the choke reticle for ranging."

"Bringing it down, Sarge. Looks like seventeen hundred meters," said Tommy Evans.

"Good. Marty, step on it. We'll fire on the go." He keyed

the armor net and called Lieutenant Baird, whose Sheridan was two hundred meters in front of him. "Blue Leader, Blue Two. Two tanks, to your right, over."

"Got 'em. You take the one on the right, Two."

"Roger." Tucker keyed the intercom. "Tommy, stay on the one on the right."

"OK, Matt. Range is in, 1,715 meters."

"HEAT, up," said Henry.

Tucker looked up and saw a bright flash from the right tank. "Jesus, Tommy, shoot it!"

The Sheridan rocked as the gun fired and recoiled. "On the way," said Tommy.

Colonel Asimov watched the American tanks turn back toward the north, and waited impatiently for the Libyan gunner to get ready to engage.

"Laser reads 1,712 meters. Gun corrected," said the gunner finally. "Sabot loaded."

"Shoot," said Asimov.

The hypervelocity fin-stabilized sabot round from the 125mm gun of Asimov's tank took exactly one second to traverse the 1,712 meters between the gun and the target. It struck Tucker's Sheridan just aft of the turret, in the engine compartment. The sabot didn't detonate; the shell carried no explosives, it was just an aerodynamically shaped solid dart of extremely dense spent uranium. The kinetic energy of the very heavy projectile traveling at five times the speed of sound simply blew the eighteen-ton Sheridan in half, scattering pieces of track, hull, and the engine over hundreds of yards. Asimov bared his teeth as he traversed his turret to seek the second vehicle. He heard a flat report followed by a louder explosion, and turned to look to his left. He saw his companion tank, its left track and turret gone, burning fiercely. "Hurry up with the loading!" he yelled into the intercom. He raised his head. He thought he could hear something like approaching freight trains above the roaring engine of the tank. He looked up and saw three dark objects, falling together toward him. He began to duck back into the turret, though he knew instantly that it would do no good. Can there really be shells so big you could see them in flight? he thought, crossing himself.

"Henry's neck is broke, Sergeant," said Tommy Evans. "He's dead."

Sergeant Tucker eased to the ground from the shattered Sheridan. His own neck felt twisted, and one shoulder howled with pain while the other was numb. "Bring him out, Tommy. I'll carry him."

Marty Grossman pulled himself up through the driver's hatch at the front of the vehicle. His face was covered with blood from a head wound. "We can all carry him, Matt."

Tucker nodded and rubbed his neck. The runway rocked beneath him as more heavy shells landed to the east. "We better boogie. The last salvo from the battleship was almighty close."

"Good shoot, Devastation," said Stuart, watching as the smoke rose off the runway to the east. Both the burning tank and the moving one had disappeared. "Fill in toward us from the gun line with the secondary battery; the colonel wants runway 11/29 taken out, cratered."

"This is Devastation. Danger Close bearings?"

Stuart gave the coordinates for the front of the army and marine positions, and for the Sheridans off to the west of the main runway. Five-inch shells began exploding on the runway, sending up dust and smoke.

Loonfeather crouched behind Stuart. "What are you shooting in front of us, William?"

"Five-inch old 38-caliber, Rufe. *New Jersey's* secondary battery."

"Why not the sixteens?"

"Can't work 'em that close. Kill us before the Libyans did."

Loonfeather rubbed his chin and closed his eyes, calling

up the image of the plan of the air base and his means to defend it. "Five-inch will need a direct hit to kill a medium tank."

"Probably. Close miss will blow the tracks and the hatches off."

"Hm. I wonder if they're coming at all?"

"You thinking of calling the helos back for the evac?"

"Yes. What do you think?"

"Sir! I have Falcon Red Leader on Armor!" said one of the RTOs Loonfeather had gathered to him.

Loonfeather snatched the handset. Red Leader was Lieutenant Connelly with five Sheridans west of runway 11/29. "Raptor Six, over."

"This is Falcon Red Leader. We can see enemy medium tanks, T-64 or T-72 type, moving across the runway. Also BTR-60s, over."

"This is Raptor Six. If they get through the naval gunfire, they're yours, over."

"The lead tanks are through, Colonel, and making smoke."

"Well, this is why we brought you, Red Leader. We can't use supporting arms any closer. If you don't stop them, it's us with a few Dragons, and then rocks and bayonets."

"Yes, sir! We're *moving*, Colonel!"

"We'll guard this net. Raptor Six, out." Colonel Loonfeather shivered. The worst thing is that we have neither rocks nor bayonets, for all the good they might do.

"Hey Colonel," called Stuart behind his spotting binoculars. "Some are coming through. There are APCs discharging infantry as they come."

"Shit. Can you walk the shells a little closer?"

"Maybe a tad. We'll ignite these wooden buildings alongside us, and maybe this one."

Loonfeather weighed it. At least we should get rid of the infantry. "One more spot, William, then tell the battlewagon to cease fire; I want the Cobras back ASAP."

"Roger, Colonel. Tell Donahue to get his people down. Tell them one more crash and it's all theirs."

Loonfeather talked to Thunder about the gunships as the
last salvos of sixteen- and five-inch naval projectiles roared
overhead. He talked to Donahue and once more to Connelly
as the last close rounds from the battleship hit the runway,
spraying concrete chips and metal fragments back on the
soldiers between the low buildings south of the Operations
Building, and onto the roof of the Operations Building itself.
Loonfeather stood and counted eleven tanks, infantry
bunched behind them, and four BTRs. I planned this formation and I'm fighting it as best I know how, he thought,
and it's all down to lieutenants and sergeants and a few tanks
and a few more brave grunts. All the firepower in the fucking
world, he thought, and they're on us.

Loonfeather looked off to the left of the Operations Building, at the apron in front, which must be held for the evacuation. Mortars began firing, spotted from observers alongside
him on the roof. In front, he heard machine guns open up
and saw the oscillating exhausts of Dragons. The veritable
whites of their eyes.

The front rank of tanks fired as one. The building in
front of them burst into flames and sagged. Loonfeather felt
the Operations Building sway beneath him as cannon fire
roared through below him—multiple prolonged cracks of
many enormous whips. Here and now, he thought. He
switched frequencies again, to Command. "Thunder, this is
Raptor Six. They're on us."

"We know, Rufus," said Colonel Brimmer. "God keep
you."

⇋27⇌
0532 (0632 Local)

Colonel Zharkov watched his men as he monitored Major
Kirov's communications with his tanks. The Maintenance
Building shook as several cannon shells struck the upper
story. The men, who had been lounging around in small
groups, smoking and talking, moved quickly back to their

tanks and armored personnel carriers and climbed inside. Many closed the hatches.

There was a lot of shouting on the tank tactical net, much of it in Arabic, of which Zharkov understood little, but he could hear the fanaticism of the Libyan soldiers. Some were ululating into their microphones like Berber horse cavalrymen as Kirov and his junior officers shouted in vain in Russian to try to restore some discipline. The screams of "Allah'u Aqbar" chilled him; they brought back the horror of Afghanistan.

Zharkov gritted his teeth as more shells struck above him, sending down showers of plaster and glass from broken light bulbs. It's only a matter of time before this building catches fire, he thought.

Captain Suslov appeared at his side. Zharkov quickly briefed him on Kirov's progress. "What will we do, Comrade Colonel?"

"Sit. Wait. This is turning into the bloodbath nobody wanted."

Suslov's face twitched suddenly, as if something the colonel said had startled him. "But Kirov is breaking through! Shouldn't we support him, assure his victory?"

"No, Suslov. Remember, as far as the politicians of the world will tell it, that isn't Kirov's column; he isn't even there. It is a Libyan column. Our orders were to take the hostages and give them to the Americans, to *prevent* a Soviet-American confrontation."

Your orders, thought Suslov, remembering his own.

The Russian lieutenant who had the duty in the office at the end of the maintenance bays ran to Zharkov's tank. He looks thoroughly scared, thought Zharkov. "Comrade Colonel, the Ambassador is calling for you on the secure land line from Tripoli."

Zharkov climbed down and followed the lieutenant back to the office, running crouched as more shells exploded upstairs. He picked up the phone and announced, "Colonel Zharkov."

"Comrade Colonel, this is Ambassador Timkin. We have just had an urgent signal from Moscow, from Doryatkin. The General Secretary has died."

Zharkov didn't speak. The power struggle would now be out in the open.

Timkin continued. "Doryatkin is very concerned about that Spetznaz unit of yours. What is your situation?"

Zharkov briefly explained where he was, and his guesses about the fighting a few hundred meters to the south. "Good, Colonel," said Timkin. "Stay concealed until it is over, if you can. If the Americans are defeated, try to keep the black-asses from butchering all the hostages."

"And if the Americans prevail, Comrade Ambassador?"

"Stay where you are. They aren't likely to search the base, are they?"

"No, I wouldn't think so, but this building is taking fire, and may burn."

"God. Well, if you have to show yourself, try to avoid a fight. Surrender, even."

"That may not be possible. The Americans will probably fire as soon as they see us." I would, he thought bleakly.

"Well, Colonel Zharkov, try to do your best. I am sure you know what is at stake in the, ah, larger arena."

He means Moscow. "I understand, Comrade Ambassador. I had better go and brief my men. However it ends, this battle will be over very quickly."

⇋28⇋
USS *America*

Admiral Bergeron read the message from the high-speed teleprinter link with Washington:

```
0219 0530Z
FLASH
TOP SECRET LIMDIS
FM MILESTONE CINC
TO TOP HAT COMSIXTHFLT
RE FIRE ARROW
```

SOV INFORM FRIENDLY REPEAT FRIENDLY SOV UNIT
ON UBN AIR BASE. US UNITS MUST NOT ENGAGE IF UNIT
CLEARLY IDENT SELF AS SOV VICE LIBYAN. FOR CINC
ROGERS RADM USN.

The admiral handed the message back to the waiting sec-
ond-class radioman. "Make sure this is passed immediately
to Lieutenant Colonel Loonfeather."

"Aye, aye, sir." The radioman ran down the ladder two
flights to Communications and handed the message to an
operator. "Watts, send this right away to Lieutenant Colonel
Loonfeather." He picked up the clipboard from the supervisor's console. "He is, ah, Thunder Two, over on *Inchon*."

"I'll get it right out." Watts took the perforated paper
tape that had been punched out by the teleprinter when
the message had been received, fed it into another machine,
and ran it. *Inchon's* code came back, signifying receipt. Watts
sat back down and put on his headphones, which were tuned
to the army's company net. *Those guys are in it up to their
necks!* he thought.

On *Inchon*, twenty miles away, the Communications
Watch supervisor logged the message, noted it was a Flash,
and called his runner. "Weeks, get this up to Flag Plot and
find a Colonel Loonfeather."

"Right, Chief," said the kid, taking the sealed red top
secret envelope. He went up the ladders to Flag Plot. Officers
and sailors and marines were milling around. Some were
shouting into microphones; others wrote on floor-to-ceiling
plastic boards. Weeks tried to ask a chief petty officer where
to find Colonel Loonfeather, but the chief brushed past him
with a "sorry, sailor." Weeks had been in the Navy only six
months, and he was awed by the commotion and a little
scared. With relief, he spotted a console in the middle of
the compartment with a hand-lettered cardboard sign that
read, "LTC LOONFEATHER USA." Weeks dropped the
red envelope on the vacant console and fled.

Commander Stuart watched as the Libyan tanks concentrated their fire on the control tower and surrounding roof.

Soldiers standing to guide Dragons at the advancing tanks
were being cut down by accurate fire from the machine guns
on the tanks. Stuart was amazed how many tank commanders
were standing in their hatches, firing the heavy 12.7mm
machine guns on the swivel mounts while Army and Marine
sharpshooters tried to shoot them down. The air buzzed and
cracked with small-arms fire and all manner of sounds from
dull thunks to metallic screams as bullets struck and rico-
cheted around Stuart's head.

The large building immediately to the west of the Operations Building was burning furiously. The flames were en-
couraged by an increasing offshore wind as the morning
warmed, blowing the smoke in from the battlefield and obscur-
ing most of it. Stuart thought it unlikely that he would again
be called upon to spot targets for the warships, and he
decided to leave the roof and see if he could be useful down
below.

Hooper and Ricardo were next to him, their faces screwed
into the roof, helmet to helmet. Hooper had been talking
into the handset of Ricardo's radio, but Stuart saw the handset
lying shattered at the end of its cord. He reached and grabbed
Hooper's wrist, and when Hooper looked up, hand-signed
"let's go." Hooper shook his head and twisted his body so
Stuart could see that the SEAL commander's other hand
held a blood-soaked field dressing against Ricardo's neck.
Ricardo's eyes were closed. Stuart pulled his field dressings
from his own pack and pressed them into Hooper's hand.
Hooper's face was a mask of pain as he took the dressings
and mouthed the word "go."

Stuart rose to a crouch and was immediately knocked
flat by the impact of several shells on the side of the building.
He felt the broken glass on the roof bite into his hands and
face as the roof buckled and began to collapse. He slid through
a crevice and tried to hold onto the edge of the torn roof
with his bloody hands. A soldier rolled on top of him and
they both fell heavily to the floor inside the Operations Building. Stuart felt a sharp pain in his back; he had fallen on

his still-slung CAR-15. He sat up and looked at the soldier. The man was dead and looked puzzled.

"Come on, William, let me help you," said Leah Rabin. She helped him to an aid station set up by medical corpsmen who had come with the marines, and got one of them to look at him. The corpsman, a short, smiling black man, hummed while he worked, even though his entire uniform was soaked with blood.

"Might need a few stitches when we get back to the ship, sir, on the hands, but you can go back up through the roof, if you want," said the corpsman with a deep laugh.

"Thanks," said Stuart, patting his face, which felt stiff with bandages. His hands were wrapped like mittens, although the corpsman had thoughtfully left the trigger fingers of both hands free. "Leah, how are the hostages?"

The hostages were huddled in small groups, mostly lying on the floor, surrounded by makeshift barricades of metal furniture. Many had covered themselves with folded metal chairs. Stuart felt that most looked surprisingly confident.

"Once we started taking casualties, several of the hostages took weapons from the wounded and went out into the alleys. These are brave people, William," said Leah softly.

"Any idea of total casualties?"

Leah gestured to a small group of men lying on the floor under gray blankets. A few had their faces covered. "Since the firing became heavy, none have been brought in from outside. I am afraid the worst will come. The Libyans are pressing hard."

"You thought they would run away."

"I really did."

"Well, only a few got through. I think the last close salvo from the *Jersey* knocked down most of their infantry."

"I am sure we can handle the infantry, William. But the tanks are inside the minimum range of the Dragons. Have you ever fought against tanks, William?" Leah's voice was softened with sadness.

"No, I haven't," he admitted.

"Tanks are incredible people-killing machines, William. If a single intact tank reaches this room, everyone in here could die."

Stuart felt chilled. We could still end up with nothing. With worse than nothing. He unslung his carbine. "I'd better get out there in that alley and see if I can help."

"I want to go with you."

Stuart looked at Leah, ready to argue. She was standing, looking at the calm faces of three hostages who appeared to be a mother and two young daughters. There was a sad tenderness in Leah's face. Stuart felt at that moment that he loved her, and he wanted more than anything to keep her from harm, just as she wanted to keep the mother and daughters from harm. "OK," he heard himself saying. His throat was choked with emotion. "Let's go, Captain."

She looked at him, and then she touched his bandaged face. It was all he could do to keep himself from weeping. "No. I will stay here, with them. If there is to be a last stand, the women will make it. It has always been that way." The mother hugged her daughters and cried a little. The girls smiled bravely. "You go, William."

William kissed her cheek. "I'll be back, Leah." He said it loud enough for the hostages to hear. As he stepped out into the alley, he felt a great rage rise in his breast, almost a lust to kill.

⇋29⇌

Major Kirov watched through his periscope as his three lead tanks reached the edge of the runway nearest the Operations Building. Four others had gone across the runway to the east. Two had been knocked out by wire-guided missiles, but two had managed to reach revetments, where Kirov had told them to stay and wait for the final pincer across the apron, once the alleys were forced. Kirov and five more tanks were back fifty meters, keeping up heavy suppressive fire on the positions being maintained on the roof of the Operations Building.

I began my advance from the end of the runway with two tank companies, thought Kirov, and a company of motorized infantry. In an advance of 650 meters, I have lost all of the BTRs, and the infantry has to dismount into this fury of fire. I would tell them to withdraw, but where could they go? Most were now taking what protection they could behind the tanks or the knocked-out BTRs, waiting for the battle to end.

And I have lost nine main battle tanks. Four disappeared in the first fifty meters of advance, blown away by a salvo of enormous shells that hit just as the last tanks crawled from their dugout positions and advanced onto the runway. One tank was damaged and another destroyed in the lighter shelling that followed, and three were lost to those damned wire-guided missiles. Kirov felt sadness fusing into anger. He didn't officially command these men; he didn't even like them, but they were fighting well against everything the Americans could throw, and Kirov wanted them to win.

Kirov spotted three small tracked vehicles as they climbed up onto the west end of runway 11/29, behind his lead elements. He recognized them as American Sheridans by their squat shape and their big-bore, stubby gun launchers, and he felt a thrill of fear. He remembered the light tanks he had seen earlier way down the runway toward Asimov. How could the Americans have got *Sheridans* into the air base? How *many* were they?

Kirov shouted a warning to the lead elements over the tank net radio, then called his own group and gave them the firing bearing. He doubted the lead tanks would hear over their own excited chatter. He squeezed the grip on his control column and took control of the turret and the gun from the gunner. The range computed at just over four hundred meters, point-blank for everyone. The gun had just been fired, so he had to wait precious seconds for the automatic loader to chamber the next round. He watched as the three Sheridans fired together, and cursed as two of his three lead tanks burst into flame. The "Loaded" light in his periscope sight lit up, and he pressed the trigger. The gun bucked and the nearest Sheridan stopped dead, its turret gone. The other two Sheridans immediately reversed and dropped back over the edge of the runway out of sight. "Shit!" shouted Kirov into the microphone. "They have fighting positions off the runway! White Two and Three, turn and go after them! Green Platoon, speed your advance!" White Platoon was Kirov and the two tanks to his left, Green the three tanks on his right.

"Leader, this is White Two. White Two and Three turning to engage."

"I will follow you. Get off the runway!"

"Green Platoon accelerating, Leader."

Damn! We had the Americans in the crushing jaws of my tanks, cursed Kirov to himself. Now we will have to deal with the Sheridans first.

⇋30⇌

Lieutenant Colonel Loonfeather switched from armor to command net. "Thunder, this is Raptor Six. My tanks have engaged; they are my last reserve. Bob, where are my gunships?"

"This is Thunder, Colonel. Four flights of Sea Cobras inbound from five miles out. We had to hold them until the Navy cleared its guns. Two minutes, maybe three."

"I hope my Sheridans can buy that much time. We're looking at enemy tanks barely thirty meters from crashing in, Bob."

"Understood, Rufus. The Snakes are coming."

Loonfeather pounded the radio with frustration as he switched back to armor net.

Lieutenant John Connelly heard on the armor net that Red Four, Five, and Six had destroyed two of the three Libyans before losing Red Six. They would reload and then pop up and shoot again. "Roger, Four. We'll get up and take a shot at the second rank now. Red Two, this is Red Leader. Let's go. I'll take the nearest."

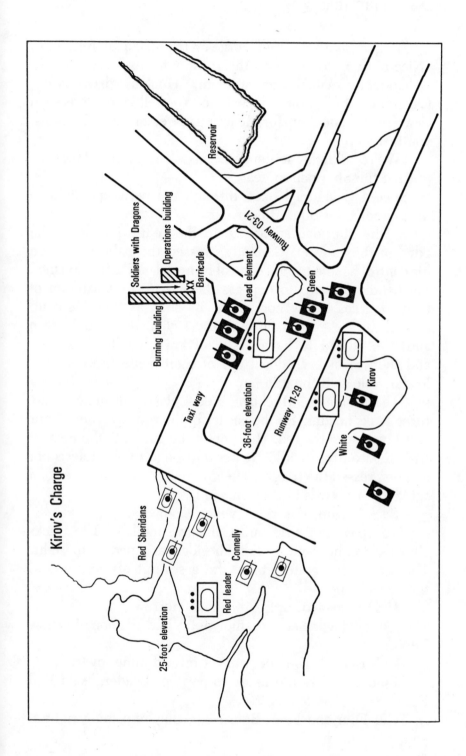

Kirov's Charge

"Roger, Leader," said Sergeant Burnside in Red Two. "Nice of them to be up on the runway for us."

Connelly switched to intercom. "Huckins, drive us up. Calandra, I'll fire from my position. You tell Huckins as soon as we're far enough up for the gun to bare, and then Huckins, you just stop."

"We're rolling, Lieutenant," answered Private Huckins, putting the Sheridan in gear.

Spec 4 Calandra looked through the periscope sight in his gunner's position. "Roger, sir."

As the Sheridan advanced up the gentle incline to the edge of the runway, Connelly pressed the palm switch on his control handle to gain control from Calandra, then pushed the handle forward to depress the gun to its maximum of eight degrees below horizontal. As soon as they were up enough to see targets through the sights, they would stop and fire. It had to be a first-shot kill, thought Connelly, and then scoot back down out of sight while Morrow, the loader, reloaded the gun.

"That's enough, Huckins!" said Calandra. Connelly saw three tanks heading for the corner of the runway where Four and Five had retreated. He trained the gun onto the nearest with the control handle. It became huge in the telescope, and he pressed the trigger. The gun roared, and the Sheridan skidded backwards in the soft sand.

"Back her up, Huckins!" yelled Connelly.

"You got him, sir!" said Calandra, jubilant. The tracks churned in the sand as the Sheridan dropped from sight. The scavenging system blew the gases out of the gun and the breech opened.

"HEAT, loaded, up!" exclaimed Morrow.

Connelly switched to armor net. "Red Platoon, Leader. Report, over."

"This is Two. You got yours; I missed mine, over."

"Four and Five are ready to pop up, Leader," said Red Four.

"Go, Four and Five. Be careful, they're coming right at you."

Major Kirov saw White Three erupt with flame as it was struck on the left side. He traversed his turret to the left, his head pressed into the padded rest above the periscope. The turret and gun of the Sheridan were just visible, and were gone before he could fire. "White Two, continue on. I am turning to attack another target."

White Two acknowledged, and Kirov told his driver to turn hard left. The tank dipped and pitched downward as it left the runway and ran down the shallow slope. "Turn parallel to the runway, and slow down, Ali," said Kirov to his driver.

Sergeant Mamani in White Two saw the Sheridans just as they emerged at the edge of the runway. They were fifty meters apart and moving fast. He trained the gun on the one directly ahead with a flick of the control column and fired. He had only a vague impression in the corner of his eye of the target exploding as he shouted to his driver to turn to the left toward the second target. He had already centered the second Sheridan in his sights and ground his teeth waiting for the bore evacuator to blow the muzzle free and the automatic loader to load. After an eternity of watching the American pull up and swing its big gun to bear, the "Loaded" light appeared in his sight and he crushed the trigger in his grip. He imagined a flash from the American's gun just as his gun fired, and then his world ended in a searing blast of heat.

"Red Leader, this is Four. There's one tank; he just blasted Five. I'm engage—"

The transmission from Four ended in an electronic hiss. Connelly thumbed the microphone. "Red Four, this is Leader, over." Nothing. "The bastard must have gotten them both," he said into the intercom.

"Red Leader, this is Blue Leader, over."

Connelly keyed the mike on armor net. "Go ahead, Baird. Where are you?"

"I'm on the taxiway, on the north edge of runway 11/29. I'm moving toward you. My radio went dead when

I fired about ten minutes ago, and we just got it back up."

"What can you see from there?"

"There's a lot of smoke blowing north from burning buildings and smoke from the battle blowing over the runway and taxiway. I can see two tanks advancing on the Ops Building on the edge of the smoke. Yablonski thinks he sees a third. He's choking the reticle for the range—Jesus!" Lieutenant Baird let go of the mike switch and traversed the turret violently to the right. They were passing a revetment and Baird, sitting up in the open cupola, found himself looking at the back of a T-72 forty meters away, deep inside the revetment. He saw the startled face of the tank's commander as the man frantically reached for his control column. Baird depressed his gun and fired, hitting the T-72 just below the engine grills.

"Jesus Christ!" said Yablonski, the gunner. "The motherfucker didn't detonate!" A cloud of white smoke rose from the engine compartment, but there was no explosion.

"Round never went far enough to arm," said Baird, awe in his voice. The Libyan tank commander continued to stare at him, then slowly raised his hands. "Doesn't matter," said Baird. "His engine's fucked; he's out of it." He swung the turret back toward the tanks advancing across the runway. The radio crackled in his ear. "Take the shoot, Yablonski."

"Got it, sir. Driver, stop. On the way!"

"We're loaded, Lieutenant," said Morrow.

"Two, Leader, you ready, over?" said Connelly, flexing his hand on the control column.

"Roge."

"Four said one tank. He might have gotten it, but if we see it, we'll both shoot. Then let's crank up and go after the tanks Blue Leader says are almost to the Ops Building."

"Roger, Leader, we're rolling."

Connelly's Sheridan jerked into motion. Two was barely visible in the swirling dust fifty meters away to his left and a little ahead. "Speed it up a little, Huckins."

⇆31⇌

Stuart crept sideways into the alley between the burning building and the Ops Building, pressing his back against the wall, which was warm even though the fire was on the upper stories. Machine gun bullets swept the alley in thick bursts. Soldiers, some carrying unfired Dragons in canisters, were pulling back. Stuart grabbed a red-headed paratrooper who looked about fifteen years old and pulled him down next to him. "What's going on, Troop?"

"There's a tank comin' around the end of this building, sir, shooting the shit out of everyone. He's too close for the goddamn Dragon to arm."

"Anybody got a LAW?"

"No. Just Dragons," said the kid, trying to pull away.

"Are there any marines down there?"

"No, sir, just Airborne."

"Hustle your ass back to the Ops Building. Find marines and tell them to bring LAWs."

"Yes, sir." Stuart sent him on his way with a gentle shove. The wall behind him was growing much hotter. There was a break in the machine gun fire as the tank's cannon roared. Stuart sprinted out of the alley and sprawled behind a metal shed. He felt a stinging sensation in his left shoulder and saw he was bleeding through a neat slit in his jumpsuit. He rolled and looked back into the alley. He could see the tank, huge and black, swinging its gun back and forth, searching as it ground its way through the crude barricade the soldiers had made, drawing ever closer to the Ops Building, impervious to the stings of small-arms fire raking it from all sides. A people-killing machine, Leah had said. Stuart shrank behind the shed as the coaxial machine gun swept the alley.

⇆32⇌
Uqba ben Nafi, 0543 GMT (0643 Local)

"Red Leader, this is Two," called Sergeant Burnside as his Sheridan topped the ridge. "Looks like Four got the guy." There was a burning hulk off to the left, past the one Connelly had shot on the first attack. Connelly looked left and right through the vision blocks. He saw a bright flash from the edge of the runway and heard a crackling roar in his earphones. To his right, he saw the shape of a tank turret and long gun backing away down the slope. He looked quickly left and saw Red Two stopped and burning. One man jumped clear.

"Floor it, Huckins!" said Connelly, his voice swollen with rage. "Drive over the edge of the runway! We have to get that motherfucker before he reloads!"

Kirov watched the baby tank tilt over the edge of the paved runway into the dirt, coming straight at him, three hundred meters away. The automatic loader of the T-72 took 7.5 seconds to cycle, and he didn't have that long. His tank was still reversing, and he heard the driver scream in panic. It didn't matter. He watched the American slow, sure of his shot, and fire. The concussion of the HEAT round killed him instantly. He never even saw the flash.

Lieutenant Baird's Blue Leader Sheridan bucked as the gun fired. He watched the target tank in his telescope and saw the shell explode on the front of the track. "Nice shot, Yablonski—" He was interrupted by a roar that shook the vehicle violently. He heard a scream of breaking track, and then the engine died. He opened the hatch above his head and stood. There was a black smudge and a shallow crater in the cracked concrete next to his left rear, and flames were starting from the engine compartment. "Everybody out," he shouted. "We're burning!"

Private Huckins had Connelly's Sheridan swaying along at forty-five miles an hour on the smooth taxiway. Through his periscope he could see two Libyan tanks pulling away from the burning hulk of a third, Blue's last target. Lieutenant

Connelly's voice came over the intercom. "Shoot the one in front, Calandra. He's practically on the apron."

"Roger. Range is in, four-four-three meters." The gun fired, slowing the vehicle abruptly.

Connelly watched through the vision blocks. The big HEAT round opened the black tank up like a melon. "One to go, guys," he said softly.

Four Marine Sea Cobra gunships from *Saipan* raced in from the sea, then spread out to hover above the middle of runway 11/29. The Cobras were the first of four flights that would soon be over the air base. The helicopters were directed by a marine lieutenant in a dugout to the east of runway 03/21. Their targets were three tanks, one advancing across runway 11/29 toward the apron from the south, one emerging from a revetment four hundred meters to the southeast of the Operations Building, and another still in an adjacent revetment, which was smoking but appeared intact. The flight leader assigned the targets. The moving tank nearest the apron was assigned to two aircraft, and the four helos each fired a TOW missile.

"Jesus, Gannet Six, just three tanks?" queried the flight leader, Capt. Ted Edwards.

"You shoulda been here two minutes ago, Copperhead Leader. There were a lot more of them, and they were beating the shit out of us."

The flight leader smiled as his gunner guided the slow missile toward the target. None of the tanks had seen them, and none were shooting back. All four missiles guided flawlessly, and all struck their targets. The tank on the runway was stopped barely 150 meters from the Ops Building. "Gannet Six, this is Copperhead Leader. Scratch three tanks."

"Nice shoot, Snake Leader. Wish you had been here earlier, out."

What's he pissed off at? wondered Edwards. "Copperhead Leader, standing by, out."

Sergeant Abdul Hasaffi had been following the progress of the Libyan tank attack on the radio. He wanted to time his arrival on the apron to coincide with theirs, so that the Americans would neither see nor hear his approach. The original mission of his company, as explained by the Russian major before he had been killed, was to capture the hostages and keep the Americans from getting them, but that was before so many of his friends and fellow soldiers had been killed. Now Hasaffi wanted only to hurt, to kill.

From the chatter on the radio, he knew the battle was going badly for the Libyan side, as the voices on the net dwindled to two, and then there were only the futile calls of one remaining tank, poised to take the Operations Building from the rear, entreating the silent network for orders. Hasaffi keyed his intercom and told his driver to pick up speed as they passed out of the barracks area and into the street that led past the Maintenance Building to the apron.

The red-headed paratrooper Stuart had spoken to in the alley found a marine captain on the apron next to the Operations Building, and repeated Stuart's request for LAWs. The captain collected a fire team of three riflemen and three men armed with thin green tubes the paratrooper assumed must be LAWs. He asked one of the marines as they started back to the alley, "What's a LAW, anyway?"

"Light antitank weapon," said the marine, a skinny Mexican with a big grin.

"Like a Dragon?"

"Yeah, but no guidance. You just point it and shoot."

"Oh, so no minimum range!"

"You got it, Troop. They're old, but us jarheads are always getting too close to things. We got Dragons, too, but we kept a few of these."

Stuart watched as the burning building collapsed inward in showers of sparks and smoky flames. The Libyan tank continued its slow advance, sweeping the alley with its coax machine gun. It seemed somehow wary, uncertain.

Stuart twisted and looked behind him as a marine captain and his fire team reached the shed in a ragged rush. Stuart crawled out of the way of the marines with the LAWs. "All yours," he said, feeling immensely relieved.

The first man pulled back the slide to arm his missile. Then he waited for the machine gun to sweep to the other side of the alley, and twisted himself into the alley and fired. A long jet of flame roared out the rear of the tube. There was a dull explosion in the alley. Discarding his tube, the marine rolled back behind the shed. "I hit the fucker in the right track. I think it stopped."

"Rose, take a shot. Aim just below the turret."

"OK, Captain." The marine named Rose rolled into the alley. The machine gun fire was chewing methodically into the metal shed now, but it was well over their heads. Stuart admired the calm way the marines went about their work. Again the jet of flame from the launcher and the dull boom of the warhead, but this time a much larger explosion followed, with the sharp, high-pitched sound of tearing metal. Rose rolled back, grinning. "He swung right from Billy's shot. I put it in right through the left track, below the turret. Blew the mother *away!*"

Rose's voice sounded unnaturally loud in the sudden still-ness. His fellow marines congratulated him. Stuart heard something else, and then they all did and became quiet. The clank of tank tracks and the crack of a cannon from north of their position. "Jesus," said Stuart. "One got through from the rear, somehow. What defense do we have to the rear of the Ops Building?"

"We're it," said the captain grimly. "Let's hustle, guys!"

Leah, thought Stuart, as he broke into a run behind the others. Dear God.

The crack of the tank cannon from behind the Ops Building sent everyone inside sprawling. The shell had passed com-pletely through the building without exploding. Next, the tank opened up with its machine guns, first the 7.62mm coax, and then the heavy 12.7mm mounted outside at the commander's hatch. When she heard the low-pitched bark of the heavy machine gun, Leah knew the commander firing the gun had to be exposed, because she knew there was no way to fire the 12.7 from inside the turret on a T-72. Her first thought was to try to get a shot with her carbine, to kill the commander. Then she remembered the RPG-7 that Stuart had used to knock out the ZSU, half a lifetime ago.

The RPG launcher and the wooden box of grenades were over on the south side of the room, where they had been left, ironically, next to the bound and gagged Abu Salaam. Leah slithered across the room on her belly, the machine gun bullets seeming to press her flatter, seeking her. She reached the launcher and took a grenade from the box and inserted it into the tube. She looked at Abu Salaam, hating him. She could not see his mouth because of the gag, but his eyes twinkled with glee.

Leah scrabbled back across the room, holding the launcher in front of her. The building's cinder-block foundation afforded some protection to the prone hostages, but the wooden structure was being shredded, as were the furniture barricades. Tracer ammunition had started several small fires.

The hostages followed Leah with their eyes as she squirmed across the room, slowed by the heavy launcher. For the first time, the eyes of the hostages were filled with fear.

Hasaffi shouted at his driver to keep accelerating. He was on the apron in front of the Maintenance Building, 225 meters from the Ops Building. His gunner and driver wanted him to turn back. He refused, and told the gunner to continue firing the coax while he fired short bursts from the heavy NSV machine gun on the swivel mount. American soldiers could be seen running toward the building from across the apron, or firing at him from positions across the runway, but he continued to concentrate his fire on the building and the hostages within. That would pain them more, be a greater revenge, he reasoned. Allah, he prayed to himself, give me victory, then take me to paradise. He intended to drive the tank right through the side of the building. He was sure he would kill everyone in the building, and he then would be killed.

Leah reached the window facing the oncoming tank. She could follow the sweeping of the coax, but the 12.7mm was firing in what seemed to be more random bursts. I will just have to guess, she decided. God of Israel, she prayed, protect me as I smite thine enemies. At least let me take the shot, and protect these innocents around me.

A burst of the heavy machine gun splintered the sill above her head. She rose quickly, the launcher already braced over her right shoulder. The tank filled the optical sight and she pulled the trigger. The grenade's rocket motor ignited after the grenade had been propelled ten meters from the launcher, and the grenade accelerated toward the tank. Leah could see the face of the commander as he swung his machine gun back toward her, too late. The HEAT grenade struck the ring joint just under the turret, penetrated the armor, and exploded inside, tearing the tank to pieces of tortured metal. The ammunition exploded in a ball of fire.

Lieutenant Colonel Loonfeather clattered down the iron staircase from the roof of the Operations Building, followed by his three RTOs with radio packs. He saw Stuart enter the building through the back door and went in after him. Most of the people continued to lie on the floor, but Loonfeather saw the female Israeli captain organizing wounded soldiers and marines to fight the fires. Stuart ran to her and embraced her, and she seemed to sag against him, but only for a moment. Loonfeather saw the RPG-7 launcher, wisps of smoke still coming from both ends, and knew who had killed the tank. "Stuart!" he called.

Leah pushed William away and returned to fire fighting. Many hostages were up and helping, but at the south end of the building the old, dry wood was beginning to burn brightly. "Yes, Colonel!" said Stuart.

"What's your assessment?"

Stuart listened to the near silence for a second before answering. "I think it's over, Rufus."

Loonfeather nodded. "I do too. Get the people off the roof, and get these people organized in here. Better evacuate. There's no way they're going to stop this tinderbox from burning with a few fire extinguishers."

"Will do, Rufus." Stuart grinned, "Hey, Colonel, that was a hell of a fight!"

Loonfeather was thinking of his casualties, especially among his Sheridan crews, and found it hard to smile, but he did. "Jesus, yes, but let's fuck off, White-Eyes! We've been here far too long."

Loonfeather took the handset from the RTO on command net as Stuart shouted to the marines and the black-uniformed SEALs to get the hostages out of the building and assembled, and to organize help for the wounded.

"Feeney," said Stuart. "Get upstairs and get everybody off the roof. Jones, make sure we don't leave anybody, including that sack of shit." He pointed to Abu Salaam, still slumped in the corner where they had left him.

Loonfeather pressed the transmit key. "Thunder, this is Raptor Six. Request the entire evac flight. Use the entire apron, over."

"This is Thunder. Helicopters are already airborne, Rufus. They'll reach you in two minutes, over," said Colonel Brimmer, on *Inchon.*

"Thanks, Bob. We'll be ready to go, I can assure you."

"Was it as bad as it sounded on the radios, Rufus?"

Loonfeather felt his whole body shake violently for a second, as though he had been suddenly drenched in ice water. He had a sudden sense of dread. His ancestors beckoned him from the back of his mind. Danger, they said. Danger is very near. Without knowing why, Loonfeather looked out the window to the north, not at the burning T-72, but beyond it. From the north will come danger, the spirits whispered. Loonfeather saw nothing but the empty tarmac and the Maintenance Building beyond.

"Rufus? Raptor Six, this is Thunder, over."

Loonfeather fought down the primitive foreboding and keyed his microphone. "It was far worse, Thunder, far worse. Raptor Six out."

Across the apron, the pool of burning diesel fuel from Sergeant Hasaffi's tank reached the corner of the Maintenance Building, which began to burn as the first helicopters crossed over the coast and descended toward the runway.

⇋33⇋
Uqba ben Nafi, 0548 GMT (0648 Local)

The first helicopters to arrive overhead the air base were twenty Sea Cobra gunships, two flights from *Saipan* and three from *Inchon*. The gunships hovered over a broad arc south of the Operations Building in the center of the base. Navy fighters and attack aircraft ranged farther south and watched the roads to the east and west. Airborne and marine units began to assemble on the tarmac as personnel were checked against lists. It was demanded by the plan that if possible no one, alive or dead, be left behind.

Lieutenant John Connelly's Sheridan rolled into the area in front of the Operations Building, greeted by cheers and a raucous blast from Sgt. Matthew Tucker's bugle. Connelly felt proud of his work, and of his men, but he wanted most to know the fate of the crews that had been hit. Tucker's Sheridan had been the first to leave the net, and Connelly's drawn, almost haggard face lit up to see Blue Two's commander and two of his men. "Damn, Sergeant, you made it! Climb up here!"

"Yes, sir. We lost my driver, sir, Bobby Henry."

Connelly felt his chest tighten. "I'm sorry, Matt."

"Yes, sir. He was good; a good friend."

"Shit, Sergeant, get up here on top, blow Assembly on that bugle; blow it over and over. Maybe some other guys got through."

"Yes, *sir*," said Sergeant Tucker, climbing up onto the turret and blowing the pure notes, first to the east and then to the other points of the compass.

"Colonel Loonfeather, we haven't met. I'm Commander Philip Hooper; the SEALs, sir."

Loonfeather turned from his radio and shook hands. "You and your team did well, Commander. Thank you."

"Make it Hoop, Colonel, please."

"OK. Rufus, then."

"Good," grinned Hooper. "Have you got a minute to run down this evacuation for me?"

Loonfeather showed him the diagram on his clipboard. "It's standard Marine Corps doctrine, Hoop. Perimeter defense is the marine rifle company, plus all those Cobras we could have used earlier." Hooper smiled, but Loonfeather couldn't; his face was set against the pain of the early casualty reports from the Armor. "We're doing this as though we're under fire, which is to say that we evacuate from the inside of the perimeter out, but the last *unit* to leave has to be strong enough to defend itself against any expected threat."

"OK, the Marines are the Critical Mass Force, the last out."

"Right, because their organization is intact—they weren't dispersed by a parachute jump—and because the helo crews are also Marines."

Hooper pointed at helicopter pairs flying in from the sea while the CH-53s continued to hover over the beach. "What about those guys?"

"Each pair—a CH-46 and a Cobra—will be vectored onto a downed helicopter, or a knocked-out Sheridan, to look for wounded or remains. Others will search the beach for stragglers from the jump, who were told to walk to the beach if they landed long. The name of every man picked up will be radioed to Major Donahue, who holds the master roster for all the units involved. The units inside the perimeter will be assigned a lift as soon as they're certified present or accounted for by their commanders. As each unit is ready, we'll call down a bird, and they're gone."

"The first bird picked up the casualties from the aid station."

"Right. The second will pick up casualties here, and then the hostages go out."

"And last the marines."

"Right. The entire rifle company will go in one last lift."

"What about your little tank?" asked Hooper, looking at the Sheridan.

"Regrettably, Commander, that gets blown up."

"How about my team, and our distinguished prisoner?"

Loonfeather shrugged. "You're intact, you can go with the hostages if you want."

Hooper frowned, remembering Ricardo's still body on the roof. We are not intact, he thought. "We've been watching you guys work for near forty minutes. We'll wait and go last, with the marines, Colonel, if you please."

Commander Hooper turned and walked back to his men. Loonfeather watched his back, fighting anger. The SEAL commander wasn't *exactly* discourteous, thought Loonfeather, stung by Hooper's abruptness, but he wasn't exactly polite either. Loonfeather knew that many would criticize the operation. Surely Hooper would have argued for a quick snatch; commandos liked to strike and be gone. Hindsight would agree with them, since the SEALs had held the Operations Building without the expected opposition from close-positioned Libyan troops before the Airborne had jumped. Hindsight and my casualties will plague me, he thought grimly. Then his mood brightened quickly as he saw Lieutenant Baird and his crew, jumping and cheering, join up with Connelly on the lone surviving Sheridan. Fuck the second-guessers, he thought behind his smile. Fuck Commander Hooper, too.

"That wasn't exactly polite, Hoop," said Stuart, following Hooper as he walked away from Loonfeather.

"Oh, fuck you, William!" Hooper stopped and faced
Stuart, anger to anger. "OK, no, I suppose it wasn't, but I
think letting the Army run this thing got a lot of people
killed."

"In what sense?"

"It was just too fucking complicated! If we could have
had three CH-53s, escorted by a few Cobras, right after we
secured the Ops Building, we would have been gone before
a single Libyan woke up. Instead, we fight a major battle
and damn near get waxed." Hooper's eyes were angry and
sad. Ricardo had died in his arms, drowned in his own blood.

"Hindsight, Hoop." Stuart sensed his friend's grief, and
he placed his hands on the big man's shoulders. "Any moving
vehicle, especially that ZSU, and we could have lost everyone."

"Yeah, I know. I'm pissed about all the casualties, and
especially Ricardo. He was a good friend." Hooper lowered
his head, his anger going. "But you know what else, William?"

"What, Hoop?"

"Maybe it was because I had nothing to do once the
Airborne took over. Maybe it was because I felt like a specta-
tor. But when those tanks came through that smoke, I was
scared shitless."

William smiled at his friend. "It did get loud."

Hooper looked up and recovered his grin. "Precisely.
Look, I'll make it right with Colonel Loonfeather."

The fire inside the Maintenance Building spread quickly,
racing up the walls and igniting the dry wooden joists and
beams. Colonel Zharkov had his men in their tanks and BTRs
with the engines running. Outside on the apron, he could
see huge helicopters landing by twos and threes and troops
loading up. Nice and orderly, he thought, but too damn
slow. We are going to have to drive out of here before the
building starts to collapse, and the Americans will not be
gone before that happens.

Zharkov climbed down the ladder from the narrow window

above the bay doors. Even though the fire was at the other end of the long building, the heat and smoke were becoming intolerable. Zharkov gestured for the duty officer to join him. "Lieutenant, get the flag from the duty office."

"Yes, Comrade Colonel!"

"Is there a sheet on the bunk in there?"

"Yes, Comrade Colonel!"

"Bring that, too." The officer looked puzzled, but he hustled away.

Zharkov climbed up onto the turret of his tank and waved for the men's attention, shouting to be heard above the rumble of the diesels. "We are going to have to show ourselves. We have been ordered to avoid direct conflict with the Americans. I wish to reemphasize that point."

He looked at each tank and BTR commander. Each nodded his understanding. Zharkov looked hard at the zampolit, Captain Suslov, who nodded gravely. Behind Suslov, out of his view, Warrant Officer Tolkin nodded vigorously. "Good." The duty officer had returned with the Soviet flag, on its wooden staff, and the wrinkled sheet from the bunk. Zharkov handed the flag to his gunner, who stuck it upright in his hatch. Zharkov draped the white sheet over the barrel of the tank cannon and fastened it with wire. He climbed into the commander's hatch and trained the gun out right to the three o'clock position.

Stuart watched Leah as the hostages jogged single file toward the three CH-53s assigned to pick them up. She waved them onward, urging each one to hurry, but the women and nearly all the children wanted to stop, to touch her, before they proceeded to the helicopters. At last, the three helos were loaded, and they lifted off under their screen of Cobras and A-7s flying above. The hostages waved from the open doors of the helos until they could no longer see the apron. The slim Israeli officer waved back, her face streaming with tears.

"Leah," whispered Stuart. She looked up at him, stripping

the tears from her eyes with the back of an angry hand. She turned from him, and he felt pain beyond imagining. "Leah, please," he began again.

She whirled and threw herself into his arms, sobbing, beyond words. He held her, fiercely tight, and he felt a tightness in his throat. "Leah."

Leah pushed her face up gently past his chin. "William," she whispered, her breath short from crying, "I have never seen such bravery as among those people."

"They're safe, now." It seemed an inadequate thing to say.

"There were so many casualties!"

"Too many. But you were very brave."

Leah pushed him back, looking at him. "Brave? I didn't feel brave."

"Brave, Leah, and beautiful."

Leah wiped away the last of her tears and seemed to stiffen in William's arms. "Are you talking of love to me, Commander?" There was the edge of forced humor in her voice.

"Yes. Please don't laugh, Leah."

Tears streamed from her eyes again, and she pressed her face into his chest. "Oh God, Stuart, I can only cry now."

"I love you, Leah."

Leah sobbed so deeply that Stuart felt his body rocked as he held her.

"OK, Rufus. The lists are complete. Last Airborne units all present or accounted for," said Major Donahue.

"Load 'em, John."

"Yes, sir." Donahue swung his arm in a circle above his head, then pumped it once. Knots of soldiers ran crouched to waiting helicopters in orderly rows, holding their weapons at port arms, across their chests. Lieutenant Colonel Loonfeather tapped Major Donahue on the shoulder. "What was the casualty total, John?"

"Thirty-six KIA, Rufus, including the aircrews picked up at sea or lost at sea."

"How many of my Sheridan crews?"

"Fifteen, Colonel. I'm sorry."

Jesus, thought Loonfeather. Fifteen killed out of a total of thirty-two who jumped. "Well, John, we knew they'd catch hell if they had to fight."

"As near as we can tell, Colonel, the seven who fought killed nine T-72s."

Loonfeather smiled between pride and pain. "Yeah, John, the hard way, too. In the open, tank to tank."

"Brave men, Colonel."

Loonfeather watched as the last of the Airborne loaded up and the CH-53s began taking off. The marines moved to the assembly points near the landing spots that had been marked on the tarmac in white paint. Such brave men, thought Loonfeather.

"Colonel?" asked Lieutenant Connelly, at his side. "Shall we blow the Sheridan?"

"Is it charged?"

"Yes, sir, but it's safe. We should back it away from the helicopters. Huckins has the radio detonator."

Loonfeather had the sudden image in his mind of danger lurking unseen. He once again heard the whispers of the Old Ones, so long dead. The feeling was so strong that Loonfeather trembled, as he had earlier. The warning had something to do with the Sheridan. "Lieutenant, let's leave it where it is. The detonator has enough range; we'll kick it off when we're airborne."

Connelly was puzzled. That wouldn't give them a second chance if the detonator failed. "Yes, sir," he said.

The last birds carrying the infantry took off and the marines began to load.

Colonel Zharkov put on his helmet and pressed the transmit key on tank net. "Radio check, by units," he said. The two other tanks and the three BTRs answered. "Ready, then. Lieutenant, open the doors."

The duty officer nodded and walked over to the switch on the electric door hoists. The overhead motors whined, the chains rattled, and the doors rolled up, impossibly slowly, thought Zharkov. "OK, Spetznaz, let's go. Move quickly, get close to the helicopters, but show no hostile intent." As soon as the door in front of his tank was high enough to clear, Zharkov ordered his driver forward. The T-72 lurched and accelerated ponderously onto the sunlit apron.

Eight CH-53s were on the ground, and the marines started toward them. The SEALs, Lieutenant Connelly's Sheridan crew, and Loonfeather, Donahue, and the RTOs on the few remaining communications nets stood together, in front of the burning Operations Building, ready to divide themselves among the last two helos. Loonfeather felt rather than heard a heavy rumbling, distinct from the scream of the helicopter turbines and the beat of their rotors. He looked north, toward the whispered warnings of his ancestors, and saw black tanks and BTRs emerge from the maintenance shed two hundred meters away on the other side of the apron. The tanks and the faster-accelerating BTRs moved into the open line between the two rows of helicopters. Marines saw the vehicles at the same moment, and the ones not already loaded instinctively dropped to the pavement and readied their weapons. The SEALs and Loonfeather's staff flattened themselves as well, while the Sheridan crew clambered back into its vehicle.

"Hold fire. RTOs, all nets, tell everyone to hold fire!" shouted Loonfeather, the only American left standing. The enemy vehicles slowed and eventually stopped under the whirling blades of the helicopters. Riflemen spilled out of the BTRs and formed behind them, their AKM carbines slung across their chests. They all stood very still, their uniforms fluttering in the rotor downblast.

Major Donahue and Commander Stuart slowly got up and walked, hunched over, to Loonfeather's side. "He has grabbed us by the belt," said Loonfeather, more to himself than to the others.

"What do you mean, Colonel?" asked Major Donahue,

his voice as close to a whisper as could be, given the noise of the helicopters.

"The North Vietnamese used to say that," said Loonfeather unemotionally, as though delivering a history lesson. "They would try to engage us so close to our artillery fire bases that we could not use the guns for fear of hitting our own men." Loonfeather turned as he heard the faster beat of the gunships moving in closer, hovering, facing the tanks. "Make sure everyone, including the gunships, gets the word, John; no firing unless fired upon."

"Yes, sir, Colonel. What are you going to do?"

"See the flags on the lead tank? The one with his gun trained out to his right? I reckon he's telling us two things: first, that he's Russian, not Libyan, and second, that he wants to talk."

"So you're going to talk?"

"Yeah." Loonfeather walked to the Sheridan and climbed up. "Lieutenant Connelly, may I have your seat?"

"Yes, Colonel," said Connelly, climbing quickly out of the commander's cupola.

Loonfeather settled in. He pressed the palm switch on the control column and traversed the gun out right to the three o'clock position, then rotated the cupola independently of the turret, so it and the .50-caliber machine gun were once again facing forward. "William, get onto Colonel Brimmer and Admiral Bergeron. Find out if we have authority to start World War Three."

"Aye, aye, sir," said Stuart, picking up the handset from the RTO on command net.

"Call me on armor net."

Stuart, already talking, gave Loonfeather a thumbs-up.

"Let's go, Huckins." The Sheridan rolled slowly toward the waiting Russian, whose red and white flags flapped in the rotor downwash.

Come to me, Old Ones, thought Loonfeather, as the distance between the rolling Sheridan and the halted T-72 diminished. He had told Huckins to drive slowly, to give him a few more minutes to think. What manner of trap is this? he asked his ancestors. The Maintenance Building erupted in a shower of sparks and smoke as the roof collapsed. They were forced to come out of hiding by the fire, thought Loonfeather. What would they have done otherwise? Shot from concealment once the helicopters were loaded, and no Americans were in a position to shoot back? Or just stayed in there until we left?

Well, now they have us. They can easily kill every one of the helicopters with their machine guns alone, and most of the boys inside them. But we have them, too. If they kill us, the Cobras will shoot, and then the Navy will flatten the base and burn it. None could escape.

"Colonel, you want a round in the main gun?" Calandra's question in his helmet interrupted the faint whisperings of the Old Ones.

"No, but have one ready. Is the demolition charge still set?"

"In the shell trays, Colonel," answered Huckins from his driver's seat.

Loonfeather watched the Russian vehicles get larger. The men in the tanks were sitting up, hatches open. The riflemen were standing in small groups, hands resting on the stocks of their weapons. They're trying not to look threatening, thought Loonfeather, but those machine guns and AKMs and grenade launchers could all be in action in less than a heartbeat.

"Load H-E Frag, Tolkin," said Captain Suslov in the second Russian tank. He felt his heart pounding inside his chest, hard enough to make his throat feel tight.

"But Captain, the colonel told us to keep the guns clear!" protested the warrant officer.

"Load it. We must fire at once if the American does."

Once the gun is loaded, the bastard can lay it and fire it by himself, thought Tolkin. He picked up the empty stub-shell case the crew used as an ashtray, laid it gently before the ram of the automatic loader, and tripped the ram. The shell case was thrust into the breech and the breechblock slammed shut. Tolkin rose rapidly through his hatch, holding his Makarov pistol just below the rim. He watched as Suslov aligned the gun on a helicopter in the middle of the near row, and saw him squeeze the trigger. Suslov's eyes were tightly shut, but they opened immediately. "Damn! Misfire! Tolkin?"

Tolkin leaned across and pressed the muzzle of the Makarov under Suslov's ribs. "You are under arrest, Captain, by order of Colonel Zharkov."

Suslov didn't speak. He didn't look at Tolkin, but straight ahead. His teeth were bared in the snarl of a cornered animal, and his eyes glowed between hatred and fear. Saliva gathered in the corners of his mouth.

"Captain, I repeat, you are under arrest—"

Suslov grasped the bolt of the 12.7mm machine gun, pulling it back and chambering a round. Tolkin shot him twice, directly through the heart, then quickly pushed the machine gun to the side in case Suslov's dying thumbs might contract on the triggers. Suslov slumped away from the gun as his eyes glazed. Tolkin climbed down inside the turret and dragged the captain's limp body inside, forcing it into the gunner's position. He then climbed back up through the commander's hatch. He looked around warily, but neither the Russians around him nor the American now slowing next to Colonel Zharkov's tank seemed to have noticed the little drama.

Tolkin breathed deeply, slowing his racing heart. *I never liked him, the dogmatic, bullying zampolit*, thought Tolkin, *and now that he has proven himself KGB, I like him less. But I'll be damned if he didn't die like a Russian.*

⇋34⇋
Uqba ben Nafi, 0559 GMT (0659 Local)

Lieutenant John Connelly watched as his Sheridan, with the broad back of Lieutenant Colonel Loonfeather extending above the commander's cupola, slowed to a crawl as it approached the lead Russian tank. He heard the colonel's voice on the armor net, soft but urgent. Connelly touched Stuart on the shoulder.

Stuart twisted his handset around his ear, still listening to command net. "Tell him Top Hat approves of his actions, Connelly. They're looking at options."

"Do they know that he's practically touching the fucking Russian tank?" Connelly said heatedly.

Stuart smiled gently, still listening to his radio. "Take it easy, Lieutenant. The colonel knows how to horsetrade."

Connelly nodded grimly. He thumbed the transmit key and whispered, "Nothing yet from Top Hat, Colonel."

USS *America*

Rear Admiral Wilson stood over the Sixth Fleet Flag Duty Officer, Comdr. William Daniels. "I ask you again, Commander, to interrupt Admiral Bergeron. We have a situation on the base that is becoming explosive."

"Admiral, the admiral has been talking to the Joint Chiefs for nearly twenty minutes. The Joint Chiefs, and I believe the President, have demanded a detailed report of the condition of the hostages, who have just landed aboard *Saipan*. The admiral told us not to break in on him unless there was a major threat to the force, or the mission."

"Dammit, Commander!" exploded Admiral Wilson. "We have a company of marines and a squadron of helicopters pinned down on that base! That's not a major threat to the force?"

"Admiral, I do not wish to argue with you, but Admiral Bergeron has given full authority to the operational commanders to deal with any threat to our forces throughout the area of Operation Fire Arrow. Surely—"

"Commander, the force threatening our marines, *directly* threatening our men and aircraft, is *Russian! Soviet,* Commander, not Libyan. I don't think the admiral's delegation of authority went quite that far!"

The duty officer rose quickly, all color draining from his face. "Where do you wish to see the admiral, sir?"

"If he's in there on the horn with the Joint Chiefs, I had better go to him."

"Right through here, sir. I'm sorry I misunderstood, sir."

"I didn't tell you all of it, Commander. My mistake. Let's find the admiral."

Uqba ben Nafi

"All right, Huckins, we can hardly delay this any longer. Pull up next to the tank and stop," said Loonfeather.

"Yes, sir." Huckins' voice came back through the intercom. Loonfeather listened hopefully for Lieutenant Connelly to break in with instructions from the fleet, but the radio remained silent in his helmet earphone. Huckins parked the Sheridan expertly spindle to spindle next to the Russian tank. Like two strange dogs, nose to tail, sniffing each other, thought Loonfeather, and broke involuntarily into a grin. Recognizing the Russian commander's collar insignia as that of a full colonel, Loonfeather saluted smartly and said, "Good morning, Colonel; I hope you speak English."

The Russian officer's stiff, even tense expression softened a bit at Loonfeather's incongruous good cheer. Returning the salute, he replied, "Good morning to you, sir. I speak English, though not well. I am Colonel Zharkov, of the Soviet Army. May I know your name, and rank?"

"Lieutenant Colonel Rufus Loonfeather, Armor, U.S. Army."

"Airborne?"

"Yes, sir. You, also?"

"Indeed. Well, we will share some understanding, then, I think, Colonel?"

"I certainly hope so," said Loonfeather, glancing at the nearby Russian vehicles and at his pinned-down helicopters. "Perhaps the colonel will tell me what is his mission?"

Zharkov swung his legs out of his commander's hatch and sat on the turret. The most dangerous phase has passed, he thought. We are talking, and the Americans recognize the stalemate, at least for the moment. He stole a glance past the American colonel to the second Soviet tank, and was relieved to see Warrant Officer Tolkin sitting in the commander's hatch. So that is over too, whatever it was. "My mission was, Colonel, *was*, to seize your hostages from the terrorists, and then our government was to effect their return to American control. Your brilliant operation rendered that mission unnecessary."

Loonfeather's jaw dropped. "You're telling me that you would have rescued our people, then handed them over to us?"

"My orders were to take control of them, Colonel. I have every reason to believe my government would have proceeded to return them to yours without delay."

"Then why in the name of God did you put up such a hellacious fight, once you knew we had them ourselves?"

"We did not attack you; the Libyans did."

"But you control—"

"Advise, Colonel, merely advise."

"Bullshit! Excuse me, sir, but you were holed up in that building. You had to hear radio traffic. You could have told your *advisers* that you had seen us go in, and to pull the Libyans back! Do you have any *idea* what casualties have been suffered on both sides?" Loonfeather heard himself shouting and fought for control.

Zharkov felt his anger swell, anger at politicians who spun their webs and got good soldiers killed, then played it however they liked afterward. "Colonel, I am not a politician—"

"Jesus, neither am I; I just want to know." Loonfeather's voice felt calmer, his rage cooler though no less intense.

Zharkov waited, arranging his thoughts. He leaned closer to Loonfeather across the gap that separated the two vehicles and spoke softly, though to his knowledge none of his tank crew understood English. "Colonel, it may seem absurd, but perhaps it is not. To the extent that terrorists harmed your people, *here*, in the territory of a Soviet ally—I am speaking as a soldier, Colonel—"

"I understand. We will both speak frankly."

"Thank you. We were not able to persuade our Libyan allies to use force to oppose *their* Arab brothers, but *we* were prepared to use force ourselves to prevent the slaughter of innocents. Do you understand that, Colonel?"

"Yes, so far." Loonfeather watched the Russian's face closely, and saw something he felt might be candor.

"However, we could not stand apart from our Libyan *ally*, and let you violate his sovereignty [Zharkov waved his arms at the men and helicopters, then pointed vehemently at the Sheridan] in such a massive way!" Zharkov felt his anger showing. This is still a dangerous situation, he thought, calming himself. I must not be misinterpreted.

"Even though your mission, and mine, were essentially identical—rescue innocent Americans."

"Yes!" cried Zharkov, giving vent to a sadness that added to his anger. "As a soldier, I beg your pardon, Colonel," he whispered, leaning still closer across the gap.

"As a soldier, I understand, Colonel. But that tidy bit of political doublethink cost me the lives of thirty-six brave men, and many wounded. Do you know how many you lost, you and your *allies?*"

"Not yet. Losses were heavy." Zharkov felt his anger dissipate, leaving only the sadness.

Loonfeather climbed out of his commander's cupola, removing his helmet and setting it carefully on the seat. "Colonel, let's you and me climb down and walk a bit. I think we can settle the rest of this, one soldier to another."

Zharkov smiled for the first time. "Yes, Comrade Colonel! An excellent idea, let us walk together."

USS *America*

Rear Admiral Wilson explained the situation at the air base to Admiral Bergeron, who, after first protesting the

interruption, sat still and silent, listening intently. The secure
link with the situation room in the White House basement
remained open, but silent. Wilson finished his short descrip-
tion, and was surprised that the commander, Sixth Fleet,
merely stared at him. The speaker from the link to Washington
hissed, and the thin but recognizable voice of the Secretary
of Defense broke through the decoder. "Admiral, we sent
you a signal—"

Admiral Bergeron pressed his transmit key, interrupting
the Secretary. After a second, the admiral spoke. "Permit
me, Mr. Secretary; we may have very little time. Thirty
minutes ago, we received a signal calling our attention to a
possible friendly Soviet force on the air base, and instructing
us not to engage it. Does that order still stand?"

"Christ! Yes, Admiral! The situation with the Soviets is
very fluid! Short of jeopardizing your mission, you must avoid
engaging Sov—"

Once again the admiral depressed the transmit key, covering the voice of the Secretary of Defense with hissing static,
then broke in. "We understand, Mr. Secretary. I'm leaving
Commander Daniels on this net. Admiral Wilson and I must
get in touch with Colonel Loonfeather at once."

"But Admiral," squealed the voice of the Secretary, "what
the fuck happened?"

"Time to figure that out later, sir. Right now we have
to prevent a tragedy." Or a world war, he thought, his heart
racing.

Admiral Bergeron handed the microphone to Commander
Daniels, who stared at it with horror. "Wilson, come on,
we have to talk to Loonfeather. Apparently he either didn't
receive, or didn't get time to read, my relay of that message."

Admiral Wilson stopped dead. "You relayed a message
to Loonfeather?"

"Yes, of course! He had just taken command of the assault—"

Wilson felt fastened to the deck. He managed to nod,
but couldn't speak.

"My God," whispered Admiral Bergeron. "Some signal-man sent that to Loonfeather on *Inchon*, got a proper acknowledgment, and Loonfeather was already ashore!"

"M-must be," said Wilson, regaining his voice and running for the ladder to Flag Plot.

"Find him and tell him, Wilson. In the clear, if necessary, but tell him!"

Wilson burst through the hatch into Flag Plot and pointed to the RTO seated under a red sign lettered "COMMAND NET-THUNDER." "Get me Colonel Loonfeather! Raptor Six!" he shouted.

"Can't, sir," said the marine corporal, startled by the admiral's outburst. "He's off the net."

⇋35⇋

Lieutenant Colonel Loonfeather and Colonel Zharkov walked west, toward the center of the apron, away from the beat of the helicopters and the rumble of the heavy diesels. Loonfeather had an idea forming, but he needed a little time. "Where are you from, Colonel Zharkov?"

"From Moscow. Originally from farther east. On my mother's side, we were Kazakhs—your books called them Cossacks."

"Great warriors."

"Yes, cavalrymen, like us, Colonel. The men of my mother's family all went into the Army of the Czars. They were hereditary majors."

Loonfeather smiled at the shorter man. "You have done much better, Colonel."

Colonel Zharkov laughed. "Universal opportunity under socialism, Colonel," he said with a lilt of humor. "But, forgive me, you do not look like Americans as we know them. Are you a native?"

"As native as you can get, Colonel. I'm an American Indian. Nation of the Dakota."

"Dakota?" said Zharkov, puzzled.

"Also called Sioux, Colonel."

"Ah, the Sioux! We are taught in school that the Sioux were the most warlike of the oppressed nationalities—ah, sorry, Colonel."

"No offense taken," said Loonfeather evenly.

"Let's see," said Zharkov, brightening. "There was Sitting Bull, and Crazy Horse, and, ah, General Custer?"

Loonfeather laughed, stopped walking, and placed his big hands on the shoulders of the Russian. "Like the Cossacks, no, the *Kazakhs*, the Dakota were great horse soldiers."

Colonel Zharkov felt the pressure of the big Indian's hands on his shoulders and decided it was friendly, though a message of power was conveyed as well. *I must gain the trust of this man, and I must know if I can trust him.* "Colonel Loonfeather, may I ask, was your operation a success?"

Loonfeather looked away. His mind's eye saw the fierce battle on the runways and the burning tanks, and he heard again the tank commanders' voices dropping off the armor net, one after another. His face registered the knowledge of the thirty-six dead soldiers and marines as he had last seen some of them, rows of green plastic bags rippling in the rotor wash of the medevac helicopters. Carefully, he controlled his voice. "Colonel, we got our hostages. We accomplished the mission. But like I said earlier, we lost too many good men."

Zharkov frowned and felt sympathy for his enemy. Major Gurevich had been a good friend. So had the dashing, humorous Kirov, and even the ascetic Colonel Asimov. How many others had died out there? "I am sorry, Colonel. Sometimes it is very difficult to know why soldiers must also be enemies."

"When we see no need," said Loonfeather, dropping his hands from the Russian's shoulders. "The officer who planned the inward defense of this airfield was a brilliant son of a bitch."

"We never anticipated that you would land armor," said Zharkov, then immediately realized he had said too much.

He braced himself for another outburst from the American.

Loonfeather looked into the Russian's eyes, slightly almond-shaped and black like his own. "You managed the defense here, Colonel?"

Zharkov wanted to lie, but his pride wouldn't let him. "I, that is, we, Colonel, assisted the Libyan commanders."

"It was brilliant, Colonel," said Loonfeather, looking back at the smoking vehicles and burning buildings. "Any of your three assault columns could have crushed us."

Zharkov followed Loonfeather's gaze across the scarred air base. Again he felt anger press back the diplomatic language inside his head. "I had a superior force, Colonel; I should have won!"

Loonfeather turned abruptly. "We had total air superiority, Colonel."

Zharkov bowed, looked at his trembling hands, and clenched them. "Yes. But even so—"

"Even so, Colonel," said Loonfeather very softly, placing his hands once more on Zharkov's shoulders, "you damn near beat us."

Colonel Zharkov forced his head up to look into the dark eyes of the American. "And now we must talk, tovarich."

Loonfeather smiled gently. "Yes, *Tovarich* Colonel, we must talk, as soldier to soldier, one man to another, with no witness other than our own honor."

The Russian's smile disappeared. "You sensed I was uncomfortable speaking freely in front of my men."

"I thought you might find it easier away from them."

Zharkov's face darkened. "It is a sad thing, when soldiers spy on each other, Colonel. Is it the same in your army?"

"No, Colonel. We have no political officers, and no secret police in our army," Loonfeather noted that the colonel seemed to wince, "although God knows we have plenty of second-guessers, especially when a commander has to make a decision without reference to higher authority, as you and I do now. That's our situation, don't you agree?"

Zharkov looked at the tall American, with his central Asian face, liking him and beginning to trust him. "I agree. What do you suggest?"

USS *America*

"Who's on the command net, Corporal?" asked Admiral Wilson as Admiral Bergeron entered Flag Plot and sat in his chair.

"Answers Black Widow, Admiral," said the marine RTO. "I think it's Commander Stuart."

"Chief, can you put him on a speaker?" The Chief of the Watch nodded, made the transfers, and pointed to one of the microphones in front of Admiral Wilson. "Black Widow, Top Hat. Is that Commander Stuart?"

"Roger, Top Hat, over," came Stuart's flattened voice through the speaker. Flag Plot was very quiet.

"This is Admiral Wilson, Stuart. Where is Colonel Loonfeather?"

"He's on the apron, sir, on foot. About fifty meters away from the point where he first met the Russian tank. The Russian commander is with him."

"Do you have any idea what they're doing?"

"The gunner on Loonfeather's Sheridan talked to Lieutenant Connelly on armor net just after the two commanders left the vehicles. He was inside and couldn't make out what was said, but at first Colonel Loonfeather was shouting."

"Are they in plain sight?"

"Roger."

"Any evidence that the Russians have taken Loonfeather prisoner?"

"None, sir."

"Can you get Loonfeather to come to the radio, Stuart?"

"Not unless he returns to his Sheridan, sir, or unless I walk out to him."

"Have the gunner on that Sheridan wave to him; try to get him back."

"Roger. Is that all, Admiral?"

"For now. For God's sake, don't you leave the net."

"Roger. Black Widow standing by."

Uqba ben Nafi

Spec 4 Calandra stood on top of the Sheridan, making the gathering motions with his arms that were the hand sign for "form on me." Loonfeather replied with the sign that meant "stay put; stay down." Calandra reported to Connelly over the radio. Connelly turned to Stuart. "Calandra says the colonel is ignoring him, sir, telling him to stay put. Calandra wants to know if he should fire a flare."

"Jesus, no, Connelly!" said Stuart, grabbing the lieutenant's arm. "God knows how the Russians might react to that! Tell him to sit tight."

USS *America*

"Well, gentlemen, what do we make of it?" asked Admiral Bergeron.

The senior staff of the Fire Arrow operation was gathered in a small briefing room adjacent to Flag Plot. Secure radio links had been established with Colonel Brimmer on *Inchon,* Captain Manero on *New Jersey,* and Admiral Bellmon on *Nimitz,* which would allow them to hear the conversation of the staff, though they would have to key in to speak.

Rear Admiral Wilson spread his bony hands on the central table. "Either Colonel Loonfeather has been taken prisoner by the Russians, or he has separated himself from his command for some other reason."

"I can't believe he would just drop off the net without a word, unless there was a gun to his head," said Rear Admiral Aarons, the Sixth Fleet N-3 Operations officer.

Admiral Bergeron leaned forward to the microphone in the center of the table. "Colonel Brimmer, you know Colonel Loonfeather. What do you think?"

There was a hiss as Brimmer keyed into the net. "My first guess is that Admiral Aarons is right. In my short time with Colonel Loonfeather, he has impressed upon me the need, especially in complex operations, to stay with the set procedure."

"Yet he gave no signal back to his RTO?" asked Maj. Gen. Carl Morton, commander of the marine corps forces attached to the Sixth Fleet.

"Not that the lieutenant recognized. Lieutenant Connelly is in Loonfeather's command; he should have recognized any covert attempt at communication."

"What was the last thing he did transmit?" asked Admiral Bergeron.

"He asked for guidance, from you, Admiral, just before reaching the Russian. Connelly had none from Stuart, and relayed that. The next time Connelly called him, the gunner answered."

"OK, Colonel, stand by and keep listening," said Admiral Bergeron. "Assuming, gentlemen, that Colonel Loonfeather *is* being held by this Russian, what can we do?"

Staff officers looked at each other uneasily. Admiral Wilson steepled his fingers and began to speak slowly. "Excuse me, Admiral, if I just ramble a bit. The Russians told us that there was a Russian unit on the base that meant us no harm. This may be that unit. If so, they may have come out, after the battle was over, because they feared we might level the base after our people were out." Admiral Wilson paused, a finger touching his lips. "In that case, Loonfeather may be trying to do a deal with them, but maybe the Russian's hands are tied. We know well the Russians give field commanders little authority to deviate from detailed orders."

"So?" asked Admiral Bergeron impatiently.

"If so, we have to let Loonfeather make the best of it. So far, there has been no shooting."

"Excuse me, Admiral," broke in General Morton. "Suppose the opposite; perhaps the worst case, but to me plausible. The Russians lied to us about their unit and its mission— set us up, even though Loonfeather never got the word. Loonfeather is theirs. We have a military *and* a political disaster on our hands. After much bloodshed and multiple acts of war, we have exchanged a group of military dependent hostages, embarrassing enough, for a fully armed marine company and a squadron of marine helicopters!"

Admiral Bergeron took a cigarette from the pack in front of Admiral Wilson. He hadn't smoked in six years. "And if that is true?"

"We can't wear it; we just can't!" boomed General Morton, slapping the table with a callused palm. "We have to fight those boys out of there, no matter what the cost!"

Admiral Bergeron let out his breath with a whistle. "Who is the senior marine officer with that unit?"

"Captain Roberts, the company commander, is the senior grunt officer," broke in Colonel Brimmer on the speaker. "He's already on one of the helicopters; we can talk to him on the helicopter control net."

"We could run it from here, Admiral," said General Morton, looking at the plan of Uqba ben Nafi taped to the bulkhead.

"What do you think would happen?" asked Admiral Bergeron.

"Some helos would get up and away. The marines on the ground would have to fight, with small arms and whatever Dragons and LAWs they have left. The Cobras would kill the Russian tanks. There would be many casualties on both sides." General Morton's expression was grim.

"Well, for now, we watch. Give Loonfeather a few more minutes. Plan it, gentlemen, as best you can. Colonel Brimmer, get in touch with Captain Roberts; see what he thinks he can do." Admiral Bergeron rose. "I'll go tell the Joint Chiefs."

Uqba ben Nafi
Lieutenant Colonel Loonfeather looked at the Russian colonel carefully, weighing the man. I have to convince him with my first words. To do that, I have to be open and fair. If he even suspects a trick, he'll fight. "Colonel, we want to pull out of here. Our mission is complete; we wish no conflict with you."

"And we wish none with you."

"Good. If you'll pull your men and vehicles back a safe distance from the helicopters, we'll take off, leaving the base in your hands."

Zharkov smiled faintly. Good, he thought, he wants to negotiate. Will his superiors in the fleet, counting up the casualties, go along with him? "We are concerned, naturally, that your helicopters and aircraft could make quick work of us once we let you depart," said the Russian slowly, as though his English had begun to fail him.

That's it, thought Loonfeather. That's the deal he wants. "I'll call the fleet. I'll get their guarantee that none of our aircraft will fire on you once we've departed, unhindered, and that all our forces, both air and naval, will leave Libyan territory as soon as we're safe."

Colonel Zharkov looked at the dark, rugged features of the American officer. I want to trust this man, but can I? He is my enemy. Given what has gone on here today, his helicopters could kill us all, and Moscow could very well choose to ignore it, rather than acknowledge the presence of a Soviet combat unit in Libya, by implication a party to the crimes of the terrorists. Yet what he offers is the only solution. How can I know he is telling the truth, or even that his commanders would be bound by his word? In his position I would give such an oath to save my men, and I certainly wouldn't trust a general far away not to ignore my promise and shoot my enemy's defenseless tanks. "Forgive me, Colonel. I feel I may trust you as an officer and a man of honor. But what guarantee can you give that some other commander, senior to you, might decide to attack us once you have gone?"

A bloody good question, thought Loonfeather. By accident or design, some hothead could order an attack, or some helo pilot with a dead radio could pickle off a missile. "Colonel, I will make sure that the operation's overall commander instructs all subordinate commanders. And I will remain with you as you move your force. If it would give you comfort, I will seek volunteers from among my officers to disburse themselves among your people. If our forces attack, they will kill us by your side."

Colonel Zharkov managed a small smile. "They would name you a hero, and give a grand medal to your widow."

Loonfeather's stomach rolled. *If our positions were reversed, would I trust him? No way.* "Colonel, they will not attack you if they say they won't. I'm giving you the only extra guarantee I can."

"And you think they will let you remain as my hostage? Here, in Libya?"

That's better, thought Loonfeather. *He's thinking of accepting me alone.* "I was hoping you would give me your guarantee that you would see me safely to a neutral country, or to the Swiss Embassy."

Zharkov hesitated. *It was everything he wanted, if it worked. The American was playing all his cards, face up. He wasn't trying to bargain. And he was betting his own life.* "Suppose I agree, Colonel. How do we proceed?"

"We go back to my tank and call the fleet commander. If he agrees to arrangements satisfactory to you, we part friends."

"Your word on this?"

"My word."

Colonel Zharkov unbuttoned the pocket of his uniform blouse and produced a flat silver flask. "I regret I have no glasses, Comrade Colonel, but I think we should drink to the success of your withdrawal."

"And to your long life, and health, Comrade," said Loonfeather, taking the flask and tilting it back. The vodka burned in his dry throat, and he coughed as he handed the flask to the Russian.

Colonel Zharkov drank. "And to your long life, and health, Colonel Loonfeather."

"To life," said Loonfeather, as they started walking back toward the tanks and the noise.

Admiral Bergeron reentered the conference room. The officers sat quietly around the table, watching him expectantly. He sat, feeling weary. His conversation with Washington had consisted mostly of angry outbursts from the Secretary of Defense, demanding to know what had gone wrong. The admiral had noticed that the Secretary's voice sounded slightly strangled, a bit like Donald Duck. After two minutes of useless wrangling, the voice of the President had been briefly heard, though too far from the microphone for Admiral Bergeron to understand his words. Then Admiral Daniels had given Admiral Bergeron his orders: avoid conflict with the Russians if at all possible, but do not surrender the marines.

Admiral Bergeron looked at the officers in the small conference room. "The Joint Chiefs agree we have to fight if the Russians will not let us withdraw. Have we a plan?"

"A very simple one, Admiral," said General Morton. "Captain Roberts has four LAWs in his helicopter, and he's fairly close to three of the Russian vehicles. He's ready, if we give the word."

"Top Hat, this is Black Widow," Stuart's voice sounded from the bulkhead speaker. "Loonfeather and the Russian have started walking back toward the tanks."

Admiral Bergeron leaned toward the mike. "Start walking to them, Stuart. Don't stop unless the Russians shoot. We have to talk to Colonel Loonfeather."

"Aye, aye, sir."

Loonfeather walked briskly toward the parked tanks, aware that the shorter Russian beside him was practically running to keep pace. Now to sell this up the line, he thought. He saw a figure in black, humping a radio, approaching from the knot of men in the far assembly area. He waved, then circled his hand above his head and pumped his arm sharply. Come to me; hurry.

The helicopters continued to sit beneath their whirling rotors, seeming to poise for flight. Stuart jogged to meet

Loonfeather and the Russian officer just as they reached the tanks. Loonfeather smiled and pointed to the radio on Stuart's back. "Command net, White-Eyes?"

Stuart was puffing in the heat of the brassy morning. "Set, Injun. Anxious to talk." Stuart dumped the heavy PRC-77 radio on the tarmac in front of Loonfeather and handed him the handset.

Loonfeather keyed into the net. "Top Hat, Thunder, this is Raptor Six, over."

⇋36⇌
USS *America*

Admiral Bergeron and his staff officers listened in silence as Lieutenant Colonel Loonfeather reported his status and laid out the deal he had struck with the Russian. The Sixth Fleet commander took another of Admiral Wilson's cigarettes and lit it as Loonfeather's voice came over the speaker, distorted and partially masked by the noise of rotors and tank engines behind him. The deal sounded reasonable, but Admiral Bergeron felt that Loonfeather was reluctant to tell all of it. The admiral keyed into the net as Loonfeather stopped speaking. "Colonel, this is Top Hat himself. You're telling us the Soviets will pull back and let you extract if we agree to leave them alone after you're out."

"Essentially, that's the deal, Admiral," answered Loonfeather.

"You'd better tell us what you mean by 'essentially,' Colonel," said Admiral Bergeron, leaning close to the microphone. He looked around the table at the faces of his staff officers, noting that their expressions varied from confused to relieved. Major General Morton looked taut and angry.

"Yes, sir," said Loonfeather. "I'm sure the Admiral realizes that the Soviets are protected from our aircraft by their closeness to us and our helos. Once they let us leave, they will have no such protection. If the Admiral agrees that we will not attack the Soviets if they let *all* of us leave *safely*,"

Loonfeather paused, and the speaker buzzed and clicked.

Admiral Bergeron suddenly had a sense of the Soviet commander standing next to Lieutenant Colonel Loonfeather, listening to at least his end of the conversation. A gun to his head? Is it possible?

Loonfeather resumed, "I suggest that we should make certain gestures, to show our good faith. My first request is that the Cobra gunships patrolling close to the south of us be withdrawn, out over the sea."

General Morton was out of his seat, shaking his head violently, his face red and contorted. Admiral Wilson gestured for calm. Admiral Bergeron waved his hands downward, demanding silence. He keyed the microphone and tilted it toward his mouth. "Raptor Six, this is Top Hat. Stand by, over."

"Raptor Six, roger, over."

Admiral Bergeron pushed the microphone aside and looked to see that the transmit key was off. He looked at each of his staff officers in turn, willing each man to calm. "Gentlemen, I see no reason why we can't pull the Cobras back." General Morton started to speak, seemed ready to burst, but the admiral held him silent with a look. "We can pull them back over the sea, have them hover below the horizon at low altitude, and still have them back overhead the air base in two or three minutes. Now, General Morton, you oppose this gesture?"

The stocky marine had got control of himself, and his face had faded from dark red to blotchy pink. "No, Admiral, if a gesture is what it is. But without those Cobras, the marines on the ground have no chance if a fight erupts. None."

"We'd lose them all?" asked Admiral Bergeron.

"Yes, sir. Captain Roberts might surprise them long enough to kill a tank or an APC with a LAW, and maybe a lucky helo with a quick pilot might jump out in the confusion, but those Soviet tanks and infantry would annihilate the grunts in the helicopters and on the ground, and many of the Russians might reach cover in the couple of minutes needed to bring back the gunships."

"In which case the ships and aircraft of this fleet would obliterate the entire base, including the Russians, wherever they tried to hide," said Admiral Wilson. "Surely the Soviets know that."

"I don't disagree, Admiral," said General Morton. "I just don't like the exchange. Right now we have a stalemate; we can bargain. Once the Cobras are withdrawn, the Russ has the undisputed advantage, however temporary."

"What would you suggest we tell Colonel Loonfeather, General?" asked Admiral Bergeron carefully. Morton hates the Russians and distrusts them without exception, but he has a point, thought Bergeron.

General Morton rubbed his hands together. His jaw worked as he tore at the problem in his mind. "It's tough. Loonfeather thinks he has a deal. Loonfeather has a good record, so I want to go with him. More important, he's *there*; he can see this Russian, and *feel* him!"

"So?" asked Admiral Bergeron, imagining the Russian and the big armor colonel, wondering how much Loonfeather trusted the Russian, and how much he should.

General Morton smiled ever so slightly. "So, Admiral, let's agree to pull the gunships back, either south, or north over the sea, but not out of sight. Let's tell Loonfeather to ask the Russ for his own gesture of good faith."

Admiral Bergeron smiled at the ruddy marine, whose nickname since the Academy had been "Terrier." More the fox today, thought the admiral as he picked up the command net microphone and pressed the key.

Uqba ben Nafi

Colonel Zharkov watched as Colonel Loonfeather finished talking to his fleet commander. Loonfeather handed the handset down to the officer who had brought the radio pack, introduced as simply, "Stuart, one of the commandos who secured the hostages before we jumped."

Loonfeather took a step closer to Zharkov, shielding the Russian from his tank crew. Loonfeather spoke slowly and precisely. "They agree in principle, Colonel. They'll pull back the gunships, out over the sea. Now I need to ask you for a gesture to reassure my people."

Understandable, thought Zharkov warily. "What do you want, Colonel?"

"The last two helicopters. The ones farthest from us. They have casualties loaded, Colonel. Walking wounded, but they need treatment. Let me fly them out as soon as the gunships pull back."

Zharkov looked up and saw the flights of helicopter gunships pulling up and veering out over the formation, to reform a short distance away, over the sea. They could be back in firing range before a tank could move ten feet, he calculated. Still, they are less an immediate menace than they were. He looked at the distant helicopters the American wanted to fly off. If a fight started, those two would have been most likely to get away, as the others blocked them from view of the Russian gunners. Colonel Loonfeather knows that, of course. "Give me a minute, Colonel." Loonfeather nodded and stepped back.

Zharkov took the radio mike handed down by his gunner, and transmitted the order to his crews that the two most distant American helicopters had been given permission to leave. He waited impatiently while each commander acknowledged, the reports from the BTRs delayed while vehicle commanders relayed the order to the squads of dismounted infantry and received their acknowledgment. He handed the microphone back to his driver and turned back to Loonfeather. "I agree, Colonel. The last two helicopters may depart at your order."

Loonfeather smiled and tried to conceal his breath whistling out between his teeth. He nodded to Zharkov, then turned to Stuart. "William, tell Top Hat we're sending out two helos."

⇆37⇌
USS *America*, 0608 GMT (0708 Local)

The two CH-53 helicopters with their cargo of walking wounded marines lifted off, then reported themselves clear of the air base and over the Med. Admiral Bergeron felt the tight feeling in his shoulders ease, and he noted that the atmosphere in the briefing room off Flag Plot had become considerably less tense. Two home, he thought; six left to get out. He thumbed the transmit key on command net. "Colonel Loonfeather, what's next?"

"Back the Cobras up a bit further, Admiral. Then Colonel Zharkov will deploy his forces to the south of the remaining helos."

General Morton motioned for the microphone, and Admiral Bergeron pushed it toward him. "Raptor Six, this is Hammer. Why south of you?"

"To protect us from Libyan stragglers, General," Loonfeather's voice floated in the smoky air. "His idea."

Morton frowned. "The Russ will be outside your perimeter, then?"

"Affirmative, General."

"And then what?" cut in Admiral Bergeron.

"Then the rest of the helos lift off, loaded, and we're out of here."

The admiral and the general looked at each other across the table. Each had a hand resting on the base of the microphone. Something's missing, thought the admiral.

Something's wrong, thought General Morton.

"OK, Colonel," said the admiral into the mike. "We'll pull the Cobras back another thousand meters."

"Roger. Raptor Six standing by."

General Morton took the microphone from the admiral and made sure the transmit key was off. "I don't like it, Admiral. I can't believe the Soviet commander is just taking our assurances at face value."

"I know what you mean, Carl. I have the strangest feeling that Loonfeather is under duress."

Admiral Wilson leaned into the conversation at the center of the table. "We did get those two helos out."

"And the Russ got our gunships backed off. If he's a desperate man, or crazy, he could blow our force to tiny fragments before we could intervene," growled General Morton.

Uqba ben Nafi

Colonel Zharkov had climbed back up into his T-72 and was giving orders into his microphone, at the same time waving and gesturing toward his own formation. Loonfeather and Stuart watched as Russian infantrymen assembled and remounted the BTRs, ready to move around the helicopters on the tarmac and to the apron to the south. Loonfeather grasped Stuart lightly by the arm and whispered into his ear. "Stand over there by the Sov tank, Stuart." Stuart nodded and moved away from the Sheridan. "Calandra!" barked Loonfeather at the Sheridan. The gunner's head popped up in his hatch. "Take off. Real slow, but don't look back. Get down to Major Donahue, then blow the Sheridan and go with the staff."

"But Colonel, what about you and the commander?" asked Calandra, leaning toward the colonel.

"*Go*, dammit!" growled Loonfeather, sneaking a look back toward Colonel Zharkov, who was still looking toward his own formation, away from the Sheridan. Loonfeather slapped the fender of the baby tank for emphasis. Calandra keyed his intercom and Huckins put the Sheridan in gear, backed it away from the T-72, turned, and headed slowly off to the south, in the direction of the assembled troops.

Loonfeather looked at his hand, which tingled and began to hurt. That was a tank you slapped, Rufus, he thought, not a pony. I have to stay calm, stay aware of the danger. Calm. He turned and walked the few steps to Stuart, standing beside the Russian tank. Colonel Zharkov awaited him, arms folded across his chest, a scowl of mistrust on his face, his almond eyes slitted. "We will ride with you, then, Colonel?" asked Loonfeather cheerfully.

"Why did you order your vehicle away, Colonel?" rasped Zharkov, glaring down at the two American officers.

Loonfeather tried to look surprised. "Why Colonel, I'm your hostage. You don't need those men, and besides, I'm sure you realize we couldn't leave the vehicle in your hands without—complications."

Zharkov relaxed. *The American took advantage of me to get his men and vehicle away. If he had asked, would I have let them go? He didn't want to ask. He is clever, but nothing has really changed.* "You may climb up, then, Colonel; we are almost ready to move. I am afraid I can't offer you any better seat than on top of the turret."

"Always been my favorite, Colonel," said Loonfeather, easing his breath out slowly. *That was tense, he thought, but we couldn't agree to give them the Sheridan. And I couldn't take the risk that Top Hat might order me not to accompany the Soviets as a hostage.*

Colonel Zharkov went back to his microphone, but kept an eye on the two American officers standing below him. The Sheridan rumbled across the tarmac toward the American assembly. Loonfeather turned to Stuart, who slapped him on the shoulder. "You're going with them, then, Colonel?"

"Yep. No sweat, just a little extra good faith."

"Well, good luck. I'll tell Top Hat as soon as you've gone."

"I'll need the radio, Paleface."

Stuart picked up the radio pack and presented it to Loonfeather. "Away you go, Colonel, and Godspeed."

"You're not getting this, Commander. You're my RTO. Up you go." Loonfeather pointed to the Russian tank.

Stuart frowned. "You can operate this radio as well as I can, Colonel."

"True, but I would feel better for your company, Commander."

"Shit," said Stuart, without inflection. He set the radio pack down heavily, a millimeter from Loonfeather's toe. "Gimme a fucking boost."

Loonfeather leaned closer. "If this really bothers you,

White-Eyes, I could have a friendly word with my pal the Russ." The colonel grinned broadly.

Stuart grimaced. "Fuck you, Loonfeather. I know it's better that two go." Loonfeather seemed to think the whole situation was terribly funny, and Stuart felt himself flush with anger. "Just give me a boost up, then pass the radio."

Loonfeather grasped Stuart's boot and hoisted. "Good man," he whispered.

USS *America*

"Top Hat, this is Thunder, over."

"Go ahead, Thunder, you're on the speaker, over," said the Communications Chief of the Watch. He pointed to a microphone in the center of the table labeled "B."

"Major Donahue reports the Sheridan is returning to him," said Colonel Brimmer, from *Inchon.* "He's in contact with the gunner. Colonel Loonfeather and Commander Stuart are still with the Russians, who are moving, backing away from the helicopters."

Admiral Wilson picked up the "B" microphone and spoke to Thunder. Major General Morton picked up the command net mike and shouted through clenched teeth. "Raptor Six, this is General Morton. Report!"

There was a short delay, then Loonfeather's voice floated in among the hisses and clicks of the scramblers. "We're fine, General. Colonel Zharkov's troops and vehicles are pulling back. We should be able to get everyone out shortly, *if nothing goes wrong,* General!"

"And what about you, Colonel?"

"We will stay with the Soviets as an act of good faith, General. Colonel Zharkov wanted assurance that our aircraft would not attack once our troop helos had gone, sir."

"So he doesn't trust us?" General Morton strained his ears to hear signs of duress in Loonfeather's voice.

"Russian paranoia, sir," said Loonfeather, almost laughing. Would *you* trust us? he wanted to add.

General Morton was cautious. "What happens to you and Stuart?"

"Colonel Zharkov has undertaken to get us out of Libya in a Soviet military aircraft, or, failing that, dump us at the Swiss Embassy in Tripoli."

"Do you believe that, Colonel?" rasped the general, mopping his red face with a handkerchief.

"I do, General. It's my gut."

General Morton paused, transmit key released, and looked at Admiral Bergeron. The Sixth Fleet commander stared back at him, then slowly nodded. Morton thumbed the transmit key. "OK, Colonel, we will ride with you. Despite thirty-two years in the Marine Corps, I do not have words to describe what I will do to you if you foul this up, and end up displayed in Tripoli in chains."

"Roger, General, understood."

"Hammer out," said General Morton, slamming the mike down on the table.

"Hammer, Raptor Six. Thank you for your support, out."

General Morton reached for the mike, then withdrew his hand. His anger faded in sympathy for Colonel Loonfeather in his precarious position. "Admiral, do you get the feeling that our intrepid colonel does not appreciate the difficult decisions we, condemned to the rear, have to make?" His voice trembled with emotion.

"Strange, General," said Admiral Bergeron slowly, around the cigarette he was lighting, "I thought he understood very well."

⇋38⇋
Uqba ben Nafi

"Call Donahue on company net, Stuart; tell him to be sure everyone is cool and ready to jump on those helos."

Stuart switched frequencies and spoke quietly into his mike. "Done, Colonel. Top Hat not too happy with our being here?"

Loonfeather sighed, his head dropping onto his chest. The T-72 rumbled underneath them, taking up the rear position behind the moving column of tanks and BTRs. "I'm afraid Hammer is the problem for me. General Morton. He is *definitely* going to have himself a piece of my Injun ass when we get back."

"Shit, Rufe, I will speak up at your court-martial," said Stuart cheerfully.

Loonfeather cracked a tiny smile. "That is why I brought you along, brother."

"Hah!" barked Stuart, watching as the Soviet formation cleared the helicopters and deployed south of the apron in front of the Operations Building.

The T-72 jerked to a halt. Colonel Zharkov turned to the two American officers seated on the back of his turret. "Colonel Loonfeather, are you confident that our bargain will be kept?"

Loonfeather took a breath. "Yes, Colonel. We will go, and then you will go."

"Is your lift ready?"

Loonfeather looked across the apron. The last marines were trotting toward their assigned aircraft in orderly lines. Only Major Donahue and three officers stood still on the tarmac. Beyond them, the last Sheridan burned fiercely. "Yes, sir. All six will go on my signal."

"Release five," said Zharkov, looking away.

Loonfeather pulled himself to his feet. "That is not our deal, Colonel." He felt the edge on his voice, anger first, and then fear.

"I know," said Zharkov. "Critical mass force; I know. But send five, please, Colonel." Zharkov continued to look away.

Loonfeather ducked down next to Stuart. "Problem. Tell Donahue to get as many as he can into five helos, and to get them off. Hold one bird." Loonfeather pressed a finger to Stuart's lips as he started to question. "I don't know, just tell him. Get the aircraft up!"

Stuart transmitted Loonfeather's words to Major Donahue. Practically immediately, the four northernmost helicopters in the formation lifted, throwing up clouds of fine dust, and banked away toward the sea as soon as they had gained sufficient altitude. Marines in the sixth helicopter moved quickly to board the fifth, which then rose and turned to follow the others.

Loonfeather watched the helicopters pass over the coast and out of machine gun range, then motioned Stuart to come close. Loonfeather mouthed "command" to Stuart, who nodded and switched frequencies. Loonfeather made a thumbing movement with his hand, which Stuart took as a signal to press the transmit key and hold it open. Loonfeather turned to the Russian and shouted above the rumble of the tank's diesel engine. "Colonel Zharkov, I must know why one of my aircraft has been detained. *We agreed that all would be released.*"

"Go and board your helicopter, Colonel," said Colonel Zharkov quietly.

Loonfeather stopped, his mouth still open. "Colonel?"

"Go and board your aircraft, please." Zharkov looked Loonfeather in the eyes, his face stiff and pained. "I trust you, Colonel, as a soldier. I regret to say I do not trust my superiors in Tripoli or in Moscow sufficiently to give you my word on your safety, if I take you with me."

Loonfeather gestured for Stuart to get down from the tank, and watched him slide off. He turned and saluted the Russian. "Stay well, Kazakh," he said simply.

"Go well, Dakota," said Colonel Zharkov, returning the salute. "When you talk to your politicians, try to say we Russians were, ah, *helpful.*"

Loonfeather nodded and smiled, then slid to the tarmac and ran after Stuart to the waiting helicopter.

EPILOGUE

⇌1⇌

Uqba ben Nafi, 20 February, 1015 GMT (1115 Local)

Colonel Hassan al-Baruni sat in the back seat of the Mercedes limousine as it drove off the Tripoli Road onto the air base. Next to him sat his oldest comrade, Maj. Abdel Salaam Jalloud. The limousine rolled to a silent stop in front of the gutted Operations Building, where a short line of tanks and BTRs, manned by Russian Spetznaz troops, was parked. The Russians rendered crisp salutes. Baruni looked toward the entrance of the gutted building. The steel doors and their frame were still standing, and he could see in his mind the face of Abu Salaam, twisted with rage, the pistol in his hand flashing. Baruni could see the look of sudden pain on the American boy's face as he fell to the pavement, and the colonel could feel the boy's blood and brains on his own hands and face.

The guard in the front seat got out and opened the door, but the colonel waved him away and pulled the door shut. The guard regained his seat, and Baruni told the driver to move on. Baruni felt his voice high-pitched and trembling.

The limousine bumped over the broken and scorched concrete, past empty firing positions, some intact and some rent apart by cannon fire. Shell casings from weapons of many types skittered away from the tires as the limousine advanced. When the Mercedes reached the intersection of the two runways, Baruni whispered for the limousine to halt, and he climbed out, following the guard. The two BTRs carrying his personal bodyguard halted behind the Mercedes, and, as usual, two of the women dismounted and prepared to follow the colonel on foot.

Major Jalloud got out of the limousine. Baruni looked so frail and agitated that the major was tempted to take his arm to support him. Jalloud looked nervously at the sad-faced guards, then back to the leader.

Baruni took a pair of binoculars from a case at his belt and scanned the runways, stopping his sweep at each burnt-out tank. He counted fifteen he could see, mostly the black

337

T-72s of his own army, but some greenish smaller tanks he thought might be American. Fire engines and ambulances patrolled slowly among the wrecks, the former spraying smoldering fires, the latter on one last sweep looking for wounded and dead. A temporary morgue had been set up in the base medical clinic, in the undamaged northern sector of the air base, and Baruni knew the count of the dead had passed 190 before his car had left Tripoli.

Colonel Baruni started walking rapidly south, down the center of runway 03/21, around the many shell craters. He knew he was expected at the medical facility, to meet with the cameras and delegations of grieving relatives and to view the fallen soldiers, but he was drawn to the southern edge of his largest military installation, to the closeness of the desert that began just beyond a low ridge some twenty kilometers inland. He walked past the blasted tanks and saw in each gutted hulk a ruined piece of his dream of leading a united Arab movement.

Baruni walked to the end of the pavement and stopped, looking at the scrubby wild grasses off the end of the runway, the shell craters and the tank tracks, the twisted metal and burnt grass, and at the dark stains where men had fallen. He turned and looked at the ruined air base under its thinning pall of smoke, and at Major Jalloud, who had followed him on his rapid march south. Jalloud was sweating and slightly short of breath. "My old friend," began Baruni, his voice shaking and his hands trembling, "I fear we have suffered a catastrophe from which we may never recover!"

"It, it was a brilliant vision, Aqid, but perhaps it is time to return."

"Return? How can we return?"

"Return to the desert, Hassan."

Baruni looked back up the runway. The Mercedes was approaching slowly, but the BTRs of his guard had remained at the intersection, surrounded by a larger group of soldiers. The two women who always followed him had disappeared. "But who will guide the Jamahiriya?"

"The Revolutionary Command Council has been reconvened. Believe me, my brother, it is only out of love that I say these things to you."

Baruni looked at his friend and smiled. He could see the anguish in Jalloud's face, and he knew he told the truth. Baruni turned his back on Jalloud and looked once more toward the distant desert. "Perhaps it is best, Abdel."

⇌2⇌
Washington, D.C., 1415 GMT (0915 Local)
The President sat in a deep chair in the morning room of the White House living quarters. He was dressed in pajamas and slippers and a long robe of deep blue silk. He had stayed in the situation room, far below, until past one in the morning, until the Joint Chiefs were able to confirm that all American units had left Libya and its waters and airspace. He rubbed his eyes, red with fatigue, and closed the red-banded "Eyes of the President Only" folder on his lap.

General Elmendorf, chairman of the JCS, and Admiral Daniels, the Chief of Naval Operations, stood on the Chinese carpet near the fireplace. They were tired as well and seemed to seek the warmth of the low fire, though the room was warm. Between them and the President stood the Secretaries of State and Defense.

"Thirty-six killed?" asked the President, "and fifty-one wounded?"

The Secretaries of State and Defense looked at each other. The President's anguish was evident. David Wasserstein spoke softly, "Mr. President, we had hoped for a minimum number of casualties, but it was a high-risk operation, and the opposition was far greater and far more effective than we expected."

The President nodded. "Why were we surprised?"

"We weren't, sir," broke in Admiral Daniels, stepping forward. I won't have these civilians apologize for my operation, he thought. "We were prepared for heavy opposition, and we defeated the enemy. Considering the opposition, we feel the casualties, while painful, were, ah, reasonable."

"Reasonable? Arch, can I tell that to the families of thirty-six men?"

Admiral Daniels stiffened. "You can tell that to the nation, sir. We can be very proud of those men."

Again the President nodded, smoothing the folder on his lap. "All the remaining hostages are safe?"

"Yes, Mr. President," said the Secretary of State. "They're at Rheinmain Air Base, undergoing thorough physical examinations, but they're safe."

"Casualties?"

"Cuts and bruises, Mr. President," said the Secretary of State.

"We may be thankful for that," said the President.

The Secretary of Defense cleared his throat. "The hostages will be flown to Andrews tomorrow, sir."

"Of course I'll want to be there. When will the dead be returned?"

General Elmendorf spoke. "Well, sir, since most of the casualties were from the 82d Airborne Division, the assault force has asked permission to escort the bodies, including those of the two murdered hostages, back to Fort Bragg."

The President nodded again, his head bowed. "Of course. I want to be there for that, too. Can that be scheduled?"

"Yes, sir," said the Secretary of State. "The ceremony of welcome for the returned hostages will be at Andrews at 2 P.M. The roll call and parade for the dead, at Bragg, will be just at dusk. Your schedule has been arranged so you can be at both ceremonies."

The President's head came up abruptly. His jaw was set, but his expression was sad. "We did the right thing, gentlemen. We got our people out. Now we must do what is right for our heroes."

"Will you say that to the nation, Mr. President?" asked the Secretary of State.

"As best I know how, Henry. Now, if you would leave me for a moment, I'd like to reflect on what I will say."

"Certainly, Mr. President," said the Secretary. The men filed from the room. The Secretary of State, last out, closed the door quietly.

Oh, dear God, prayed the President silently. He closed his eyes and saw the line of flag-draped coffins on the tarmac at Pope Air Force Base, under a gray and blustery sky. Thirty-six. *Did* we do what was right? he prayed, seeing the mourners' faces beyond the coffins. Were we *just* in doing so, Lord?

The mental picture of the coffins faded. The President saw men and women and children, rescued hostages, leaving an airplane and running to embrace family and friends. Thank you, dear God, he thought, reaching for a yellow pad and a pen.

⇌3⇌
Moscow, 1500 GMT (1800 Local)

Ministers Doryatkin and Tikunin sat in a low leather settee in Doryatkin's office. Across the vast room, aides were packing the contents of Doryatkin's desk in boxes and sealing them with red wax. Workmen collected the boxes and the metal filing cabinets, similarly sealed, lifted them onto handcarts, and wheeled them out.

The room was quiet, the movement of the workmen silenced by thick Shirazi rugs. The lighting was dim, and the two ministers were serving each other from a liter bottle of export-only vodka. They clinked their glasses and watched the snowstorm lash the high windows. The events of the long day had left them almost too tired for speech.

Chairman Nevsky of the KGB walked quickly into the room and stopped. The aides and the movers recognized him, bowed deferentially, and silently departed. Nevsky crossed the dim room to the two ministers, neither of whom rose. "Comrade General Secretary, if I may intrude?" asked Nevsky, his voice soft, careful.

"Of course, Comrade," said Doryatkin. "Sit. Marshal, give our good friend some vodka."

Marshal Tikunin poured a glass of the clear spirit and passed it elaborately to Nevsky, who perched on a high upholstered chair. The glass was full to the brim, and Nevsky spilled a bit raising it to his lips.

"It is good of you to stop by, Comrade Chairman," said Doryatkin, with a little bob of his head.

"I—ah, naturally, I wanted to congratulate you, Comrade, upon your election as General Secretary of the Communist party of the Soviet Union!"

He runs it off like a drumroll, thought Doryatkin, smiling broadly. "Thank you, Comrade!" he said, lifting his glass. "And I thank you especially for, ah, *encouraging* your friends to make the vote unanimous."

Nevsky's face was concealed behind his glass. "Unity is paramount in difficult times, Comrade."

"Quite," said Doryatkin, waiting for Nevsky to continue.

"Well," said Nevsky. Tikunin bent to fill his glass, then filled Doryatkin's and his own. "So you have turned the disaster of our arms in the Libyan desert to your advantage. Good!" Nevsky raised his glass.

"Disaster, Comrade?" said Tikunin, reddening.

"Well, we lost nine officers and forty-nine tanks. Surely—"

"The black-asses lost forty-nine tanks, *Comrade*," said Tikunin, masking his face with his uptilted glass. He set the glass down carefully and riveted Nevsky with his narrow-set eyes. "A far different thing."

Nevsky felt chilled by the old marshal. It was a feeling he was used to inflicting upon others.

"Comrade Chairman," interrupted Doryatkin mildly, "did you come here to *consult* about something, ah, *specific?*"

Nevsky struggled to regain his composure. "Comrade, my wife—"

"Yes, Nevsky?" said Doryatkin, an edge in his voice despite his smile. Marshal Tikunin filled the glasses.

"—Has a cousin, Comrade General Secretary. The mother of one Suslov, a captain, killed. He was supposed to be with Colonel Zharkov, yet Zharkov's special detachment fought no engagement, suffered no casualties."

"Really!" Tikunin said, containing a belch. "This Captain Suslov has been named a Hero of the Soviet Union!"

Doryatkin turned to the marshal. "Can he have been away from his post, Comrade Marshal?"

"Must have been!" growled Tikunin. "We must have a full investigation! I will summon Colonel Zharkov in the morning; he will explain."

"Colonel Zharkov is in Moscow?" asked Nevsky, raising his glass to his lips in both hands.

"Yes. Surely he can tell us if this man left his post—or was on another assignment. . . ." Doryatkin let his voice trail away.

"That may not be necessary, Comrade," said Nevsky, his smooth voice cracking.

"But surely," offered Tikunin, "if the KGB has an interest?"

"No, no," said Nevsky, waving his empty glass. "It is— was, only for my wife's cousin. Let the poor man rest as a hero."

Doryatkin raised his glass. "It will be as you wish, Comrade Chairman."

"Thank you, Comrade General Secretary." Nevsky rose, bowed, and backed out of the room.

The old marshal picked up the nearly-empty bottle of vodka, his big body shaking with silent laughter. He poured the remainder into Doryatkin's glass and his own, with just a ceremonial drop into the KGB chief's abandoned glass. "Your eternal health, Comrade," said the marshal with a bark of laughter.

"*Nalivay*," said Doryatkin, settling back into the cushions.

⇋4⇌
London, 2000 GMT

Commanders Hooper and Stuart were ushered to a quiet corner table in the dark, red-plush and polished wood interior of Simpson's Restaurant, next to the venerable Savoy Hotel on the Strand. Hooper wore his dress blue uniform, which he had left in the care of the Air Force at Upper Heyford during a stop on his long trip from Norfolk to Israel less than one week before. Stuart wore a dark blue, almost black business suit with a fine chalk stripe. Stuart was known to the maître d'hôtel; he entertained clients at Simpson's frequently, but as always when they had dined together through their fifteen years of friendship, Hooper commanded all attention. As they reached the table, the captain appeared, and Hooper ordered champagne before they sat down.

"Veuve Cliquot Ponsardin, Commander," said the captain, presenting the bottle with its orange label.

Hooper glanced at the bottle and nodded, smiling happily. "Appropriate, eh, William? How much of this stuff did we pour down our necks in the Officers' Clubs of Subic Bay and Da Nang during the Dark Days?"

The captain poured the wine and Hooper tasted it carefully. "Never varies. Excellent stuff. Please give my dear father a glass, and leave the bottle close to hand, Captain."

"Sir," said the captain, filling both glasses. He placed the bottle next to the table in a silver bucket filled with cracked ice, and withdrew.

Stuart raised his glass. "Absent comrades, Hoop."

"And your health, William. And to mine, and to the intactness of our skins after our most recent adventure."

Stuart drank slowly, savoring the wine. His left hand had required seventeen stitches and remained heavily bandaged; his right hand and face showed only red swellings and surface scratches around small bandages. A waiter rushed up, withdrew the bottle from the ice, and refilled the glasses. Hooper graced him with a brilliant smile.

"How much longer can you stay in London, Hoop?"

"Not sure, old man. My Sealies go home tomorrow. I sent a signal through the embassy that I might be called on to contribute to your after-action report."

"I didn't know I had to write a report."

"Of course you do! You have to write for Black Widow! Surely you wouldn't leave our place in history to an illiterate brute like me?"

Stuart chuckled. "Well, it will be nice to have you around, anyway. I will check with the DIA at the embassy tomorrow and find out what is required."

"Excellent. Now, a final toast, to your expense account, which will doubtless pay for this fine dinner, even though it *is* your sworn debt of honor, and then let's get to the serious drinking."

"Excuse me, Mr. Stuart." The maître stood next to the table.

"*Commander* Stuart," growled Hooper in mock outrage.

"Really? We didn't know, sir. Commander Stuart, then."

"Mister is fine, Mayer. What is it?"

"There is an officer in the bar, sir. A Colonel Loonfeather. He wishes to join you, just for a moment."

"Colonel Loonfeather! Of course, Mayer. Ask him to join us. Perhaps you could arrange another chair."

"Sir."

"And more important, Mayer," said Hooper, "another glass."

"At once, Commander."

The tall American Indian followed the maitre to the table, a grin opening his bronze face. He was in service dress green uniform, his dark raincoat draped over his shoulders. Stuart thought he looked tired, even drawn. Stuart and Hooper stood and shook hands. Hooper pressed a full glass of champagne into the colonel's hand. They drank, once again to absent friends, and sat.

"You must join us for dinner, Colonel," invited Hooper. "Stuart is paying."

"I would like nothing more, gentlemen," replied Loon-feather softly. "I am flying to Washington tonight. The embassy put me up at the Savoy, and I saw you two walk past."

"You're going tonight?" asked Stuart.

"Yes. Air Force, special flight." Loonfeather grimaced. "I'll be asked to explain myself—my casualties, I think—tomorrow. At least they'll let me fly to Bragg to meet the troops when they come in."

"Where are your men, Colonel?" asked Hooper, his good humor extinguished by Loonfeather's sad tone.

"At Rheinmain. They fly tomorrow morning, direct to Bragg. There will be a last calling of the roll for the dead. The President will be there."

"Excuse me once again, Commander." The maître touched Stuart's shoulder lightly. "The telephone. I'm sorry."

Stuart excused himself and followed the maître. Loonfeather sat in silence, his head downcast. Hooper pulled the bottle from the bucket and refilled the glasses. "You think they're going to get rough, Colonel?"

Loonfeather sipped his champagne. "I'm informed that the Secretary of Defense assured the President that casualties would be minimal."

"You ran a brilliant operation, Colonel."

Loonfeather looked up sharply, though he detected no hint of irony in Hooper's voice. "Really, Commander? I had a distinct feeling that you disapproved."

Hooper smiled. "OK, I did. I thought it could have been done with much less fuss, and I was rude. I meant to apologize, and then the Soviets popped up and we all got real busy. I apologize now, Colonel. The operation was right, and you may be assured that I will say that to any REMF who asks me."

"Thank you, Commander, though I doubt anyone will ask."

"I have ways of being heard. Stuart even more so. You know we will back you up."

"Thank you again, Commander—"

"Please, make it Hoop. Even my Sealies can't call me commander without a smirk."

"Hoop. But I didn't come here to ask you two to testify. It won't come to that; the country is wiser than our leaders, and the people are proud of what we did."

Stuart returned and slid into his chair. "As well they should be, Colonel."

Loonfeather smiled, but his eyes wrinkled with grief. "I want to know, just from you two, because you could see it all, whether the operation was proportionate, appropriate— I don't think either word is right, but—"

"It was a good operation, Colonel. We could have los with less," said Hooper.

"You beat a better force than we planned for, Rufus. You know that," said Stuart.

Loonfeather rose and extended his hand to Hooper and then Stuart. "Thanks. That's what the Russian commander said too, for what it's worth."

"Good luck. You get trouble, you call, OK?" said Hooper.

"The embassy driver is waiting. Enjoy your dinner, gentlemen, and thank you." Loonfeather turned and marched to the polished brass doors of the restaurant and out into the rain.

"That's sad," said Stuart, picking up his glass.

"Yeah. Everybody got what they wanted: hostages home, moderates in power in Moscow, President gonna make a stirring speech over the remains of the brave—"

"And Baruni is apparently out of power."

"Yeah. It *looks* like we did good!"

"Hoop, do you think the politicians will really get at Loonfeather?"

"Not directly; they can't. They will make him a hero— give him a big medal, and probably a full colonel's eagle. But down the line, they'll fuck him over, because he fought too hard and offended their sensibilities."

"Shit, Hoop! You and I both know how close we came

to being overrun! We could have been wiped out! What would our jolly politicians have made of that?"

Hooper twirled his glass by its long stem. "Kinda takes you back, doesn't it?"

Stuart nodded slowly. "Nam all over again. The politicians fuck up, then dump on the low orders in the trenches. It isn't fair."

"Never is, lad. But this topic is depressing. You don't look too happy yourself, for an intrepid warrior fresh from victory come."

Stuart shook his head, his mouth tightening. He stared at the champagne flute, watching the fine bubbles.

"Did you see Leah before we came back here?" asked Hooper with infinite delicacy.

"Yes. On *Inchon*. I asked her to come to London." Stuart looked up, his face curiously devoid of expression. "To have dinner with us."

"And?"

"She declined. No, she more than declined. She said that she—cared for me, but that I could never enter her life."

"Why, if that's what you want?"

"She said she admired—us, fighting against terrorism. Our spirit, and especially our bravery. But that for us it was a quick response to a single insult. To her, it's life. Israel and the army are her life." Stuart drank the last drops from his glass.

"What did you say to that?" Hooper's voice was almost a whisper.

"I—I asked if I could come and visit her, in Israel. She said again that I could not be part of her life." Stuart dabbed the corners of his eyes with his napkin.

Hooper felt the pain and looked away. "Did she say anything more?"

"She just cried. Cried to wake the dead."

Hooper took a deep breath and felt the rush of despair envelop him. Ricardo's body in the green bag, and all the others. "Let's have some more champagne, William," he said gently.

Stuart's head snapped up. His jaw was firm and his eyes were dry. "Of course, Hoop. To honor absent comrades."

⇋5⇌
USA, a year later

The man who styled himself as Abu Salaam was brought to trial in the Federal Court for the District of Columbia two months after his capture. He was charged with one count of air piracy, two counts of murder, and sixty-five counts of kidnapping.

Abu Salaam repeatedly disrupted the court's proceedings, denying the court's jurisdiction and calling upon the Arab nation to demand his release. The wave of hostage-taking by revolutionary factions that he had confidently predicted did not occur; in fact, the Arab world took very little notice of the trial. The judge finally had him removed, to view major portions of the trial on closed-circuit television from his cell.

The prosecution presented its case in exhaustive detail. Thirty-one of the hostages testified, all of whom had either seen Abu Salaam fire the fatal shot at Lance Corporal Stevens or had seen the terrorist Walid kill Seaman Cummins, clearly under orders from his commander. The defense attacked the constitutionality of the law that allowed non-U.S. persons to be brought to trial for crimes not committed in the U.S., and argued that because of the notoriety of the hijacking, the defendant could not receive a fair trial anywhere in the United States. The jury found the defendant guilty on all counts after deliberating for less than fifty minutes. The judge conferred the sentence of death.

The Circuit Court of Appeals agreed to review the case immediately and affirmed the lower court's decision. The Supreme Court similarly agreed to a prompt review and to decide the constitutional issue. During the months of review,

Abu Salaam was confined at the military stockade at Fort Leavenworth, Kansas.

The Supreme Court completed its review in January, upholding the lower court's decision. As to the constitutional issue, the justices reasoned that while Abu Salaam had never set foot upon the United States aircraft, he had undoubtedly controlled and commanded the kidnappers, and that the murders had grown out of the acts of piracy and kidnapping. The court's decision was unanimous.

On February 15, a year to the day after the hijacking of World Airways flight 41a, Abu Salaam was led to the gallows outside the walls of the prison at Fort Leavenworth. He had two last requests, first, that he be executed by a firing squad, as befitted a soldier. The request was denied by the commandant of the prison. He then asked to be left without the hood and to be allowed to address the witnesses. That request also was denied.

At five minutes past six in the morning, beneath a cold and rainy sky, Abu Salaam was brought before six witnesses drawn from the Officer's Duty Roster. His hands were tied behind him, at the wrists and at the elbows, and his legs were tied at the ankles and at the knees. Over his gray prison uniform he wore a black hood, held securely by the noose around his neck. The prison commandant read the execution order, stepped back, and Abu Salaam dropped as the trap opened beneath him. Ten minutes later, he was pronounced dead by the prison's Chief Medical Officer.